THE WHISPERING NIGHT

A Medieval Romance

By Kathryn Le Veque

Printed by Dragonblade Publishing in the United States of America

Other Novels by Kathryn Le Veque

Medieval Romance:

The White Lord of Wellesbourne
The Dark One: Dark Knight

While Angels Slept
Rise of the Defender
Spectre of the Sword
Unending Love
Archangel
Lord of the Shadows

Great Protector
To the Lady Born

The Falls of Erith
Lord of War: Black Angel

The Darkland
Black Sword

Unrelated characters or family groups:
The Whispering Night
The Dark Lord
The Gorgon
The Warrior Poet
Guardian of Darkness (related to The Fallen One)
Tender is the Knight
The Legend
Lespada
The Wolfe
Lord of Light

The Dragonblade Trilogy:
Dragonblade
Island of Glass
The Savage Curtain
The Fallen One
Fragments of Grace

Novella, Time Travel Romance:
Echoes of Ancient Dreams

Time-Travel Romance:
The Crusader
Kingdom Come

Contemporary Romance:

Kathlyn Trent/Marcus Burton Series:
Valley of the Shadow
The Eden Factor
Canyon of the Sphinx

The American Heroes Series:
Resurrection
Fires of Autumn
Evenshade
Sea of Dreams
Purgatory

Other Contemporary Romance:
Lady of Heaven
Darkling, I listen

Note: All Kathryn's novels are designed to be read as stand-alones, although many have cross-over characters or cross-over family groups.

Novels that are grouped together have related characters or family groups.

Series are clearly marked. All series contain the same characters or family groups except the American Heroes Series, which is an anthology with unrelated characters.

There is NO particular chronological order for any of the novels because they can all be read as stand-alones, even the series.

CHAPTER ONE

The month of January
1197 A.D.

Chepstow Castle was a bastion that sat along the edges of the Wye River, protecting the English borders like a great lion. It was a foreboding place, with dungeons and soldiers and a feel about it that reeked of power.

On this night, the moon hung low in the sky and there was ice in the air. Sentries walked the wall, watching the surrounding countryside for hints of danger. There was a light in the keep, a single glow emitting from a lancet window near the top of the structure. It was the only warmth in the silence of the dead, cold night.

This was William Marshal's fortress. He was the Lord Chancellor of England, appointed by Richard the Lionheart. From this place, William issued commands and directives that controlled most of the kingdom. He was the law while the king was away battling the infidels in the Holy Land. Until Richard returned, there was no man more powerful in England, save the king's brother. And therein lay the danger.

In the solar of the great keep, smoke curled up from the hearth in ribbons of gray and white. The Marshal sat near the heat, in a chair that was designed for a much larger body; his weight tended to rise and fall with the seasons. He was an old man and his health suffered at times. But in his youth, there had been none stronger in the land. Those were the days of old, when men were larger than legends, fighting for the new country and living to tell the tales.

Now, this man of legend had eyes that were yellowed with years. He still counseled men, great men in the current day. He sat in the chair, gazing across the room at a familiar figure lurking in the shadows; it was a man who had the potential to be one of the greatest of his time. A protégé of the Marshal, groomed with the greatest of care. Bright silver glints of mail reflected off the figure in the corner; every time there was movement, the Marshal could hear the grate of the armor. It was a tense, uneasy sound.

"So you have no comment on my suggestion?" William finally broke the silence. "It would be a tremendous opportunity and a tremendous honor for you. Have you nothing to say?"

7

The profile in the shadows waited a nominal amount of time before emerging into the light. A massive knight materialized, moving with the stealth of a panther, stalking the older man huddled before the fire. He didn't speak, but the expression on his handsome face said enough. He was displeased.

The Marshal fought off a grin at the sight of him. "So you do not like the idea of marriage."

"That is not true."

"Then you like it?"

"Under the proper circumstances."

"And you do not consider these the proper circumstances?"

The warrior pursed his lips. "When I entered the knighthood, I was prepared to die for my liege. When I came into your service, I was prepared to die for my king. I am not, however, prepared to marry for him."

"So you consider that a fate worse than death?"

"It could be," the man shot back softly. In truth, he was off-guard by the Marshal's suggestion and fading fast. When he had been summoned this night, a marriage, especially his own, had been the last thought on his mind. "You are speaking of something far beyond the call of duty, my lord."

"How?"

The knight was frustrated to realize that he could not adequately debate the subject. "Simply that. To fight, to kill, and to die for one's king is honorable and expected. But to marry for the king... I am, after all, only a knight, the son of baron, and...."

"The barony of Anglecynn is older than England herself and you will inherit it when your father dies. You are descended from Saxon kings. Your forefathers conquered England with William the Bastard and married Saxon princesses." The Marshal's voice tightened. "You are Sir Garren Beaupre le Mon of Anglecynn and Ceri, heir to an ancient and rich kingdom had we not been united by the Normans. You're more than suitable for this task."

The Marshal made it sound as if he was someone of importance. But Garren knew differently. "Then if you place such significance on my heritage, let me point out that the woman you suggest is no one of any particular consequence."

William jabbed a wizened finger at him. "She is the daughter of one of John Lackland's most powerful supporters. Her father serves the Earl of Norfolk. To position you within the House of de Rosa as her husband puts you in direct communication with her father."

"And the prince's plots."

"That is the hope."

Garren fixed the Marshal with an icy stare. He was a big man, will over six feet in height, with shoulders so broad that he sometimes had to turn sideways to enter a door. He was accustomed to using his size as an intimidation tactic, but that particular method failed to work on William. The old Marshal had battled kings and princes and was not about to be put off by a mere knight, no matter how large or powerful.

"Your father knows Bertram de Rosa," William said steadily. "They served together as young knights under Henry the Second, and, as I recall, supported the sons against their father in their quest for the throne."

"Until my father realized what an unscrupulous character John was."

The Marshal knew all of that and nodded his head. "Yes, yes, and then he married your mother and withdrew from politics all together, which is no easy feat in this world."

"And what makes you think that Bertram will be at all receptive to my father and his suggestion of betrothal?'

"Because your father saved Bertram's life once, and any honorable knight will consider that a life debt." William pointed his finger at him. "You will bring your father to me and I will tell him what is to be expected."

Garren growled low in his throat and turned away, stomping off across the room. He knew the decision had already been made no matter of his protests. Ignoring the tantrum, William picked up his pewter chalice and swirled the last of the red liquid, watching the dregs at the bottom of the cup. Had he been a fortune teller, perhaps he could have divined the future of this particular venture. There was much at stake.

"Garren," he said quietly. "When you became an agent for the king, it meant that your life was no longer your own. We must do as we must to preserve England and Richard's throne. Your particular calling in this is a great one that I cannot leave to a novice. It requires your wisdom and skill."

"Marriage requires no wisdom and skill," Garren rumbled. "It requires the hide of an ox and the loins of a rutting bull. We have a number of younger men in the king's service that could do as well as I or better."

"Untrue," the Marshal countered. "I have known you for eighteen years. You have served me and your king flawlessly with your strength and cunning. This could be perhaps the most important task you have yet to undertake. Can you not see that, lad?"

Truthfully, Garren could. Going into the de Rosa lair was an enormous risk. But he would have rather faced a thousand rabid men in battle all by himself than plunge into matrimony.

"My lord," he tried to soften his tactics. "I am not the marrying sort. My life has been dedicated to the service of the king. I am not a lover, nor am I

9

particularly comfortable with women. Although I appreciate the seriousness of this mission, as Bertram de Rosa is indeed a formidable supporter of John's, I sincerely believe there are others better suited to a marriage."

William wasn't swayed. "You are perfect, foremost because your father and Bertram fostered together when they were squires. They have known each other many years. What could be more natural than your father proposing a marriage contract between his son and Bertram's daughter? There is no one else I can trust with such a coincidental connection. Bertram will never suspect a thing."

"That you're planting a spy in his midst."

"For all he knows, he is simply gaining a son." He put his cup down and sat forward, his yellowed eyes intense. "Can you not see the importance of this? What we learn from de Rosa could quite possibly bring about the end of John. For months the prince has been working towards something big, a move against his brother that we cannot seem to determine. With you in the de Rosa stronghold, it is more than possible that you can discover the prince's plans and put an end to all of this. Is that not what we are all fighting for?"

Garren took a long, deep breath. He ran his fingers through his short, sand-colored hair, trying desperately to contradict William's assertion. But he could not. The Marshal was correct, and Garren saw the logic of it. Being a logical man, it was difficult for him to continue resisting. He was dedicated to the service of Richard, and if the king required him to marry to aid his cause, he was sworn to obey.

"Christ," he finally hissed. "I could handle this task very well if it did not involve a woman. Useless, petty, clinging...."

William put up a quelling hand. "The Lady Derica de Rosa is a beautiful woman, so I am told."

"A viper can also be beautiful until it bites you."

William could do nothing more to convince him. The man was set. William stood up, his back curved with age. Once, he had almost been as tall as Garren himself. Now he found himself looking into the man's chin.

"You will bring Allan le Mon to me by the end of the week so we may discuss this proposal," he said with a finality that could only come from William Marshal. "I plan to have you wed to Derica de Rosa by late spring. Do you have anything further to say?"

"Would it do any good?"

"No." William was moving toward the door of his solar, a strong indication that their meeting was over. "I shall look for your father in a few days to discuss the arrangement."

Garren was angered, resigned to his future. The most important task of his life would probably also be the most taxing. He wasn't fearful of the mission in the least; what concerned him was a spiteful, suspicious, conniving wife. It would cause him to be on his guard on both fronts, and he did not relish the thought. It would make the undertaking twice as dangerous. When he paused at the door to bid the Marshal farewell, he noticed an odd look to William's eye.

"There is something more I should probably tell you, Garren," the old man said, "and though I am reluctant to do so, it is only fair. The Lady Derica is the only female in her family for generations. I am told they treat her as if she is the Virgin Mary incarnate. She is protected, pampered, and coddled."

Garran rolled his eyes. "I *knew* it. A spoiled, petty female. Of all the...."

"Wait," William laid a wrinkled hand on his arm. "I am not finished. She has three uncles and three brothers in addition to her father, and I am told they guard her with the ferocity of a pack of wolves. You must know that acceptance as her husband will not be a simple thing. There will be much trial and tribulation with it and you must be amply prepared."

Garran snorted, an ironic smile on his lips. "Nothing about this is going to be simple. What is one more obstacle?"

"You must be ready for the scrutiny, on all sides."

"Could I not be assigned a simpler task? Abducting the Pope, perhaps?"
William shook his head. "Garren...."

"Or perhaps you would like me to march into Windsor and, announcing I am a spy for his brother, and challenge John to a game of 'catch me if you can'?"

"You jest," William smiled weakly. "Good. As long as your sense of humor remains intact, I know you will be successful. It takes humor to temper the serious nature of this endeavor and keep your sanity. I hesitate to suggest it may be the most important one of your life."

There was something in William's tone that caused Garren to sober. "You have already done that."

"I know. But I will suggest it again."

Garren left Chepstow in the dark of night, wondering if he shouldn't keep riding until he reached the sea and still, keep going. He suspected that his life was going to change dramatically. He wasn't used to feeling uncertain about any task he was preparing to undertake, but this particular venture had him reeling. Give him battle, gore, blood, and men set to kill him, and he was in his element. But suggest a marriage in the line of duty, and he felt like a novice.

Above him, a bird of prey hovered against the night sky, calling to its mate. Garren glanced up, noticing the bird was directly over him as if preparing to swoop on his head and peck his eyes out. It couldn't be a good sign. Bad omens abounded in the whispering night, and for the first time in his life, Garren le Mon thought he had a true taste of fear.

CHAPTER TWO

Spring was in full bloom. It was a clear day, if not cold, with great puffy clouds scattered across the sky. The land below was growing green with new sprigs. Norfolk was lovely country in the spring with its gentle fields and relatively flat lands, conducive to the farmers that plowed into the thawed earth. Everywhere there were signs of life, peasants going about their chores, and animals in the field. It was a lovely place to live.

The hulk of Framlingham Castle dominated the landscape, its cold stone facade a strong contrast to the brilliant life surrounding it. It was the only bastion for several miles and the gates remained open for the peasants who conducted business within the walls. And massive walls they were; fourteen enormous towers linked the curtain wall nearly thirty feet in height, creating a huge circle around an equally large inner ward.

Each tower was designed to function autonomously should the castle fall under siege. Two of the towers were particularly large, one on the middle section of the western wall, and one on the east. They were longer, more spacious, and the tower on the western wall harbored a great hall. There were also several outbuildings and stables to house the four hundred men-at-arms needed to maintain the safety and structure of the castle.

Framlingham was the property of the Roger Bigod, second Earl of Norfolk, but the earl chose to live at Norwich Castle to the north rather than in the wilds of Framlingham. He entrusted his castle to Bertram de Rosa, a knight who had served his father, Hugh, for many years. Bertram and his sons were essentially part of the earl's family and the castle belonged more to them that to the earl himself. They took great pride in the place and ran it with power and efficiency.

On the third floor of the larger western tower, a lone young woman sat in her chamber running a brush through long, honey-colored hair. She had been listening to sobs and wails all morning. Had she not known better, she would have suspected the person emitting them to be in some manner of horrible pain or grief. But she knew too well of the dramatics behind them. As the day wore on, it grew annoying and her patience waned.

The young woman sighed, making a face that no one would ever see, expressing her irritation at the screeching. The brush strokes grew more furious as she used her hand to form curls from the strands that cascaded down her back. She scrunched up her pert nose when a particularly loud cry pierced the air, rolling her eyes in disbelief.

In the corner, a serving maiden was sewing on a gown of pale yellow and silver. When another chorus of cries filled the air, she slapped the sewing in her lap.

"I cannot take this any longer," she groaned. Into the air, she thrust the needle. "I would sew his mouth shut, my lady!"

The young woman glanced over her shoulder, an expression somewhere between tolerance and agreement.

"Weddings always affect him so," she sighed heavily. "Especially mine."

The serving maiden's countenance softened. "Forgive, my lady. I did not mean to...."

The woman shook her head. "You did not upset nor offend me, Aglette. Do not worry. I have had months to come to terms with my future and surely time enough to come to terms with whatever angst I may have felt."

"Three months, to be exact, my lady."

The young woman paused in her toilette, gazing at her reflection in the polished pewter mirror before her. A sweet oval face looked back at her, bright green eyes with long dusky lashes. She had been called beautiful since the day she was born, yet the term had no meaning to her. It hadn't for years. Her uncles and brothers and father were biased and she knew it. But there were times when other men had come, a few suitors, and had called her beautiful as well. Still, she wasn't sure if she believed them, though the reflection said otherwise.

She wondered if she would hear the same praise from her new husband. Certainly she was curious about him as well, as she had never even seen him. His father, an old friend of her father's, had initiated the betrothal proposal and she had never once seen hide nor hair of her Intended. All she knew was that he was a knight of independent wealth, newly returned from the Crusades. And they would be wed in one week.

A well-arched brow lifted. "The Lady Derica de Rosa le Mon. Has a rather musical sound to it, does it not?"

"It does, my lady."

"The House of le Mon is an old, distinguished family."

"It 'tis, my lady."

"I shall be a baroness someday."

"Indeed, my lady. Most honorable."

Derica thought she sounded very much like a woman trying to convince herself that everything would be all right. With Aglette echoing everything she said, she realized they were both trying to comfort her. She set the brush down and stood up. Her long day-robe trailed along the cold floor as she went to her maiden to see how her wedding dress was coming along.

"What if he is hideous?"

Aglette looked up from her work. "Who, my lady?"

14

"My husband... what if he is hideous?"

Aglette could only shrug. "I suppose we shall find out soon enough, my lady."

"I suppose." Derica's gaze moved from the exquisite gown to the young serving woman she had known her entire life; Aglette's parents had both served the de Rosa household for many years. Derica reached out and stroked the girl's red head before turning away, wandering across the chamber with no true destination in mind.

"Garren le Mon has been fighting in the Holy Land for several years," she said, more to herself than to Aglette. "He could have been injured, or disfigured somehow. Mayhap that is the reason he did not come with his father during the betrothal negotiations. Mayhap... mayhap his father was afraid I would refuse if I saw what his son truly looked like."

Aglette looked up from her fine stitching. "I believe you were told that Sir Garren was not yet returned from Jerusalem during the negotiations. He has only just set foot back on English soil."

"Ah, or so they would have you believe," Derica held up a finger as if correctly surmising the situation. "Or, if he is not disfigured, mayhap he is an ogre. Or a simpleton. Or he has a great pimpled face that frightens young children."

Aglette giggled. "Anything is possible, my lady."

"I shall wager there is something wrong with him. There has to be."

"It matters not now. The contract is done."

Derica's composure took a hit. She was always in control of herself, sometimes unnaturally so. Being a woman, it was expected that she would be an emotional creature. But not Derica. Growing up among men had given her that element.

"Aye," she agreed softly. "It is done."

"Are you afraid?"

Derica thought a moment. Was she? "I am not. But I am apprehensive. And a bit surprised. I truly never thought I would ever wed."

Aglette smiled; she knew the reasons behind that well. "Your new husband will have his hands full with your male kin."

"It 'tis the truth."

They smiled at each other. Perhaps that was why Derica was not frightened of her marriage; any hint of abuse or threat from her new husband, and her brothers and uncles would take care of him directly. There was comfort in the thought. But more than that, she did not have a fearful nature.

Sounds of a commotion wafted up through the lancet window. It was enough to catch their attention. Crowding around the thin slit, Derica and Aglette struggled to catch a glimpse of what was going on; they could see a flurry of activity around the open gate. There was the glint of armor that passed across their line of sight that was just as quickly gone. From the sounds of shouting, the women correctly surmised that the mysterious Garren le Mon had just made an appearance.

From mild apprehension to a case of full-blown panic, Derica moved away from the window, her heart in her throat. The sounds of the wailing, momentarily ignored, was suddenly back with a vengeance. Aglette looked at her mistress, fear in her own eyes. The moment they had waited for had come all too soon.

"I must be strong," Derica struggled to regain her control.

"Aye, my lady," Aglette agreed fervently. "You will be."

"He must know that I am a woman to be respected."

"Aye, my lady."

"Yet I will also be respectful."

"Aye, you will."

Derica stopped pacing and looked at her. "There is only one thing to do."

Aglette blanched. "Saints help us," she whispered. "I am afraid to know what that may be."

***

"You heard me correctly. I would see my bride before we wed."

Bertram de Rosa was looking into the face of a very large, very stubborn man. He could see a bit of his friend in the son's expression, but for the most part, Garren le Mon had a look and feel all his own. Having never met the man before, Bertram wasn't sure what to think. But he certainly sounded like a man who was eager to get a look at his fair English bride after having spent the past two years in the sand and sun with only dark women to view. In that respect, he could hardly blame him.

But he was careful with his reply. In the solar of Framlingham where the castle business was conducted, the only move he made was to pour himself a cup of wine. There was no desk, and only one chair. Bertram usually took it, leaving whomever he was conducting business with to stand and be scrutinized. It worked amazingly well. But he did not take his seat this time. Even with his three sons and two of his three brothers in the solar with him, Bertram wasn't at all sure he would hold the advantage.

"Allow me to introduce your future relations," he said evenly. Moving from his left, he indicated the men standing. "These are my brothers, Alger and Lon. And next to them stand my sons, Daniel, Donat and Dixon."

Garren had stormed into Framlingham as if he were lord and master. He, his father and the Marshal had determined that it would be the only way to give himself a level playing field against the aggressive de Rosas. He was an aggressive man naturally, so the strength he put behind his manner was hardly an act.

He scrutinized each man indicated in turn; Alger was missing an eye, a battle scarred warrior. Lon was also apparently seasoned, shorter than his brothers, with a challenging manner. The three brothers stood next to one another; Daniel was tall, slender, and held no animosity in his expression, whereas Donat and Dixon seemed quite hostile. The middle son was bulky, wearing a mail suit and, very strangely, no shoes. The last son, a little man, stared at Garren as if he was going to throw knives at him at any moment.

Garren glared at all of them before turning back to Bertram.

"I have been months out of England, my lord," he said. "I would see this woman my father has chosen for me."

So the man wasn't much for pleasantries. Bertram remained cool; he'd dealt with amorous suitors before. "You will go through the formalities with me first, as her father. It is my right and duty to inspect you as my daughter's future husband."

Alger walked up and stood next to Bertram in mute support. He looked like a brigand with his missing eye and dirty appearance.

"You will respect the House of de Rosa, le Mon," he growled. "We have no patience for your demands."

Garren's jaw ticked. "Since when is a man's right considered a demand? Have I been from England so long that all propriety is ignored?"

Alger bristled but Bertram stopped him. "We are not ignoring your demands, Sir Garren. But do we not have a right to question my daughter's future husband? Would you not expect that formality were it your daughter?"

Bertram wasn't being particularly obstinate; he was simply asking a question. Garren thought perhaps it was time he softened his stance a bit and allowed the man to have a look at him. But he had no doubt that any of them would think twice before challenging him in any way. With a faint nod of his head, he then accepted a cup of wine that Bertram extended. Alger stood there and grumbled until Bertram silenced him.

"Sir Garren," Bertram began. "Please tell us of your adventures in the Holy Land. You are the first crusader we have seen in many months. What news is there?"

Garren did not drink the wine; he simply held it in his hand. It was a nominal insult, accepting the wine but not drinking it, suggesting it was sub-standard or that there could possibly be poisoned laced in it. In any case, it was to further stress that he was no one to be manipulated or trifled with.

"The news is that the men grow weary of fighting," he said. "One out of every two Englishmen die from either illness or hunger, and the sands are littered with more knights dead from disease than from Saladin's arrows."

"What does the king have to say about the condition of his men?" Daniel's deep voice came from behind. "Surely the king would be concerned for the men who have followed him on his quest?"

Garren looked at the young, dark-eyed man. "Richard spends his nights in his tent with his lovers. He cares little for those who have sworn service to him. It is a dirty, bloody undertaking and I am more than glad to be free of it." He turned back to Bertram. "If there are no more questions, I would see my bride."

Bertram stared at him. Then, he snorted ironically. "Not like your father, are you?"

"What do you mean?"

"Andrew is the congenial sort."

"As I am not. And I am not happy with the fact that I return from the Levant a committed man."

"You have never been so fortunate," Lon, the youngest uncle, spoke up. "Every man in England would kill for the chance to become Derica's husband. Had you not been off killing infidels and bedding pagan whores, you might show more manners with civilized people."

Garren cast him a long glance. "Are you suggesting that I am uncivilized?"

There was great threat in his tone. Lon smiled thinly. "I suggest nothing of the sort. I say it plainly."

Garren had been forced to leave his weapons at the door. But that did not prevent a great arm from shooting out, grasping Lon around the neck. Everyone leapt to aid him, but Bertram's shout stopped the onslaught.

"Enough," he roared. "Le Mon, you will release him immediately. I forbid you to show such disrespect in my house. One infraction is forgivable, but do it again and I shall throw you in the vault myself. Is that understood?"

Garren's gaze moved to Bertram. He still held Lon in his massive grip. Ever so slowly, he released the smaller man, but the implication was obvious. It was a pack of wolves against one Alpha male, and there would be a war if all sides did not quickly come to terms.

"I do not disrespect the House of de Rosa, my lord," he said. "But if you expect such reverence from me, I would expect the same from you. I will not be called uncivilized by men who stay in England, clinging to her shores as a child clings to his mother's skirts."

Every man in the room flared except for Bertram and his eldest son. "Do you call us cowards?" Donat bellowed.

18

Garren didn't back down. "You are either cowardly or too brainless to serve your country when needed, so I will hear no more talk of my being uncivilized. We all make choices in life, only to be judged by God and not by others."

Lon rubbed his neck, grumbling, but was wise enough to move out of Garren's striking range. The others in the room grumbled and bickered to each other, deeply insulted, deeply angered. Bertram, however, seemed to be focused on something deeper in Garren's meaning.

"You mentioned the service of your country rather than your king," he said after a moment. "An interesting choice of words, Sir Garren, that you would rather serve your country's needs over those of your king."

"England is my king, my lord."

"And that is where your loyalties lay?"

Garren knew that question had to come at some point; he was simply surprised it had come so quickly. He smiled, without humor. "I returned to England to get away from the politics that threatened to pervert all of the good that the Holy Crusade is trying to accomplish. Yet I see I cannot escape it."

"Politics are like life, Sir Garren. One cannot escape either."

Garren took a step at that moment by drinking his wine. It was a signal, very cleverly, to his host that some level of communication and comfort was being established. It was a ploy he had developed during his years of service for the king, when a gesture or word could determine the course of his undertaking. He was well adept at such things.

"Agreed, my lord," he replied. "And also like life, Politics can make a man wish he was never born. Sometimes it is better to simply walk away."

It was more brilliant strategy to direct the conversation as Garren had intended. Though he would not come out directly and swear he had no political affiliation, a hint in this regard was enough for the moment. Still, Bertram was shrewd; Garren could see it in his eyes. The man was no fool.

"Sometimes you cannot walk away," Bertram said quietly.

"Sometimes you must."

Bertram acknowledged the statement by slightly lifting his cup in Garren's direction. Perhaps the old man was being particularly congenial because Garren was the son of his old friend. Or perhaps he genuinely agreed with him. In any case, he didn't seem quite as aggressive as Garren had been led to believe. But, then again, it was only their first meeting.

"Then I see that you do have much of your father in you," Bertram said. "He would rather stay out of the political climate than risk himself. There is no shame in that, of course. Sometimes it is more than prudent. But I would have thought a knight like you to be fiercely loyal to the king."

Before Garren could reply, the door to the solar creaked open and a woman burst forth. Apparently oblivious to the fact that there was a roomful of men around her, she planted herself squarely in front of Garren.

The men didn't react initially, but Garren was momentarily taken aback; she was the most beautiful woman he had ever seen. And she was glaring at him. He could see, faintly, that she resembled Bertram, for they both had the same pale green eyes. She had her father's expression, too; an appraising sort of look that one had when inspecting a side of beef.

The woman put her hands on her hips, looked up and down the length of Garren, and then turned to Bertram.

"Sir Garren, I presume?" she asked.

Bertram looked at the woman with little patience, yet with the same expression, appeared resigned to her behavior. He sighed heavily. "Sir Garren le Mon, may I present my daughter, the Lady Derica Isabela Fernanda Elspeth de Rosa."

Derica turned back to Garren. Her expression hadn't wavered one way or the other. "Welcome to Framlingham, Sir Garren."

"Thank you, my lady."

A tense silence followed as Garren and Derica sized one another up. "Sir Garren and I were just discussing business," Bertram said. "Perhaps it is best if you leave us, my dear."

Derica, predictably, ignored her father. "Sir Garren," she said. "I understand that you have just returned from the Holy Land."

The woman had the manners of a raging bull, but he almost didn't care. She was positively delightful to look at and at that moment, Garren knew he was in a huge amount of trouble. A mediocre or even ugly woman would have been far easier for him to deal with objectively.

"Aye, my lady," he said evenly.

"Tell me about it."

"What do you wish to know?"

Derica cocked a well-shaped brow. "Well... the women, for instance. I hear they act like a pack of wild animals."

"No worse than a daughter barging into her father's solar uninvited."

Garren heard a few titters, though he could not be sure where they came from. He thought perhaps the brothers. Derica, however, simply cocked her head. A challenging smile creased her lips. "I am welcome anywhere in my father's house, invited or not."

Garren smiled back. They simply smiled at one another, like hungry wolves, a standoff that made Garren want to laugh out loud. She was amazingly audacious. He looked at Bertram.

"Do you raise your daughter to behave so, my lord?" he asked. His gaze disapprovingly returned to Derica. "No wonder she has had no husband yet."

Before Derica could verbalize her outrage, Bertram spoke. "She knows how to behave, I assure you. At the moment, she chooses not to."

Derica would not be left out of the conversation. "I am not in any way insolent. It is my right to inspect the man who would be my husband, is it not?"

"It is not," Bertram said flatly. "Leave us now. We will send for you when the time is correct."

"I will not be discarded, Father. I have every right to inspect Sir Garren just as you are."

"Later, Derica. Do as I say."

"I will not. I have every right to...."

Bertram took her by the shoulders and turned her back towards the door. Before they reached it, however, a large figure in flowing silks and perfume appeared and threw massive arms around Derica. The largest woman Garren had ever seen held Derica, weeping hysterically.

"My darling, my sweetling," the woman wept in a deep, husky voice. "I told you not to come down here. Your fate will come soon enough; you do not have to hasten it."

Garren looked at the woman; he could hardly believe it was Derica's mother. She had a huge wimple on with miles of sheer fabric, flowing all about her like waterfalls of color. She also wore an appalling amount of rouge on her lips in an attempt to make herself more attractive. But no amount of color could disguise the obvious. As Garren looked more closely, he swore he saw stubble on the fat cheeks.

"Remove her," Bertram waved his hands at the pair. "Both of you, leave us."

The huge woman wept and wept. Derica removed herself gently from the embrace and in turn, embraced the woman. She cast a long glance at Garren; he would never forget the look in her eyes. He didn't know why the expression affected him so, but it did. Her eyes seemed to reach out and grab him. Quickly, thankfully, she left the room and he could refocus on the task before him. Still, the Marshal's words echoed in his head.

I hear Derica de Rosa is a beautiful woman.

God help him, he had been right. The stakes of the game grew.

***

It had been, in fact, one of the longest afternoons of his life. Bertram de Rosa, having been the more congenial out of the group of de Rosa men, had

21

turned into something of a barracuda when his daughter had left the room. It was as if, suddenly, a taper had been lit in his mind and he pounded Garren with questions for several hours. Politics, religion, and education-no subject escaped him. It was if he suddenly had to know everything about the man, immediately. By the time the sun set, Garren was exhausted. Sup was a few hours off, but he fully expected the interrogation to resume at mealtime. At the moment, he was grateful for the intermission.

It was the first time he had been to Framlingham and discovered it to be an enormous place. The wall walk seemed to go on forever. He had made his way up onto the battlements, watching the last of the sun, the dancing colors across the deepening sky. It was peaceful and he welcomed it. Now and again a sentry would pass him and hardly give him a glance.

A chill breeze was kicking up. Garren leaned back against the stone, his big arms crossed and his brow furrowed in thought. The Lady Derica de Rosa, he repeated over and over in his mind. He pondered the long honey-colored hair, silken-looking with its loose curls. He thought about her great green eyes, huge things that stared back at him as if they could read into his soul. He mulled over the shape of her face, the way her lips curved into the shape of a rosebud. He even liked the contours of her nose. She was rather tall for a woman, and rather robust, with delicious curves. Not that she was heavy by any means, but she wasn't a frail little thing, either. She was quite tasty in his opinion. The Marshal hadn't lied in the least.

A gust of cold wind came up, whistling past his ears. He was standing near the northeast tower when he heard something that didn't sound at all like the wind. There was someone lingering in the shadows of the tower, just inside the top of the stairs. He didn't flinch or try to see who it was; he simply stood there and waited. Whoever it was would make themselves known soon enough. His dagger, well-concealed, was within easy reach.

Another gust of wind arose and he caught the distinct scent of flowers. He didn't know which kind because he wasn't very good at that sort of thing. But the scent alone told him who was lying in wait for him.

"You know," he said casually, "if your father finds you out here with me, without an escort, we would both be in for a good deal of trouble."

There was no immediate reply. After a moment, he heard soft footfalls coming towards him. Very leisurely, he turned his head to see Derica emerging into the moonlight. She looked beautiful, dressed in a burgundy surcoat and a matching heavy cloak. Garren wasn't sure if he should smile at her or just look at her. He settled for just looking at her.

Derica gazed back. She wasn't sure what to say to him, or why she had even followed him for that matter. The only reason she could manage to pinpoint was curiosity. Pure, wild curiosity.

He wasn't as she had expected or imagined. Garren was taller, taller than any of her uncles or brothers, and his shoulders were enormously wide. He had sand-colored hair with a hint of copper in it, cut close to his head. His eyes were clear blue, she had noticed, and his jaw was very square. It gave him a rather brave appearance, she thought. She could believe that he spent so much time in the Holy Land, fighting the infidels. Surely those dark-skinned natives must have been afraid of him.

He wasn't deformed, maimed or pimple-faced, as once suggested. He was, in truth, a large and quite handsome man, and therein laid her curiosity. The moment she had set eyes on him, everything she had feared had taken flight and now she found herself with an entirely new set of fears. The fear of attraction.

They gazed at each other in the ghostly gray light, each appraising the other. It seemed that all they had done in the two times they had met one another is stare at each other in an attempt to satisfy the insatiable interest about the person they were going to spend the rest of their lives with. It was a hunger that grew by the moment.

"Well?" Garren finally said.

Derica seemed to snap out of whatever silly trance she found herself in. She'd never in her life experienced anything so strange. "What do you mean?" she asked.

He wriggled his eyebrows. "About your father. If he finds you here, he'll berate us both."

She acted as if she hadn't heard the question. "Why is it you have never married?"

Garren couldn't help it; he laughed softly, his straight white teeth gleaming in the moonlight. "I must say, you are direct."

Derica realized she sounded like an idiot and her cheeks grew hot. Trying to recover, she leaned back against the wall a few feet from him, trying to act as casually as he was.

"I simply meant that you're obviously old. Why is it you have never married?"

Garren laughed harder. "Old, am I? How old do you think I am?"

"Thirty years, at least."

He was greatly amused. "Thank you for the compliment, but I am nothing of the sort."

"Oh. How old are you, then?"

"Thirty-one years."

Her jaw dropped, just as quickly shut. "Good Heavens. I had no idea...."

"That I was as old as God himself, eh?"

She shrugged; he grinned. Garren turned back to the night sky, noting that the wind was picking up.

"It is getting rather cold," he said. "Mayhap you should return to your chamber."

"You did not answer my question."

"What is that?"

"Why have you not married?"

"I have never had the time or the inclination. Had my father not set up this betrothal, I would not have considered it."

"Why not?"

"I just told you. I have never had the time nor...."

Derica looked at him, then. "You mean to say that you have never met a woman you have wanted to marry? Not even in all of your travels?"

It was Garren's turn to shrug. "I have met a few interesting women in my lifetime. But it would have been unfair to marry any one of them and then leave her while I go about my vocation."

He could see the thoughts racing through her mind. "Then you are telling me that you plan to give up your vocation? That you are ready to stay in one place? Is that why you have agreed to our betrothal?"

He could sense something behind her questions, something he couldn't quite single out. "I agreed because my father went to a lot of trouble to secure this marriage for the future of my family lineage," he said carefully. "At some point, I will need to produce an heir to carry on the le Mon name."

It wasn't the answer she was looking for. "So that's all I am? A breeding cow?"

"I wouldn't put it quite that way."

Derica wasn't quite sure what she had been driving out, but the breeding stock line hadn't been it. She felt insignificant the way he described his views on the marriage. Pushing herself off the wall, she headed back toward the tower and the stairs. Garren called after her.

"Lady Derica?"

She didn't answer. With every step, she felt more and more distress and had no idea why. Garren called out to her again and she whirled on him just as she reached the steps.

"I am not breeding stock, Garren le Mon," she nearly shouted at him. "If all you wanted was a broodmare, you should have had your father select someone else. I am not interested."

She had a lot of fire, Garren would admit. He moved away from the wall and walked towards her, slowly, watching her body language. He was a man who had made a living from watching the twitches of others and he could tell just how furious she was, though he wasn't entirely sure why.

24

"Isn't that what marriage is, my lady?" he asked. "To perpetuate the family lines, to strengthen allies? If there is something else involved, then I am ignorant of it."

Derica felt as though she had been slapped. She didn't understand why she suddenly felt so hopeless. He had entirely logical views of their marriage. She wasn't sure what her views were at all.

"As am I."

Garren watched her fade down the steps, into the darkness of the tower. He knew that somehow he had offended her, but wasn't sure how. Still, he wished he knew her well enough to ask for her forgiveness for whatever it was that he had said. At this moment, he felt the distinct twinge of regret for something he didn't fully understand.

CHAPTER THREE

"I am not going to sup," Derica said. "You may tell Father that I am feeling ill."

Dixon de Rosa was thirteen months older than his sister. They had always been exceptionally close. He watched her as she sat before her vanity mirror, the slow movements of her hands as she braided her long hair, and knew something was wrong with her. Illness had nothing to do with it.

"He'll not disturb you, I promise," he said. "Garren le Mon is an arrogant buffoon. We'll chase him away before the night is out, just as we have done the others. You will see."

Derica's expression was pensive, thoughtful, as she braided the ends of her hair. Her fingers would move quickly, then slow, then speed up again, then more slowly as her thoughts progressed.

"I have a feeling he'll not be run off," she said after a moment. "He is not like the others who have come to call upon me."

"Of course he is. We'll have him gone in the blink of an eye."

Derica cast her brother a long look in the reflection of her looking mirror. "You cannot run him off, Dix."

"Why not?"

"Because we are betrothed." She secured the end of the braid and turned around. "The other suitors that have come were merely that-suitors. Sir Garren and I have a contract to be married, legal and binding. You cannot get rid of him, no matter how much you want to."

Dixon chewed his lip angrily. "Hoyt will."

"He doesn't like to be called that and you know it."

Dixon rolled his eyes. "I have never been able to call him that."

"What?"

"That."

Derica fought off a smile. "He is not been right since that blow to the head three years ago, has he? It still takes some getting used to."

"I cannot call him Lady Cleo Blossom, no matter how much he wants me to."

Derica stood up, facing her brother. "It matters not what you want. What matters is that if we do not call him Lady Cleo Blossom, he will become quite angry and, you will recollect, quite violent. He is perfectly harmless as long as you do as he wishes."

Dixon put up a hand. "I know, I know," he sighed. "For the greatest warrior among us to take a blow to the head at a tourney and wake up thinking he is a woman is... is...."

"I have heard this before, darling."

"It is tragic!"

"I know. But it 'tis God's will that our beloved Uncle Hoyt has become the Lady Cleo Blossom. We may not know the reasons now, but perhaps in time, it will become clear."

Dixon grumbled. "Woman or not, he still packs a wallop. And as protective as he is over you, perhaps Sir Garren will feel that wallop before the night is out. The beauty of it is that he wouldn't dare strike a woman back."

Derica didn't say any more. Her brothers and uncles were always hostile where suitors were concerned. Normally, they had her blessing to do anything necessary to drive the fools away. But Sir Garren was different; half of her wanted him to leave, but the other half was quite interested in him.

She thought about him, standing on the battlements, the soft breeze blowing through his hair and the moonlight reflecting off his features. He had laughed at one point and the sight of his smile had made her feel strangely weak. No man had ever had that effect on her, and she'd known many to come to Framlingham on the quest to gain her hand. They'd tried every known trick, every known charm. But she hadn't fallen for it.

What made Garren different, she didn't know. But she didn't feel like seeing him this eve. She didn't want him to go, she didn't want him to stay, she didn't want to speak with him, yet she felt the strange urge to be in the same room with him. She decided, at that moment, that she was going mad.

"Go down to the hall and give father my message," she didn't want her brother standing there watching her in her moment of dementia. "Tell him I have retired for the night."

"You're sure?"

"Absolutely." She smiled at her brother's dubious face. "Please. Go now."

He left, reluctantly. Aglette slipped in when Dixon left and began preparing Derica's bed for sleep. One of her duties was to brush out her mistress' hair. Even though Derica had recently done just that, she was so lost in thought that she hardly realized when Aglette unbraided her hair and began running the comb through it again.

***

27

"I fear I have said something to upset you."

The voice came from the shadows. Derica was so startled that she nearly fell off her chair. She'd been dozing by the fire in her chamber, having no idea how long she'd been in the twilight between thought and sleep. She knew it was le Mon before she even saw him. When he finally emerged from the darkness, her heart leapt into her throat.

"You...," she gasped, patting her chest to restart her heart. "How did you get in here?"

He came to a halt, a respectful distance away. "Forgive me for startling you. But when your father told me you were feeling ill, I knew it was not the truth."

"You didn't answer my question."

"What question?"

"How did you get in here?"

His blue eyes twinkled and he gestured at the door. Derica, calming somewhat after her initial fright, slowly shook her head. "That door was locked. I bolted it myself."

"I did not say I came through the door."

"But you pointed to it."

"I did not. I merely pointed to the obvious."

She was becoming irritated. "The obvious door? You're not making any sense."

He remained cool, almost amused. "Does it matter how I got in? I would say that you should be more concerned as to why I am here."

Derica was still looking over at the door, almost hidden in the darkness. There was a lancet window near it, the oilcloth partially peeled back. It took her a moment to realize that the window was what Garren had meant. Her eyes widened.

"Do you mean to tell me that you came in through the window?" she was astonished. "I am four stories up. How in God's name did you climb up the side of the keep?"

He smiled faintly. "I came to apologize if I said something to upset you when we met on the battlements. Whatever it was, I did not mean to. I sensed that you were perturbed when you left, and then when you did not appear at sup, I knew I must have offended you."

She eyed him. "Are you always so evasive?"

"What do you mean?"

"I want to know how you came in through the window, and you want to discuss some silly conversation we had on the battlements."

"It wasn't a silly conversation at all, I assure you. It was the first true conversation you and I have had, and I suppose I conducted it badly."

Derica cocked an eyebrow. She was coming to suspect he was not going to tell her how he came in through the window. But she was off-guard at his appearance and had no desire to continue a conversation with him.

"My father will throw you in the vault if he finds you in here," she said. "You'd better leave the way you came so no one will see you."

Garren stood there, watching the light reflect off her features. He also knew it was dangerous for him to be here, but for the duration of sup he had been seized with the determination to see her. A small seed of confusion was glowing somewhere in his mind, something that he suspected at some point would make it difficult for him to keep his mind on his mission unless he kept it in check. Maybe if he could talk to her, to find out just how spoiled and petty she was, he could learn to dislike her. He needed to find a reason to dislike her in order to maintain his focus.

He took a couple of slow steps, moving towards the other chair in the chamber and being very careful not to appear threatening.

"You have no interest in me, my lady," he commented quietly.

"I beg your pardon?"

He took the chair, lowering his big body. "I said, you have no interest in me. This marriage is as much a duty to you as it is to me."

He was a safe enough distance away and Derica was feeling more composed, enough so that she found herself responding to him.

"Unless a young woman is intended for the convent, it is expected she would wed," she replied. "I have no desire to become a nun or an old maid."

"But you were disturbed by my observation that one of marriage's primary purposes is to produce heirs."

Derica shrugged, toying with the ends of her hair. "Sometimes the truth is disturbing."

"It is. But why should the production of a child disturb you? All women want children, do they not?"

"My mother died giving birth to me."

"I see," Garren understood. "Then childbirth frightens you."

Derica looked up at him, feeling an odd warmth coarse through her as their eyes met. "Not particularly," she tried to sound uncaring. "It is a fact of life. One cannot avoid it."

Garren sensed she was putting up a front but he let it go. "Many, many women survive it," he said. "True enough that some die, but the same pertains to any risks you take in life. Some live, and some die, but it is better to have taken the chance than to have had no chance to take."

For the first time since they met, he drew a smile from her, however reluctant. It was a beautiful gesture. "You speak like someone who has taken many chances, and has perhaps regretted the ones he never had."

He met her smile, feeling the same warmth that she was feeling. "I think that can be said for all of us, not just me," he said. "But there are things I wish I could have done, and things I wish I hadn't done."

She laughed softly, her straight white teeth reflecting the fire. "This conversation is becoming too philosophical for me. I am but a simple woman, after all."

"You are indeed a woman. But I doubt you are simple."

"So I have been told." She was again feeling those familiar feelings associated with him, wildly curious to know more about him. "You never did answer my question when we were up on the battlements."

"About what?"

"Whether or not you planned to stay in one place after we wed, or whether you plan to continue your wandering ways."

The answer was obvious, for his mission. He had to say, act, or do anything to convince her he was who he said he was. But the answer that came forth was the honest truth, an inherent response before he could think it through.

"I will stay with you."

She lifted one of those shapely eyebrows at him. "Is that a fact? You intend to stay here, with me, at Framlingham?"

He realized there was a fantasy life here for him to play out, to make plans that would never come to past and to tell her that the future would be as bright and wonderful as he said it would be. He shouldn't have indulged the fantasy, but gazing into her sweet face, he couldn't help his natural male instincts to give in to the role.

"We will not stay here," he shook his head. "Do you think I want your father, uncles and brothers breathing down my neck at every turn; scrutinized like an ibis in the midst of alligators?"

Her eyebrows drew together, though she was smiling. "Ibis and alligators?"

"Creatures in the Holy Land. The latter always eats the former. Quite fascinating, really, but also quite deadly."

"I would like to hear about them sometime."

"We shall have plenty of time to talk about things like that."

"I am sure we will, in this mysterious place you intend for us to live if we will not be here at Framlingham in the midst of alligators."

She was sharp of wit. He liked that. Grinning, he leaned forward with his elbows on his knees as if somehow that would move him closer to her.

"We shall not live in a mysterious place, I assure you. My father's castle is to the north and east of Oxford, a very old place. Parts of it are hundreds of years old, but it is very comfortable."

"Sounds intriguing. Does this castle have a name?"

"Two, actually," Garren was warming to the conversation. "The origins of the castle, as I said, are very old. Parts of it were built at least three hundred years before the Normans came. It was part of a village back then, the house of the king, and was called Culthberg because Culth was the king who built it. But when the Normans came, they called *le chateau de le roi*, or the house of the king. So Chateroy Castle it became."

He had a deep, rich voice. Derica liked listening to him. He was not at all like the arrogant, aggressive man she had seen in her father's solar earlier that day.

"A fascinating story," she said. "How long has your family lived there?"

"Culth was my ancestor. When the Normans came, a king by the name of Ael ruled the province. He surrendered to the Normans without a fight and gave his only child, a daughter, to a general serving William the Bastard. They had thirteen children, the eldest of which was my grandfather several times over." He grinned. "Funny thing about the Norman general; his name was not le Mon when he married the Saxon princess. All he could say about his new acquisition was 'mine, mine', so William took to calling him 'mon', which is 'mine' in French. So the name le Mon was born."

Derica laughed softly. "A name borne of greed."

"I certainly can't blame the man being excited about his just reward."

Derica shrugged in agreement. The conversation lulled and she couldn't think of any more questions to ask him at the moment. He had been quite open with her and she was, in truth, feeling comfortable with him. He seemed to be a likable man in spite of her original impression. She was coming to regret not attending sup; yet if she had, she knew they would not have been able to converse as they were now with her brothers and uncles hanging over them.

A twinkle came to her eye. "Now," she said. "Are you going to tell me how you got in through that window or are you going to dazzle me with more talk of the history of the le Mon family?"

"I am going to dazzle you with more talk."

She shook her head, a reproachful gesture. Yet there was humor in it. "Then talk. God's Bones, you risked your life to come to me. You may as well make it worth the risk."

"It is worth the risk already."

Derica could feel her cheeks grow warm. Lowering her gaze, she moved her chair back, away from the fire. "You may as well sit across from me rather than in the darkness, then. Let us be comfortable."

Garren didn't need to be told twice. He picked up his chair and moved it. Sitting an arm's length away from her was much better than sitting an entire room's width from her. He just sat there, looking at her, smiling when she would meet his gaze, looking at his hands when she looked away, both of them trying to think of something to say. It was not uncomfortable, but more than once they chuckled when they realized the flow of conversation did not come so easily.

"Is Chateroy a beautiful place, then?" Derica finally asked.

Garren nodded. "I think so." He couldn't think of much else to say to that. "Have you lived at Framlingham all of your life?"

"Aye," she replied. "I was sent away to foster when I was eight years of age, but my family missed me so that they sent for me when I was twelve years and I have been back at Framlingham ever since."

Garren cocked an eyebrow. "If they think to send for you when you and I go to Chateroy, they had better think twice. I will not return you."

She was pleased by his statement. "It will be difficult for them. Being the only female in the family, I am something of a prized commodity. Women tend not to survive long in the de Rosa house."

"Why?"

She shrugged. "It is rare for a female de Rosa to be born. For several generations back there has been nothing but males. My father has three brothers and his father had one, and his father before him had six, and so forth, for seven generations. I am the first female in well over one hundred years."

"And well worth the wait," Garren said quietly.

Derica burst into embarrassed laughter. "You certainly are free with your flattery, Sir Garren."

He shook his head. "Not really. It does not come easy to me, as I am not particularly comfortable with women."

"You seem very comfortable with me."

"That is because you are easy to talk to."

She dipped her head graciously, to thank him. The conversation quieted once again, but there was no discomfort to it. Garren's gaze moved back and forth between Derica and the dying fire. He was appalled and thrilled to realize he could grow to like this very much. She'd given him no reason to dislike her; if anything, the entire conversation had produced the opposite effect. The seed of confusion that had sprouted in his mind was growing in to a nice, healthy sapling, one he should like to rip out by the roots before it grew into a mighty oak and obscured his vision completely.

"Well," he said softly, rising. "I suppose I should leave you to your sleep. I have taken enough of your time."

Derica rose with him. "Strange, I am not tired at all, but I am sure you must be after your long journey today."

"I am, a little," he gazed into her eyes, longer than he should have. If only she had been the petty, spoiled female he had hoped for. "I will bid you a good eve, then, my lady. Pleasant dreams."

"Thank you, Sir Garren," she said. "Good sleep to you as well."

He stood there looking at her just as she stood there looking at him. Garren couldn't seem to move his feet. He felt like an idiot.

"Well?" she asked.

"What?"

"I thought you were leaving."

"I am."

"It doesn't appear so."

"In good time, my lady."

She smiled coyly. "Then perhaps we should sit again until you are completely ready," she turned back to her chair. "I would not want you to think me rude by hastening you out of my chamber, although propriety demands that I must. Still, it has been a...."

As she sat down, she looked up to see that Garren was gone. Startled, not to mention disappointed, she bolted up and ran to the lancet window. Hoisting herself up on the sill, she looked down but saw nothing. All was quiet and dark in the ward below. Glancing up, she caught a glimpse of boots disappearing over the top of the battlement directly above her head. A small rope dangled down the side of the keep, which was quickly retracted as she watched. All evidence was removed, and Sir Garren was gone as if he had never come at all.

Derica lowered herself from the window and pulled the oilcloth back over the window, keeping out the cool night air. She stood there a moment, thinking on Sir Garren and grinning like a fool. It had been a most eventful evening.

She wasn't sorry that she missed sup in the least.

***

"He *what*?"

"He came to my chamber last night. We had a wonderful conversation."

Aglette was beside herself. Derica put her hand on the woman's elbow and forced her to continue walking. It was a sunny morning and the bailey was alive with activity. Villains were bringing in wagons of food and goods for the castle and soldiers milled about as the women strolled through the compound.

"I... I simply cannot believe...," Aglette stammered. "How scandalous!"

"He was afraid that he had offended me and came to apologize," Derica said evenly. "We talked at length."

"But how did he get in?"

"Through the window."

"The window?" Aglette gasped. "Good Lord, how did he manage that?"

Derica smiled at the thought of his boots disappearing high over her head. "With a rope. He lowered himself down from the top of the keep. Quite clever, actually."

"And all of this does not distress you?"

"Why should it?"

Aglette looked at her mistress with her mouth agape. Derica wasn't the least bit concerned with the behavior of a man she barely knew. She suddenly knew why.

"You're smitten with him," she accused.

Derica's smile vanished. "I am not."

"You are! I can see it in your face."

Derica looked away from her so the woman could not read her expression. "You see nothing. He came, he apologized, and we spoke. It was pleasant. The man is to be my husband, after all. Should I not know something about him?" She glanced up, seeing her brother Donat on the battlements. He glared down at her, his usual expression. "Do you think it would be a simple thing to talk to the man with the alligators hanging about, waiting to devour him?"

"Alligators?"

"A story for another time. Suffice it to say that if I am to be married to the man, I would come to know him at least somewhat. I know that is a ridiculous notion in this day and age, but I would like to establish some manner of rapport with him."

"Why?"

"Because we are going to spend the rest of our lives living together. Is it wrong to want to know the person I will be living with, the father of my children?"

Aglette looked uncertain about the whole thing. "I suppose not, but... if your father hears that he has visited you in your chamber, and you without an escort, he'll...."

Derica put up a silencing hand. "I know. It is too horrible to think of." She paused a moment, looking about the bailey, realizing that she hoped to see Garren. "I believe this is the one man I do not want them to chase off."

Aglette was astounded. The Derica she knew had no use for men, in any way. For her to show interest in one was astonishing. She started to reply, but the expression on her mistress' face stopped her.

"There he is," Derica murmured.

Aglette looked across the bailey towards the cluster of buildings that housed the stables. As tall and strong as an oak, Garren was crossing the compound, apparently heading from the knight's quarters to the stables. He hadn't seen the ladies and Derica came to a halt, watching him stroll away from her. His moves were graceful and powerful.

"How do I look?" she hissed.

Aglette peered at her. "Look what?"

Derica elbowed her in the ribs. "My dress, my hair. How do I look? Am I presentable?"

"As presentable as you always are," Aglette replied. Her gaze moved between her mistress' face and the massive man in the distance. "You are smitten with him."

"I am not. I just do not want to appear unkempt or slovenly to the man I am to marry. What kind of bride do you think I am if I am anything less than composed?"

It wasn't the reason and Aglette knew it, but she kept her mouth shut. She watched Derica as the woman's green eyes focused on Garren like a cat watching a mouse. Even after he disappeared into the stable, she didn't move. She continued to stand there, waiting and watching, until quite some time later he reappeared.

Suddenly, she was moving. "Come along," she whirled for the keep. "Let's go inside."

Aglette almost had her neck snapped by Derica's abrupt movements. "Why the hurry?"

Derica didn't answer. She was determinedly walking toward the keep. But in a matter of a few moments, they heard a deep male voice behind them.

"Good morn to you, ladies."

Garren walked up, his handsome face shining in the morning sun. Derica came to a halt and turned around, very casually.

"Sir Garren," she put up her hand to shield the sun from her eyes. "Forgive me, I did not notice you. Where did you come from?"

Aglette lifted an eyebrow at her. Whatever her mistress was up to, she was playing the game quite coyly. It was a surprise coming from a woman who, under normal circumstances, gave no thought to such things. But she wisely kept quiet.

"The stables," Garren answered her question. "My horse was acting strangely yesterday and I wanted to see if he came up lame."

"Did he?"

"Slightly. He'll be no good to me for a day or so."

"I am sorry to hear that," Derica said. "My father has several chargers. I am sure you can borrow one should you need to."

"Perhaps."

Garren studied her in the bright of the day; she was dressed in pale yellow brocade, quite becoming with her coloring. He'd spent a sleepless night, tossing and turning with thoughts of her on his mind; the sapling of confusion had grown into a yearling of stunning strength, with branches that reached into his mind to cause mass disorientation. But he had fought the branches, the tree itself, and in the morning had awoken with the resolve to distance himself from her as much as possible. No more sneaking into her chamber, no more private conversations. He had to draw the line if there was to be any hope of him keeping his mission in focus.

It had been easy to reason so with distance between them. But gazing at her, he knew that line would be extremely difficult to draw. He was attracted to her, more than any woman he had ever met. Knowing she was to be his wife, and he would be entitled to all of the husbandly pleasures thereof, was enough to seriously disturb him. A woman like this could make him forget everything he had ever worked for and he was coming to comprehend something he'd never understood his entire life; why men over the centuries had died for the affection of a beautiful woman. Suddenly, it was blatantly obvious.

He knew he had to get away from her before he forgot everything he had resolved himself to over the past several hours.

"If you will excuse me, I will not burden you ladies any longer with my presence," he said. "Good day to you."

He walked away from them, almost too quickly, but Derica's voice stopped him.

"Sir Garren?"

He paused, turned, and would have had to have been a blind man not to see the expression on her face. She looked as if someone had just stolen her best friend.

"My lady?"

"Have... have a pleasant day as well."

"Thank you."

It was harder than he could have imagined to turn and continue walking. But he had to. In fact, he had to do more.

CHAPTER FOUR

"Have I ever asked this of you before, my lord?"

"You have not."

"Then I would hope you would take me seriously when I ask that you reconsider assigning me to this task."

"Of course I take you seriously, Garren. But you have only been at Framlingham one day. How do you know this mission is impossible?"

"You must trust me when I tell you that it is. I know my limitations and I am telling you that I believe this mission will fall into serious jeopardy."

"So you have told me repeatedly. But what you have failed to tell me is why."

Garren sat in William Marshal's solar, gazing at the old man with the yellowed eyes, wondering how he was going to explain this to him. Months in the making and he was running from his assignment like a coward. He'd never run from anything in his life.

Outside, the night was becoming early morning. He'd ridden for hours to get from Framlingham to Chepstow and he was exhausted. But he'd never felt so strongly about anything in his life, so much so that he was willing to yank William Marshal from bed and beg him to reconsider the task at hand.

"Suffice it to say that, for various reasons, it is not something I can do," he muttered. "There are too many factors...."

"Rubbish," the Marshal snapped softly. "Tell me the truth. What has you spooked like a skittish mare?"

Garren looked at him, wondering if he should tell him the truth, but knowing in the same breath that he would sound like a complete idiot. Still, the Marshal deserved to know. Garren was the best agent he had and had served flawlessly up until this point. He knew he could confide in William but was reluctant to do so. With the truth came admission.

"Send someone to infiltrate the servants," he said. "I need support on this task. I fear that my attention may not always be where it should and I need assistance that I can depend on should I be indisposed."

William studied him a moment, a wise man with many years of living and loving behind him. He suspected he knew what the problem was. "Is it your bride?"

"Aye."

"You have expressed reservation about this betrothal from the beginning. What is it that still disturbs you?"

Garren took a deep breath, staring into the fire, trying to think of the right words. They came to him in pieces. "I am not sure. There's something about her...."

"Is she unpleasant?"

"Nay."

"Fat? Lazy?"

"Nay."

"Then what?"

Garren was hesitant. "From the onset, I feared the woman would be a distraction," he said quietly. "I have never been comfortable with women, you know that, and I saw the entire marriage element as unnecessary to this mission. I could have infiltrated the House of de Rosa another way, for instance, as a bachelor knight searching for a house to pledge my fealty."

The Marshal nodded patiently. "You suggested that, as I recall."

"I did. But you were convinced the marriage aspect was the most convenient and secure."

"It still is." He threw up his hands. "Garren, where is this leading? I do not understand what the problem is."

Garren sat a moment, trying to piece together his thoughts. He finally stood up and began to pace. "Derica de Rosa is no ordinary woman," he said softly. "If I were the marrying kind, she is someone I would choose to marry."

"And that is a bad thing?"

"Aye," Garren whispered. "I have known the woman all of a day and already she haunts me."

"In what way?"

"In a way that makes me feel as if I cannot breathe every time I look at her."

The Marshal was silent, contemplating what Garren has so haltingly told him. "Then I think I understand," he said quietly. "At first you feared being married to a woman you hate. Now you fear being married to a woman who takes your breath away and you fear that your loyalties will be torn."

"Something like that."

"I am sure this is a foolish question, but do you think you could grow to love her?"

Garren looked sick. "Christ, I don't know," he hissed. "All I know is that the very moment I lay eyes on her, one set of fears was replaced by another and with as much attraction as I feel towards her, I am afraid that I cannot guarantee the sanctity of this mission. If she is a distraction to me now, God only knows how I will feel about her a week, a month or a year from now."

William fell silent as the long moments ticked away. "I am not sure how we can break this betrothal, Garren."

"Therein lies the confusion," he said, agitated. "I don't want to break it, for all of the wrong reasons. But I also do not believe I can perform to the best of my abilities, which will greatly compromise me and the success of this task. Yet, I am sworn to the king and to my vows as his servant. Never, in all of my years of service, have I faced a situation like this and I find it bewildering."

The Marshal stood up from his chair, moving his weary body across the floor as he contemplated Garren's situation. As he saw it, there was only one way to deal with it.

"You are my greatest asset," he said. "You have never failed me. Yet I have also never known you to act like an addle-brained schoolboy, which is exactly what you are doing. Is this woman so attractive to you that she could ruin everything you have worked to achieve over the past eighteen years? Is she more important than your king and country? Is she so important that you would let it all slip through your fingers to see John Lackland on the throne, running the country into the ground? In one day, do you give your loyalties to a woman you don't even know simply to sate your lust?"

He was bellowing by the time he finished. Garren remained characteristically cool, yet at the same time, he felt ashamed.

"It is more than that, my lord."

"What more could there be?" he shouted. "By this foolish behavior, you have already compromised your position. Do they, in fact, know where you have gone? Don't you think they will discover that you're missing, run off liked a frightened child?"

"They know I am gone. I told Bertram that I had business to attend to. He did not ask what it was, and I did not offer. All they know is that I shall return sometime in the next couple of days and the wedding is set to take place on the sixth day of this month."

"Of course it will take place," William hissed. "This is what we have worked for these past months. Now, pull your head together; otherwise, we are all dead. Is this clear to you? Stop allowing yourself to be led by your loins and think with that clever mind I know you have. This woman is a tool of your trade and nothing more."

Garren's jaw ticked. "You are correct, of course."

"Indeed I am," William calmed. "Garren, I am not unsympathetic, but this entire conversation is ridiculous. You're a knight in the service of the king. Anything else is secondary, including any personal feelings you may have. While I appreciate that you are communicating these concerns to me, my answer is the same- you have a job to do. Do it, and do it well, and perhaps when this madness is finished, you and Lady Derica may have a chance at some manner of life together. She will be, after all, your wife."

Garren smiled ironically. "How much of a life can we have knowing I married her to betray her and her family? My sole purpose is to destroy everything they believe in."

"You can't seriously expect me to believe that it worries you."

Garren could see that the Marshal was hardening. Perhaps the honesty aspect had been a mistake. He shook his head. "It does not. It was merely an observation." It was time to make the long ride back to Framlingham and he would waste no more times. "Thank you for your attention, my lord. I am sorry to have disrupted your sleep."

"You did not," William replied. "But I will do one thing for you; I will send someone to infiltrate the servants at Framlingham. Perhaps another set of eyes and ears is a prudent move and can be great assistance to you."

Garren wanted to leave. He felt foolish for even coming, but the Marshal lay a hand on his broad shoulder in a rare gesture.

"Do not be ashamed of what you are feeling, Garren," he said quietly. "We have all had moments of lust and fear when it comes to a woman. I know you, and I know what you are capable of. I have nothing but confidence in your abilities to see this through. All of this foolishness about Lady Derica shall pass."

Garren could only smile weakly. He hoped the man was right, but on the other hand, he hoped he wasn't.

***

When she realized he wasn't going to look at her, Derica hung her head and focused on her food. The great hall of Framlingham was lit with tapers as the family and senior soldiers dined on a great pig stuffed with apples and nuts. Garren had arrived an hour or so before the evening meal, much to Derica's delight, but he'd barely said a word to her since his return. He sat next to her on the dais, wine in hand, making tight conversation with Bertram.

No one else would talk to him. They all sat, glaring at him to various degrees. Derica had no idea why, after he had left her chamber, he had become so cold towards her. He had seemed genuinely sincere and friendly during their visit, but in the presence of others, he ignored her.

"Eat, pigeon," came the deep voice beside her, "Your food is growing cold."

Derica glanced up at her uncle, Hoyt, clad in a gown that was lavish and expensive. The rouge on his cheeks was too bright and he smelled of strong perfume. She'd long since gotten over the shock of him thinking he was a woman; in fact, at times, he was very comforting in an odd sort of female way. He was like a great, protective nanny.

"I am not hungry," she pushed her trencher away.

Hoyt put it back in front of her. "You must eat. You must maintain your strength for... for...."

He suddenly burst into loud tears, clapping a wisp of a handkerchief over his mouth to muffle the cries. All conversation at the table stopped and they looked at Hoyt, carrying on pitifully.

Bertram wasn't particularly tolerant of the brother who dressed in the gowns of a queen. "Lady," he gruffed wearily. "You will not distract us with your wailing. Leave us."

Hoyt cast him a pathetic glance and continued to sob. "How can you be so cold?" he sobbed. "Your only daughter will be married on the morrow. Do you show no compassion to her plight?"

Bertram sighed heavily. "'Tis only your theatrics that intimate it 'twill be something horrible and fiendish. Marriage is an event of satisfaction and progression."

"There is no satisfaction in marrying a stranger," Hoyt insisted. "To allow this... this man access to your daughter in the Biblical sense is barbaric. You have protected her with your life since the day she was born only to turn her over to someone we do not know? I find your callousness shocking."

"I will not discuss this with you."

Hoyt continued to weep and put his arm around Derica protectively. Garren watched it all carefully, noting the size of the lady's hand, suggesting what his first instincts told him that this was no lady at all. Suspicion filled his mind; he wondered seriously what game he was playing. He didn't like the implications at all.

"And you, Sir Garren?" Donat entered the conversation from across the table. "Do you find it barbaric to wed a woman you do not know, someone who obviously has no interest or need for you?"

Garren was cool. "I have no need or interest, either, but I will attend my duty. The barbaric nature of the deal has no bearing on my personal feelings for the matter."

Donat and his brothers were working up a righteous flare. "Derica deserves better than the likes of you," Donat hissed. "At least we do not have an ancestor that surrendered like a coward to William the Bastard. Suppose cowardice runs in your blood, eh?"

"Would you like to find out?"

"Indeed!"

"Sit down, Donat," Bertram bellowed. "There will be no fighting on the eve of your sister's wedding."

The table was growing unruly. Hoyt's weeping grew louder. Donat's green eyes blazed at his father. "'Tis not fighting, Father. Call it a test of worthiness."

"He is worthy else I would not have agreed to a contract."

It was apparent that Donat was surprised not to have his father's support. "You agreed to the contract based on your friendship with his father. As le Mon clearly stated, he is nothing like his father. Doesn't Derica at least deserve to know what kind of man she will be forced to spend her life with?"

Bertram wouldn't dignify the challenge to his authority as head of the House. His gaze was steady on his middle son. "Take your seat, Donat. We will speak of this no further. "

Donat wouldn't give up without a fight. He thrust a hand at Derica. "But look at her; she is clearly miserable. She clearly despises this man."

Derica's head came up sharply. "You do not speak for me, Donat de Rosa," she snapped. Realizing what she had just said, her cheeks flamed as she looked at the surprised faces around her. "That is... I mean to say that...!" She suddenly bolted to her feet, throwing her napkin to the table. "I think you are all horrid. Each and every one of you."

She tripped over Hoyt in her attempt to flee the table, knocking his wimple into the subtlety in front of him. The tumbling wimple also managed to clip a chalice, which tipped over and splashed red wine onto Donat's linen tunic. Donat, trying to evade the spilling liquid, leapt up and knocked Dixon across the side of the head with his forearm. Dixon, outraged, threw a punch into Donat's face that sent the brother tumbling. In seconds, a full-scale fight erupted at the head table. It seemed that the de Rosas needed little provocation to leap into battle, with others or just with themselves.

Garren pushed himself back, away from the flying fists. The only family member not fighting was the eldest brother Daniel, and he immediately excused himself. Meanwhile, Derica was tangled in Hoyt's skirts and Garren reached over, unwrapping the material from her ankle. Before she stumbled further in her haste to leave the table, he grasped her hand to steady her, but she jerked her arm away.

"I do not require your assistance," she hissed.

Garren allowed himself to look at her for the first time since arriving back at Framlingham. He'd spend the past several hours attempting desperately not to think of her, much less look at her. Now, in the midst of a melee, he could think or see nothing else.

"My apologies," he said. "I did not want you to fall and hurt yourself."

Derica glared at him, gathering her skirts. Before she could reply, they were both startled by Hoyt's flying fist, sending his younger brother Lon to the floor when the man spilled more wine on him in his attempt to stop his nephews from fighting. Hoyt had an enormous hand and an enormous punch, and in spite of Derica's declaration of no assistance needed, Garren took firm hold of her and half carried her, half pulled her, off the dais.

The table was in a nasty uproar. Garren took Derica to the small alcove directly behind the table, shielding her from the violence. He watched the fight a moment before shaking his head with disapproval.

"Are they always like this?" he asked.

Derica tried to stay focused on her need to get away from Garren, but she found that she couldn't. She didn't want to admit that she simply liked being around him, but she did. After a moment's struggle, she resigned herself, feeling like a fool.

"Aye," she muttered. "The de Rosas tend to be a riotous bunch. You may as well know that events like this are not unusual for us."

Garren had a good grip on her, just in case bodies came flying in their direction and he needed to move her, quickly, to a safer haven. His eyes were sharp at the fighting going on, in particular, watching Hoyt clobber a nephew and brother to the point of unconsciousness. With the wimple off, there was no longer a question of the overly-made up creature being a man. He was colossal, with deadly fists.

A chair crashed against the wall near them, splintering. Above it all, Bertram was shouting for the disturbance to cease. No one was listening, however, and the punches continued to fly.

"I think we should leave," Garren began to look around for an escape route. "I do not like the shift in winds."

Derica shrugged. "This will calm soon enough, once they've blown off their anger."

He spied an opening at the far end of the hall. "Perhaps. But I will not risk the potential for your injury." He put both arms around her, shielding her with his massive body as they moved from the alcove. "The sooner we get out of here, the better."

Derica permitted him to drag her along the wall until they reached the exit. It led into the servant's passage that skirted the hall and led to the entrance of the larger tower. It was a cold night, with the stars bright above, and Garren took her down the wooden steps into the ward. At the base of the stairs, however, Derica removed herself from his protective grasp.

"I do not believe I am in any danger now," she said crisply. "In fact, I believe I can make it back into the hall and up to my chamber without any horrors befalling me. But I thank you for your concern."

Garren didn't know what to say. Her manner was abrupt and he knew it was because of his behavior. Warm one minute, cold the next. He wished he could explain the reasons for his actions, but he truthfully wasn't sure he fully understood them himself. He just looked at her and Derica began to suspect he was never going to reply. Gathered her skirts, she turned to the stairs. Garren continued to stare after her, her name on the tip of his tongue, knowing he should let her go but unable to.

"Derica," he called softly.

She paused, her manner stiff. "What is it?"

What is it? Garren felt a strange pressure in his chest, tight, as if he couldn't breathe. He couldn't be truthful and tell her what it was. He felt himself weakening again and wondered, if this time, there would be no point of return.

"I am sorry if I have been rude to you," he said.

"I am sure I do not know what you mean, Sir Garren. Good eve to you."

She turned up the stairs again but he stopped her. When she turned this time, he appeared a few steps below her. He had mounted the stairs and she had never heard him. The expression on his face was surprisingly unguarded.

"You must understand something," his voice was low. "How I behave with you privately and how I behave with you in front of your family are two different matters altogether."

She almost did not want to be drawn into this line of conversation, so deep was her insult and confusion. But a large part of her needed to know why he had been so nice to her then had changed as abruptly as day to night.

"Why?" she demanded softly.

"Because if they see that I am kind to you, interested even, then it will suggest weakness. And right now, your family is putting me to a test of strength. I must not fail that test. Can you comprehend that, in any manner?"

She did, somewhat. Her father and uncles and brothers were a group marred by male shortcomings. Another male into the fold only fueled their fires. Garren was doing what he had to do in order not to be trampled by them.

Her hurt was easing. "But you were...," she tried to find the right words. "In front of Aglette, you acted as if I had done something to offend you. Only the evening before, you had been warm and kind in my chamber, yet when I saw you in the bailey, you were...."

He put his hand up to silence her. "I know," he said softly. "But your servant could also be a witness for your family. Were they to ask her, she could say that she saw me demonstrate kindness toward you, something that could, again, be perceived as weakness. I want nothing to be used against me."

"Aglette is not a servant. She is my friend, and loyal to the death."

"My apologies, then. But I could not make that assumption."

She wondered if she should believe him or not. "So what you are telling me, in essence, is that in public you cannot show me any kindness so long as my family is around? Only when we are alone, is that it?"

"While your family still gnashes their teeth every time they see me, I am not sure there is any other alternative."

"Are you so concerned they would think you weak that you would rather have me think you a cad?"

"No," he shook his head slowly. "But I pray you understand my reasoning."

"But those things you said in the hall, how you have no need or interest in marrying me. Is that true?"

"No."

"Then you do have interest?"

"Can you not see it in my face, even now?"

She could, but she was terrified of this man she did not know, yet was enormously attracted to. He had the power to bend her emotions like grass in the wind.

"I see a man who says one thing, yet demonstrates another," she said after a moment. "I think you make excuses to soothe me. I shall not be made a fool of."

He sighed, feeling like he was losing a battle. This one involved feeling and he hadn't a sword big enough to fight it.

"I understand your reservation. What would convince you that I am a man of my word?"

She looked at him, thoughtfully. "Would you consider yourself a strong man, Sir Garren?"

"Stronger than most, I suppose."

"Then if you are so strong, what should it matter what my family thinks? If you are so strong, their opinion should mean nothing to you. You can stand on your strength alone."

He gazed at her a long moment. Then, he smiled. "Wiser words were never spoken, my lady."

"Perhaps. But will you heed them?"

"I can see that it will cost me your respect not to. And your respect means more to me than theirs."

She was surprised. "It does?"

"It does."

His expression made her feel giddy. They stood there on the sturdy wooden steps, gazing at each other, feeling a tide of new emotion sweep through them. Garren knew it was unhealthy for him, but he couldn't help it. It was far easier to give in than to resist. Perhaps he should just learn to work with his traitorous emotions so that they did not interfere in his thought process. He had always been the adaptable sort. With that thought, he let go of his fear and simply enjoyed something he'd never felt before in his life.

It was a bold move to reach out and take her hand. It was even bolder to place a tender kiss on the inside of her wrist. He could feel her hand tremble and it pleased him tremendously. He wanted so badly to kiss her lips, but he wouldn't dare. Her soft hand in his calloused one, for the moment, was enough.

"There you are!"

The roar came from the entrance to the larger tower. Startled, Derica and Garren looked up to see Alger and Lon standing in the doorway, swords in hand. One-eyed Alger leapt onto the steps, pulling Derica away from Garren.

"So you take her out here with lustful intentions," he growled. "I shall teach you some manners, le Mon. Women in the Holy Land may respond like dogs in heat, but civilized English women do not."

Alger was armed, but Garren remained cool. "I am without my sword. If you would allow me to collect it, I would be happy to teach you a lesson of my own."

A weapon came flying at him, courtesy of Lon. Garren deftly caught it, noting it was nothing the size or strength of his own sword. Alger didn't permit him to take a breath before he was flying at him, sword wielded high.

Garren easily deflected the blow, but he was at a disadvantage. He was halfway up the wooden stairs and to lose his balance would cause him to tumble several steps. So he descended carefully, unable to take the offense against Alger as the man pounded him mercilessly. But once they were on the level ground of the ward, the tides turned.

"Uncle Alger," Derica begged. "Please stop this. You're being foolish."

Alger growled and grunted, once landing blows, now deflecting them. He ignored his niece, who pulled away from Lon and scampered down the steps.

"Stop this, I say!" she hissed. "You're going to be injured!"

"The only one who is going to be injured is...," he grunted, warding off a strong blow aimed at his head, "... your intended. Any man who attempts to sully your honor gets the same."

"He didn't attempt to sully my honor," Derica insisted. "He was a perfect knight. In fact, he is the one who removed me from the hall so your boyish games would not injure me."

"You mean that he removed you from the hall to take advantage of you," Lon said behind her. "He is had his way with whores in the Holy Land and now he wants to have his way with you."

Somehow the thought of Garren being intimate with dark-skinned women didn't sit well with Derica. In fact, the thought of him with any woman didn't sit well with her. She watched Garren toy with her uncle, convinced he could kill the older man if he wanted to.

"Tell them you were not trying to have your way with me or they'll nip at your heels like dogs for the rest of your life," she told him.

Garren distracted Alger with a thrust while managing to get his foot in behind the man. Alger tripped and fell heavily, and his sword went into the mud.

"Gladly," he said, hardly winded. "I was not trying to have my way with your niece. I was simply talking to her."

Alger was furious and humiliated. "You are a liar. We saw you touch her."

"Her hand," Garren lowered his sword. "You saw me touch her hand. Harmless, I assure you. And if I wanted to ravage her, do you think I would do it out here in the bailey for everyone to see? I would have taken her somewhere where no one could find us."

Alger struggled up from the mud, glowering. It was enough of a distraction to allow Lon to race down the steps and leap onto Garren's back. Derica shrieked, unwisely entering the melee by trying to pull Lon off of Garren. Garren had no idea she was behind him until he brought his sword up in an attempt to dislodge Lon and ended up striking Derica instead.

She cried out, the upper portion of her right arm sliced by the weapon. The men forgot their battle, their eyes wide at the sight of her blood.

Garren was the first one to Derica's side. "Let me have a look," he took her arm gently. "Come on... that's a good girl. Let me see what I have done to you."

There were tears in her eyes, making their way down her cheeks as he peeled the tatters of her sleeve away. The wound hurt tremendously and she wasn't very good at hiding it. "I am sorry, Garren."

Garren's expression was warm and reassuring as he examined the injury. "Sorry for what?" he asked gently. "I am the one who struck you, therefore, I am the one who is sorrier than words can express."

"But I got in the way...."

"You were attempting to help me. That is noble and courageous, and I am indebted to you."

Lon had bolted off, screaming that Derica had been mortally injured. Alger remained, trying to gain a look at the injury.

"It is a decent cut," he said. "Better to take her inside to clean it."

Garren agreed; it was a long nick and somewhat deep. It was going to need a few stitches. He swept Derica into his arms and carried her into the tower. By this time, the place was in a panic and there were several anxious faces to greet them. Garren ignored the worry, more concerned with tending Derica than answering foolish questions. He snapped orders to the servants and sent them running for healing supplies, ignoring Derica's family as they tried to stop him and inspect her injury for themselves.

"What happened?" Bertram demanded. "How was she struck by your sword, le Mon? Give me answers, I say!"

Garren growled at him. "She was trying to save me from your foolish brothers. If you have anyone to admonish, better spend your breath on them. Were it not for their stupidity, none of us would be in the position we now find ourselves in."

Bertram cast Lon a long look. Alger refused to look at him at all, appearing more concerned with his niece. Garren shoved past Bertram and the others, mounting the steps to the upper floor; he would have been angry about the blockade were he not more concerned about Derica's mental state at this moment. She was pale and weepy, trying to be brave. He doubted she could have handled a confrontation of any kind.

Once in her chamber, he laid her upon the bed. The menfolk were crowding in behind them and once she was out of his arms, he was more forceful about chasing them back. Aglette squeezed in through the door, bearing water and witch-hazel.

"I will see to my daughter, le Mon," Bertram insisted. "You will not stop me."

Garren was not to be trifled with. "I have no time to waste with you, so I will make this clear. Derica does not need a gaggle of men hanging over her right now and I can guarantee that I have treated more battle wounds than you have seen in your lifetime. Leave her to me and trust that she will be properly cared for."

Bertram glared at him. "She is my daughter. You have no right to touch her, in any fashion, more than I."

"She is my wife, in the eyes of law if not yet in the eyes of God. But that, too, shall be reckoned two days hence." He planted a big hand squarely on Bertram's chest and pushed the man back, through the chamber door. "Be gone. I shall send word when she is well enough for visitors."

He slammed the door and bolted it before Bertram could respond. Ignoring the raving on the opposite side of the door, he returned his focus to Derica.

She was sitting up in her bed, pale, but the tears had subsided. Garren smiled gently as he approached, all but shoving Aglette aside and taking the stool from her. He peeled away the remaining material as Derica sucked in her breath, pained by his touch.

"I am sorry," he murmured. "I know it hurts."

She shook her head, biting her lip and looking away from the blood that stained her gown. "Not much, it doesn't."

He knew she was lying but he would not contradict her. He inspected the wound more closely, seeing bits of material in it. He had to clean it out quickly and sew it up.

"Derica," he said softly. "I need to clean the wound and put a few stitches in it. Be brave just a while longer and we'll be done with this foolishness. Are you with me?"

Derica had tended wounds before like this, on her brothers and uncles. She knew they healing sometimes hurt worse than the injury, but she nodded to his question.

"Aye," she whispered. "Hurry and get it over with."

Up until this moment, Garren had ignored his guilt at having done this to her, however accidental. Now he was seized with remorse. Tending her wound was going to hurt him far more than it would hurt her.

"I brought this, my lord," Aglette shoved a bottle at him. "If we get her drunk on wine, she'll not feel a thing."

Garren knew that wasn't quite the truth, but he took the bottle from her anyway. "My thanks," he held it up to Derica. "It might help, my lady."

Derica took a few large gulps, as if the faster and more she drank, the less the shock and pain. It was strong and tart. Garren watched her take another gulp before moving in on the wound. He would have liked to have taken the time until she was properly fortified, but there was no time to waste.

Some of the material was imbedded deep. Garren used a long pair of tweezers that Aglette had brought to pull out the bits and pieces, listening to Derica gasp and then finally sob softly in pain. More than once, he put his hand on her shoulder, gently rubbing, apologizing for the pain he was causing her. Derica would only nod her head to acknowledge him.

After an agonizing eternity, Garren was finally ready to stitch the wound. He set his tweezers down, apologized again to Derica, and poured some of the ale on the wound to cleanse it. She emitted a piercing shriek and abruptly fell silent. Garren hurriedly put five neat stitches in her soft skin.

49

"It is over," he said quietly, taking a strip of clean linen from Aglette to bind Derica's arm. "Your bravery astounds me, my lady. I have seen battle hardened knights handle pain not a morsel as well as you did."

Derica was beyond the crying stage. Lying back on the pillows as Garren expertly wrapped her arm, she didn't respond. The wine had taken its toll and she hovered in fitful unconsciousness.

Garren took longer than he had to tying off the binding. His gaze moved between Derica's white face and his work. When he was done wrapping the arm, he kissed it softly. His guilt was overtaking him completely and he was deeply sorry for her agony.

"Sleep well, sweetheart," he murmured. "You have earned it."

He collected the basin and linen next to the bed, preparing to leave her in peace. But Derica's weak voice stopped him.

"Do not go," she whispered.

He handed the bloody rags to Aglette. "I thought you were asleep."

"Please stay."

Her face was the color of the linen upon which she rested. Garren sat back down next to her.

"I will not leave you," he murmured.

"Promise?"

"On my oath. I will never leave you."

Her eyes opened and her head lolled in his direction. Garren smiled at her as their eyes met. Derica's only response was to open her hand, slowly, and lift it with great difficulty. Garren saw the gesture meant for him and he quickly took her hand, holding it tightly. With that, Derica closed her eyes once more and sleep claimed her.

CHAPTER FIVE

"I am in no mood for foolery. My daughter has been injured this night and my patience is at an end."

"I assure you, I bring no foolery, my lord. Fourteen hundred men have landed at the mouth of the Welland River. Nottingham is a two day's ride from there. Can you imagine such a force for our cause, my lord?"

A man dressed in shabby clothes and a patched eye sat near the hearth, warming himself. The bugs that found a home in his garments and against his skin were jumping off of him due to the searing heat. Bertram watched small, black things fall onto his stone floor. He moved his foot when a dark dot with legs moved too close.

"You're sure?" Bertram asked.

The man nodded. "I have eyes everywhere, my lord. I trust their word."

Bertram digested the information. The man was a spy, someone who had worked for the prince's cause for several years. He looked and acted like a mad peasant, making him the perfect spy. He could go almost anywhere and glean whatever knowledge he could. His network was laced with relatives and other unscrupulous acquaintances on the prince's payroll. More often than not, the information they provided was startlingly accurate and Bertram was well aware of the fact.

Which was why he considered the man's statements carefully. "Teutonic mercenaries," he muttered. "Fat, evil, well paid murderers."

"Moving for Nottingham Castle."

"Then it is up to the Earl of Nottingham to amass them until the prince is prepared to move. Any news of the Irish mercenaries?"

The dirty man shook his head. "I have not heard, my lord. The hope is to move them through Liverpool, far to the north and away from Richard's ever-present eyes. Their destination is Bolton Castle and the prince's supporter there."

Bertram knew that, but the Irish mercenaries were not his concern. Neither were the Teutonic. His direct concern was a mass of French mercenaries due to arrive at Great Yarmouth sometime before the month was out. Weather was unusually turbulent this spring, making crossing the channel difficult. Time frames for the prince's paid armies had been sorely distorted by it, making future plans difficult to calculate.

Bertram stood up, clasping his hands behind his back. In the shadows, Lon and Alger listened intently; they were the only family members allowed to witness the exchange. They had known when they saw the spy ride into the ward earlier that evening that something was afoot. Alberic always brought with him information, bugs, gossip and intrigue.

"So we wait," Bertram said slowly. "The Irish at Bolton, the Teutonic in Nottingham, and the French at Framlingham. Other castles will house more mercenaries when the time comes and when we slip the noose around England's midsection, we will divide Richard's country. If all proceeds as it should, John should have the throne by Christmas."

"Nothing except Richard's armies," Lon rumbled. "You speak as if his supporters sleep while we amass. You know as well as I do that if we have spies, then so does he."

"I have been in the prince's service since the days he rebelled against his father," Alberic scratched his cheek where an insect bit at him. "There is an entire community of those who secretly serve the prince and his brother. We are as shadows, flitting between sunrise and sunset, ghosts that appear and then disappear just as quickly. We are fleeting figments of the imaginations, as deadly as a viper if one draws too close. Sometimes I believe our task is more difficult than the knights who fight with weapons and fire."

"I cannot disagree," Bertram said. He watched more bugs leap onto his floor. "If there is nothing else, then I say you should leave. 'Tis unwise for you to remain here for any length of time."

Alberic stood up, stiffly, feeling his age this night. It was cold outside, threatening rain, but he dare not ask for shelter from de Rosa. They both well understood his role, and he was clearly not a guest. Slipping from the solar without another word, he made his way out of the tower and into the bailey. The gates were still open, even in the night, and his worn mule was tethered outside the walls. As he hurried across the ward, trying to remain as inconspicuous as possible, something caught his attention over by the western tower.

Alberic paused, dipping into the shadow of the wall as he was so used to doing. Hiding was second nature to him. He watched a large figure cross from the large western tower and into the stable block. Puzzled, he tried to follow but stopped short of the wooden steps into the structure. He could not risk entering the stables and being cornered. He stood there a moment, unsure what to do, unsure of what he had seen. But he knew he must seek Bertram.

Bertram and Alger were still in the solar, deep in discussion. Lon had since vanished. Alberic paused at the solar door and removed the soiled cape that covered his head.

"My lord?" he said.

Bertram looked up from his conversation with his brother, somewhat annoyed to see the dirty spy standing in the doorway.

"I told you to leave."

"I was, my lord," Alberic took a hesitant step into the room. "But... I saw something...."

"Well, what is it, man, and be quick about it."

The spy wasn't sure where to begin. "As I was leaving, I saw a man come from the western tower and enter the stables."

"What man?"

"He was large, quite large. Young and strong, with light-colored hair."

Lon looked at his brother. "He must mean le Mon. If he has left Derica's side, then she must be doing well enough."

"Now is our chance to see to her ourselves."

"Agreed. The man was as unmoving as a guard dog."

"My lord?"

The spy was demanding attention, interrupting their conversation. Bertram snapped at him impatiently. "So you have seen my daughter's intended. What of him?"

Alberic appeared taken aback. "He is to marry your daughter?"

"Yes, what of it?"

The spy would not be intimidated; he was, in fact, growing suspicious and disturbed. "I know that man, my lord."

Bertram's temper took a strange, cooling twist. "You do?"

"Aye, my lord."

"Where do you know him from?"

Alberic thought carefully on his reply. "As you know, my lord, I have been in the service of the prince for many years. I have seen many things, and many people. Those of us who covertly serve our masters tend to hear of one another, if only by reputation. It is wise to know one's enemies. Sometimes, however, we are fortunate enough to put a face to the name or reputation."

"Get to the point."

"What do you know of your daughter's intended, my lord?"

Bertram's temper flared again. "Alberic, if you do not tell me your meaning, I will throw you from this room. You waste my time."

The spy cocked a long, dirty eyebrow. "I think not, my lord," he said coolly. "I think you betray your prince."

Bertram moved for him, but Alger stopped him. In spite of the insult, he suspected there was true motivation behind it. "Explain yourself before I let my brother gut you."

"Gut me and you will not know who your daughter's intended truly is."

"Le mon?" Bertram glanced at his brother, a thousand unspoken words of doubt and fear in his expression. "Who is he?"

Alberic put his filthy hood back on and turned for the door. His plan was to go directly to the prince with what he had just seen. But he would do de Rosa the favor of letting him know that his fate would soon be sealed, and his loyalties questioned.

"That man," he said slowly, "works for William Marshal."

***

"My lady?" came the whisper. "My lady, are you awake?"

Derica heard the murmuring, a soft voice in her ear. She sighed deeply as she emerged from her warm slumber, opening her bleary eyes to see Aglette's pale face. Blinking, she struggled to orient herself in the bright room.

"Aglette?" she yawned. "What is it? What time is it?"

"'Tis nearly noon, my lady," Aglette said. "Something awful has happened!"

"What's so awful?" She gasped as she moved her arm the wrong way; it was stiff and sore but, thankfully, had no signs of poison yet. She looked around the room. "Where is Sir Garren?"

Aglette was obviously distraught. The more lucid Derica became, the more she realized her servant had been crying.

"He is in the vault," Aglette whispered.

"What for?"

Aglette burst into sobs, struggling to contain them. "I have heard they are going to kill him!"

Derica was instantly awake. "What on earth for?"

The maid shook her head. "I do not know, my lady. I only heard from the soldiers that your father and brothers captured him early this morning and placed him there."

Derica was seized by confusion and anger. Sitting up, she bolted from the bed as fast as she could, looking for some manner of clothing to wear. The room was swaying and moving was difficult, but she would not let it stop her. She had to find out what had happened to Garren.

"Please, my lady," Aglette begged. "You are unwell. Perhaps you should...."

Derica waved her off harshly. "I swear that my family is no better than a pack of mad dogs. The moment Garren is alone, they descend upon him like vicious beasts."

She yanked off the gown she wore with the tattered, bloodied sleeve and struggled to step into a garment of soft gray lamb's wool. Aglette rushed to help her, both of the struggling to pull the sleeve over her bandaged arm. Fortunately, the sleeve was loose enough that it fit, but barely. The tight material caused Derica some pain, but she fought it. She had no time for her discomfort.

Aglette tried to run a comb through her long, tangled curls, but Derica would have no part of it. Fumbling a pair of slippers onto her feet, she moved from her chamber as fast as her shaky legs would carry her. Aglette stumbled behind her, fastening the dress so that it would stay on her mistress. By the time they entered the ward, Derica was flushed and weak, but her determination speared her on. The day was bright and cool, and she received some curious looks from soldiers and peasants alike as she sprinted across the bailey in a disheveled mess.

The vault of Framlingham was located in the bowels of the gatehouse tower, an enormous place that smelled like rot. A soldier guarding the entrance tried to keep her away, but she ignored him and descended the narrow stone stairs.

The steps came to a leveled room, cold with stone and mold. Torches lit the walls and there were several people standing about, making the small chamber crowded. Two iron-grated cells were at the far end of the room and a hole in the floor held a pit dungeon. Derica's eyes adjusted to the dimness, recognizing her father and uncles.

Bertram spoke first. "Derica! What...?"

She cut her father short. "Where is he?"

Bertram moved towards her, his arms outstretched. "Derica, my love, you must...."

She slapped her father's hand away; it was sharp movement that strained her bad arm and she winced as pain shot through her.

"Answer me. Where is Sir Garren? Why is he in here?"

Bertram glanced at his brothers, undeterred from putting his arm around his daughter. She pushed against him, but he was insistent.

"Derica, you needn't worry about Sir Garren any longer. There will be no forced marriage and you will be free to marry a man worthy of you. I am so sorry you had to...."

Derica pulled away from him sharply, looking at her father as if he had gone mad. "No marriage? What are you talking about?" Her father tried to hold her again and, this time, she roughly slapped his hand away. "If you do not tell me what is going on here, I shall pummel each and every one of you until I have my answers."

Alger tried to comfort her. "Derica, you're ill and distraught. 'Twould be better if you retired to your chamber and allowed us to do what needs to be done."

Derica could see that she would receive no answers. With a growl of frustration, she pushed past her father and uncle and moved towards the cells. Her brothers tried to stop her and she fought with them, too; it seemed that no one wanted to answer her or help her find Garren. Even rational, gentle Daniel wouldn't help her. When she finally pushed past Donat after threatening to restructure his nose, she caught a glimpse of a large body chained to the wall of one of the cells.

It was Garren. He looked as if he had been thrashed within an inch of his life, blood on his face and matted in his hair. His arms were bruised and bloodied, and the iron cuffs that held him to the wall had chaffed huge red welts around his wrists.

Derica suddenly felt very ill and weak. Bertram didn't try to stop her as she entered the cell.

"Dear God," she whispered as she surveyed Garren's wounds. "What have they done to you?"

Garren hated for her see him like this. She appeared weary and exhausted, and he knew she shouldn't be here. Nasty dealings were afoot and he didn't want her bearing witness. But he was glad to see her nonetheless.

"It took several of them to capture me," he was trying to lighten the grim situation. "Your father, uncles, brothers, and a few soldiers for good measure. One moment I was in the stables, and in the next I was being set upon. Without you there to protect me, the alligators snared the ibis."

Derica could not give into his attempt at humor. "But why? I do not understand."

Before Garren could reply, Bertram answered. "He is a spy, Derica," her father said quietly. "You must not interfere in what needs to be done."

Confusion flickered across Derica's face. "Spy?" she repeated. Her focus remained on Garren. "What are they saying about you?"

Garren took a long, deep breath. "They believe I mean to destroy them."

"Destroy?" Derica mouthed the word as if she had never heard it before. "Why in the world would they think this?"

Garren shook his head. "I was not given the courtesy of being told their reasons. They seem more intent on beating a confession out of me."

Derica's confusion faded and her fury returned, worse than before. She whirled to her father. "You're mad," she hissed. "I have known you to be suspicious and belligerent, but this accusation against Sir Garren is pure madness."

Bertram remained calm. "We know this for truth, daughter."

"From whom?"

"A reliable source. Suffice it to say that...."

"Who told you this?"

"It does not matter. What matters is that I trust this word." He nodded towards Garren. "Your intended is sent from William Marshal to spy against us. He comes to destroy everything we have, including you."

"That is not true," Derica turned back to Garren. "What insanity would cause them to say this against you? Tell them they are lunatics!"

"I am not here to destroy you," Garren said softly. "When I came through the gates of Framlingham five days ago, my only intention was to gain wealth and status through marriage. Now my only intention is to marry you, wealth or no. You are the only wealth I will ever want."

Tears filled her eyes. She reached up with her good arm, touching his battered face, feeling his lips against her fingers. Anger such as she had never known filled her.

"Release him, father."

"I cannot. He must be punished."

"You mean killed."

"Spies are dealt with in such ways."

Derica exploded. "If you kill him, I shall flee from Framlingham and you will never see me again. I will whore for every nobleman that serves King Richard and shame the name of de Rosa such as you have never dreamed." The tears escaped and found their way onto her face. "This foolish paranoia that feeds your soul must come to an end. For all of these years I have ignored it because you were my father and I love you. But now you attack me directly, and you attack my happiness. Release Sir Garren or I swear I will make you sorry until the end of your days."

The entire vault was deathly silent by the time she finished. Bertram was pale; he'd never seen his daughter in such a tirade. She had always maintained such control over her emotions. His natural instinct was to do whatever she wished, but at the moment, he was torn. He didn't want her to follow through on her threats; he wasn't sure she would, but, being a de Rosa, she was stubborn and willful and he wasn't entirely sure that she wouldn't.

"Derica," he said quietly. "You're sick. You're not thinking clearly. You must understand that this is a man's matter. It does not involve you."

"It clearly involves me if Sir Garren is to be my husband," she countered. "You will release him immediately and I will forget this ever happened."

As much as Bertram loved his daughter, he would not be pushed around by her.

"I cannot."

Derica stared at him for several long, painful moments. He had been right about one thing; she was ill and not thinking clearly. In a fit of momentary insanity, she swooped upon the brother standing nearest to her and unsheathed his sword. Before anyone could stop her, she pressed the blade against her stomach.

"Release him now or I drive this into my belly!"

Everyone shouted at her to stop, including Garren. She had a wild look to her eye and there was no one in the chamber that had any doubt she would do as she threatened.

Bertram pleaded. "Derica, no. It is not as bad as all that. Please... give the blade back to Donat."

Her response was to grip it more tightly. "Release him. I shall not tell you again."

Bertram looked at Garren. Strange how mortal enemies had, in a fraction of a second, suddenly became allies. Garren could feel the father's panic; he had quite enough of his own.

"Derica," Garren said softly. "Put the blade down, sweetheart. Please."

Derica looked at him. "Do you not understand that they mean to kill you? I will not let them do that. I cannot."

"So you would kill yourself instead?" Garren smiled. "Do you think that would give me pleasure to watch? As much as you do not wish my death, I do not wish yours even more. To know you died on my behalf would fill me with grief as I cannot comprehend. My life would be meaningless."

"As mine would be were you to leave me," her lip quivered. "I cannot let them do this to you."

"If you thrust that blade into your belly, they are going to kill me anyway. Your death would not stop them. It would more than likely cause them to insure that my death was as painfully long and slow as possible. Did you think of that?"

She knew he spoke the truth. Tears spilled down her cheeks as she looked at her father. She knew how her father and brothers were, that honor and service to the prince was nearly everything to them. She could not imagine who told them Garren was a spy, or how this wild idea took root, but one thing was for certain; if they believed Garren was a spy, for whatever reason, nothing on earth could convince them otherwise. But bargains could be struck, and for the sake of Garren's life, she knew what she had to do.

"Release him and I will not kill myself. His life for mine, father. That is the bargain."

Bertram eyed his daughter. He couldn't stand the thought of her driving that cold blade into her soft belly. He weighed his choices.

"Do as she asks."

The command came from the steps leading up into the gatehouse. Everyone turned to see Hoyt standing at the base of the stairs, without his makeup or fancy gowns. He looked as they all remembered him, a massive man who had been the best warrior of them all. Bertram hadn't seen his brother this serious, or this normal, in some time. It was unsettling.

"He is a spy," Bertram said to his brother. "If we let him go, the consequences could be lethal."

"If you do not, the same could be said." Hoyt entered the vault, slowly. His eyes were on Derica. "Look at her, Bertram. She means what she says. Let him go or we shall all be sorry."

Bertram knew that his brother was correct; there was only one choice to make. He found himself cursing the day his only female child was born. At that moment, something between them changed.

"Then I shall release him," he said. "But I shall also say this; there will be no marriage. I will never again hear the name Garren le Mon and if I ever see him again, I will kill him. Make no mistake. My mercy is given only once."

Derica was not surprised. Her terms had been accepted; now her father was extending his own. It was a compromise of the greatest proportion, but Derica considered it a small price to pay for Garren's life.

"As you say," she whispered.

She kept the sword against her stomach as she watched Hoyt unlatch the shackles around Garren's wrists and ankles. It was sorry to say that she didn't trust her family, but she did not. She had lived with them too long and knew too well of their ways. She had to maintain the threat even though, deep down, she would not have done it. It was bluff that, with the mere thought of her death, had worked against her father. She didn't feel the least bit guilty.

"Sir Garren is free to go to the stables and collect his horse," she said pointedly to the men around her. "He will not be touched."

The younger men grumbled, kicked at the ground, but dare not dispute her. The older men glared. Only Hoyt stood there, with no discernible expression, but the message was obvious; his support was with Derica and, subsequently, with Garren. The tides of the de Rosa household were shifting.

Garren rubbed his wrists. Hoyt was standing next to him and their eyes met, silent words of understanding passing between them; Hoyt had seen Garren tend Derica and had seen the tenderness in the man's eyes. It was more than courtesy or infatuation; there was genuine emotion there. Whatever his brothers were cooking up now against Garren was not only detrimental to Derica, but to them all. Walls were being built with little hope of ever being torn down again.

Garren turned to Derica. "I will not leave you here."

Derica could feel her anguish welling. "I cannot go with you. Be fortunate that you leave with your life."

He was going to argue with her but thought better of it; surrounded by the de Rosa clan, she had a point. He was indeed fortunate to be leaving with his life. But in his estimation, it wasn't over. Not as long as there was breath left in his body.

"Then the last time I see you will not be with a sword against your gut," he said softly. "Take it away and let me see you one more time the way you were meant to be."

That was all it took for Derica to throw down the sword. She wanted to run to him and throw herself in his arms, but she dared not. It might set her father off and she had no way of knowing. They gazed at each other, a thousand unspoken words between them.

"You haven't asked me if it is true," Garren said.

"If what is true?"

"If I am a spy."

She shrugged weakly. "That is because it doesn't matter. You are Sir Garren le Mon of Anglecynn and Ceri, a man who came to me with kindness and compassion such as I have never known. That is who you are to me." She could read the longing in his eyes and her heart was broken. "Now, go. Please. While there is still time."

"I shall not forget you, lady."

"Nor I, you."

His expression said everything that his lips could not. Derica watched him walk from the cell, listening to his boots until they faded away. Her father, uncles, brothers stood there, unable to move, unwilling to say anything. Everyone stood in a dark, brooding mass.

"Derica," Daniel said softly. "You must understand that Father was only doing what he thought he had to. To protect you."

Derica held up a hand to him, a gesture to be silent. She was not prepared to speak to any of them at the moment, not even the eldest brother who seemed to go against the grain of the de Rosa personality traits. Now, she simply wanted to get away from all of those who had turned her once-happy future into a nightmare in a matter of hours.

When enough time had passed, she wandered from the vault and into the sunshine. Garren had long since passed through the gates. She stood there, in the middle of Framlingham's massive ward, watching the green countryside beyond the gates as if expecting him to reappear any moment. She was beyond tears, beyond exhaustion, and every fiber of her being cried for the future she would never have.

It was difficult to comprehend what this short week in her life had brought to her. Nothing seemed worth the living any longer.

CHAPTER SIX

Yaxley Nene Abbey
Leicestershire

As a child, the place had always frightened him. A dark structure, made from dark stone and covered with dark ivy, it always appeared like something out of a religious nightmare. He had come here with his father on a yearly pilgrimage when very young. Even at his advanced age, he came still on that pilgrimage, now more from a sense of wanting than a sense of duty.

Tonight, it was a different sort of pilgrimage. It was important that he come because he could think of nowhere else to go. He had been riding for an indeterminate number of hours and his charger, the great red beast with the pale eyes, was exhausted. There was a wall around the abbey and a gated opening that reminded Garren of the gate to hell; sharp spikes jutted up from the iron grate like fanged teeth. Garren shuddered involuntarily as he passed through, as he had since he had been a child. It was as though the gate had eaten him alive with all of those sharp teeth.

The moon had disappeared by the time he arrived. Dawn was near. Garren left the charger grazing on the grass near the wall as he approached the great oak door that kept the secular world from the women inside. He rapped on the door, heavily, and waited.

A pale face wrapped in white appeared. Garren announced himself and the tiny nun allowed him entrance. Garren knew what was expected of him and he stopped just inside the door and planted his big feet, unmoving. He was not permitted to go anywhere inside the structure unless the nuns indicated. Right now it was a waiting game, and his patience, fed by exhaustion, was brittle.

Yet he knew he would be waiting awhile, so he closed his eyes and inhaled deeply of the musty scent that reminded him of his days as young boy. The carefree days of his youth came back to his weary mind in bits and pieces, remembering the father who doted on him, the mother who died when he was so young that he could barely remember her. He remembered a pet goat he had when he was perhaps three or four years, the one who had butted him and trampled him until he grew big enough to outrun it. His eyes opened, and he found himself smiling about that idiotic goat. He had named it Henry, after the king, much to the amusement of his father.

Revelry took his mind off his wait. He remembered having to leave the goat to foster at Sandhurst Castle, more crushed about leaving the animal than his father. He remembered some of the other pages teasing him because he used to cry in his sleep for the goat. His memories began to drift towards his days as a squire, when he outgrew the boys who teased him and turned into their worst fear. He smiled wearily at that memory, too, until soft footsteps roused him from his daydreams.

The small nun in the white garments returned. She didn't say a word, but she motioned for Garren to follow. He did so, listening to his heavy boots echo off the walls as they entered a darkened corridor. Two doors down, there was a room; the nun indicated for him to enter, which he did.

The chamber was completely dark but for a small taper burning on a well-scrubbed table. As he eyes adjusted to the darkness, he saw a figure seated near the wall.

"Garren?"

He knew the voice very well. Dropping the saddlebags he had slung over one massive shoulder, he went to the silhouette and dropped to one knee.

"'Tis me," he said. "I am sorry it is so early."

The figure moved into the light; an older woman with fine features surrounded folds of white material. "You needn't apologize, little brother. Early morning or midnight, I care not. I am most thankful for your presence."

She smiled, her hands reaching for Garren. He smiled in return, kissing her hands before embracing her. The former Lady Gabrielle le Mon, or now more correct Sister Mary Felicitas, put her arms around her younger brother's neck.

"Garren," she gasped, patting his shoulders. "You grow larger by the year. Have you found a wife to feed you well, then?"

He shook his head even though she could not see him. Gabrielle had been blind since birth, committed to Yaxley Nene Abbey at eleven years of age, months after her brother, and only sibling, was born. Though they were far apart in age and had never lived under the same roof, the yearly pilgrimages to Yaxley had seen them form a bond that ran strangely deep. Garren adored her.

"No wife," he said. "Not yet, at any rate. But let's not talk about me. I want to know about you; how have you been?"

"Well, little brother," she held his hands in her warm, tiny ones. "And you?"

"Well enough," he said. "I have been quite busy, but I have written to you some."

Gabrielle lit up. "Diaries!" she exclaimed softly. "You know how much I look forward to your visits when you read to me the chronicle of your life. How long has it been? At least a year since you were last here. I am sure so much has happened since then."

"Much indeed."

Garren left her long enough to retrieve small rolls of vellum from his saddlebags. His sister was the only outsider, other than his father, who knew his true role in the scheme of Richard's cause. He knew his secret was safe with her and made it a point to write letters to her, chronicling the adventures that his life sometimes took. It was dangerous writing should it fall into the wrong hands, but he never left any identifying marks on the parchment other than a name here and there. Certainly nothing traceable. Settling his bulk beside her, he unrolled a spool of yellowed parchment.

"I am not sure where to start," he said. "I spent some time in London, but there is not much to say about that other than a grand feast I attended where a woman wore jewelry she said was smelted for the gods. She had this necklace in the shape of a vulture and many colored stones to adorn it. She also wore solid gold rings in the shape of bugs."

"Bugs?"

"Strange, is it not? But she said ancient kings used to wear these adornments and she was quite proud to show them off."

"Garren?"

"Aye?"

"What is wrong?"

He paused in his chatter. "What do you mean?"

Gabrielle took his hand again. "I know you well, my baby brother. Something is troubling you. I can hear it in your voice."

"I am not sure what you mean."

"I am not a fool. When you come to me before dawn, when your voice trembles and you talk too much, something is wrong. What is it?"

Garren felt a huge sense of depression sweep him. He had indeed come for a reason, not simply to see his sister. She knew that, and he felt doubly guilty. He set the vellum down.

"It is that obvious?"

"Tell me."

He felt as if he was at confession. He had truly meant not to delve into the problems in his life immediately, but he couldn't seem to help it. Gabrielle was soothing, comforting, and wise. Before he knew it, everything from the past week was spilling out and he could hear the anguish in his voice as he spoke. It frightened him. Gabrielle held his hand and never said a word. By the time he was finished, exhaustion claimed him and he leaned back against the wall, positive he would never rise again.

"It would seem that much has happened, little brother," Gabrielle said softly.

Garren snorted at the irony of it. "I can face any battle with confidence. Give me a sword and I shall emerge the victor. But give me emotion, give me a woman whom I am undeniably attracted to, and I fall apart like a weakling. My heart hurts and I cannot repair it; my anger knows no bounds, yet it is directionless. I have no one to blame, yet everyone to blame. I feel as if I am in everlasting damnation, in love with a woman I should have never loved in the first place."

Gabrielle didn't say anything for a moment. "And your Lady Derica," she murmured. "Does she feel the same for you?"

"I see it in her eyes every time she looks at me."

Gabrielle nodded silently. Garren prayed that she was thinking through the situation far more logically than he could at the moment. "Then I suppose the question is, what do you want?" she said." To marry her? Have you thought on the consequences of that action, my dear?"

"I want to marry her, yes," Garren said quietly. "I want to get her out of Framlingham and take her some place safe."

"Where would that be?"

"I do not know. I cannot go to Chateroy, as it is the first place they would look. Father must not know anything of my actions."

"For his own safety, I agree," Gabrielle said. "But what will happen to her if you take her from her family and marry her? Do you intend to continue in the Marshal's service? You know as well as I that your service takes you all over England and beyond. Do you expect your bride to stay alone, hiding from her family the rest of her life, while you go about your duty?"

Garren removed his helm and ran his fingers through his short hair. "I will resign my service to the Marshal," he muttered. "I would rather be with Derica, hiding from her family until the end of our days, than be away from her for one more minute. I serve a king who has not spent a day of his reign in England. I fight and fight for a man who is not even here to know that we are all fighting for him. He battles the infidels in the Holy Land while we battle for his very life as a monarch at home. Am I tired of it? No. But I have seen something, felt something, I never thought I would see or feel, and although I love my king, I want to love Derica more."

"Truly now, Garren?"

"Truly."

Gabrielle was thoughtful. "I have never known you to speak of any woman, much less one you wish to marry. Are you sure this is not an infatuation, quick to flame, quick to pass? The thoughts you voice would surely end your illustrious career."

"Well I know it," he said. "And, no, I am sure this is not an infatuation. I felt something different for Derica from nearly the moment I met her, something I have not felt before."

"Feelings enough to incur the Marshal's wrath?"

Garren sighed heavily, gazing up at the dark ceiling. Outside, the sun was beginning to rise, soft gray light coming through the lancet window.

"I begged him not to send me on this mission," he murmured. "God, I begged and pleaded until I could say no more and, still, he sent me. I would love to blame William for this mess, but I cannot. The fault is my own."

Gabrielle smiled. "Do you believe in the Will of God, Garren?"

"I do."

"Then you surely must know that this was planned for you a long time ago. You begged and pleaded with the Marshal not to send you on this mission, but still he sent you. You knew from the moment you met the lady that there was something different about her and in the matter of a week, you have found yourself hopelessly entangled in something that men only dream of. Perhaps this was meant to happen, all of it. Perhaps you were indeed sent on a mission, simply not the one you had planned for."

Garren was interested in what she was saying. "What do you mean?"

"Precisely that. You stated that your mission was to infiltrate the de Rosas in the hope of discovering the movements of Prince John's rebellion. What if... what if your true mission was to simply marry Derica de Rosa and, as a result, perhaps affect Richard's opposition in a way you never dreamed possible."

"I do not understand."

"Nor do I at the moment. Sometimes we cannot see God's Wisdom until well after the fact."

She had a point. Garren mulled her words, watching the room turn shades of gray and white as the sun continued to rise. There was fog outside, shrouding the countryside, dampening his mood. Finally, he pushed himself from the wall and rose wearily. Gabrielle's sightless eyes tracked him.

"What are you going to do?" she asked.

He lifted his arms in a helpless gesture. "The only plan I can come up with is storming the castle and spiriting her away, which is not particularly wise. I am too tired to think right now." He looked at his sister. "Tell me; what would you do?"

"Do you truly wish to know?"

"I would not have asked otherwise."

She smiled faintly, a gesture shaped somewhat like her brother's. "I would suggest you plan carefully for this, Garren. You must not make any rash decisions."

"What plans do you suggest?"

Gabrielle folded her hands. "You cannot return to Framlingham for her. They would kill you. You cannot storm the castle, as you cannot amass enough men in a short amount of time. So it is logical that perhaps you know of someone, a trusted friend or knight, who could infiltrate Framlingham and whisk her from the castle. Do you know of someone?"

Garren was listening intently. "I do. Then what?"

"Have them bring her here, to me. That way, if her family tracks her, it would lead to the abbey and not even the de Rosa's would dare breach the sanctity of the abbey. I will keep her here with me until you come for her."

"Where am I going to be?"

"After you tell the Marshal that you no longer wish to be an agent for the king, you will find a place for you and your wife to live. You cannot run the rest of your lives. Find a place in Scotland or Wales, something well off the path and fortified, and take her there. Swear fealty to whichever king you wish, raise a sizable force and recruit bachelor knights, and live there with your lady for the rest of your life. If that is what you wish, Garren, then make it so."

Garren just stood there and smiled. "A sound enough plan, madam. How is it that your mind works so?"

"My brother taught me."

Garren knelt down beside her again, kissing her softly on the cheek. "I am glad to have come to you," he said softly. "You help me to think clearly when my entire world is in turmoil."

Gabrielle patted his hand. "You have no time to waste, Garren. I suspect even now that your lady is living anxiously. If she supported you against her family, she cannot be in their good graces. The sooner she is removed from Framlingham, the better. The sooner you are reunited with her, the better."

Garren collected his saddlebags, his mind was racing with possibilities, of hope, where moments before there had been none. He had another mission now, perhaps greater than any he had ever undertaken. He took his sister's hand, trying to think of the proper words of gratitude.

"To express my thanks seems quite inadequate," he said simply.

She waved him off. "None needed, Garren."

"I do not know when I shall return. I do not know when Derica will arrive. Of the future, I can say nothing for certain. Only that I will do my very best."

"I know you will. And I shall be prepared for any event. I shall welcome it."

He gave her hand a squeeze before quitting the room, marching into the early morning light with more purpose he had ever felt in his life. Back in the small chamber, Gabrielle swore she could hear his charger race off even though she knew she could not. She sat there, wondering if she had given him advice that would end his life. But the man's heart was in turmoil, and she gave the only advice she knew she could.

There was nothing to do now but wait.

***

Garren had known Fergus de Edwin since they had been boys. They had fostered together at Sandhurst Castle and had formed a friendship that had lasted all of these years. They had served together, and at times had gone years without seeing one another, but somehow they always found each other again. Garren knew, in any circumstance, that Fergus was the only man who would postpone his own funeral if Garren needed him. That manner of friendship was few and far between, and Garren valued it.

Fergus was a bachelor knight and something of a free spirit. His fealty shifted from time to time with different lords. His cause also happened to be any cause that Garren had, and at the moment, Garren needed his friend desperately for a cause that he never thought he would support. In this crisis, Garren could only turn to one man.

Fortunately for Garren, he had last heard that his friend happened to be serving Walter de Lacy at Longton Castle in Herefordshire. The nearby village, Haverhill, was a two-day's ride from Framlingham. Garren had taken a room in a tavern in Haverhill and found a youth to run a message to the castle. It was the middle of the night by the time he sent the message.

He suspected it would be dawn before Fergus arrived, if he was even still at Longton. Having not slept in well over two days, Garren stripped off his armor and fell down on the bed of his rented room. The straw inside the mattress was damp and old, but he didn't care. He was beyond exhausted and asleep before he realized it.

As a knight, his life depended upon his reflexes. Knights were notorious for sleeping lightly. But the sun was up and there was someone in his room before he was fully oriented. His sword was near his hand and the blade came up. He heard it clang against metal, followed by what sounded suspiciously like a yelp. Rolling off the opposite side of the bed in a flash, he saw a man with bright blue eyes standing on the other side, rubbing his left arm.

A bolt of relief ran through Garren and he lowered the sword. "Christ," he muttered. "Fergus, you idiot...."

Fergus stood there, still rubbing his arm. "Did you have to try and cut my head off?" he complained. "You send for me and this is the welcome I receive? Even from you, that is cold."

Garren tossed the sword on the bed and wearily scratched his head. "What did you expect, sneaking into my room? I will wager that you were standing over me trying to decide how best to smother me as I slept."

Fergus broke into a wide grin. Garren did the same. The men embraced each other as one would a brother.

"You're as ugly as ever, Garren."

"And you're still as stupid as I remember." Garren rubbed the sleep out of one eye and indicated the only chair in the room. "Please, sit. So you're still at Longton, after all?"

Fergus took the chair as Garren lowered himself back onto the bed. Fergus was a nice looking man with brilliant blue eyes and dark blond hair. His teeth protruded slightly and his skin was rough from sun and cold. He shrugged to Garren's assertion.

"De Lacy is fond of me and pays me well," he said. "I have no reason to leave yet. And you? Last I heard, you were wandering somewhere between Dover and Hastings."

"I still am."

"So why are you in Herefordshire?"

"Up until yesterday, I was to marry a local heiress."

Fergus' eyebrows lifted; he liked money. "Is that so? What did you do to make her break the betrothal?"

Fergus snickered at Garren's expense. Garren grinned at his friend's sense of humor. "It wasn't her, but her father. Seems he didn't take too kindly to me, after all."

"Do tell."

Garren's smile faded and the conversation took a serious turn. He explained everything, from the beginning. Fergus had no knowledge, nor had he ever, of Garren's true vocation, so the details about the Marshal were left out. For all Fergus knew, Garren's father had negotiated a marriage contract, which was broken when the de Rosa's concocted some foolish story about Garren being a spy for the king. Garren made sure to point out, without much embellishment, how suspicious the clan was and how protective they were of Derica.

Fergus was grim. "So you want revenge for them breaking the contract?"

"No."

"Then what?"

"I want her."

Fergus didn't quite understand. "You want her? But why? Lady Derica without the inheritance is hardly worth the trouble."

"You don't understand, Fergus. I am in love with her."

Fergus looked shocked. "I see," he muttered. "Are you sure, Garren?"

"I am."

"Perhaps it was something you ate. It made you ill and affected your thoughts. Perhaps you simply think you are in love with her."

Garren grinned. "I am fairly certain that it is not my imagination."

"A spell, then. She cast a spell to bewitch you."

"I sincerely doubt it."

"But love," Fergus stood up. "Garren, you of all people cannot succumb to something that makes the strongest of men weak and ineffectual. Love has destroyed more lives and kingdoms throughout the ages than can be counted. Are you not terrified?"

"Absolutely."

"Then let me help you," Fergus grasped his arm. "Let me beat it out of you. I shall not let this destroy you, Garren, I promise."

Garren laughed as his friend tried to jerk him off the bed. "You can't beat it out of me. But if you don't let go of me, you're going to get a beating of your own."

"I am trying to help you. Do not resist me, you fool."

"Fergus, trust me. This isn't something that can be bashed away with a fist or reversed with magic charms. It is something deep inside that can never be erased."

Fergus let go of him. "Something has indeed happened to you, my friend. The Garren le Mon I have known all of these years would never speak like that."

"The Garren le Mon you knew no longer exists," Garren said quietly. "This is serious. I need your help."

Fergus cast him a long look as he reclaimed his chair. "I see. So you sent for me not to socialize and become disgustingly drunk as we remember old times, but to put me into service."

"Aye."

He signed with exaggeration. "Very well. What will you have me do?"

"Go to Framlingham and abduct Derica for me."

"And then can we get disgustingly drunk?"

"I shall buy you your own winery."

Fergus grinned. "For my own winery, I would abduct the Queen herself." He sobered, his manner serious for the first time since his arrival. Things like abductions, raids and sieges didn't bother him in the least; he'd done worse. But the true motive behind the request plagued him. "Are you sure, Garren? This isn't just some manner of infatuation, is it?"

Garren shook his head. "Why does everyone keep asking me that?" he muttered to himself. He focused on his friend. "No, this is not an infatuation. I want this woman to be my wife because I love her and her family is not going to stop me. How much clearer can I make this?"

Fergus didn't have an overly suspicious mind, nor was he a deep thinker. He more often than not simply accepted what was said.

"If that is your desire, my friend, then I shall ride to Framlingham today for your ladylove." He scratched his head. "You do have a plan, don't you? What do I do with her once I have her?"

"You worry about getting her out of the castle. When you do, ride for Yaxley Nene Abbey and deliver her to Sister Mary Felicitas. Beyond that, there is nothing you need concern yourself over. I shall pay you, handsomely."

"I am not worried over the money," Fergus said. "I would do this for nothing at all, simply because we are friends. But there is one thing that concerns me."

"What's that?"

"If her family is as protective as you say, then you are going to need help keeping her. Even if I manage to get her out of Framlingham, I am willing to wager that the hounds will track us and follow."

"That is why you are taking her to the abbey."

"But she can't stay there forever, and neither can you. Eventually, you are going to leave with, I suspect, her family in pursuit. What then?"

"That part of my plan is a little less clear. I shall know more when I return to Chepstow and discuss options with my liege."

"What for?"

"The Marshal controls several bastions along the Marches. I shall request transfer to one of the remote ones, easily defended. I shall keep her there with me until her family grows weary and returns home. The Marches are a long way from Norfolk and, do not forget, her father serves the Earl of Norfolk. He cannot be gone overlong on a siege using the earl's resources."

"Unless the earl gives his blessing and sends more reinforcements to aid him. Then, you will have a battle that will basically pit the Earl of Norfolk against the Marshal of England over a reason that has absolutely nothing to do with either of them. Do you want to risk that now when tensions are already so high between Richard and John's supporters?"

"Not particularly."

"Then I would suggest that you take her someplace remote, with no soldiers, no connections whatsoever. Just the two of you. Wait until the

70

situation cools. As it stands now, running to a fortified castle is basically inviting her family to follow and bring on a full-scale war. It is a tease."

Garren thought on his words carefully; Fergus may have been flighty and scatter brained at times, but he had the heart and soul of a true warrior. In battle, the man was invaluable, which was why an undertaking of abduction didn't faze him in the least. He would have battled through fire if Garren asked him to.

"I appreciate your point of view," Garren said after a moment. "But the de Rosa's are powerful. It will be imperative that Derica and I have ample protection against their onslaught, which I have no doubt will come. My hope and inclination is that, after a time, the de Rosas will tire of any siege they may undertake and give up. Furthermore, with Derica and I married, the Church will undoubtedly support our position. Were the de Rosas able to retrieve her, however remote, the fact remains that she would still be a married woman."

Fergus shrugged. "Anything is possible. But if you are trying to avoid being tracked and thereby avoid the entire siege scenario, then surely keeping a low profile is best."

"I cannot disagree."

"Do you want a battle, Garren?"

"To teach those bastards a lesson, perhaps. But that would certainly not be in Derica's best interest."

"Nor yours. People tend to die in battle."

The men fell silent a moment, pondering the immediate future. "Your family is from Wales, Fergus?" Garren ventured.

"Aye."

"Then if I were to maintain a low profile, as you suggest, perhaps...."

Fergus was already thinking ahead of him. "A half a day's ride from the village where I was born lies an abandoned castle," he said, excitement in his tone. "When I was a lad, it was fairly intact but neglected. Story has it that Rhys, a Prince of Dyfed, built Cilgarren Castle for his new bride, but that he abandoned it shortly after her death. So there it sits, massive and unused. My father could direct you to this castle. It would be a perfect hiding place for you."

"You're sure? An entire fortress completely unused?"

"In all of the years my family has lived there, they have never seen it inhabited except for immediately after its completion. Legend has it that the place is haunted, and the princes of Dyfed will not go near it. And, being that nearby castles like Cardigan and Carmarthen are far more threatening, the English have no desire to claim it at this time. They have got their hands full with manned castles much less unmanned ones."

Garren felt better than he had in some time. A plan, a place. With Fergus to help him, he was positive the outcome would be favorable. Now to the get man to Framlingham and claim the prize. He suddenly snorted, softly.

"Cilgarren," he muttered. "It is fate that I go there."

"Why do you say that?"

"Because the castle bears my name."

Fergus grinned. "Indeed it does," he agreed. "Perhaps in the years to come, people will forget the 'Cil' altogether and simply call it Garren's Castle."

Garren nodded vaguely, his mind mulling over Fergus' advice. "Your clear thoughts and suggestions are much appreciated, my friend," he said. "Strange thing about Love; it muddles your head like fog. I have not been able to think objectively about any of this. I needed you more than I realized."

"My offer still stands to beat it out of you."

Garren laughed softly. "I think when you meet Derica, You will change your mind."

Fergus stroked his chin. "Is that so? Then perhaps I will abduct her for myself."

Garren cast him his best intimidating glance. "You will rue the day you were born, I assure you."

"Very well. That threat, coming from you, is enough to cause me to reconsider. I shall stay the course and then you shall name your first born son after me."

"Fair enough."

"Then let us make this so, my friend. Time waits for no man."

Fergus' confidence reassured Garren. But deep down, he was anxious for something that would be completely out of his hands until the moment Derica appeared at Yaxley. Until then, all he could do was wait and ignore the nameless fears that attempted to seduce him. So many things could go wrong and thinking such thoughts would surely drive him mad. All he wanted to do was see Derica again, and truly hold her for the first time. If he thought about it, he'd never done anything more than kiss her hand. The longing to touch her, hold her, experience her was almost more than he could bear.

He didn't like waiting.

CHAPTER SEVEN

It was a lazy day. The sun gave muted warmth, accompanied by the rising humidity that came with summer. It was early in the year to experience the moist heat, but it was present nonetheless. Perhaps it was an indication of the unbearable summer to come.

Derica lay on a day couch, fan in her hand. Her chamber was warm and damp. Every so often, the fan would wave back and forth and then collapse against her breast. The bright green eyes were half-lidded, with thought and boredom, staring into the room as if her mind had been spirited away somehow. Ever since that dreadful day, nearly a week ago, that she had made the bargain for Garren's life it was as if something had left her. The spirit that was normally present had vanished. Those who knew her well were unsure if it would ever return.

Aglette had long since hidden away the yellow wedding gown that she had worked on so diligently for all those months. She thought about burning it simply to erase the memories, but she wasn't sure that would be wise. She was currently working on a summer gown for her lady, a pale blue garment made of light fabric. They had purchased the material last year at a fair in Bury St. Edmunds. Yards of it had lain in Derica's chest, disregarded, until Aglette rediscovered it. She thought that a new gown was something her mistress might need at this time. Anything to brighten the dark days they were all suffering through.

Derica wouldn't see anyone but Uncle Hoyt and her brother Daniel. They were the only two members of the family who didn't represent Garren's departure. Her Uncle Hoyt had spent a good deal of time with her, brushing her hair, stroking her back, talking to her about things like goddesses and flowers. Any mention of anything remotely romantic would send Derica into fits, so Hoyt avoided the mythological love stories he was so fond of. Cuchulain and the other Celts who had fought so hard for love and kingdom were put aside in favor of discussions on roses and lavender. It was all Derica could tolerate. Hoyt hurt for her, but deep down, he could not truly understand what she was going through. None of them did.

Daniel's visits could be particularly brittle because he almost always carried a message from the rest of the family. As the brother who stayed the furthest away from any manner of politics or family squabbles, he had been coerced into playing peacemaker. He would bring her meals to her and sit with her while she picked at the food, discussing things like the weather and the quality of the spring foals.

Unlike her emotional outburst in the vault of Framlingham from the week prior, she had reverted back to her normal character of controlling her emotions, only now it was darkly so. There was no emotion in her face whatsoever. She mostly lay upon her day couch, staring up at the ceiling and ignoring everything around her. She had no use for her family at the moment, those people who had ruined her life.

Aglette had stuck to her with the faithfulness of an old dog. She had known Derica her entire life and had never seen her so miserable. It was difficult to comprehend that she was making herself ill over a man she had known less than a full week. Aglette had seen suitors come to Framlingham for weeks on end and Derica had never so much as said more than two words to them. Garren le Mon, clearly, had been different. They all knew that now.

So the little maid sewed the blue dress and chattered, even though she knew she would receive no answer. Eventually, she gave up chattering all together and simple sewed. In fact, the pretty blue dress was almost done save hemming the length. Perhaps now was a good time to focus her mistress on something other than her misery.

"There we are," Aglette stood from her stool and held the dress up. "What do you think of this, my lady? Beautiful, is it not?"

Derica didn't respond, though the fan lifted and waved back and forth a few times. Aglette tried not to become discouraged.

"My lady," she said, more firmly. "I will need for you to try this on so that I may hem the bottom. Will you do that, please?"

Derica continued to fan herself. Aglette was about to try again when Derica's head moved, very slowly, towards the dress. The green eyes that focused on it were lifeless.

"The sleeves are sheer."

"Aye, they are," Aglette was thrilled that she was getting a response. "In the warmth of summer, it will make it much cooler for you."

"But everyone will see the scar on my arm."

Aglette hadn't thought of that. "Not much, my lady. Not unless they look closely."

"It is healing quite nicely. Garren did a remarkable job tending it."

"Aye, he did."

The fan stopped. "Where do you suppose he went, Aglette?"

Aglette lowered the dress. This was as much conversation as she had gotten out of Derica in a week and she wanted to tread carefully. "I do not know. Perhaps back to Chateroy."

Derica clasped the fan against her breast and sat up. Her shoulders and forehead glistened in the moist weather. "Do you suppose... if I had Uncle Hoyt write to him, that he would write back?"

"I do not know, my lady. But you can certainly try."

"Father would not permit it, I am sure."

"Then perhaps we could sneak a missive out somehow."

Derica fell back against the couch once more, closing her eyes in anguish. "He said he would not forget me. But I shall wager that he has. What would he want to remember about this horrid place and the horrible way he was treated?"

Aglette didn't want to argue with her, and she did not want her mistress to fall deeper into despair with the present line of conversation. She laid the blue dress aside.

"I am going down to the kitchens to fetch some cool water. A sponge bath will do you a world of good. Then we shall try on this dress."

Derica didn't reply and the fan lay still against her chest. Aglette quit the chamber and descended to the second floor where she took the steps into the ward. The kitchens were located towards the rear of Framlingham's bailey. Her thoughts centered on Derica as she commandeered two kitchen servants to help her carry the water buckets up to her mistresses' room. Before she left the area, however, she collected a plate of bread and cheese, hoping to coerce Derica into eating something. With the bath and dress, perhaps she would feel better. One could only try.

She sent the servants bearing water on ahead as she collected one last bit of fruit for her mistress' plate, some small green grapes. The cook also gave her some boiled fruit juice flavored with cloves and honey. As Aglette crossed the ward towards the western tower, a sharp whistle pierced her ears. Then the sound came again. Thinking it was one of the soldiers on the wall walk above, she ignored it until she passed near the kiln and saw a figure bundling bunches of straw for the kiln fire.

"Mistress," the man was on his knees, his face half-obscured by a dirty cloak. "Mistress!"

Aglette was used to aggressive men; it happened quite often. "Go about your business. I have no interest in you."

"I have been waiting here the better part of a week, waiting for the chance to speak with you," the man hissed. "You're Lady Derica's servant."

Aglette didn't answer; she kept walking. The man stood up, a bundle in his hands.

"How has your mistress been feeling this past week?" he asked.

Aglette paused, looking at him pointedly. "I do not know who you are or what you want, but if you do not leave me alone, I shall send the soldiers after you."

Aglette continued walking. After two steps she had forgotten about the conversation until she heard the man's voice behind her once again.

"Aglette," he said slowly. "I bring your lady a message from Garren."

Aglette came to a dead halt. She turned, eyeing the man with the bucked teeth and bright blue eyes. "What... what do you mean a message?"

Fergus could see the fear in her eyes. "Garren said you are someone to be trusted."

Aglette was shaken. "I... I serve my lady faithfully." She lowered her voice. "Who are you?"

Fergus knew there time would be short. He glanced around, seeing that their conversation was going unnoticed for the moment.

"I am Sir Fergus de Edwin, a friend of Sir Garren's," he said quietly. "He has asked me to come on his behalf."

"You are a knight?"

"Aye. You must bring your lady to me so that I may deliver the message in person."

Aglette's heart was thumping in her chest, with fear and excitement. "How do I know you are who you say you are?" she whispered. "You cannot possibly expect me to rouse my lady simply because you, a stranger, say that you bear a message for her."

Fergus turned around, back for the kiln, and picked up another bunch of straw. "I shall be at the stables in one hour. Bring her there so that I may deliver the message."

Aglette glanced around, wondering also if someone was noticing their conversation. She felt as if she was in the midst of something horribly treacherous.

"I will not," she was afraid. "I have half a mind to run and tell Sir Bertram that you are here."

Fergus didn't look at her, continuing to bind the straw. "If you do, I shall swear that you helped me gain entrance and that it was you who plotted to spread the rumor that Sir Garren was a spy. I shall tell your lord that you are the root of the resistance within Framlingham and that all covert dealings pass through you. Even if he didn't believe me right away, I can guarantee you that your days at Framlingham are numbered. Suspicion has a way of killing all it stalks."

"You wouldn't dare!" Aglette gasped.

"Try me."

Aglette was aghast. She blinked tears of fear and fury away. "But how do I know you are who you say you are?" she repeated. "Everyone at Framlingham knows of Sir Garren. You could simply being trying to trick me."

Fergus looked at her; she was a pretty girl in a pale sort of way. "Tell your mistress that the ibis has returned," he said, more gently. "She will understand and will assure you that my presence is no trick. Go, now. Tell her."

Aglette didn't know what to say. She turned so quickly for the tower that she nearly dropped the plate with food on it.

"One hour," Fergus called after her. "At the stables."

Aglette had no idea how she managed to carry the tray up two flights of stairs with her quaking knees, but she managed somehow. By the time she reached Derica's chamber, she was a mess. The kitchen servants were filling a basin with the water they had brought and Aglette chased them from the room furiously. Even Derica, in her stupor, looked surprised when her red-headed maid slammed the chamber door and threw the bolt.

"Aglette?" she said. "What is the matter?"

Aglette looked like a frantic chicken. She threw her arms up in the air and struggled not to shout.

"A man in the ward," she gasped. "He said... he said that Sir Garren sent him."

Derica's expression grew serious, confused. "What do you mean? Who is he?"

"He said his name was Sir Fergus," Aglette stammered. "And... oh, my lady, he said that Garren has sent you a message. He wants you to meet him in the stables in one hour!"

A week of lethargy was erased in a matter of seconds. "Garren has sent me a message?"

Aglette shook her head fearfully. "That is what he said, my lady. I am frightened!"

Derica didn't know what to feel at the moment. "Is that all? Did he say anything else? How do I know it isn't a trick somehow?"

"But who would trick you?"

"I do not know. But how can I know for sure that it isn't?"

Aglette seemed to calm strangely, though there were tears in her eyes. "He said to tell you that the ibis has returned," she whispered. "He said that you would understand."

Derica's eyes widened enormously. "Dear God," she murmured. "Ibis and alligators."

"Then you know?"

She closed her eyes and, as Aglette watched anxiously, tears suddenly streamed down her cheeks. They were like rivers. But accompanied with the tears was a smile so bright that it lit up the room. Derica suddenly shouted and began spinning around the room like a madwoman.

"Aye!" she cried. "I know!"

Aglette's fear began to fade, replaced by some of the happiness her mistress was feeling. "Truly? He has sent you a message?"

Derica's answer was to throw her arms around her maid. The two of them danced jubilantly around the room. They hopped and cried and Derica bumped into the couch, stumbled, but kept going. She could have flown from the window at the moment and not been aware of it. But her dancing came to an abrupt halt.

"I must get dressed," she began rushing around the room. "I must wash. Where is my soap?"

Aglette kept a cooler head, helping Derica wash quickly with a cake of rose-scented soap. The blue dress, a form-hugging garment without a hem, was Derica's choice simply because it was there. As she pulled up the sleeves, Aglette fastened the stays with trembling hands.

"'Tis too long!" Derica exclaimed as she shoved her feet into doeskin slippers.

She was already heading for the door, tripping on the garment. Aglette struggled after her with a comb. "I told you that I needed to hem it, my lady," Aglette said with irritation.

"I shall trip on this and fall to my death before I can hear Garren's message."

"Then pull it up. Higher."

Derica had the front of her skirt bundled in a wad in front of her as she took the narrow stairs. Aglette ran the comb through her tangled locks. By the time they entered the ward of Framlingham, Derica let the skirt down just enough to be decent and struggled to calm herself.

"I will do this myself from here," she said. "Return to my chamber and keep watch for my family. I do not want them trying to follow me."

"How shall I keep them from looking for you should they come?"

"Think of something. Anything. I shan't be long."

Aglette watched her mistress scurry towards the stables. She was shaking with fear, and hope, and didn't think it appropriate for her lady to go alone. But she respected her wishes. Dutifully, she turned back for the tower, hoping the annoying de Rosa men would not want to console Derica yet again. She doubted she could hold them off long and for that, her fear mounted.

Derica tried to keep from running to the stables. She was so excited that she could scarcely breathe. The stable block was a long, low series of buildings attached to the outer wall. The wall walk was twenty feet above, soaring into the sky. She entered the first building and, seeing only horses and a few servants, went into the second and third. The fourth block was dim due to the shadows cast from the wall above. Derica passed through it, not seeing a living soul. She was about to exit when she heard someone clear their throat behind her, softly yet firmly.

Startled, she swung about. A man in a dirty brown cloak was in the shadows, hidden behind a large pile of hay. He pushed the hood from his face slightly, revealing bright blue eyes and a handsome face.

"Lady Derica, I presume?"

Derica nodded, hesitantly. "Are you....?"

"I am."

"I was told that you have a message for me."

He nodded. "I am Sir Fergus de Edwin. Sir Garren has sent me. He told me to tell you that the ibis has returned to the alligators."

She smiled at the words from their private world. "Is he well, then?"

"He is."

She sighed, visibly relieved. "I am so glad," she murmured. "He went through so much here... I have prayed for him."

"He is well enough that he has done nothing but speak your name," Fergus said. "Garren and I go back many, many years, my lady. When he asked me to help him in a matter involving a woman, I did not take it lightly. Garren is not the sort to be infatuated with a female."

Derica was pleased to hear him say that. "Nor I a man. What message did he give you for me?"

"He has sent me to bring you to him."

"Bring me to him?" Derica repeated. "For what purpose?"

"To marry you."

"Marry?" she sounded stunned. "After all that happened... after everything my family did to him, he still speaks of marrying me?"

"It is his heart's desire." Fergus regarded her carefully; she was a strikingly beautiful woman. He didn't blame Garren in the least. "But is it yours?"

"Why do you ask?"

"You seem hesitant."

She shook her head. "'Tis not that. 'Tis simply hard for me to believe that he would still want to marry me after all that has happened."

"My lady, if you do not wish to go to him, I am not here to abduct you. I am merely here to help you should you wish it."

"Is that what he told you to say to me?"

"Nay. But I am an honorable knight. I do not abduct unwilling women."

"I am not unwilling, Sir Fergus," she said quietly. "I want nothing more in this world than to be Garren's wife. If he sent you for that purpose, then it is my pleasure to go with you."

"Good," Fergus smiled. "Then we shall arrange it. A time and place, when there is little chance of your absence being discovered too quickly."

"Why not now?"

Fergus peered from the open stable door. "Where is your family?" he cast her a long look. "I understand you are surrounded by a host of guard dogs."

"I do not know where they are," she said. "But we can leave Framlingham without being noticed. There are always peasants coming and going and we can blend in with the crowd. Where is your horse?"

"In the woods to the south," he replied. "Are you certain you wish to go now? Do you not wish to pack lightly, or to collect anything of personal value?"

Derica shook her head firmly. "The sooner I see Garren, the better. He is the only thing of personal value to me." She could see the indecision on Fergus' face and she put her hand on his arm. "Sir Fergus, I have done nothing but eat, sleep and dream of Sir Garren since nearly the moment I met him. He is all that I have dreamed of and more. I must be with him. Do you understand that?"

Fergus could see her sincerity and he felt a stab of envy; he wished a beautiful woman would speak so fondly of him. But he pushed those thoughts aside, quickly, and removed the dirty cloak from his back. Swinging it over Derica's shoulders and pulling the hood over her honey-colored hair, he began to pile straw on her back.

"Let us do this the best way possible, then," he said. "I think I have a plan."

Derica was so excited at the prospect of being with Garren that the weight of the straw on her back couldn't dampen her spirit. Although she was angry with her family, she still loved them and felt a moment of sorrow that she would never see them again. She also felt sorrow at the prospect that Aglette would take the brunt of their anger. Still, she had to do this. She knew in her heart she would have risked death to go to Garren. But hopefully, it would not come to that.

***

Leaving Framlingham would have been easier had they left a few moments earlier or later. As it was, the timing was right so that Daniel and Dixon were in the ward, speaking to the guard captain. Derica spied them the moment she and Fergus left the stables, and Fergus saw her hesitation.

"What's the matter?" he asked.

The hood was down over her face, the huge cloak covering her body. "My brothers," she whispered. "Over by the main gate, talking to the guard."

Fergus had no such cover for his face, as he had given his cloak to Derica. But he was dressed like a peasant. Still, he was a knight and projected a higher image than most of the dirty people around him. He knew this was going to be tricky.

"There is my handcart," he pulled her towards the small card heavy with straw. "I used this to gain entrance a few days ago. It is been an effective cover."

"A few days ago?" Derica allowed him to lift her onto the edge of the cart. "You have been here that long and have only now tried to contact me?"

Fergus grinned as he secured the straw with a length of rope. "It wasn't as if I could charge into the tower and announce myself," he said, eyeing Daniel and Dixon in the distance. "I had to make myself familiar with the place and determine who had access to you and who did not."

"Like Aglette?"

"Exactly. I was told she was your servant."

"Who told you that?"

"One of the peasants, a man who sells his grain to the castle. You'd be surprised what these people know about you."

His eyes were twinkling as he secured the last of the rope. Derica pulled the hood further down over her face.

"Like what?"

Fergus grabbed the end of the handcart and lifted it. With little effort, he turned it around and began steering it towards the open gates.

"I hear you're something of a spitfire," he said.

Derica scowled. "That's not true."

"Shhh," Fergus snapped softly. "Keep your voice down unless you want those two brutish brothers to hear you."

She lowered her head, trying to make sure every identifiable mark was covered. Her blue gown, unhemmed and long, trailed out from underneath the cloak.

"My gown," she hissed. "They'll see it!"

Fergus could feel his apprehension rise; he was close now and to fumble with her gown would be to draw attention to them. Carefully, he set the cart down and pretended to adjust his load of straw.

"Pull it up," he whispered. "If I touch you, it will look too obvious."

Derica fumbled with the gown as much as she could without being too noticeable about it. She was feeling her panic but forced herself to calm, knowing that it would do no good to fall apart. With a pull and a tug, she managed to toss a length of cloak over the escaping pale blue. Fergus collected the handle of the cart, lifted, and began to push again.

Derica lowered her head and closed her eyes, saying a soft prayer. Gradually, she could hear Daniel's voice. She didn't dare look over. Peering up from the edges of the hood, she could see Dixon's boots as they passed by. It was too close, and too nerve wracking. Her palms were moist with anxiety. But they went unnoticed through the gates and down the road, and Derica lifted her head slightly to watch the great open gates of Framlingham slip further and further away. She felt, not strangely, as if a part of her life was slipping further and further way, too.

"I think we are safe," Fergus broke into her thoughts. "I shall push the cart into those trees. My horse is about a quarter of a mile into the woods."

Derica was bumped around as the cart rolled over the grass and into the trees. Fergus set it down and she slid off. Her eyes were on the silhouette of Framlingham, half-hidden through the trees. Fergus could see where her thoughts lay.

"'Tis difficult to leave the only life one has ever known," he said quietly.

She shrugged. "'Tis not so much that," she said. "I love and respect my father and brothers, but sometimes, they cannot be reasoned with. This is one of those times. Although I am not happy to disrespect their wishes, I feel very strongly that they are wrong in this case. Garren is a good man with a good heart and to the Devil with the politics of the king and his brother. I hate politics."

"Politics are a fact of life in this day and age, my lady."

"That may be. But I do not have to be a part of it. The only reason they will not allow Garren and I to wed is because someone told them that he was a spy for William Marshal. They will not tell me who; therefore, I say they are wrong. They are wrong to destroy my happiness based on their prejudice." She caught Fergus staring at her when she had finished her little speech. "Why do you look at me so?"

"Because the peasants were right; you are a spitfire."

She made a face at him, quickly gone. "Am I wrong?"

"I am not sure there is any right or wrong in matters of the heart."

After a moment longer, Derica turned away from the only home she had ever known. She refused to dwell on the regrets she might have; all that mattered was that soon, she would be with Garren. Fergus had her by the elbow, helping her walk through the heavy grass, when they suddenly heard the thunder of hooves.

Fergus immediately pulled her down, as if they could hide behind the thin green stalks. His hawkish gaze caught sight of a host of chargers at the gates of Framlingham and they could hear shouting in the distance. The men-at-arms were mobilizing. He knew immediately what had happened.

"Run."

He grabbed Derica's arm and pulled her along with him, the both of them flying through the trees and into the bramble.

"They've discovered me!" Derica gasped as they tore through the grass.

Fergus didn't answer her; he knew their luck had been too perfect. If they guarded the lady as much as Garren had told him, then they had lived on God's good graces for all of this time they had not been discovered. He had taken the chance, quickly, and now he wasn't at all sure that had been wise. All he could think of was getting to his horse and on to Yaxley Nene Abbey before they were stopped.

He prayed that God's good graces lasted just a bit longer.

***

"You are pacing is like the roll of wagon wheels, Over and over again, never ending, never...."

"I get your meaning. I shall sit if it will stop your complaining."

Gabrielle suppressed a smile, listening to her brother's grumpy mood, and knowing he had a very good reason for being anxious. She was simply trying to eliminate some of the tension.

"You should have gone on to Wales, as Fergus suggested," she said, her hands feeling at the sewing in her lap. In spite of her complete blindness, she sewed extremely well by touch. "To come back here, simply to wait, will drive you mad."

Garren glanced over at her; it was sunset, on the seventh day since he had left Framlingham. He'd left Fergus five days ago with the intention of riding to William Marshal to inform him of the change in his mission. But a day into that journey, he had turned back for the abbey; he wasn't so sure the Marshal would allow him to return for Derica. The man was driven and forceful, and Garren was his vassal. Whatever the Marshal ordered, he was obliged to follow, and he could not risk an order that took him far away from Yaxley and far away from Derica. So he had decided to return to the abbey and wait for Fergus to bring her. He wasn't sure how long that would take, but after four days of waiting, he was beginning to show distinct signs of impatience. All he wanted to do was hold a woman he had never held before.

"I would say the nuns have been quite accommodating to have me here," he said. "They've not tried to remove me once."

Gabrielle grunted. "That is because you sit with me and cause no problems. But they still force you to sleep outside at night."

"It is not been bad."

Gabrielle fixed a couple of stitches, running her fingers over her work as if she was playing a harp. "Tell me again of this castle where you plan to take her, Garren. The place where kings used to live."

He settled back in the old chair, crossing his massive arms. He was without his armor this day, as the nuns refused to let him wear it, or bring any weapons, deep inside the abbey. All of his protection was by the front door. He felt a bit naked without it, but he also felt very free.

"It is called Cilgarren," he tilted his head back, closing his eyes wearily. "As I told you, it was built for the princes of Dyfed. But the wife of the first prince died and now the place is supposedly haunted. Fergus tells me that it has been vacant for years."

"Is it big?"

"I am told it is massive."

"Cilgarren," Gabrielle repeated softly. "So you intend to take her there?"

"I do," he muttered. "Do you know that I have never even kissed her?"

"Who?

"Derica."

No matter how Gabrielle had tried, for days, to speak of other things, the conversation always came back to the lady.

"'Tis well and good that you haven't," she chided gently. "You are not married to her yet."

"But we are betrothed."

"Of no matter. You have no rights to her until you are properly wed."

Garren opened his eyes and stood up. His pacing started anew. "My entire life, I have lived by the sword and the code of Chivalry. I have been in the service of the most powerful man in England and have done some things during that service that I am perhaps not so proud of. But I have always been confident in my decisions. I can truthfully say there is nothing I look back upon that I regret, knowing that I made the right choice at that point in time." He stopped pacing and looked at his sightless sister. "But I cannot know for sure that what I do now is the right thing. To love a woman so much, to be consumed with her to the point of madness. I cannot know for certain that the choices I have made over the past several days have been the right ones, with surely more choices to come. How do I know that in a month or a year she will not come to hate me for taking her away from her family and forcing her to marry me?"

"You cannot know," Gabrielle said quietly. "Be good to her, treat her well, and love her. That is all you can do."

Garren was having a tough bout with indecision at the moment. His anxiety was getting the better of him. He sat down again, next to his sister, and patted her hand.

"I am sure that I am driving you mad with my incessant whimpering," he said. "I thank you for your patience and advice."

Gabrielle smiled. "I envy you. You have such a wonderful future ahead of you, with happiness and children, married to a woman that you love. How many people in this world are fortunate enough to experience that?"

"I feel extremely humbled," he admitted. "Never did I imagine my life would take the turn it is apparently taking and my happiness would be complete but for one thing."

"What?"

"I still must face the Marshal with what I have done."

Gabrielle didn't say anything for the moment. "Perhaps you should not," she murmured. "Perhaps you should simply take Derica to Wales and stay there for the rest of your lives."

Garren smiled ironically. "As much as I would like to, I cannot. I am a knight and I am sworn to serve my king above all. I must confess all to the Marshal and pray I have not caused over-much damage to Richard's cause. There are other agents, of course, other men who can infiltrate and uncover information, but the Marshal had high hopes for my mission. I am, after all, the best he has."

"But it wasn't your fault your mission failed. Someone told the de Rosas who you are."

"I know. But I am making somewhat of a mess of it by abducting the Bertram de Rosa's daughter."

Gabrielle shrugged; she couldn't disagree. "So you plan to continue working for the Marshal and Richard's cause even after you wed her?"

"Eventually, after the de Rosa's have cooled and I can safely travel England again without the threat of them on my tail seeking vengeance."

"What of your wife, then?"

"What of her?"

"She doesn't know that it is true."

"What's true?"

"That you are an agent for her father's most hated enemy."

Garren inhaled deeply, regretfully. "I will have to tell her and pray she can forgive me."

The conversation died after that. Gabrielle was left to wonder what would happen to her brother if his ladylove did not forgive him.

CHAPTER EIGHT

Derica had never been out of the walls of Framlingham without her brother, father and uncles riding close escort. On those occasions, which had been rare, she had looked at it as something of a grand adventure.

But her harrowing ride with Fergus de Edwin was no grand adventure. It had been terrifying. Fergus had ridden north for the rest of the day to elude the search parties from Framlingham; when nightfall came, he had dared not risk putting her up at an inn and, instead, made camp in a small vale outside the village of Thetford. Although he tried to make it as comfortable as possible for her, it was nonetheless cold and damp and he would not light a fire for fear that the search parties might see the smoke. Derica was cold and wet, wrapped in her new gown and Fergus' old peasant cloak, and tried not to let her misery show.

Fergus built a little shelter for her to keep the damp off and she had slept fitfully. For warmth's sake, he lay close to give her some of his body heat and in the morning they had made jokes about not telling Garren of their improper proximity. Derica was kidding, but Fergus was mostly serious. He'd seen Garren in battle too many times not to fear the man greatly, especially where a woman was concerned.

It was slow going once they turned west for Yaxley. Fergus estimated it would take them at least three days to reach the abbey. They stayed to the untraveled roads and footpaths, and Fergus slipped into a small town on the second day to buy bread and cheese for the lady. So far, she hadn't complained, but he knew she was cold and hungry and uncomfortable. He felt very badly about it.

The second day blended into the third and, even though their travel had been slower than he had estimated due to the fact that they had swung far to the north, they had nonetheless made good time. The closer they drew to the abbey, however, the more relieved Fergus was becoming. It was certainly no offense to the lady that he was eager to drop her off and return to Longton; he simply didn't like feeling of being hunted.

On the afternoon of the third day they stopped at a stream that transected a small, lush valley. There were trees about, offering shelter and shade from the sun that had decided to appear. In truth, it was pleasant and they needed the rest. Derica immediately took her slippers off and waded out into the stream, hooting at the freezing water. Fergus watered the horse, grinning at her, trying to keep his eyes averted from tantalizing flashes of ankle.

"Fergus," Derica called to him as she hopped onto a slick rock.

"My lady?"

"Tell me something."

"Anything, my lady."

"You have known Garren a long time, have you not?"

"Since we were squires."

"Tell me what he was like back then."

Fergus let the horse graze. "He was a somewhat small boy, very quiet, very sharp. He never needed to be given an order twice."

Derica hiked her skirt higher as she stepped from the rock back into the water. "Garren was small?" she giggled. "I cannot imagine that. He is absolutely enormous."

"That happened very quickly," Fergus said. "Because he was small and quiet, some of the other squires used to taunt him. But the moment he entered youth and his voice deepened, it was as if he woke up one morning a head taller than even the knights. From working with the sword and other weapons, his arms and shoulders grew enormous. Woe betides those who had teased him when he was small."

"He punished them?"

Fergus smiled at the memories. "In very subtle ways. They never knew they had been punished until it was all over. But he made sure each and every one had their day."

"But he is not a vengeful or wicked man."

Fergus looked over at her; she was standing in the stream, the filtered sunlight glistening off her hair. He'd never seen anything so beautiful.

"No, my lady," he said quietly. "He is not a vengeful or wicked man. In fact, Garren is one of the few men I know that will be honorable 'til the death. He is what every knight hopes to be but seldom is. I have nothing but respect and admiration for him."

Derica smiled, thinking of Garren, her heart swelling with happiness and longing. "I hope to find that out for myself."

"As you shall. You are a most fortunately woman, Lady Derica."

She knew that. Gathering her skirts closer, she timidly picked her way out of the stream.

"Then we should not keep him waiting any longer," she said. "The sooner we get to Yaxley, the better."

Her foot slipped on the bank before the last word was out of her mouth. With a whoop, she tumbled into the chilly water, landing flat on her backside. Horrified, Fergus dropped the horse's reins and rushed to help her, but she just lay there and laughed.

"Are you all right?" Fergus asked. "Did you hurt yourself?"

Derica shook her head. "Of course not. But I am as wet as a mud hen."

Her laughter was infectious. Fergus was smiling as he reached down and pulled her out of the water. "I can see that," he picked up the edges of her gown and tried to wring some water out of it. "You don't have a change of clothes, my lady. I am sorry...."

She cut him off. "Don't be silly. I shall dry if you spur the horse fast so that the wind swishes through the material like a storm." She made wide, sweeping motions with her arms and they both laughed.

"I shall do my best to create the tempest."

"Good." Pulling away from him, Derica found her slippers and, drying her feet off on the dry portions of the cloak, put them off. "Come along, Fergus. I want to get to the abbey before dark."

"Aye, my lady," he shook his head, thinking she was very adept at giving orders and knowing that Garren would have his hands full with her. He was about to help her onto the charger when shouts in the distance caught his attention.

They both froze, ears peaked, listening with the trepidation of the mouse awaiting the cat. The shouts came again and Fergus didn't wait to interpret them.

He tossed her up onto the horse and mounted in front of her. Spurring the charger through the trees, he struggled through the stream and rocks in an attempt to wipe clear their trail. Behind, Derica clung to him fearfully.

"They've found us," she hissed.

Fergus nodded to the obvious. "They must have undoubtedly heard your scream when you fell in the water."

"Sweet Lord," she murmured. "I am so sorry, Fergus. I didn't know...."

"Of course you didn't."

"What are we going to do?"

"Create that tempest I promised."

Fergus reined the steed out of the stream and into the forest. The horse began to thunder through the bramble, plowing a path and leaving a host of broken branches in its wake. It was an obvious trail to follow, one plowed with furious speed.

"We're close to the abbey, perhaps a few miles," Fergus said after several moments. "I am going to leave you there and then try to lead the search party away. Perhaps they will follow my trail and bypass the abbey all together."

"You're going to be a decoy?"

"I did not come all of this way simply to have them grab you before you can enter the abbey walls."

Small branches were whipping her in the face; the green of the trees whizzed by her head as the horse galloped through. She held on tightly, praying that they would reach the abbey before her family caught wind of their trail. She was sickened to think they had come this far, this carefully, only to be discovered at the last possible moment.

Closing her eyes, she could see Garren's face and she prayed, harder than she had ever prayed in her life, that she would see him again. It was with certainty, she knew, that if her family caught up to her she would be sequestered the rest of her life. She couldn't bear to think of what they would do to Fergus.

Derica couldn't hear anymore shouting but she wasn't convinced that her father wasn't right behind her. Fergus thundered across a meadow and skirted what looked and smelled like a bog. Derica kept her face buried in his back, holding on tightly, trusting that he would get them safely to the abbey. She lost track of time as they raced along, through the trees and, at one point, across a farmer's field. But suddenly, they emerged onto a road and Fergus let the horse have his head.

Rocks pelted Derica's legs and feet. The wet part of her dress lay across the back of the charger, sticking to the horse. Abruptly, the horse slowed and began to lope in a strange, sloppy gait. Fergus looked about the animal in a panic before pulling it to a sharp halt. He leapt off the horse.

Derica's gown, unhemmed and long, had wounds its way around the horse's back legs. Fergus unwound the dress and pulled Derica off the animal.

"Listen to me," he made sure she was looking him in the eye before pointing over to his right. "The abbey is through those trees and down a small hill. If you cut through, it will keep you off the road while I lead them on a wild goose chase. When you get to the abbey, you are to ask for Sister Mary Felicitas. Do you understand?"

Derica nodded, the fear in her eyes momentarily replaced by gratitude. "Fergus, I cannot possibly express my thanks adequately. What you have done is...."

"Is nothing more than Garren would not do for me." Fergus smiled at her, briefly. "It was a pleasure, my lady. I wish you and Garren all of the happiness in the world. He is an extremely lucky man. Now, off with you and don't look back."

Impulsively, he kissed her on the forehead and mounted the steed. With the charger hurling down the road, Derica tore into the trees as fast as her shaking legs would carry her.

***

Nine days. Nine long, miserable days.

Garren knew that, in the grand scheme of things, nine days was a trifle. He would trust Fergus and his judgment completely as to the right time to whisk Derica from Framlingham, so it was quite possible that he was looking at weeks. It was a depressing thought. He didn't know if he could take it.

It was an hour before sunset. He had been in his sister's chamber since just after sunrise. Over the past nine days, they had spent an indeterminate number of hours talking about so many things he could hardly keep track. It was the most time he had ever spent with his sister at one time and, in spite of the circumstances, he had enjoyed it. Gabrielle had kept him calm and occupied and, for that, he was grateful.

But on this ninth day, He is spent his waking hours resigning himself to a long wait. When Gabrielle was summoned to help with the evening meal preparation, Garren excused himself and wandered to the entry hall of the abbey. He wasn't allowed anywhere else. He stood there a moment, muddled and unfocused. Thinking that he should perhaps check on his horse to occupy himself, he opened the door and stepped out into the fading sunlight.

The horse was tethered with some other animals in a small shelter the abbey used for a stable. Garren wandered through the ward, glancing up into the trees when he heard a hawk cry. The branches over his head were thick with greenery and moisture, filtering the weak rays of the sun. He was nearing the stables when he heard the abbey gate swing open and shut heavily. Knowing some of the nuns had been out in the trees gathering mushrooms, he didn't give the squeaking gate a second thought. He was learning to control those impulses that had him running to the door every time he heard the iron-clad sound of the gate.

The horse's hindquarters were facing him. He put his hands on the beast and shoved it sideways. Ever since his trip to Framlingham, the horse had shown a tendency to come up lame on the right front leg and he wanted to check it again. The horse was still favoring the leg, but not nearly as it had been. He was deep in his inspection of the fetlock when a voice filled his ears, a sweet note that he thought he surely must have dreamt. He heard it again, louder this time, and some familiar part of him inside ignited like a roaring flame. Someone was calling his name. He looked up from the horse's leg and turned around.

Derica stood several feet away, dirty, disheveled, with tears streaming down her face. She said his name again, so choked she could hardly speak, and Garren nearly came apart.

Somehow, he managed to stumble over to her. It was odd how everything seemed so dreamlike, as if time itself had slowed. He could hardly believe what he was seeing. But the moment he touched her, the dream burst and she was very real and very warm. He pulled her into an embrace that threatened to crush her.

"Derica," he whispered. "My God... are you real?"

She was sobbing. "I am." Her arms were around his neck so tightly that she was in danger of strangling him. "Garren, I have missed you so. I did not know you would be here. Fergus said...."

His bruising lips cut her short. In a short matter of seconds, his mouth was on hers, kissing her as if he had been doing it all of his life. She was sweet and soft and he kissed her until she gasped for breath.

"You have no idea how I have longed for you, how much I have thought of you," he murmured in between heated kisses. "The day I walked from Framlingham I was sure that my life was over." He paused, holding her face in his hands, drinking in the sight of her. "My God, you are more beautiful than I had remembered."

She smiled through her tears, running a finger over his delicious lips. "I could not believe it when Fergus came for me," she murmured. "He said that you wanted to marry me."

He kissed her furiously, again, because he could not get enough of her. "If you will have me."

"I will have none other."

He squeezed the breath out of her. For an eternity of sweet moments, they said nothing. Their words were in their kisses, in their touch. Garren was so delirious that it took him some time to realize the entire back of her dress was damp and cold. Like a man waking from a dream, he struggled to get a grip on reality. And the reality was that she was cold and wet. He let her go long enough to turn her around to see just how bad off she really was.

"Why are you all wet?" he asked.

Derica was swooning with happiness and exhaustion. "I fell into the creek when Fergus...," her eyes suddenly grew wide with fear. "Garren, Fergus is in trouble."

"What trouble?"

"My family has been chasing us since we left Framlingham, three days ago," she said. "They almost caught up to us earlier today. Fergus sent me on to the abbey while he went to lead them off our trail."

Reality settled more firmly on Garren; were they to leave the safety of the abbey while the de Rosa patrols were still in the area, they risked running into them. However, as the only abbey in the area and place of safe haven, it would be inevitable that, at some point, the de Rosa band would come knocking at the door. Even though Derica could claim sanctuary, still, it would make for an ugly situation, especially if they knew that Garren was with her. He couldn't risk being discovered.

"He is buying us time to get away," Garren took her gently by the arm. "We must get out of here. Did you bring anything with you?"

"No, nothing. We left hastily to avoid being followed, but we were followed anyway."

Garren didn't say anything to that; he simply patted her hand. Derica followed him across the ward and into the abbey. It was cool and dark, the smells of cooking wafting on the air. Her damp dress was causing her a chill and she shivered. Garren could feel her twitch.

"First things first," he said. "We must get you into something dry and get you something to eat."

"It has been a while since I last ate."

"Didn't Fergus feed you?"

"Of course he did. But the last of our bread ran out this morning."

"I hope he was chivalrous. He didn't eat everything, did he?"

"He ate hardly a thing. He let me have most of it."

"As well he should." He kissed her again, just because he wanted to. "You have no idea how glad I am to see you again. Although I hoped for the best, I wasn't sure if the best would come."

She smiled and grasped his hand, tightly. He took her into a small corridor and into the second chamber on the right; it was empty but for a cot, a small table and two chairs. It was dark, and somewhat creepy.

"I shall see if the nuns have something you can wear while your gown dries," he said. "Sit down and rest a moment, sweetheart. I shall return shortly."

She sat down, but she continued holding his hand as if she was fearful to let him out of her sight. He knelt down beside her and kissed her hand gently.

"I promise, I shan't be long," he kissed her lips. "Everything will be all right, Derica. I swear it."

Their gazes locked and she smiled, putting her hands around his neck affectionately. "I know it will," she said. "Do you remember when we were up on the battlements of Framlingham, right after we'd first met, how you told me that we would be in for a good deal of trouble were my father to find us alone and unescorted?"

He grinned. "I do."

"I think this is a bit more serious than that."

"Agreed."

"But even if they were to break the door down this moment, for the feeling that I have right now when I look at you, it would be well worth the price."

He was deeply touched. "I can tell you now that I intend there should be many more moments like this one," he whispered. "You shall never be out of my sight, ever."

Derica knew he meant every word of it. "But what about Fergus? Aren't you going to help him?"

"Fergus can take care of himself. To go chasing after him right now would only ruin what he is trying to accomplish."

She understood, but still, she worried for him. "He is a good friend to you."

"The very best. I am concerned for him, of course, but I would do more harm than good in my attempt to help him right now."

Derica smiled sadly and let go of his hand so he could search for something dry for her to wear. With a wink, Garren left her in the cold, silent room.

She must have been more exhausted than she'd realized. She was aware that she was on her back, still in that dark little room, with soft voices around her. She stirred a bit before sitting up, groggily.

Garren was sitting across from her on a small chair. There was a tiny figure swathed in brown and white beside him, and the two of them were talking softly. Garren caught sight of her and smiled.

"I am sorry, sweetheart," he stood up and went to her. "Did we wake you?"

She shook her head. "No," she rubbed her head. "How long have I been asleep?"

"A few hours," Garren sat down next to her and put his arm around her. "I came back with something dry for you to wear and you were asleep sitting up. So I laid you down on the bed. You never woke up."

Derica yawned delicately, trying not to be rude. "I did not realize I was so exhausted, but this is the first bed I have slept on in days. Fergus was afraid to put us up at an inn for fear we'd be discovered, so we slept in the woods."

Garren hugged her gently. "You have had a rough time of it."

She grinned, rubbing the sleep from her eye. "Not really. It is all been rather adventurous."

The tiny figure in brown and white twitched, reminding them that it was still there. Garren looked over at the silhouette.

"I would like you to meet someone," he said to Derica. "This is Sister Mary Felicitas."

Derica stood up; she did not want to be rude and greet the woman on her backside. "Sister, it is an honor to meet you."

Gabrielle moved into the light and Derica could see, immediately, that her eyes were sightless. "And you, Lady Derica. I have heard nothing but your praises for days. I feel as if I know you already."

The nun's hand was outstretched and Derica took it; it was tiny and cold. "I hope we will indeed get to know one another," she said.

Gabrielle smiled. "I like her, Garren," she said to her brother. "I can hear it in her voice. She will be good for you."

Garren's eyes twinkled as his gaze moved between his sister and Derica. "She has been that already."

Derica smiled coyly, feeling the nun squeeze her hand tightly. "Fergus told me that when I came here, I was to ask for Sister Mary Felicitas," she said. "Do you help run-away maidens by way of habit, then?"

Gabrielle laughed. "No, my lady. Just the ones my brother happens to be in love with."

Derica looked at Garren with such an expression that he felt his heart leap strangely. Though he had never said the words, surely she suspected his love for her. It was the first time such emotion had been put into words, and he could see that it did not displease her. He reached over and, taking Derica from his sister's grasp, pulled her onto his lap. She curled up like a kitten against him, all warm and soft and round in all of the right places.

"Now," he said, though he was having trouble maintaining his train of thought with her sweet body pressed against him. "My sister and I have been talking and I would seek your approval of our conclusions. Firstly, I have had the sisters pack a bag for you to take with us."

"Pack a bag? With what?"

"Three garments, my lady," Gabrielle said helpfully. "Though I know the standards of the garments are not what you are used to, still, they will be serviceable. We have given you two durable broadcloth dresses, plus a finer gown made from lamb's wool and dyed a lovely shade of blue, I am told. We have also managed to locate some calendula soap, plus a comb and a few other personal items. I hope it will be adequate."

"Considering I have nothing but the clothes on my back, sister, I am sure what you have given me will be more than adequate," Derica said. "Your consideration is very much appreciated."

Gabrielle smiled in response and Derica turned back to Garren. He was so warm and comfortable that she snuggled closer to him, allowing her nostrils to become accustomed to the musky, intoxicating aroma. He was heavenly.

Garren was becoming accustomed to her feel, too, far too quickly. He never wanted to let her out of his arms. But his mind was whirling with thoughts and he forced himself to continue.

"Secondly, I think It is best we leave this place tonight," he said. "We have got several days travel ahead of us and the sooner we can get away from the de Rosa patrols, the better."

"Agreed. Where are we going?"

"Wales."

She pulled her face out of his neck, looking him in the eye. "Wales? Why so far away?"

"Simply because it is a safe place for us. 'Tis far away from your father and I believe it would be best for now."

"And then what?"

"When their anger has cooled, we go to Chateroy."

Derica thought on that a moment. "My father can stay angry a long time. It might be years before we can safely live at Chateroy. Even then, if we are discovered, I cannot guarantee that he will not lay siege in order to avenge me. He will consider me, after all, stolen property."

"The lady is as smart as she is beautiful," Garren winked at her. "But Chateroy is my home, and my inheritance, and I intend to occupy her as such in time. Besides, my father has so much money that who is to say we cannot buy your father off given time. For his troubles, so to speak."

Derica shook her head. "You cannot buy my father's pride or loyalty."

"Then here is your choice; you may ride home tonight and beg his forgiveness and live your life in peace. Or, you can stay with me and spend the rest of your life avoiding your family. Well?"

He was half-serious, half-not. Derica cocked an eyebrow. "Will you let me think on it?"

"No."

She scowled; he grinned. When he began to pepper her cheek and neck with kisses, and finally gentle bites, she squealed and began laughing. In the shadows of the room, Gabrielle cleared her throat softly.

"Temperance, my good knight," she admonished her brother softly. "The lady is not yours yet in the eyes of God. Better to finish what is necessary so that you may be free to do with her as you please."

Garren and Derica stopped their play, knowing she was correct. They had been so thrilled with the reality of seeing each other again that the larger formality had been momentarily pushed aside. The sooner they were married, the better for all concerned.

"I assumed we would find a priest on our journey to Wales," Garren said. "I am not sure there is time at the moment to do this properly."

"If there is time to play, there is time to wed," Gabrielle said firmly. "Four miles to the north is a Jesuit monastery. I would have you become man and wife before you leave this place, Garren. I ask this of you."

"Then let us send for a priest. I, too, am eager to claim this woman as my own in the eyes of God."

Near dawn, Garren and Derica were married by a disheveled priest who smelled strongly of sacramental wine. All of the sisters in the convent were witness. The Mother Abbess even gave Derica a simple silver wedding band, the kind that the nuns received when they took their final vows and became brides of Christ. When Garren slipped the ring on her finger, she couldn't remember ever having been so happy.

As the priest droned on in Latin, Garren and Derica lost themselves in each other's eyes, feeling emotions they'd never felt before, elated that they were going to spend a lifetime together. Upon their meeting a week prior, neither one of them could have imagined what their marriage would have truly become. When they knelt for the final prayer and received the Blessing, Derica could hardly concentrate on what was being said. All she could think of was her husband and the blissfully happy life they would have.

It never occurred to her that happiness would come at a price.

CHAPTER NINE

Riding with Garren was far different than riding with Fergus. For instance, she had always ridden behind Fergus in the saddle, but Garren put her in front of him. He held her tightly with one hand and reined the muscular charger with the other. As dawn broke on the first day of their wedded life together, they found themselves on a misty road surrounded by dripping trees. It was wet and cold, but wrapped in Garren's arms, Derica had never felt warmer, or more content.

The nuns had worked furiously during the night to clean and hem the pale blue gown that had caused so much trouble. It was packed away in the borrowed satchel the sisters had filled for her. She was dressed in a heavy broadcloth peasant gown that was a bit too snug, the very same garment she had taken her vows in. Her waist was narrow, her hips shapely and her breasts full, and she filled out the dress better than a peasant ever could have. The bodice of the gown was crisscrossed with a series of string ties, which Sister Mary Felicitas and another nun had worked furiously to cinch up across her rounded breasts. She had spent a good deal of time exhaling to shrink down while they pulled. Finally, the garment was laced, but Derica was clearly squeezed into it like a cork ready to pop.

Garren had thought the dress quite pleasing on her figure. He had no complaints whatsoever. But she was obviously out of place in such a plain dress, like a beautiful painting set in a latrine. With her hair plaited into a long braid that tumbled over one shoulder, she looked positively angelic. He couldn't take his eyes off of her, and he made sure that he always had hold of her with one hand or the other. Never in his life had he felt more fortunate, and the more time passed, the more deeply attached he could feel himself becoming. Gone were the fears he had possessed when he had first met her; he had surrendered fully to his emotions and had never been happier in his life.

Derica fell asleep less than a half hour into their journey. Garren scanned the countryside with his trained eye, every so often glancing down at the lady in his arms. She was wrapped in the brown cloak Fergus had given her, also cleaned by the nuns along with the blue dress. Her head was cradled in the crook of his right elbow, her face pressed against his cold armor as she snored softly. Every so often, she would shift and her left hand would come into view, the silver ring gleaming in the misty light.

Garren smiled every time he looked down at her; he could hardly believe she was his.

She slept well into the day. He never stopped, traveling in a southwesterly direction. The fog lifted eventually, giving way to a semi-clear day. Garren stayed clear of the towns as Fergus had, choosing instead to stick to the trees and less-traveled paths. He expected to make terrible time this day, hardly to where he would have liked to have been. But Derica was sleeping, exhausted, and he wanted to be considerate of her. Still, his senses were painfully attuned to everything around them. He knew they were not safe from her father's patrols and was torn between doing what he knew needed to be done for their own good, and wanting to be indulgent of his wife's exhaustion.

Sunset came and there had been no signs of de Rosa' patrols. He could only hope that Fergus had been successful in diverting them. The berg of Kettering loomed up ahead. Going against his instincts of staying to the woods, he wanted their first night as husband and wife to be spent in a place that was warm and comfortable.

There were three inns in the town. At sunset, most of the avenues were closing up for the night and there was little traffic on the streets. Garren reined his charger towards the largest of the three inns, a place called the Rough Head. It appeared good enough for his purposes.

When the charger came to a halt, Derica roused immediately. She blinked her eyes and sat up so quickly that she bashed Garren in the chin.

"I am sorry," she said, rubbing the spot she had hit. "Are you all right?"

He let her massage it. "I have been hit harder," he quipped. "So I see that you have awakened, Lady le Mon. Are you ready for a decent meal and a decent bed?"

She nodded gratefully. "More than you know." She yawned. "I could sleep for a week."

He dismounted the charger and lifted her off, kissing her twice before he set her feet on the ground. There was a boy sitting in the dirt outside of the inn; Garren tossed the boy two pence and asked him to feed and stable his charger for the night. The boy eagerly took the money and led the beast around the side of the building. Collecting Derica's bag and his own saddlebags and weapon, they proceeded inside the establishment.

It was a smoky, loud place. Men and women were everywhere, eating and drinking and relieving themselves on the floor. Derica had never been in a tavern before; were she not used to the wild ways of her brothers, she might have been shocked. As it was, she was not easily startled. Garren was pleased to see that she was observing the happenings without stress. Holding her by one arm, he made his way through the madness to the barkeep.

He asked for a room and was told there was none. But a gold piece on the counter proved that there was indeed a room to be had. At the top of the stairs and to the right, Garren and Derica found themselves in a small room with a small bed. Oddly enough, it seemed relatively clean. Garren closed the door, bolted it, set their bags down. The noise from the room downstairs was a distant roar.

"I shall start a fire," he said.

The fireplace was small and dark, but Garren soon had it smoking with a weak blaze. Derica sat down on the only chair, watching the flames glisten off of Garren's coppery-blond hair. The events of the previous days seemed like a dream to her, but the reality of the silver ring around her finger told otherwise.

"It must have been a very uninteresting ride for you today with me passed out like a drunkard," she said.

He turned from the fire, smiling at her. "It wasn't uninteresting at all. I spent the entire day staring at my new wife."

"And?"

"And I think I have married an angel."

She blushed. "Oh, but you do flatter me, Sir Garren."

"I speak the truth."

He set the poker down and stood up. Derica watched with anticipation as he came over to her and pulled her to her feet. He took her in his arms, gazing deeply into her eyes before kissing her with such tenderness that Derica's knees went weak. He suckled her top lip, her bottom lip, before his tongue carefully entered her mouth. Derica had never been kissed like that before, but took to it with eager abandon. She was eager to experience anything he wished to teach her.

He slid the cloak off of her shoulders and let it fall to the floor. With his wife in his arms, he moved to the small bed and carefully set her upon it. Slowly, he pushed her back until she was laying down, with his big body over her. He wrapped her in himself, feeling and tasting something he would gladly risk his life for a thousand times over.

Although he didn't want to scare her, he was eager to explore her. But he restrained himself for the moment, kissing her, acquainting her with his touch and taste, before gently moving to the laces that his sister had struggled so to cinch up. With a tug, he released the tie and her bodice instantly loosened. She didn't resist him, nor did she utter a word of protest, so he continued.

He was careful about loosening the bodice. But soon it was falling off of her shoulders and his hand snaked inside, stroking the silky flesh of her collarbone. Moving lower, he could feel the swell of her breast and he could not restrain himself from gently stroking, touching, moving toward the swollen nipple. When his fingers finally moved across the hard, red peak, he let out a ragged sigh. Had he possessed any less self-control, he would have taken her at that very moment.

His desire was beginning to overwhelm him. Her gown came off in inches, moving down her torso, exposing her breasts, before moving to her waist. He tugged gently, removing his own armor in pieces even as he undressed her, which was no easy feat. He kept his lips on hers constantly, kissing her until she could hardly breathe, tasting her deeply. In time, her gown was off and his tunic with it. His leg armor was a bit trickier and more than once he apologized, left her mouth, and unlatched something. Sections of armor hit the floor like metal rain drops.

When his breeches finally came off and they were both as naked as the day they were born, he stopped long enough to look at her; she was all he had known she would be. Her breasts were round and white, her stomach flat, her legs smooth and shapely. He admired her as one would have admired the most magnificent of sculptures, a work of art that could never be duplicated.

"What's wrong?" Derica whispered.

"Nothing, sweetheart."

"Then why do you stop?"

"To look at you."

It was her first flash of self-consciousness and Garren gently grasped the hand that came up to cover her nakedness. He kissed her hand, her lips.

"No, sweetheart," he murmured. "You will not hide from me. You're the most glorious beauty I have ever laid eyes on."

His kisses had fogged her mind. But when he stopped, the fog cleared and Derica was becoming uncomfortable with her state.

"Garren, I...."

"What?"

She wasn't sure how to put the words. "I... I have never let anyone, save Aglette, see me without clothing. I am not sure...."

"I am your husband. 'Tis my right, and only mine, to see you unclothed. Does this disturb you?"

She shrugged. "It should not, I know, but...."

"If you are uncomfortable, we can stop. I shall be content to hold you in my arms all night long, with or without clothing, however you wish."

She looked into his eyes and steadied herself. "I do not want to stop," she assured him. "I have been waiting for this moment for as long as you have."

He touched her face, her hair. When he spoke, it was almost a prayer. "Christ, what have I done in my life to deserve someone like you?"

She smiled timidly, trying to be brave, anxious of what was about to happen between them. All she knew was that she wanted him, although she knew not how.

His body was big, hard, warm and musky. Though she'd never known a man intimately, she knew he was something she would come to crave. As he kissed her strongly, his hands moved to her breasts and he fondled her tenderly. His mouth moved down her neck, biting her gently, until he reached her nipples.

Derica gasped as his warm and wet mouth began to suckle her, gently at first but with increasing ardor. When he finally took her, it was with little pain. She thought the sensation a bit uncomfortable at first, but that quickly passed. The fog of passion quickly shrouded her mind again and her body began to behave in a way she never thought possible. She clung to him, wrapped herself around him, relishing every move he made. She could hear herself gasp with every touch, every stroke, and it oddly excited her.

Excited was not an adequate word for Garren. He'd never had anything so sweet. It was as if they had been doing this together their entire life, so brilliant the sensations. Although he'd always exhibited remarkable control, he knew he would not last much longer with her. He could feel his loins burning with a fire that could not be controlled. When he touched the place where their bodies joined, Derica stiffened and cried out as though seized by the most exquisite pain. It was his undoing, and he allowed himself a tremendous release. His thrusts slowed until they stopped completely as their first frenzy of passion was sated.

It was dark in the room, quiet but for the crackling of the fire. Wrapped in Garren's arms, melded to his flesh by heat and sweat, Derica lingered in the wonderful world between a dream and reality. She never wanted the night to end; to lie with him, as they were, for eternity would have been fine with her. Garren continued to caress her, rub her, his kisses soft against her forehead.

"Are you all right?" he whispered.

She sighed contentedly, snuggling closer to him. "I have died and gone to heaven."

He laughed softly. "I know how you feel."

There were no more words spoken for some time. Garren's touch said everything words could not. Derica fell asleep in his arms, waking abruptly when he stirred.

He was out of the bed, pulling the coverlet over her before she was aware of what he was doing.

"What's wrong?" she asked sleepily.

"Nothing, sweetheart." He was over by the window, peering out of the oilcloth. "Go back to sleep."

She sat up. "Did you hear something?"

His eyes were riveted to the street below the inn. He didn't say anything for a moment. "I heard horses," he let the oilcloth fall back. "Just a merchant. I doubt your father and his horde would be in disguise."

She heard his words, but her focus was centered on the sight before her; frankly, she'd never seen a nude man before. Garren's shoulders were impossibly wide, his neck thick and his chest muscular and broad. His torso was narrow and rippled with muscles. As he turned to look for his breeches and weapon, she noticed the perfect roundness of his buttocks and the defined muscles of his legs. She felt her cheeks grow hot and her heart race, slightly embarrassed but wildly attracted at the same time.

Garren noticed she was staring at him. He picked up his broadsword and leaned it against the wall, grinning. "Is there something I can help you with, Lady le Mon?"

"What do you mean?"

"I mean that you are staring at me as if I am a prized bull. Is there something I can do for you?"

She blushed furiously. "No."

His grin widened as he made his way over to the bed, breeches in hand. "Are you sure? I would be happy to...."

"No!"

She flopped back down on the bed and pulled the covers over her head. Garren laughed softly, tugging at the covers she was holding so tightly.

"Are you sure?" he teased. "Do you require my services again, perhaps? Or maybe you would like me to parade around so that you may stare at me until you have had your fill."

She growled at him. "Go away."

"You can touch, you know. Anything you want."

She shrieked softly in frustration and he continued to laugh at her. He finally stopped trying to pull the covers off of her and, instead, bundled them up all around her and gave her a massive hug. She squealed like a child, with delight, and yanked the covers off of her head. Her hair was wild over her face and they grinned at each other, playfully.

"I am thinking on going down and getting us some food," he said. "What say you?"

"I am famished."

"Then I shall return shortly."

"Can I come?"

"You don't want to rest here, in bed, and have a man serve you?"

She made a face at him and tossed off the coverlet. Garren helped her cinch up the peasant bodice, not so much helping her as stealing a touch of her skin now and again. Their entire world now was filled with discovery, laughter, and new sensations. Derica grabbed the comb and tamed her hair, securing it at the nape of her neck with a piece of cloth the sisters had packed for her. Garren stood behind her as she groomed, running his hands down her torso, around her waist. He watched her face as she fumbled with her hair. He was completely fascinated by her.

He left her long enough to put on his tunic, boots, and strap the sword to his waist. With his wife in hand, he quit the room and descended the stairs in to the loud, smoky hall.

It was more crowded than when they had first arrived. People were laughing, eating, and becoming riotously drunk. Garren kept hold of Derica as he ordered food from the barkeep and went in search of a table for the two of them. Derica wanted to eat in the hall, since she had never been to a tavern before. Garren hoped that one meal in such a place would cure her of any further curiosity. He couldn't see any charm to it, but she did.

The only table they could find was a small one by the hearth. Garren sat with his back to the wall, facing the room, and Derica within arm's length. She was chatting on about something, but he was only half-listening. His attention was on two knights on the far side of the room. Knights tended to have a special sense around each other, always knowing another knight, another potential enemy or ally. But Garren's circumstances were slightly different in that his knightly duties took on a more subversive role. It was essential he be completely aware of his surroundings at all times.

"Did you hear me?"

Derica was asking him a question. Garren looked away from the men in the corner and smiled at her. "I am sorry, I did not. What did you say, sweetheart?"

"I asked you if you'd ever been to Rome. Surely coming back from the Holy Land, you must have passed through?"

He shook his head. "I have not been to Rome." It wasn't the time to tell her, yet, that he'd never been to the Holy Land. "Is that some place you wish to go?"

She nodded. "I hear they have all manner of ancient buildings, built by the gods of some olden race. And there is a huge theatre where men fight to the death."

"I have heard of this also," he said. "Perhaps we will go there some day, if it would make you happy."

Her face lit up. "Do you mean it?"

"Of course."

She leapt up and threw her arms around his neck. "Oh, Garren, I am so happy. Thank you for being so wonderful to me."

He held her, flashes of the truths he must eventually tell her filling his mind. He'd pushed everything aside in light of recent events, but now with the event of their marriage and life together, he knew that he must tell her the truth of the matter soon. It was not fair to hold anything back from her. He struggled not to be fearful of how she would react, knowing he had basically lied to her.

"We will go anywhere you wish," he gently sat her back in her chair; the knights in the corner had noticed him and eye contact had been made. He didn't want Derica between him and any hostilities that might erupt. "Is there somewhere else you might like to visit?"

She was a-gaggle about their potential travel. Most definitely, she wanted to visit Spain and Corsica. Greece was another place she would like to go. Garren lost track of all of the places she had heard of as his study of the two knights intensified.

"But what if we have children right away?" she was saying. "Will we take them with us? Certainly we cannot leave them behind. Do you suppose...?"

Garren didn't hear her after that. The knights in the corner were shifting; both of them were looking at him. Suspecting something might erupt, Garren took her by the hand and pulled her from the chair.

"Let us eat in our room," he said. "I do not wish to share you with these ruffians out here."

"But...," Derica looked disappointed. "Very well, then. If that is your wish."

He barely got her to the stairs before the knights were on them. Derica was on the first step when the growling voice came.

"Le Mon."

Garren was cool. He turned, placing himself between his wife and the knights. The men tossed their cloaks off, revealing the swarthy features of one and the clean shaven features of the other. Garren immediately recognized them, and his heart sank. He knew them both, and not on good terms.

"De Claare," he wanted them to know that he was not off-guard. "I see you have brought your trained dog with you."

The swarthier knight snarled in response, but the other, a man with short black hair, smiled thinly.

"Torres is indeed a dog," he said. "And he bites. Imagine finding you here in the wilds of Northampton. What are you doing so far from Chepstow?"

"Nothing worthy of your notice."

"Ah, but you are in my territory. My liege is Leicester and you, my friend, are far from the support of Richard's great Chancellor. I am sure my liege will be very interested to know you are here."

"Leicester is a traitor. He defiles England with the very air he breathes."

"A matter of opinion." De Claare cocked an eyebrow. "Tell me something, le Mon; why would a knight of your reputation and stature fight for a king that has barely set foot on English soil? I do not understand it."

"That is because you are too stupid to realize the truth." Compounding his current concerns was the fact that Derica was hearing tantalizing clues to his true self. "Leave peaceably now and you leave with your life, de Claare. I shall not make the offer again."

De Claare shook his head. "When last we met at that skirmish at Corfe Castle and you forced my men to surrender before the Marshal's armies, I told you that if I saw you again I would kill you. I meant it."

Garren smiled humorlessly. "You could not do it then, even when you outnumbered us two to one. What makes you think you can do it now?"

De Claare's gaze moved to Derica, standing on the steps above her husband. He pointed at her. "Your lady wife, I presume?"

Garren's sword came out faster than the blink of an eye. "I was merciful on the battlefield at Corfe. Mention the lady again and my mercy is at an end."

The two knights laughed in sinister fashion. Behind Garren, Derica came down to stand behind her husband. He felt her hand on his shoulder.

"Come with me, now," she murmured in his ear. "We'll bolt the door and wait for them to go away. Please, Garren."

"She is a delightful morsel, le Mon," de Claare said. "A gift for your faithful service, no doubt."

Garren knew there would be no getting rid of them until someone's blood was spilt. "Go back to the room and lock the door, sweetheart," he told her. "Do not open it for anyone but me, and do not come down here no matter what you hear. Is that clear?"

Derica's heart filled with terror. She'd been around warring men too long and knew what they were capable of. And she was also smart enough to know that her presence was a distraction in a vocation where distraction could be deadly.

"Please, Garren," she was beginning to cry. "Come with me. Leave them here."

Garren could feel her fear. "I cannot. Please, go. I beg you."

Derica would not argue with him, though she desperately wanted to. She looked at the men threatening her husband, hating them with every fiber her small body possessed.

"Then if you are to fight him, allow him to regain his armor," she said strongly. "You are fully protected and fully armed. There is nothing honorable about fighting a knight without his protection."

Garren took his eyes off his opponents in an attempt to hush her, but de Claare spoke first.

"The lady knows something of knights," he said. "Have you, perchance, had much experience with them?"

Torres and a few men surrounding them snickered lewdly. Derica could feel her anger outweighing her fear.

"My father and uncles and brothers are knights," she growled. "The House of de Rosa is well known for their fighting."

De Claare's smile vanished. "De Rosa?" he repeated. "You are of the House of de Rosa?"

"Bertram de Rosa is my father."

The knight was clearly puzzled. He looked at Garren. "You married into the House of de Rosa?" he asked, incredulous. "Le Mon, could it be that your loyalties have changed?"

"They have not."

"But you married your enemy's daughter."

"I married a woman whom I adore. And our marriage is none of your affair."

De Claare and his knight were confused. They wanted Garren in the worst way, yet they were unwilling to provoke the wrath of de Rosa. Anyone who supported John Lackland, as Leicester and Norfolk did, knew of the warring de Rosa clan. To attack a member of that clan, even a daughter's enemy husband, would cause problems and it was a chance de Claare did not want to take.

With a long look, the knights backed away. Sheathing their swords, they quit the inn without another word. Garren stood, sword still in hand, watching the door to make sure they did not return. He was not surprised the de Rosa name had held such weight with them.

"Come on," Derica said quietly. "Let us return to our room. They will not come back."

Garren's eyes lingered on the door a moment longer. When he turned to follow his wife up the stairs, she was already half way to the top. Entering their room on her heels, he closed the door quietly and bolted it, wondering what he was going to say to her in explanation to she had just heard. He prayed that she would understand.

Carefully, he set his weapon against the wall. "Derica," he began hesitantly. "I know you heard things that might have confused you. I would like to explain, if you would allow me."

Derica stood by the window, peering through the oilcloth as her husband had done earlier. "I think they have left." She let the oilcloth fall back and looked at him. "I told you once that it didn't matter to me if you were a spy or not. It still doesn't."

He felt more relief than words could express, but she deserved to know all of it. He sat down on the mattress and motioned her over. When she came close, he pulled her down onto his lap and held her tightly, just for a moment.

"Whether or not it matters, you deserve to know all of it," he said quietly. "Few people know what I am about to tell you, simply because my life would be in jeopardy if the truth were widely known. But as my wife, it is your right."

Derica curled up on his lap. "Is it awful?"

"That depends."

"Was my father right about you being a spy, then? Did I unwittingly lie for you?"

He paused. "Aye."

Surprisingly, she wasn't upset by the knowledge. He was being honest with her, for better or for worse.

"I have been in Richard's service for many years," he said. "In my younger days, I fought for him in France as well as in England. I fought for him against his father, against his brothers, and in support of both his father and his brothers. Sometimes royal families have a strange sense of loyalty."

"Go on."

"Some time ago, I went into the service of William Marshal. William is not only Richard's chancellor, he is his most ardent supporter. In doing so, he retains experienced knights like me for tasks he considers vital to Richard's rule."

"Like what?"

"Anything that conventional means cannot accomplish. I do what is necessary to further Richard's cause, be it on the battlefield or in a more covert venue."

Derica thought a moment. "My father is a supporter of the king's brother."

"I know."

"Then I would guess that your coming to Framlingham was in the line of duty. You were sent to spy on my father."

"Aye."

"And you were to marry me to accomplish that."

He looked her in the eye. "That was the original plan," he said. "But, as you can see, it did not turn out that way. Somewhere in the process of

107

accomplishing my mission, I fell in love with you and my motives for the Marshal were forgotten. For you, I am willing to risk everything I have ever been, everything I have ever believed in. I could not and would not betray you, not even for the sake of my king."

Derica fell silent, her mind whirling with this new information. She stroked his neck, the back of his head, feeling his soft hair drift through her fingers.

"Richard," she murmured.

"What about him?"

She lifted her shoulders, weakly. "I was simply thinking that all of the talk that you were in the Holy Land with the king was a lie."

"For necessity's sake, it was."

"And your father; was he in on the deception?"

"It was difficult for him to be less than truthful with his friend, your father, but he was indeed a part of the deception for my sake. It was by sheer coincidence that my father and your father knew each other."

"Then I suppose I should be angry about all of this."

"I would not fault you if you were."

Her expression grew thoughtful as she tried to put together the pieces to the puzzle. "And Fergus? Does he work for the Marshal, too?"

"No. He has no knowledge of the truth of my vocation and I prefer to keep it that way."

She looked at him, his strong face and beautiful eyes. After a moment, she simply shook her head. "It is my opinion that politics are a deadly game and something I have no use for, and it does not please me that you are involved in such intrigue. But I understand that you must do as you must." She smiled, timidly. "Perhaps I am a stupid woman and simply cannot see past my emotions, but I cannot hate you for this."

It was more than he had hoped for. With a sigh of relief, he kissed her deeply. "I am so sorry I lied to you in the vault," he murmured against her lips. "I did not want to, but I saw no other way at the time. Your father was prepared to hang me."

"I do not care about any of that," she whispered. "All that matters is that you are truthful with me now and will forever be so. Promise me, Garren."

"I swear it."

They held each other, tightly, and Garren thanked God for the sense to marry this amazing woman. He settled back on the bed with her clutched against his chest, thinking about nothing in particular beyond what had just occurred. He knew there would be other nights like this one, coming up against people who wanted to see him come to harm. He was glad Derica knew the truth, and tremendously glad for her strength. He knew he would need it in times to come.

"Garren?"

"What, sweetheart?"

"Does the Marshal know what's happened? With me, I mean."

"No."

"You must tell him."

"I will as soon as I am able. But my greater concern right now is getting us to a safe haven."

Derica sat up, looking at him. She suddenly looked like a child, small and vulnerable. "I am afraid," she said. "What will happen if...?"

He put his fingers on her lips. "Hush, now," he murmured. "No fears. The Marshal will be sated and your family will eventually come to terms. Everything will turn out fine, given time. We simply need to let the situation cool a bit."

Derica lay back down against his warm, comforting chest. She didn't want to voice her doubts. Though she heard his words, she wasn't sure she agreed.

CHAPTER TEN

"I shall not ask again."

He'd been burned, beaten, poked, slapped and moderately cut. Tied to a gnarled oak tree somewhere south of where the de Rosa's had caught up to him, Fergus hadn't yet become impatient with the situation. For the moment, he was tolerant. Bertram de Rosa was missing his daughter and he was understandably brittle. Besides, Fergus had suffered worse wounds at the hands of scorned women. Most of what he'd received thus far had been child's play.

"If I have told you once, I have told you a thousand times," Fergus said patiently. "I know nothing of your daughter's disappearance. I am a bachelor knight in the current service of Somerset. I was attempting to return home when you and your brigands ambushed me."

"You are a liar," Donat snarled in his face; the middle de Rosa brother had inflicted most of the torture. "We know you were at Framlingham. We found your handcart by the side of the road and followed your tracks."

"I have no knowledge of any handcart, though I was in the vicinity of Framlingham. I have friends in Saxmundham and was passing through. That is why you found my tracks."

"Liar! What did you do with her?"

"I have done nothing."

"If she is lying dead somewhere in a ditch, you will curse the day you were born. I swear it on God's Holy name."

"If she is lying dead somewhere, it is not by my hand."

Donat shoved his fist into Fergus' stomach once again. It was the latest blow in a long line of many. Fergus coughed in pain, trying to convince himself it wasn't so bad. He'd felt worse. But when a strike came to his face, he saw stars and thought, perhaps, that it was indeed bad.

Bertram stood with Lon and Alger, watching Donat beat their prisoner senseless. Dixon helped his brother now and again by thumping the captive on the head when he was particularly uncooperative. Only Daniel stood off by himself, watching the beating without emotion. He had tried to intervene once to suggest reasoning was a better method of interrogation, but he had been ignored. Now he said nothing. If his brothers beat their only suspect into oblivion, then they would never get any information out of him. Their brutal methods would cause their failure.

Bertram was already feeling failure. Five days without Derica suggested that the trail was growing cold. He suspected that le Mon had everything to do with her disappearance. When they had asked their captive about le Mon, they had received nothing by way of answer. It was becoming a maddening game. Watching his son split the prisoner's lip, he turned to his brothers.

"I wish we had Hoyt with us," he muttered. "He had a knack of being able to gain any information he wished."

"That is because he used methods that Donat has yet to aspire to," Lon said. "A hot poker up the arse has a way of making a man talk."

Bertram grunted. "Aye, but my sons still feel that beating a man is the only way. Pure strength."

"They're young. They will learn."

"Learn indeed. But they will not learn from the best."

Bertram had flashes of his larger brother in times past, pouring scalding water on a man's eyeballs in order to gain vital information. Before the blow to his head, Hoyt invented new ways of creating pain to all those who opposed the de Rosa will. Bertram found himself cursing that day when Hoyt took a blow so hard in the tourney that his helm had to be pried from his head. He was never the same after that. He could have used the old Hoyt now, very much.

"If they want to learn how to dress and fold laundry, Hoyt can teach them very well," Alger mumbled.

Bertram sighed. "I had hopes when he chose to ride from Framlingham in search of Derica, in the manner of days of old. But the moment we tracked down this thief, he disappeared without the stomach for doing what needs to be done."

"Where do you suppose he went?"

"Who can say? To the nearest town to buy fabric, or perhaps he went home. I do not know. I am coming not to care any longer."

The senior de Rosa brothers nodded in silent agreement. The continued to observe as Donat pummeled the hostage. It was having no effect. Finally, Bertram himself moved forward. He was tired of waiting. Grabbing his captive by the hair, he looked into the swollen blue eyes.

"I shall make this brief," he said. "If I do not receive the answers I seek, then I will allow my son to do whatever he wishes to you. Keep in mind that he young, lacks discipline, and had a fondness for creating as much pain as he can. With that said, I will make you a proposition; whatever le Mon has promised to pay you, I will double it if you tell me where my daughter is."

Fergus didn't reply; he continued to stare at him. Bertram's attempt at good will was fading. "Have you no answer for me?" he pressed.

Fergus didn't say a word, and it was clear that he was not going to. Bertram let go of his hair and turned towards the men.

"Lon, Alger, backtrack his trail and leave no stone unturned," he snapped. "If there is a house, search it. If there is a town, raid it. Take enough men-at-arms with you to satisfy that."

The uncles moved for their horses, shouting to the company of soldiers that had accompanied them. Ten were singled out for the hunt. Bertram turned back to his sons.

"Daniel," he addressed his eldest. "Go back to Framlingham. Mobilize two hundred men and prepare them for a march to Chateroy Castle. We are going to pay my old friend a visit and see if he knows the whereabouts of his son."

Daniel didn't say a word as he turned for his horse. Bertram watched him a moment, wondering if he would actually do as he was bade. The man was the least violent of the de Rosas and the most likely to disobey his father in that regard. When Daniel rode off, Bertram turned to Donat and Dixon.

"As for this one," he tilted his head in Fergus' direction. "Do what you must to wrangle information from him. But be mindful that he is our only link to your sister."

For the first time, Fergus felt a distinct sense of despair as he watched Bertram de Rosa walk away. He knew that the old man had been the only thing stopping the sons from unleashing on him. He glanced at the two de Rosa brothers; they stared back with the eyes of something without a soul. In that moment, Fergus knew that he was in a good deal of trouble.

***

It was a cold, misty morning. Garren had awakened before Derica and had built a fire to warm the freezing room, but it hadn't been nearly warm enough by the time she rose. Hissing with chill, she went in search of her clothing. With the coverlet wrapped around her, she looked like a giant baby in too much swaddling. Garren grinned as she banged about, pulling out the pretty blue lamb's wool gown that the sisters had given her. It was very warm, something she desperately needed at the moment.

"Cold, is it?" he quipped.

She groaned, trying to hold the dress with one hand and keep the coverlet about her with the other. Garren took mercy on her.

"Let me help you," he said. "I shall hold the coverlet and you hold the dress."

Derica's teeth were chattering. Garren took hold of the coverlet, pulling it back just enough to get a peek at her nude body as she fumbled with the gown. It was too much for him to take.

"I know how to warm you, and quickly," he said softly.

She was having a hard time manipulating the dress with her quaking hands. "H-how?"

He dropped the coverlet entirely and put his arms around her. She squealed as he pulled her down on the bed, but quickly succumbed to his heated kisses. He explored her with his burning hands, stroking her nipples that were hard from both his touch and the chill. His body was big and warm, enveloping her. Derica surrendered to him, each sensation new and wonderful. He seemed to take delight in stroking her inner thighs, feeling her quiver and laughing softly when she did so. When he finally took her, it was tenderly and far more slowly than it had been the previous night. Now, he could be patient and experience everything he had been too crazed to experience their first time. In reflection, he had been selfish. He would not be selfish now.

For Derica, it was as if they had been making love for a sweet eternity, yet it still wasn't long enough. When the rapturous spasms overtook her body once again, she was disappointed and elated at the same time. Garren's rapture came shortly thereafter, and they lay entangled in sweat and glory in a world where time had no meaning. They were only aware of each other and their bliss. But, as it did so often in their world, reality settled as the day grew light around them.

"Are you hungry?" Garren kissed her temple.

Derica yawned, snuggling against him. "Always."

He kissed her again. "Then let us break our fast and depart. As much as I would love to languish with you all day in bed, I am afraid we cannot spare the time."

They dressed in warm silence. The lamb's wool gown was absolutely stunning on Derica's figure. The nuns had even managed to stir up a pair of warm hose for her, which she gladly put on even though they were a bit too small. She braided her hair, smiling shyly when she caught her husband staring at her. By the time she pulled on her soft slippers and swung the cloak over her shoulders, Garren had everything packed and waiting for her.

There were bodies sleeping in the tavern below, strewn about the floor and tables. It smelled of smoke and urine. Derica wrinkled her nose at the pungent smell as Garren sent a servant to bring about his charger and procured a hunk of bread from the serving woman. He handed the food to his wife, who promptly tore off a piece of the bread and chewed happily.

Garren wondered aloud if there would be anything left for him to eat and she shook her head playfully.

It was misty and cold when they stepped outside. Derica pulled the hood of her cloak around her tightly to ward off the chill. The destrier was brought around by the same sleepy lad who had taken him the night before. Garren loaded their bags on the steed and lifted his wife into the saddle. Derica put a piece of bread in his mouth to thank him for his efforts. He gathered the reins and was preparing to lead the horse off when a figure approached through the mist. Neither Derica nor Garren saw until it was too late.

"Derica," came a familiar voice.

Derica nearly jumped out of her skin. Uncharacteristically startled, Garren made an instinctive move for the broadsword strapped to the front of his saddle.

Hoyt de Rosa emerged from the shrouding fog, covered with a black cloak and looking like the Devil himself. Derica and Garren immediately noticed something different; the flamboyant de Rosa was dressed in armor and not the usual fine silks. He looked as he had before his accident, an enormous knight to be feared and hated. Their anxiety deepened.

Hoyt came to a halt several feet away. Garren put himself and his weapon between the elder de Rosa and his wife, bracing himself for what was surely to come.

"I wish no trouble, my lord," he said. "But another step and I will be forced to defend myself."

Hoyt's gaze moved between his niece and Garren. He shook his head, long with hair that he had not cut in years. Without the rouge and eye makeup, he looked quite masculine.

"Do you have any idea how worried your father is?" he asked Derica. "We have been searching for days."

Derica was torn between shame and defiance. "How did you find us?"

Hoyt crossed his arms thoughtfully. "'Twas not a matter of finding you, but following you." He looked at Garren. "My brother captured the man you hired to abduct Derica."

Garren's heart sank, thinking of his friend Fergus and remorseful that the man's loyalty had gotten him killed. "Did his death bring you the information you sought?"

"I do not know. I did not interrogate him. While my nephews were intent on inflicting pain, I rode back along his trail and found small footsteps branching off into the forest. There was an abbey over the hill. So I lay in wait and was rewarded, the next day, to see you both ride from the abbey. As I said, it was simply a matter of following you and biding my time."

"I am not going home, Uncle Hoyt," Derica wasn't sure how to address him, but it didn't seem right calling him Lady Cleo Blossom when he was dressed in armor. "Garren and I were married yesterday. I am his wife and I am staying with him."

"I suspected as much."

Garren watched his body language carefully; he was armed, but had yet to unsheathe his sword. It hung at his side. In fact, he'd made no aggressive moments at all.

"If you have come to take her home, you have wasted your time," Garren said. "You may report back to her father than she is well and happy, and we intend to have a good life together."

Hoyt shook his head. "I have not come to take her home, nor do I intend to tell my brother anything at the moment."

"Then what do you want?"

Hoyt was silent a moment, as if contemplating something very deep. "Garren," he said slowly. "Does the Marshal know what you have done?"

Garren's guard went up, higher than ever. He was very good at denying his true vocation and used that experience.

"So you still think I am a spy, is that it?"

"Games are not necessary, sir knight. I know that you are sworn to William Marshal and that he sent you to Framlingham to spy on my brother. Did he not tell you that there would be another set of eyes at Framlingham?"

"I do not know what you mean."

Hoyt smiled ironically. "I thought you would not," he said. "But do you know this? *La lealtà alla morte. Onorare soprattutto.*"

Garren stared at him, long and hard. He had no idea how Hoyt de Rosa would know that unless the Marshal had told him. There was a code with the Marshal's men, something that identified them to one another. Each man had what was termed his 'phrase', a specific combination of words that another agent would speak to him to let him know he was an ally. In a startling twist, Hoyt had just spoken Garren's phrase, and there was only one reply possible.

"*Lungo vive il re,*" Garren said softly.

"Then you believe me."

Garren wasn't sure how to reply. Although he did not lower his sword, his manner was less defensive and more curious. "Why did you not identify yourself earlier?"

"I did not want to give myself away, so to speak," Hoyt replied. "I am sorry I could not be of help when my brothers' persecuted you. Had I intervened any more than I did, surely they would have suspected something. I could not risk it."

Garren lowered the sword. He glanced at his wife; he wanted to see how she was reacting to all of this. From her expression, it was clear that she was shocked.

"But...," Derica hardly noticed her husband looking at her. "I do not understand, Uncle Hoyt. Do you mean to say that you serve William Marshal?"

"It would seem so," Hoyt walked towards them, slowly. "Many years ago, I served John and Richard's father. When Henry died, my loyalties naturally fell with John because he was Henry's favorite and, I believed, rightful heir to the throne. But over the years I have come to see what a weak ruler he would be. Already, the man tears this country apart and he is only a prince. What would happen if he were king?"

"You sound like my father," Garren said quietly.

"Your father is correct," Hoyt agreed firmly. "At a tournament a few years ago, I came into contact with William Marshal. I knew him from when he served Henry, as we both fought for the king in our prime. After a few hours conversation, I realized I was in complete agreement with him. Richard was our best choice for king. So, with a convenient bump on my head at the very same tournament, suddenly I am crazy and my brothers pay little attention to me. Better to observe for Richard's cause in such a way and never be suspected."

Derica's jaw hung open. "Then the dress, the rouge, was an act? You were spying?"

"Nay; not really. I never completely gave over my support to the Marshal, as my loyalties to my family were stronger than my loyalties to the king. But, as I saw necessary, bits of information made their way to the Marshal for the king's cause. I walked a fine line between betraying my brothers and helping England. It wasn't until very recently that I decided to lend full support to Richard. From now on, the Marshal will know everything that I know. I hold back no longer."

Garren listened to the very clever explanation, but he couldn't help probing for his own peace of mind. "What finally caused you to lend full support?"

Hoyt looked him in the eye. "Two thousand French mercenaries due on the shores of Norfolk within the week."

"You're sure?"

"Positive. With the several thousand Teutonic and Irish mercenaries already at Nottingham and Bolton, they'll create a formidable army for the prince."

"How do you know this?"

"The same spy who identified you to my brother also reported this. The man is a frequent visitor to Framlingham. When I saw him skulk through the front gates, I knew something was amiss. I heard everything he said."

"Spy? What spy?"

"His name is Alberic. He has worked for the prince's cause for several years. He knew you on sight and told my brother of you."

Garren nodded in understanding as it became clear how Bertram knew of his loyalties. "As I would probably know him on sight as well," he muttered. "'Tis wise to know the face of the enemy even if you do not know his name."

"Precisely."

Satisfied with that mystery solved, Garren returned to the subject at hand. "How soon do you estimate that the mercenaries already on English soil will merge with the French?"

"Within four to five weeks."

Garren was grim. "They will tear England apart."

"Exactly."

"Does the Marshal know?"

"No," Hoyt said. "That is why you must go to him immediately. I must return to Framlingham and resume my place. It is up to you, Garren. You must tell him."

Garren tore his gaze away from Hoyt long enough to look at his wife. She was ashen with fear.

"I must get my wife to safety first," he said after a moment. "I will tell the Marshal once she is settled."

Hoyt could not disagree. "I do not dispute you, especially with my brother on the rampage. I will try to hold him off as best I can, but I cannot promise success." He looked at his niece and his manner softened. "I will not ask where you are going. I do not want to know. But I do hope that you are truly happy, wherever you may go."

Tears filled Derica's eyes. She had always been particularly close to her uncle. Dismounting the charger, she embraced him, drawing strength from the Hoyt of old and not the strange creature he had been over the past few years. Yet she understood his reasons; politics and deep beliefs were strong motivators for men's loyalties.

"God be with you, Uncle Hoyt," she murmured. "I pray we meet again, very soon."

He kissed her forehead. Derica went back to the charger and Garren lifted her up once again. He could see how upset she was and kissed her hand to comfort her. By the time he turned around, Hoyt was disappearing into the mist.

"De Rosa," he called. "We shall meet again."

"I am sure we will. If you do not take good care of my niece, it will be sooner than you think."

Garren could barely see the man's outline through the sea of white. "There is one last thing, my lord."

"Speak."

"The man your nephews captured... he is an old and dear friend. If you could discover what's become of him, I would be grateful."

"Consider it done."

Garren was satisfied. As he adjusted his wife's cloak and finally gathered the reins, it was Hoyt who called out to him.

"Garren?"

"What?"

There was a lengthy silence. "There is something I should tell you. There are more of us."

"What do you mean?"

"In the de Rosa house. There is another who shares our views and is willing to help."

Garren thought on that. "My advice is caution, my lord. Men such as us do not live long if our trust, even in family members, is given easily."

"Prudent advice."

The morning mist swallowed them up as they went their separate ways.

***

When the soldiers had cleared an all other de Rosas were gone, Donat and Dixon advanced on their captive. Donat balled his fists while Dixon carried a club. Fergus saw them coming and he lowered his head, closing his eyes against what was surely to come.

His body was taut with expectation. But he found it strange when he heard a dull thump, followed by a grunt, and it did not come from him. Opening an eye, he saw one of the de Rosa brother's on the ground. The man was unconscious. Puzzled, Fergus opened both eyes and looked up.

Donat rubbed his knuckles, glancing down at his brother. When he saw that Fergus was looking at him, he shook his head.

"Hated to do that," he said. "But he was about to bash your brains in. Are you badly injured?"

Fergus didn't know what to say. "W-what?"

"I asked if you are badly injured. I tried not to be too harsh, but for appearance sake, I had to do a nominal amount of damage."

Fergus' puzzlement grew by leaps and bounds. He looked at Dixon, sleeping forcibly upon the grass. "What is happening? Why is your brother on the ground?""

Donat replied as he untied the ropes that bound Fergus to the tree. "I had to do that. He meant you great harm."

"And you didn't?" Fergus jerked his hands free, stepping away from Donat as he rubbed his wrists. "Just what in the hell is going on here? You pounded me for the better part of a day and now you knock your brother cold when...?"

Donat put his hands up in a supplicating gesture. "I know you do not understand any of this, but let me explain. I am not against you, man. I am with you. What I did, I had to do for the sake of my family. It wasn't anything personal against you."

Fergus was about to explode. "What you did?" he clapped a hand to his forehead. "Perhaps you'd better start from the beginning. Why did you just release me?"

"Because you took my sister to be with le Mon."

Fergus sneered. "Eh?"

"Le Mon and my sister. You took her to be with him, did you not? I had to pretend to beat you in order that my father and uncles wouldn't have a go at you. Then you'd be in a world of pain right now, my friend. I had to put on a show."

"What on earth for?"

"Because my father wants to see this country torn apart by a greedy bastard of a prince. Le Mon serves the one man who can save this country. I believe in that cause."

"What cause?"

"William Marshal, of course. The same man you serve."

A glimmer came to Fergus' eye. "I serve Longton, not Richard."

"There is no need for secrecy. I know that le Mon serves the king's inner circle. I would assume you do the same." When Fergus didn't react, he held up his hands. "I even know the phrase. La lealtà alla morte. Onorare soprattutto. It is le Mon's phrase, is it not?"

"I do not know what you speak of."

Donat shrugged his shoulders. "As you wish," he said. "But I must know where my sister and le Mon are so I can keep my family away from them. They'll search to the ends of the earth for her."

Fergus cocked an eyebrow. "Is this some clever ploy? To trick me into believing you are my ally when, in truth, it is simply another tactic to force me to reveal all that I know? I am not as stupid as I apparently look."

"Nor am I," Donat said. "Sir knight, I realize this situation appears morbidly strange. But you must believe me when I tell you that the beating you took, at my hands, was purely an act for the benefit of my family. I was protecting you, if you will believe it. But they are off now, searching for my sister and preparing to lay siege to le Mon's castle. If le Mon and my sister are heading there, then they must be warned. Do you not understand?"

He was imploring him, but Fergus had seen some great actors in his time and was not taken in. Still, there was something urgent about the man's manner.

"I will believe you if you let me go," Fergus responded, confident that his request would be met by a refusal.

"Is that they only way?"

"It is."

"Go, then," Donat replied. "I will not follow, and I will do my best to keep the others off your trail. But, for God's Holy sake, if you know where le Mon is, you must tell him what is happening. He must be warned. Use his phrase and he will know that you speak the truth."

Fergus stared at him. The circumstance was as strange as any he had ever encountered and he did not trust the man in the least. But he was not about to contest his freedom. With his eyes still on Donat, he made his way to the trees where a destrier was tethered. Confiscating the horse, he tore off through the bramble, heading in haste for the road.

Donat watched him go, hoping the knight was loyal enough to le Mon to warn him but wondering in the same breath if he had just made a foolish mistake.

"*Pour Richard de Dieu et Roi*," he whispered softly.

Donat picked up the club that his brother had held and promptly smacked himself in the nose. When Dixon eventually regained his wits, he found his older brother unconscious on the ground and the prisoner escaped.

CHAPTER ELEVEN

This time of the year, Wales was a place soaked in perpetual gray. The land was gray, the sky gray, even the water. It was cloudy for days on end, making travel cold and miserable.

It took Garren and Derica nearly a week to make it to the border of England and Wales, the desolate area of the southern marches. They watched the landscape move from flat, fertile farming soil to rocky, hilly land that seemed to be the distinguishing characteristic of this part of the country. Still, there were moments when the sun broke through the cloud cover and produced spectacular yellow beams that fingered the slumbering landscape. In those moments, it was beautiful, and Derica would make Garren stop the horse to observe the precious moment.

For a woman who had spent her entire life given any luxury she could possibly want, Derica had traveled incredibly well with hardly a comfort. There were times when she would want to walk because her backside ached, but Garren never heard a compliant other than that. She was, however, constantly cold and many were a time when her icy fingers would snake inside his tunic to seek warmth against his skin. He would grunt and make faces, but she would giggle and tell him to quiet. Such was the price he had to pay for her company.

Quiet wasn't a word she knew much of herself. Although it wasn't annoying in the least, she talked constantly as the charger lumbered over the landscape. While Garren listened with interest, Derica would prattle on about her life back at Framlingham, the day her brothers accidentally killed her dog in a drunken brawl, or the time when her entire family went to a tourney in Saxmundham and another knight, not knowing that she was a de Rosa, had asked for her favor as she sat in the lists. Garren grinned as she relayed how the entire clan cornered the knight and his pages in the knight's tent, collapsed the tent, and then proceeded to beat everyone caught within the folds of material with the tent stakes they had ripped up from the earth.

He came to learn quite a bit about the woman he married in the two weeks that it took them to travel into Dyfed. He found her to be more of a delight than he could have imagined. He knew that she desperately wanted to learn how to read Latin. He also learned that she loved to draw sketches of castles; not simply to produce artwork, but of how to build them. They would sit by the fire at sundown and he would watch her sketch in the dirt. He had to admit that she had some brilliant ideas.

Garren had never been much of a conversationalist, or so he thought. Whereas he believed he had been doing most of the listening, it seemed that he had done some talking, too. He spoke of his father, a short man with bad eyes who had doted on his only son. Derica heard about the young page who had missed his pet goat when he had gone to foster. She heard a few antics that had involved Fergus, but Garren would become sad upon remembering the friend who had sacrificed himself and Derica would change the subject in a well-meaning way. It had been, after all, her family who had murdered Fergus. She hoped that the event would never cast a shadow over her and Garren, even though Garren had never so much as uttered a word to that effect.

Carreg-wen was the home of Fergus' birth, the village on the outskirts of Cilgarren. Garren and Derica had spent the night in the woods a few miles out, making love before the fire and talking well into the night. When dawn broke, they made their way through the mist and fog into the small town. It was an unspectacular place. Garren had made up his mind to seek out Fergus' father not only to inform him of his son's fate, but also to seek his aid in locating the castle. A few inquiries in town pointed the direction to a small cottage at the north-western end of the berg.

The rain was falling harder. Water formed in puddles all around the small, mud-brick dwelling. A heavy thatched roof dripped rain onto the ground as Garren walked up to the warped door and rapped on the splintering wood with his great gloved fist. Derica sat astride the charger, her lips unnaturally bright in the freezing weather, trying not to let Garren see that her teeth were chattering. He glanced at her when he received no immediate answer, winked, and rapped on the door again. He almost pounded on the head of the man who swiftly opened it.

Garren took a step back, noting the shock in the man's eyes. "Emyl de Edwin?" he asked.

The man had Fergus' eyes. They were bright blue and suspicious. "Who asks for him?"

"Fear not, my lord," Garren said. "I mean you no harm. I am a friend of Fergus'."

The man looked slightly less suspicious. "If you are looking for my son, I do not know where he is. He could be in France, or perhaps the Holy Land. If he owes you money, be assured that I have none to pay his debts. If I had, do you think I would be living here?"

Garren had to smile. He put up his hand to silence the man. "My lord, I come not to collect a debt your son owes me, though I am not surprised you have had experiences like that. Fergus had been known to make a promise or two that he had no intention of keeping."

The man cocked an eyebrow. "Ah, well, I see that you do indeed know my son."

"Well enough not to lend him money, my lord. May we speak?"

"That depends. What about?"

Garren glanced up at the sky. "I would prefer not to discuss business out here in the rain. My wife is freezing and I would hope to gain her some shelter."

The old man's eyes drifted to the charger, to Derica sitting cold and wet in the saddle. "No," he said after a moment. "I don't suppose you have come here to collect any debt with your lady in tow. 'Twould be bad manners. Bring her in by the fire."

The old man stepped back inside the cottage. Garren lifted Derica off the horse, carrying her across the mud and into the cramped, warm quarters. Closing the door behind them, he helped her pull back the soaking cloak. Near the hearth, the old man motioned them over.

"Take the cloak off and give it to me," he held his hands out. "I shall dry it by the fire. Lady, sit here, on the stool. 'Tis warm here."

Derica gratefully took the offered seat. Her hands were blue with cold and she held them up before the flame. The old man laid out the cloak, glancing at Derica with appreciative eyes. She caught his stares and he shrugged sheepishly.

"Forgive, my lady," he said. "'Tis been a long time since I have seen such beauty. I am Emyl de Edwin, and you are welcome in my home."

Garren removed his helm and pulled off his wet gloves. "I can see that you are indeed Fergus' father. The gift of flattery must run in the blood."

Emyl shrugged. "'Tis not flattery, but truth." He looked at the enormous knight. "And you, my lord. Your name?"

"Garren le Mon. And this is my wife, the lady Derica."

A flicker came to Emyl's eye. "Garren," he murmured. "I remember you as a lad. Now I see you as a fine, strong man."

Garren smiled. "And I remember you as a loud man who tried to thump us on the head with the butt of your sword on the occasions when you came to visit your son."

Emyl took Garren's outstretched hand and held it tightly. "You used to run from me."

"I am no fool."

"Did you come to seek vengeance, then?"

"No," Garren snickered. "Though you surely deserve it. I have actually come for another reason."

"Name it, then."

"I would ask that you direct me to Cilgarren Castle."

Emyl's eyebrows lifted. "Cilgarren? That derelict, beautiful old woman?"

"Then you know of it."

"Of course I do. What do you want at that place?"

Garren took a long, slow breath, listening to the rain pound on the walls. "'Tis a long story, my lord, one not worthy of delving into. I would be indebted to you should you tell me the way."

Emyl was either wise enough not to probe. "Very well. Take the road through the town out to the west. When you come to the River Teifi, go south along the bank. Where the ground rises, look to the sky. You will see the castle above you. In fact," he pointed a finger at Garren. "I will take you there myself. In this fog, 'twill be difficult to see. I should not want you to get lost."

"That is not necessary, my lord," Garren assured him. "We can find it, though your offer is appreciated."

"Nonsense," Emyl waved him off. "'Tis the least I can do for Garren le Mon, the boy who once ran from me in terror. I should make up for my bad behavior."

Derica's hands were warming, as was her smile as she listened to the conversation. "You must have been an awesome knight, my lord."

Emyl turned to her. "Indeed, Lady le Mon. I was indeed formidable at one time. But that was before..." he looked slightly uncomfortable. "That was before the ravages of drink and foolishness set upon me. There was a time when I was an honorable knight in the service of the Earl of Shrewsbury. My ancestor arrived at Dover with William the Bastard many years back. Once, the de Edwin name meant something."

Derica glanced at Garren, uncertain what to say to a man who had apparently ruined himself. "Perhaps it shall again," she said with soft encouragement. "We plan to live at Cilgarren Castle. Perhaps you could serve Garren and help us make it a fine, strong place."

"Truly, Garren?" Emyl said. "Have you been granted the lands?"

Garren shook his head. "No," he said. "Suffice it to say that the lady and I are in need of finding a safe place for a time. Your son suggested the derelict castle of Cilgarren for this purpose."

"Safe place?" Emyl repeated. "Have you committed a crime, then?"

Garren cast his wife a wink. "Marrying this woman against her father's wishes is crime enough. We need to find safe haven until his anger cools."

Emyl laughed. "I see now. Well, I cannot blame you in the least. Were I younger and prettier, I might have done the same thing." He reached over by the hearth, collecting a large earthenware jug. "A drink, then. Let us toast your criminal activities."

Emyl took a huge swallow, reminding Garren very much of his son. Derica smirked as her husband reluctantly took the container and ingested a long swallow of the bitter, dark liquid.

"Do I get to drink to my own criminal activities, too?" she asked.

Garren cocked an eyebrow at her but dutifully handed her the jug. Derica took a gulp that spilled over her lips. She coughed and laughed at the same time, making a face at the strength of the liquor. Garren, grinning, shook his head at her and took the jug away. Emyl crowed happily.

"Garren, she is wonderful," he took another drink. "Too bad you married her before my son had a fair chance. And where is my prodigal boy these days? Not visiting his father, I can tell you. I haven't seen his swarthy hide in years."

Garren's jovial mood vanished. He didn't dare look at his wife, who was suddenly looking at the fire. He didn't want to tell this lonely old man that his only son had died as a result of Garren's crime. As he struggled to find an answer, Derica spoke.

"The last I saw of him, he was riding to the south of Yaxley Nene Abbey," she said softly. "I do not know where he went, but he was in good health last I saw him."

Garren shot her a strange look, his jaw tense and his eyes narrowed. She turned away from the fire, facing her husband as if daring him to disagree with her. He wouldn't back down and neither would she. After a moment, she looked at Emyl.

"Do you know that your son rescued me from my prison and delivered me to Garren?" she said. "He was brilliant in his plans. Why, had it not been for him, Garren and I would still be separated, longing for one another. "Tis a horrible thing to love someone you can never be with. Your son saved us from that fate."

Emyl looked pleased and surprised. "Truly, now? My son was noble for once in his life?"

"Verily," Derica said. "He is as clever as a fox and as loyal as a hound. Garren and I are both eternally grateful to him."

Emyl scratched his thinning hair. "Perhaps the lad has become a worthy knight, after all. He wasn't always so, you know."

"How so?" Derica asked.

Garren knew he was foolish not to stop the charade this instant. But Emyl's expression was so that Garren didn't have the heart. He rationalized his lack of truth by telling himself that he did not know for sure that Fergus was dead; Hoyt had never actually seen his body. But the implication was such that the de Rosas had finished him off in their zeal to locate Derica.

Garren listed to Emyl go on about Fergus' shortcomings. His son was rash, young and foolish, to be sure, but he was also strong and virtuous to a point. Drink and gambling were his vices, as were his father's.

Garren finally sat down in an old chair, watching his wife's profile in the firelight as she listened to the old man, noticing the wrinkle in her nose when she laughed. His thoughts soon turned from Fergus to Derica, and his heart began to swell so that he thought it might burst from his chest. Outside, the rain pounded harder, distracting him from his thoughts.

"Derica, sweetheart," he muttered. "We should be on our way. Are you warm and dry enough to continue?"

She nodded, her cheeks rosy from sitting so near the hearth. "I am."

Emyl fingered the cloak, laid out before the flames. "'Tis nearly dry," he stood up. "Give me a moment to gather my things and we'll be off."

Garren could have very well found the castle himself, but he allowed Emyl to feel useful. He was sure the old man didn't get much chance at that. Moreover, he was still feeling guilty about Fergus. In very short time, Emyl was cloaked and carrying one of the biggest swords Garren had ever seen, save his own. As Derica donned her drying cloak, Garren indicated the old man's weapon.

"A fine piece," he said. "Where did you acquire it?"

Emyl held the weapon up for Garren to inspect. "'Twas a gift from my liege, Shrewsbury." He beheld the sword as if it were the most beautiful thing in the world. "De Braose was an evil bastard, the most wicked marcher lord on the border. But he rewarded his faithful well. He gave this to me for meritorious service, probably stolen off of a dead Welsh prince."

Garren knew well the marcher lords, past and present. The Marshal was also a marcher lord. They were often the most ruthless men in the kingdom simply because the Welsh border was the most disputed.

Outside, the thunder rolled, and Emyl sheathed his sword. Garren put his helm on, adjusting it on his head so that it did not chaff against his skin. Just as Emyl opened the door of his warm hut, lightning flashed across the sky.

"The weather worsens," he commented. "Are you sure you won't stay here until this passes?"

Garren swept Derica into his arms. "If the castle is as derelict as your son said it was and provides no immediate shelter, then perhaps we shall. But for the moment, I would like to see it. I feel more secure within stone walls." He glanced as his wife. "Should the lady's family be tracking us, I would not want to be caught in a cottage that would be easily burned to the ground. And I would not want to jeopardize you."

Emyl threw up his hood. "Pah," he spat. "They'd have a fight on their hands, I can tell you."

Garren didn't reply. He followed the old man out into the driving rain, placing Derica upon the wet back of the charger. As he mounted up in front of her, Emyl disappeared around the side of the cottage and emerged a short time later astride a small, pale-colored donkey. Garren remembered Fergus' father coming to visit his squiring son, perched on the crest of a mighty red charger. To see him like this, a worn out man on a worn out steed, was disheartening.

They followed Emyl out onto the road that led through the town. They were heading west, into rain that stung with its ferocity. Garren shielded Derica as best he could, providing a huge windbreak from the elements. She huddled behind him, well protected, her cheek against his back as she watched the road pass by. When the charger began its jaunty trot, she had to lift her head otherwise it would bang against Garren's body. The rain fell hard, wetting her already cold nose.

It was slow going in the bad weather. Eventually, they reached a decline in the road. Derica peered around Garren and saw that the road descended to the banks of a river, running full with rainwater. Ahead of them, Emyl directed his donkey off the road and into the thick, grassy mud.

There was so much fog and rain that it was difficult to see for any distance around them. Garren followed Emyl into the sludge, realizing it was not so much a muddy field as a muddy path. The grass, as far as he could tell, was simply overgrown on to it. Ascending the path, he craned his neck back to see what he could through the haze. Gradually, an ominous sight came into view.

Cilgarren Castle loomed like a great ghostly beast on the hill high above them. Garren had seen many castles in his life, and it was clear from the onset that Cilgarren was no ordinary castle; as they mounted the path, he could see how the path cleverly paralleled the structure, making it convenient for defenders to shoot down invading forces.

Men would be picked off like sitting ducks. Massive round towers connected the curtain wall, arrow slits evident in the rounded stone fortifications. The west side of the castle was protected by a steep cliff that disappeared into the river below, while the northern side with the path was protected by a steep, unmanageable slope.

With every muddy step his destrier took, Garren became more impressed with what he was witnessing. It was apparent that this huge gray beast was built by for greatness. In the same breath, he was baffled why it should sit, unused and unwanted, when it could be a major force to be reckoned with.

The path crested at the top of the slippery hill and a large curtain wall stood before them. At first glance, Garren estimated it was easily twenty feet high. There was no telling how thick it was until they came closer. They edged the horses forward and Emyl spoke with reverence.

"I had forgotten the beauty of her," his eyes grazed the structure. "Why the princes abandoned it, I shall never understand. But they say ghosts chased them away."

"Ghosts?" Derica echoed. "What ghosts?"

Emyl gestured at the fortress shrouded in mist. "Legend says that Cilgarren was built by a prince of Dyfed named Owain," he answered. "He built it as his seat of power, given to him by his father, Madog ap Gruffyd. Owain had a wife named Bryndalyn, the most beautiful maiden in the land. One day, shortly after the castle was finished, Owain went off to fight one of the many skirmishes that hamper the Welsh. Men returned from the battle saying that Owain had perished. In her sorrow, Bryndalyn threw herself from the cliff that overlooks the river."

Derica's mouth was open in sorrow. "Poor lady," she murmured. "If Garren were not to return to me, I...."

She trailed off, unable to continue. As Garren reached around to pat her hand, Emyl shook his head sadly.

"Aye, my lady, but the truth was that Owain did not die. He returned, quite sound, only to find his lady dead. 'Tis said he went mad, locking himself in a room with her body. He neither ate, nor slept, but kept himself in with her corpse. Eventually, he died of a broken heart." The old man looked at her. "But God punishes those who take their own lives, as Bryndalyn and Owain did. So the two of them spend eternity searching the rooms of this place for each other, never in the same place at the same time. On still nights, one can hear them calling for each other. They come so close, but are ever damned to be a just breath away."

"So they can never be together, ever?"

"So it is said."

Derica looked as if she was about to cry. "That is the most awful story I have ever heard."

Garren held her hand, smiling faintly at the old man's story and at his wife's gullibility. The mood was growing heady and he had no intention of letting it get the better of them.

"Are you willing to face the ghosts to get out of this rain?" he teased. "Boo!"

She frowned at his attempt to startle her. "How can you make jokes about this? 'Tis a horrible tale, Garren. Tragic."

"I am sorry," he kissed her hand and spurred his charger towards the entrance. "You're right, It is tragic. I believe I shall go off and cry myself ill right now."

She couldn't see his expression, smirking at her, but she could feel his humorous snorts against her body. "Stop laughing at me. How would you like it if we were separated like that, through all eternity?"

"I wouldn't. Tell me if you plan on doing something foolish like that, will you?"

"I don't think I shall tell you anything. I think I shall go back to Framlingham and leave you alone with your bad sense of humor."

"As you wish, my lady."

He turned the horse around and she squealed, laughing as he reined the horse in a couple of tight circles. Finally, they were heading back for the gate and she smacked him, lightly, on the shoulder.

"Stop fooling, Garren," she said. "If anything of what Emyl says is true, then this is a revered place. We should be respectful."

Emyl had watched the interaction, smiling at their antics. Garren was a serious knight, he knew, and put no stock in ghost stories as his lady apparently did. Emyl didn't know if the legends were true or not himself, but one thing was apparent; no one had lived in this massive place for years. There had to be a reason.

There was an enormous ditch surrounding the outer curtain wall. It was wide across and partially filled with muddy rainwater. Garren surveyed the trench and could see that, at some time, there had been a bridge over it. He could see remains of it floating in the muck. There was no way the horses could cross, so he dismounted and stood at the edge of the ditch, trying to figure out the best way to cross. Emyl came to stand beside him and together, they mulled over the problem.

The gatehouse and wall were directly on the other side. Garren couldn't think of anything else but to climb down into the ditch and see how deep it was. He took off his helm and began to remove his armor.

"What are you doing?" Derica asked.

He unlatched his breastplate. Emyl took it from him and he began to unfasten the protection around his shoulders.

"I am going to find out just how deep this trench is," he told her. "If It is too deep, I shall sink to the bottom with all of this armor on."

Derica climbed off of the charger. She went to stand next to her husband, eyeing the trench, eyeing him as he removed every last scrap of protection. The rain soaked the woolen tunic he wore and water dripped off of his face. She wiped a drop from the end of his nose, smiling timidly when he looked at her. Garren gave her a quick kiss before lowering himself into the ditch.

"Be careful," she admonished him. "There may be spikes in there that you cannot see."

He almost slipped on the sides, warily regaining his balance. "I shall be careful."

"Don't fall!"

"I won't."

Derica winced and twisted her fingers as he slid down the muddy side and into the water. He stopped sinking when he was up to his knees. Surprised but cautious, he took a few more steps across the ditch.

"It looks like this is all there is of it," he announced. "Still, we can't get the horses across. The sides are too steep."

Derica immediately began to descend into the ditch. "I am coming with you."

He slugged back across the water. "Wait, sweetheart, don't get your feet wet."

He carefully took her in his arms and carried her to the other side. Derica deftly climbed to the top of the bank with a strategic shove from her husband. Emyl, his hands full of swords, slid down the muddy incline and trudged across the water as Garren hoisted himself out on the opposite side. Lowering a helping hand, he pulled the old man out of the ditch and took his weapon.

The great gatehouse loomed overhead. Derica stood there a moment, inspecting it, wondering if she could hear Bryndalyn and Owain calling to each other. Garren whispered a ghostly moan in her ear to tease her and she made a face at him. He took her hand as they crossed under the half-raised portcullis.

Inside the curtain wall was a massive outer bailey. The ground was muddy and uneven, and there were no outer buildings. But there was another, taller, curtain wall several hundred feet away. There were also three massive towers they could see set within the wall. Most of all, another ditch lay between them and the inner wall.

"Another trench," Derica observed. "They were certainly obsessed with entrenching this place, were they not?"

Garren cocked an eyebrow. "When an enemy is laying siege, one is grateful for all of the protection a castle can provide."

"You saw the walls around Framlingham. They are enormous. But since I have lived there, we have never truly seen a siege."

"But you would be grateful for them in such an event, I can tell you from experience."

They had crossed the outer bailey and now stood looking down into the deep, stone-lined ditch. It was wider than the first ditch, filled with water and debris. Garren glanced over to his far left and could see, almost butted against the outer curtain wall, a drawbridge crossing over the ditch and leading into another gatehouse. They made their way over to the bridge and gingerly walked across the wet, rotting wood. Garren inspected the chains that fastened it and they were old and rusting. He wasn't comfortable with the bridge and made sure Derica was quickly off it.

The passage beneath the second portcullis was long and damp. It smelled of rot. When they emerged on the other side, it was into a smaller inner bailey where the true scope of Cilgarren came to light. There were four massive towers including the gatehouse, all of them at least three stories into the sky. To Garren's right stood several buildings; a great hall, perhaps a chapel, and then kitchens off to the left of the larger structures. Over by the north tower was another building, possibly the stables. There was also a kiln.

"Amazing," he breathed.

"What do you mean?" Derica asked.

He was at a loss where to begin. "This place is a massive, fully-functioning fortress that has been abandoned. Why, in God's name, would someone just abandon this?"

Derica didn't have an answer. The place was indeed large and intricate. She let go of his hand and pulled her cloak more tightly around her, wandering through the bailey and inspecting the towers from a distance. While Garren kept an eye on her, she went to the long, low building that held the great hall and peered into the open door.

It was dark inside, but there was enough weak light that she could see a few broken stools, a table that was missing a couple of legs, and other debris scattered inside. The hall itself was good sized with a massive stone hearth. She took a step inside the door, smelling the dampness and mold. It was eerie.

She thought of Bryndalyn and Owain. Perhaps they sat at this table once, long ago, and toasted their happiness. Perhaps they had enjoyed the fire in the hearth or danced across the floor to lively minstrel music. She could almost hear their laughter if she listened hard enough. Derica wasn't quite sure why the tale of the pair sat so heavily on her mind except for the fact that, for the first time in her life, she knew what it was to truly love someone and she could never imagine losing that love. Bryndalyn did not survive the loss and she doubted she would, either. There would be nothing to live for.

A low, desolate sound suddenly pierced her thoughts, howling eerily through the musty air. It echoed off the walls, lifting the rafters with its mournful sound. Startled, Derica bolted from the room and into her husband's line of sight. Though Garren's expression was unreadable, he had heard the sound, too, and unsheathed his weapon in a deliberate motion.

"Derica," he said calmly. "Come to me, sweetheart."

Another wail filled the air and Derica didn't need to be told twice; she darted back over to Garren, panting with fright.

"Garren, what is it?" she gasped. "Ghosts?"

He shook his head, his eyes riveted to the structures around him. "I am sure nothing so unearthly," he said evenly. "Stay close."

He handed her the charger's reins and paced into the center of the ward. Emyl also had his weapon wielded, the old man as calm as Garren was. Once a knight, always a knight, no matter how long it had been since he'd last whiffed the scent of battle. Both men were acutely vigilant as they visually inspected their surroundings for the origins of the noise.

The wail came again. Garren turned, hearing it come from the north tower, or so he thought. He motioned to Emyl to flank him as he made his way to the entrance of the tower. Derica huddled against the charger out of fear and warmth, watching her husband with anxious eyes. It took her a moment to realize that Garren had not put his armor back on after removing it to cross the first trench. Not wanting to call out to him and distract him, she could only watch and pray that whatever situation he was about to face did not injure him.

Her first indication that all was not well was when the charger suddenly started. Derica would have fallen to the ground had hands not grabbed her. Trouble was, they were not her husband's hands. A scream erupted from her throat.

Garren swung around in time to see someone grabbing his wife. He took a step in her direction when a body suddenly came flying at him, a man dressed in dirty rags that blended in with the gray sheets of rain. The man had a weapon and Garren brought his sword up instinctively, deflecting a heavy blow. He was involved in his own fight, terrified for his wife, furious at the inconvenience of having to battle for his life. He was about to shout for Emyl when he saw that the old man, too, had been set upon.

Derica was howling, swinging fists and kicking feet. A fine lady though she might be, having grown up with three older brothers had taught her something about self-defense. She was desperately trying to find eyes to gouge her fingers into. When that failed, she took to kicking furiously at the knees of her attacker. One foot made contact with a kneecap and the man released a growling yelp. It was enough of a break for Derica to swing around and kick him, as hard as she could, in the lower abdomen.

The man fell into the mud and Derica scattered like a frightened chicken. She was terrified her attacker was going to rise up and come after her again, so she grabbed the first heavy rock she could find and raced back over to the man wallowing in the muck. She smacked him on the head and stopped his squirming.

With her assailant subdued, she took a look around her; a glance to Garren saw him in serious combat with a man nearly as tall as he was, yet infinitely more slender. Emyl seemed to have the more immediate problem, grunting and groaning as he battled for his life. Derica couldn't stand by idly; she lifted the rock and made her way over towards Emyl. Careful not to get in the way or take the chance that the enemy would turn on her, she hung back, clutching the rock, until Emyl's opponent turned his back on her. With a cry, she hurled the rock and hit the man on the nape of the neck. It was enough of a blow to cause him to fall down, whereupon Emyl finished him.

The sight of the blood made Derica nauseous. In spite of her warring family, she'd never seen a man killed before. Emyl went to her, trying to take her someplace safe, away from the fighting, but she would not leave Garren. She and Emyl watched with trepidation as Garren launched a powerful enough blow to dislodge his opponent's sword completely. When the man tried to retrieve his weapon, Garren shoved the tip of his razor-sharp blade at the man's neck.

"The game is ended," he growled. "Leave the sword and I shall be merciful. Attempt to reclaim it and my mercy is at an end."

The man slowly lifted his hands to show his submission. Garren gazed into deep brown eyes and a handsome face. The man was young, but he had handled the sword well. He took his eyes off of Garren long enough to look at his dead companion in the mud.

"Did you have to kill him?" he whispered.

Garren responded. "What did you expect? You were trying to kill us. It was necessary to defend ourselves."

The man dropped his hands and made his way over to his companion. His movements were slow with defeat. Emyl and Derica moved to stand with Garren as the three of them observed the man in the rags. He fell to one knee, putting his hand on the wet corpse.

"He was just a lad," the man muttered. "A child."

"A child who was trying to kill me," Emyl didn't feel guilty in the least. "If you were that worried over his health, you should not have allowed him to attack us."

"We were protecting ourselves," the man in rags suddenly boomed. The dark eyes flashed. ""Tis you who invade our home."

Derica looked at her husband with big eyes. Garren's expression was neutral, though he could feel her stare. "You live here? On whose authority?"

The man in rags stared at him for a moment. "On my own. No one has lived here in decades; there was no reason why we should not."

The man that Derica had smashed over the head suddenly groaned and sat up. He shook his head as if waking up from a deep, ugly sleep. Garren heard the noise and glanced over at him.

"Tell him to be still," he commanded quietly. "Any provocative movement and he shall meet the same fate as your companion."

The man in the rags eyed his disoriented comrade, but he could see that provocative action would be the last thing to occur. He looked at Garren, more closely than before.

"You are a knight," he stated.

Garren cocked an eyebrow. "And as such, you will answer my questions or face the consequences. Tell me your name."

The man in rags signed deeply, with resignation. His hand came to rest protectively on the head of his dead friend.

"David," he whispered.

"Who is the dead man?"

"My brother, Guy."

Garren heard his wife gasp softly, but he didn't look at her. "And the man over there?"

"My uncle."

"Does he have a name?"

"Offa."

"Offa," Emyl repeated, looking closely at the man covered in mud. "Offa van Vert?"

The round, dirty man grunted. "The same."

Emyl's mouth popped open. Then he threw up his hands. "I should run you through, you idiot. Why in God's name would you attack me?"

Offa blinked his eyes, trying to rid himself of his double vision. "Emyl?"

Emyl sneered. "Dimwit! Of course it is me. Can you not see that through those bloodshot eyes?"

"I cannot see anything at the moment," Offa shook his head again. "The lady was true in her aim."

"Emyl," Garren cut into the conversation. "Who are these people?"

Emyl looked ill, as if a horrible situation had suddenly been made clear to him. "Offa van Vert was a knight, Garren. He served Cadell ap Gryffud. We grew up together, in this region. I simply haven't seen him in years." He glared at the muddy knight. "I thought you'd died, you old goat. What are you doing here?"

Offa struggled to one knee. "The Welsh rebellion hasn't much room for an aged knight. My youth is gone and so is my money. I knew of this place, too. My nephews and I have lived here for three years."

Emyl looked at Garren; he didn't know what more he could say. The entire circumstance was sickening. Garren stood there a long while, watching David grieve over his brother. Finally, he sheathed his sword.

"Your brother did not have to die," he said quietly. "You should have determined my motives before attacking us."

David wiped his eyes. "My delay might have given you the upper hand had you been intent on killing us."

"Are you a knight?"

"No."

By now, Offa was on his feet and walking unsteadily towards his nephews. "My sister married a common man. There was no opportunity for the boys to foster in a proper house. I have schooled them the best I can."

Garren took a few steps, retrieved David's old sword, and extended it to the man.

"You have done an admirable job," he said. "I am impressed with David's skill and strength."

Offa knelt beside his other nephew, putting a tender hand on the lad's head. "Guy will never know his potential," he whispered ironically. "He could have been great."

Garren glanced at his wife, seeing the sorrowful expression on her face. He was feeling guilty when he knew he should not. "An unfortunate happening." He came as close to an apology as he could.

"Unfortunate indeed," Offa stroked the dark hair. "It was my fault. I am a foolish old man. Foolish and stupid. The boys fought against me in their training and I most always allowed them to win, giving them a sense of confidence. It was Guy's undoing."

Emyl sighed heavily, making his way to the man he had once known. His gaze moved between the dead lad and the uncle.

"You did as you felt best, even as you moved to defend your home," he tried to comfort him. "You did not know our intentions were peaceful. But Garren is correct; you could have determined them first. 'Twould be best to teach David that lesson today. A costly lesson though it might be."

Offa nodded his head silently. Emyl stood over him, knowing there was nothing more he could say. Observing the scene, Derica slipped her wet hand into her husband's.

"We should help him bury his nephew," she said softly.

Garren gazed down at her, her sweet face pinched pink with cold and wet. She did not understand the warring ways, the event that one did not usually bury his enemy, but he knew this was a different case. In spite of himself, he was beginning to feel very guilty about the whole thing. The Garren of old never knew the meaning of the word.

135

"As you wish, my lady," he said softly.

He helped Offa and David dig the grave. By the time the sun settled, the rain had let up somewhat. Still, it was the end of a very long day, and a very long trip. As he fell asleep beside his wife later that night in the shadows of the old great hall, he felt a sense of peace for the first time in days. But he knew that would be short-lived.

CHAPTER TWELVE

"I thought I should inform you. I doubted he had the opportunity yet."

William Marshal sat at his great desk, listening to the words. Many times over the years he had heard news, good or bad, from this exact spot. Tonight, the news was not encouraging. He felt disappointment deep in his gut.

The old man sighed, scratching the chin with a day's growth of white stubble. He tried to remain calm. He should have seen this coming, and in a sense he had. He had tried to discourage a man who had never known the joys of love from exploring the temptation of it. He thought he'd been firm enough, candid enough. But apparently his words had been in vain. Of all the men in the world to succumb to insubordination, he never thought he would live to see the day it would be Garren le Mon.

"So he married her." It was more of a statement.

"Aye, my lord."

"Against Bertram's wishes?"

"Aye."

The scratching of the stubble turned into rubbing the forehead. "Do you know where he and his bride have gone?"

Next to the desk, Hoyt de Rosa shook his head. "Nay," he mumbled. "Last I saw, they were leaving the inn at Kettering. I did not ask where they were going, and he did not offer. The point is that you should know that my brothers were informed that Garren is a spy. His cover was destroyed and he was lucky to have escaped Framlingham with his life."

"But he married your niece without her father's permission."

"He did. But that was secondary to my brothers discovering his true identity."

"Somehow I believe the two are related. Is it possible that he told her of his true identity and she told her father?"

"Not at all, my lord," Hoyt insisted. "I can assure you that Derica knew nothing of his mission. In defense of Garren, I will say this; he accomplished what he set forth to do. He posed as a suitor for Derica. He performed superbly. The only complication, which was not his fault, was that my brothers were told that he was a spy. His only choice was to flee. They would have killed him had he not."

"Then who told them he was an agent?"

"A spy for Prince John, a man I have seen at Framlingham on more than one occasion. He apparently recognized Garren and told my brother of his suspicions."

"Why was the man at Framlingham?"

"Informing my brother of all I just told you. Garren's recognition was incidental."

The Marshal absorbed the words. It was a true accounting of what had happened, more than likely. But the fact remained that his most prized agent was missing.

"Garren, Garren," the Marshal muttered regretfully. After a moment, he shook his head, trying to shake off the shock of it. "Very well: I shall accept your explanation for now. But I must speak with Garren. Unless he has fled from the service of the king completely, I expect him to show himself and explain his actions. If there was ever a time I need Garren, it is now."

"Aye, my lord."

"For it seems now that we have a greater problem."

"We do."

"Several thousand Teutonic and Irish mercenaries at Nottingham and Bolton."

"Aye."

"And two thousand more French due next week."

"That is true."

"And you said you told Garren this?"

"I did."

The Marshal shook his head faintly. "I cannot believe he would abandon Richard in his hour of need."

"You know his character better than I."

"I thought I did," William murmured. He gazed across the room, to the lancet window where the cold night swirled beyond. "But a woman has been known to do strange things to a man's sense of duty."

Hoyt couldn't argue. He'd seen the looks between Garren and Derica, but he was afraid to voice his opinion. He could only pray that Garren would do what was right.

***

"Garren?"

Garren looked up from the small piece of vellum he was writing on. Derica was smiling back at him, a large bundle of vegetation in her arms. Before he could answer her, she shook her head at him.

"You did not hear a word I said," she set the bundle down on the table, next to his writing. "I asked if you would move aside so that I may set this down."

He smiled, rather sheepishly, and moved the vellum well clear of her burden. "I am sorry. I was writing to my sister."

Derica knew that. Over the past week, they had worked hard to settle in to Cilgarren and she could not fault her husband a bit of quiet time. Offa and his nephew had become gracious hosts, working alongside Garren and Emyl to make the great hall livable for the lady's sake. The table had been restored and everyone had a dark corner of the room to sleep in. Garren had eventually told them of their reasons for being there; it was only fair should the de Rosas show up. Instead of being upset by it, Offa had seemed strangely excited as if he would once again be provided the chance to prove himself a warrior.

"And just what are you saying in your missive?" Derica nodded at the vellum. "Complaining about me, were you?"

He laughed softly. "Absolutely. You are too sweet, too wonderful and too generous for your own good. What a burden you are."

"Then it is your misfortune to have been foolish enough to marry me." She grinned, peeling back the cloth of the bundle she had been carrying. "While you were loafing about, I went hunting. I found wild lentils growing on the slope above the river. Someone must have planted them there some time ago, when this castle was lived-in, because the hill is covered with them. And see what else? Blackberries. Lots of them."

He plucked one out of her pile and popped it in his mouth. "Delicious." Snatching her around the waist, he kissed her cheek. "As are you."

She let him kiss her a few times, affection that quickly grew into passion. As he nibbled her neck, she put her hands on his chest in a half-hearted attempt to stop him.

"Not now, Garren," she muttered. "Someone might come in."

"Let them," he growled, but she somehow found the strength to dislodge him and he sighed with mock frustration. "You are a cold wench."

She ignored him, focusing on the harvest before her. "I am afraid that I am not much of a cook, as you have no doubt discovered. Other than supervising the kitchens, father would never let me learn the craft. He was afraid the knives would cut me or the fire would burn me, or I would somehow get hurt. So all I can do is hunt for food, and not much more. At least I feel as if I am contributing something that way."

Garren put a hand on her shoulder. "No worries, sweetheart. I learned to do for myself at a young age, as you no doubt have discovered."

It was her turn to smile sheepishly. "So you can cook whatever I gather."

"Precisely."

"Will you at least go with me to forage?"

"I think I can spare the time."

They carefully divided up the lentils from the berries before heading out again. It had stopped raining a few days hence, but the ground was still wet and soft, and the moats were filled to brimming. Garren carried the cloth she used to bundle up whatever she gathered, keeping the conversation light as they made their way over to the north tower next to the kitchen. The cooks of Cilgarren had apparently planted their gardens on the steep slope above the river, knowing that it would be relatively safe from invasion from the river below.

Garren had hold of his wife's skirt as she scavenged about, fearful she would lose her footing in the damp soil and plunge into the water far below. But she was quite surefooted, chattering as she collected more lentils and found a few wild turnips. He remained mostly silent, listening to her talk, watching the dull sunlight glisten off of her hair and wondering how he was going to tear himself away from her long enough to conduct his business with the Marshal. No doubt, William was wondering what had become of him by now. Time was not his friend in this matter. As reluctant as he was to leave her, he knew equally as much that he had to.

Emyl took the duty and cooked a nice lentil stew that night. The lentils, turnips and a few old carrots from Offa had made a tasty feast. After sup, Derica dozed by the fire as the men rolled a pair of die across the floor. Garren wasn't much for gambling, but Emyl had insisted and now Garren owned nearly everything his three comrades had.

"Now that you are so wealthy, do you think we could go into the town and buy some flour?" Derica had been listening to her husband win. "I have a fancy for bread."

The men looked up from their game. "I think that could be arranged," Garren said. "But it would be wiser to send Emyl into town. He would be far less noticeable to your family should they happen to be in the area."

Odd how days had passed and she hadn't thought of her fanatical family. But thoughts of them suddenly filled her mind and she was unsettled again. How people who had professed to love her could wish such unhappiness for her by wanting to destroy the man she loved was beyond her comprehension.

"Do you think they've managed to track us here?" she asked.

Garren shrugged. "'Tis hard to say. We're far away from Framlingham, but if they've a true desire to track us, there is no telling how far they'll go. 'Tis best to be safe right now and stay where we are."

"We'll go," David passed a nervous glance at Derica. "If there is any news of visitors in town, we'll discover it."

140

Garren tried to keep the smile from his lips. Over the past few days, David had shown a noticeable interest in Derica and seemed absolutely terrified by it. Garren could hardly blame him. The young man had spent years in isolation and suddenly there was a beautiful young woman in his midst. Derica wasn't oblivious, but she had been polite about it.

"My thanks," Garren said. "But in case there are, make no provocative move. Return to the castle immediately and I shall decide a course of action."

David nodded his dark head. "We'll defend you, have no doubt."

"I don't. Your loyalty is appreciated."

David didn't say any more. He was uncomfortable saying what he had, afraid he'd sounded like a fool. Offa slapped his nephew on the shoulder. "You needn't worry, my lady. Even if they make it to the castle, we know many places to hide and avenues of escape. They'll never get you."

Derica smiled in thanks. "I hope we're not too much of a burden."

"Not at all. David and I crave the excitement."

"But your life was so quiet before we came."

Offa snorted. "It was dull. At least now we have something to look forward to."

"A battle?"

The old man's eyes lit up, memories of glory from long ago filling his mind. "Indeed. Fine adventures of bloody battles!"

Derica looked at her husband and they smiled at each other. After a few more moments of languishing before the fire, she forced herself to stand. "I believe I shall go to bed." She stretched her shapely body. "Good eve to you, my lords."

The men responded politely. David stole a quick glance but just as quickly turned away. Garren excused himself and followed his wife up the narrow steps the led into the minstrel's gallery above the hall. He'd fashioned a large screen out of wood and rushes, hiding them from the view down below. A pallet of more rushes and bedding from Emyl's humble home lay upon the floor, comfortable enough for the two of them. Garren felt bad that he had nothing to offer her other than borrowed goods and the bare minimum of comfort. She deserved so much more. As his wife lay down, he tucked the worn coverlets in around her.

"Someday, we'll have a massive castle and the finest bedding money can buy," he said softly. "You will only touch satins and silks, I swear it."

She smiled. "I have had that. It matters naught if you are not with me to share it."

"So you prefer rushes that scratch and poke?"

"As long as they scratch and poke you, too."

141

He sat there a moment, gazing down at her, torn between tremendous joy and tremendous sorrow. He could not delay the inevitable; the longer he put it off, the harder it would be.

It was quiet in the gallery. He tucked the covers in tighter around her, trying to think of the correct words, when she interrupted his thoughts.

"I have something to tell you," she said softly.

"You do? What?"

"You're going to be leaving soon."

He lifted an eyebrow. "I am?"

"Aye," she nodded. "You must attend William Marshal. He needs to know all that has gone on at Framlingham during the past few weeks."

"Hmmm," he looked at her with interest. "You are correct, madam. The security of this country is at stake. When must I leave?"

"I would think tomorrow," she said as if issuing orders. "The sooner you leave, the sooner you return."

He nodded, a warm twinkle in his eye. "I cannot tell you how much is pains me that I must go alone. I wish I could take you with me."

"I am safe here," Derica was trying to be brave. "I have Emyl and Offa and David to protect me."

An eyebrow lifted. "Mind that David keeps a respectful distance. I would hate to have to kill him."

"David is afraid of me. I swear that if I winked at him, he'd faint."

"I have spent my life being suspicious of the motives of others. Though he seems harmless enough, I cannot discount his thoughts should I not be here as a thwarting presence."

"I am my own thwarting presence. I have thwarted many an amorous suitor in my time."

He grinned. "But not me."

She returned his smile. "Nay, not you. You were the only man who lowered himself from the roof into my boudoir. With such dedication, how could I discourage you?"

His smile faded as he gazed into her eyes. "Christ, I am going to miss you. I am so sorry that I must leave, even for a short time."

The longing in his voice squeezed her heart, making it difficult to be brave. "How long do you think you shall be away?"

He ran a finger down her cheek, onto her shoulder. "'Tis difficult to say. Perhaps ten days, perhaps twenty."

"Twenty days," she breathed. "Why can I not go with you if you are to be away that long?"

"Because I shall travel much more quickly without you. Furthermore, there are threats on the road I have no desire to expose you to. Bandits and murderers, to name a few. I would rather know you were here, safe, waiting impatiently for me to return."

She knew he was right, but that didn't help the tugging in her chest. When he pulled her up and took her in his arms, it only increased the ache. Derica held him tightly, afraid to let him go.

"Promise you will return," she whispered.

His fingers were in her hair, his mouth against her forehead. "I swear it."

She kissed him once, twice. "Do you realize that since we were reunited at the abbey, we have never been apart? It will be strange not waking up to you every morning. It has become a part of me, like breathing."

"I know," he said. "But after this temporary separation, I shall never leave you again. Ever."

She was quiet a moment. "But what if William Marshal insists you continue in his service?"

"I have been in his service for many years. I have dedicated my entire life to the king. It is time that I dedicate myself to my own life now and he will have to understand that."

"What if he doesn't'?"

"He has no choice."

She sighed, hearing his determination. But she also knew that he had a strong sense of duty to Richard. A man who would chose to be a spy for the king would have nothing else. She wondered if his love for her would outweigh his sense of duty if he were pressured to make a choice.

"Whatever happens, my love," she ran her fingers through his hair. "This night belongs to us."

He couldn't think of a reply other than to make love to her.

***

The next morning dawned dismal. Rain was coming down in sheets, creating a blurry white landscape. Emyl had loaded Garren's charger and had it waiting outside the outer wall. Both bridges were still in a state of disrepair and the horse could not be brought any closer.

A fire burned in the crumbling hearth in the great hall, sending smoke to the ceiling and escaping from gaps in the roof. Garren and Derica had eaten a cozy meal near the fire, greedily soaking up the last few moments they would have together until he returned. They kept the conversation positive, talking of trivial things, unwilling to face the fact that time was drawing short.

Derica was in control of her emotions until Emyl came with Garren's armor and began helping him dress. She sat atop the old table, huddled in the woolens that the nuns had given her as she watched her husband transform from a strong, sweet man into a terrifying vision of a knight. She well remembered the first time she ever saw him, in her father's solar. Although he had worn his armor, he had not been allowed his weapons inside the castle; even so, he had been an impressive sight. Having lived in a household full of knights, she had long gotten over being impressed by a bold man in a steel suit. But watching Garren as he adjusted his breastplate, she felt giddy and warm as she hadn't felt in years.

Garren noticed her watching him and his eyes twinkled. "Why do you look so?"

She blinked at him, puzzled. "How do I look?"

"Like you are day dreaming."

She grinned. "I am, in a way. Tell me something; why is it that you do not have horns jutting from the armor on your shoulders? Uncle Hoyt used to."

He snorted. "Because I do not need them. Men with spikes on their armor aren't merely looking to defend or attack honorably; they are seeking to maim and destroy."

"Then you say that Uncle Hoyt is dishonorable?"

"I say nothing of the sort. I simply mean that he has them because, I would imagine, he derives a good deal of pleasure at men being terrified by the mere sight of them. 'Tis a good intimidation tactic, mentally unsettling an enemy before the battle has even begun. What sane man would not fear a knight with spikes all over his armor?"

She thought on that a moment. "Father's helm has a horn that comes out of the center of his forehead, like a Unicorn."

Garren merely wriggled his eyebrows, in approval or disapproval she could not tell. When Emyl finished struggling with a strap that finally decided to latch, Garren stepped away and shook himself slightly, like a dog shaking its hide. The armor clinked and settled on his big body.

"Your weapon and helm are with the charger," Emyl said.

Garren nodded at him, then looked at his wife. She was smiling at him, but it was forced. Emyl, sensing the farewell to come, excused himself and left them alone.

The silence was expectant. Derica struggled to keep the smile on her face. "It is time, I see."

"Aye," he agreed. "Will you walk with me to the door?"

She slipped off the table and slid her hand into his enormous one. Together, they walked to the open door where the rain pounded outside. Derica was about to walk outside but he held her back.

"Not outside, sweetheart," he said. "I shall take my leave of you here, where it is dry."

She looked at him, those enormous green eyes bright with emotion. He smiled at her, memorizing every last line of her sweet face. He committed it to memory, to keep him warm on the long cold nights to come. He ran a delicate finger along her jawline, touching the honey-colored hair that tickled her face. He couldn't discern any other emotion at the moment other than deep, agonizing longing.

"I hope to make good time, but this weather is a bit of an obstacle," he realized he was struggling to keep his emotions in check. "If all goes well, I should be in Chepstow in three or four days. I plan to meet with William, explain the situation, and beg my leave. Hopefully he will be gracious about it, but if not, 'tis of no matter. I shall try to make my stay at Chepstow no longer than a day. With luck, I shall return in a week, mayhap ten days."

She nodded. "Then we shall look for you then. What happens if it takes longer? Will you send word?"

He shook his head. "I don't dare. I cannot be certain that the de Rosa's aren't lingering somewhere around Chepstow, thinking that perhaps I may take you there. I doubt they would move on me if you are not at my side. The object is to find you, and if they kill me, they will eliminate all hope. I cannot take the chance that a messenger would be followed."

"And lead them right to me," she murmured.

"Exactly."

She digested that. "They will try to get you somehow. My father is very clever."

"I know," Garren gazed up at the gray sky. "For that very fact, I wonder if he will not go to Chateroy to abduct my father. He may anticipate a hostage-for-hostage exchange."

"Your father for me?"

"Something like that. I cannot rule out any possibility."

Derica fell silent. She traced the lines of his armor, running her fingers over his breastplate, simply to keep her hands busy. "Garren, what happens if you do not return?"

He looked at her. "I swore to you that I would."

She met his gaze. "But you cannot guarantee it. Certainly, I am not asking you to because I know that you cannot. But if you do not return in a month or two or three, what should I do?"

He sighed, heavily, realizing she was more willing to face the reality of it than he was. "You're not going to like my answer."

"What is it?"

"Have Emyl take you back to Framlingham."

She stiffened. "I will not."

He tightened his grip before she could pull away. "Listen to me, sweetheart. 'Tis the safest place for you, and I want you safe and well-cared for. Your father is after me, not you. He'll forgive you should you return. 'Tis the most logical solution."

Her brow was furrowed like an angry child. "I will not go home. There is nothing for me there. They'll simply try to marry me off again and won't have any part of it, do you hear? I won't marry ever, again."

"Then what would you suggest?"

"That I go to the abbey with your sister."

He had to admit that her answer pleased him, but he was positive that it was because he was being selfish. "You have a right to be happy in life should I not be at your side. I want you to be happy. Do you think you would truly be happy in the cloister?"

"I do not know. But I believe I would be happier there than married to some pompous fool whose only ambition is to be politically linked to the de Rosa name." She stopped struggling, gazing deeply into his eyes. "Garren, do you think if I returned home that I would be a desirable marriage prospect? Of course not. My father would more than likely sell me to an arrogant French mercenary who can pay for the de Rosa name. Marrying me into a decent family was lost the moment I fled Framlingham. Is that the kind of life you would hope for me?"

She had turned it around on him admirably. He knew the political game of noble marriages as well as or better than she did, and knew she spoke the truth. His heart sank to think of what would become of her should he not return.

"Nay," he said quietly. "And I suppose I should be more pragmatic than I have been. Truly, my intention is to return to you. It is my only thought. But if by chance the fates are against us, then you should know your next move. If I do not return within six weeks, then go to Yaxley Nene and stay with my sister until you have decided what you wish to do. No one can touch you there, especially your family. If you wish to devote yourself to the cloister, then so be it. But if you wish to return to your family, then I shall support your decision."

"You're sure that is what you wish me to do?"

"I believe it is a sound plan."

With the most difficult of subjects decided upon, Garren's impending departure began to weigh heavily enough that she could hardly breathe. Derica always believed she was the strongest of women, but suddenly, she didn't want to be strong. She wanted to be weak. Resting her forehead against his armor, she cried silent tears of longing. The warm droplets fell on his protection, little salty rivers running their course. Garren stroked her hair, silently, feeling her pain and then some.

"The longer I delay, the more difficult this will become," he murmured.

She sniffled, struggling to regain her composure. "I know. 'Tis best you go, now, before I cling to you like a great anchor and you have to drag me across the yard."

It was humor in a moment of agony. Garren kissed her deeply, tasting her tears. Abruptly, he broke away, leaving her standing in the doorway as he marched across the muddy inner ward. He didn't dare look back, fearful that he would retrace his steps back to her and be unable to break away a second time. He got half way across the yard when two figures emerging from the crumbling gatehouse caught his attention. Garren's pace slowed as he assessed the forms; one was Emyl, but it took him a moment to recognize the second. When he did, he froze dead in his tracks.

"Fergus!"

***

The hearth smoked and spit embers into the dark room. Fergus didn't care if he did catch a few red-hot particles on his skin, so long as he was warm again. It seemed like it had been ages since he had last been warm and fed, or safe for that matter. But the great hall of Cilgarren had a massive, protective quality that soothed him after his harried adventure.

"For once, the blows did not come from someone with a grudge against me." He was trying to be glib. "At any rate, not a gambling grudge. The de Rosas certainly had another grudge, especially when I wouldn't tell them where Derica was."

Derica sat at the crumbling table, wincing as she thought of her family imparting the bruises and welts on Fergus' face.

"Oh, Fergus, I am so sorry," she said. "They've always been as such. Ruffians in every sense of the word. Did they break any bones?"

He shook his head. "No one can crack this skull, my lady. Many have tried. It would take better men that the de Rosas to break my bones."

Garren stood next to his friend, his great arms crossed. He analyzed every movement, every word, thinking there was far more to the story than what Fergus was saying. It was just a feeling he had, knowing his friend as well as he did. But the sheer fact that the man was alive was a miracle, and a welcome one. Still, there was something very odd about him, something Garren couldn't quite figure out.

"But they didn't follow you," Garren said. "You're sure of it?"

"I would stake my life on it."

Garren didn't question him further. That was all he really cared about at the moment, and there would be time for more detail later. He slapped his friend on the back. "I, for one, am amazed to see you. We thought for certain the de Rosas had devoured you."

Fergus stood from the fire, a weak smile on his lips. "Not hardly, though they tried. " He rubbed the stubble on his face. "Although I would like nothing better than to tell more stories of my persecution, I would truly like a bit of food and perhaps some sleep. It has been a long few days."

Derica leapt up, rushing around for the leftovers from their morning meal. David and Offa helped her gather the items while Emyl sat at the old table, his old eyes drinking in the sight of his only son.

"'Tis been a long time, lad," he said. "A long time indeed."

Fergus was genuinely glad to see his father. "I am a bad son, I know. I stay away for years and only come to you when I want something."

Emyl shrugged. "If that is all I can have of you, I shall accept it. At least you acknowledge what a rotten lad you are."

Fergus grinned as Derica placed some cold stew and berries before him. He shoved food in his mouth and continued. "I directed Garren to Cilgarren, you know. It is the safest place for him." He eyed his friend. "But now I see he is leaving, after all this trouble I have been through. Where are you going, pray?"

Garren had spent many years of his adult life avoiding that question from Fergus. He was quick to make a believable excuse. "I am afraid the de Rosas may go after my father. I intend to go home and scout the situation for myself."

"And if they have?"

"I shall deal with that situation if and when I come upon it."

Fergus shoved another bite in his mouth. "Let me finish this feast and I shall go with you."

"How?" Garren asked. "You have been on the move for weeks, Fergus. You're so weary with fatigue and lack of food that you can hardly stand. You need to rest and regain your strength. I have enough to worry about without wondering if you are going to drop dead any moment."

Fergus pointed his stew-covered knife at him. "I have been worse than this. Hell, Garren, you have been worse than this and still rode fifty miles into battle. I have seen you myself." He turned back to his food. "It is settled. I ride with you."

Garren didn't refute him right away. To do so would to have looked suspicious, but he clearly didn't want Fergus coming with him. He needed a plan. Straddling the old bench, he sat, hearing it groan under his weight. A gloved hand scratched his forehead.

"Fergus," he said quietly. "I need you here."

Fergus' mouth was full. "Why?"

Garren glanced over at Offa and David, talking softly by the smoking hearth. "Do you see that dark-haired man?"

Fergus glanced in David's direction. "That young whelp you introduced me to? The one who has been living here?"

"Aye."

"What about him?"

"He is fond of Derica. Too fond, if you get my meaning."

Fergus' eyebrows rose. Then he laughed. "Idiot. His life shall not be a long one."

"He is the nephew of an old friend of your father's. I should hate to have to kill him were he to press his intentions on my wife while I am away. As it stands, only your father stands between my wife and a potential problem. But with you here, there is no doubt that David would be in way over his head were he to attempt something. It would give me more peace of mind than you know."

Fergus swallowed the last of his food. "So, once again, you expect me to pay nursemaid to your wife."

"I ask you, my friend."

"You do not want my sword at your side?"

"I want your sword here, in my stead."

Fergus signed heavily, wiping at a smear of food on his chin. "Very well. If that is your wish."

Garren smiled. "Many thanks."

"But you owe me."

"The usual?"

Fergus nodded firmly. "A hog's head of ale, deliverable upon your return."

Garren stood up and reseated his helm. Derica had been standing a respectful distance away, allowing the men sometime between the two of them, and Garren extended a hand to her. It would be their second painful farewell of the day.

Fergus watched them walk from the hall, Garren's arm protectively around Derica's shoulders. He rose from the table, told his father he was going to find shelter for his weary horse, and went out into the yard. His movements didn't seem so weary anymore. He casually melted into the shadow of a wall, watching Garren and Derica take their leave of each other. When Derica finally went back into the hall, wiping her eyes, Fergus followed Garren into the old gatehouse.

"So I finally get you all to myself."

They were sheltered from the elements in the dank passage. Garren stopped walking and turned around. "So it seems." He moved back towards Fergus. "I assume you have information for my ears only."

"What makes you say that?"

"I just do. I know you, Fergus. There's something else."

"Perhaps," Fergus regarded him. "I have a question for you."

"Ask it."

"Where are you really going, Garren?"

It was more a statement than a question. Garren answered evenly-. "What do you mean?"

"I mean exactly that. You're not going back to Chateroy, are you?"

"I said I was. What makes you think otherwise?"

Fergus' pale blue eyes glittered. "Something that one of the de Rosas said to me."

"And that was?"

"That perhaps you are going to see William Marshal."

Inwardly, Garren flinched. "William Marshal? Why would I want to see him?"

"As a member of his inner circle. As a man who is loyal to Richard in the most sworn sense."

Garren snorted. "So they told you I was a spy, did they? They accused me of that to my face."

"You do seem to wander a bit, Garren. It would explain a great many things about you."

Garren rolled his eyes. "Not you, too," he growled. "Fergus, listen to me. The de Rosas think that everyone is somehow involved with William Marshal, especially the man who eloped with their only female kin."

"He seemed terribly certain. He said to tell you that he was on your side, and he wanted me to warn you against returning to Chateroy."

Garren grew serious. "The de Rosas are waiting for me there."

"They're going to raze it. They are probably laying siege as we speak. I did not want to say anything in front of your wife for fear of upsetting her."

"That was wise," Garren said. "And you say it has been at least a week since you saw the de Rosas?"

"Aye," Fergus replied. "They've already had time to amass and reach Chateroy by now."

Garren fell silent, mulling over his options. Fergus watched him closely. "What are you going to do now?"

"I must defend my father's house, of course."

"By yourself?"

"My father has two hundred men at arms. It is a sizable force."

"Against the de Rosa thousand?" Fergus shook his head. "That's madness, Garren. Chateroy will fall if it hasn't already. And if you go back there now, they'll kill you. What about your wife?"

Garren's eyes turned in the direction of the great hall, as if he could see her through all of the stones that separated them. "I must deal with the consequences my actions have brought upon my family," he said softly. "She understands that."

"She'll understand everything until you get yourself killed, and then she'll go mad," Fergus said. "Trust me, my friend, when it comes to women. They never mean what they say."

"So what do you suggest?"

"Do you have anyone with an army you can call upon for support?"

Garren wouldn't be sucked into that line of conversation again, and he wondered seriously why Fergus was trying to probe him. Knowing Fergus, it was purely nosiness.

"Let me think... I could call on my father, I suppose."

"Oh... right."

Garren didn't like being toyed with, especially not by Fergus. He cocked an eyebrow at him, his manner sarcastic. "I suppose you could ask Longton for help, but being allied with John, I don't suppose he'd respond."

"Not bloody likely."

"Any other suggestions?"

"Sorry, not at the moment."

The thought of Chateroy under siege was growing increasingly disturbing. Garren suddenly felt a strong sense of urgency. He turned from Fergus.

"I must go and see what they've done to my father."

"Garren," Fergus took a step after him. "I wish you wouldn't. It is a trap."

"Be that as it may, my father would not be in trouble were it not for me."

Fergus watched him until he was nearly out of the gatehouse. "Garren, there's something else. Another message from the de Rosa brother that saved my hide. He said that if I speak it, you will know the truth."

"What?"

"I am sorry, my friend. So sorry."

Garren came to a halt. "For what? Fergus, I don't have time for this."

It was odd how the expression on Fergus' face had changed. Garren had never seen such a look, something between wisdom and sorrow. It was an expression that cut through Garren like a knife.

"For this," he whispered. "La lealtà alla morte. Onorare soprattutto."

The sledgehammer hit. Garren was confused and suspicious. Had Fergus been an agent for William, Garren would have known long ago. Or perhaps he wouldn't; there were those in service that even Garren didn't know about. Something wasn't right and his guts churned with dread. It occurred to him that the probing Fergus had been doing was for a definitive reason, an overshadowing motive that Garren was slowly coming to understand. Something told him not to respond.

"What does that mean?"

"Your phrase, my friend."

"The last I recall, I don't speak Italian."

"You are obligated to respond."

"Fergus, what are you talking about?"

Fergus gazed at him without saying a word. Then, he smiled weakly. "Nothing," he said. "Forget about it. In fact, it is best you do not respond."

"Why not?"

"Because... well, because 'tis best, that's all. I do not want to know that you know what I know."

Garren could have done of two things at that moment; he could have continued his ignorant charade, or he could have let his guard down. He had known Fergus far too well and long to let it go.

"What in the hell are you talking about, Fergus?" he rumbled.

Fergus shrugged weakly. "Nothing, my friend. Nothing at all. 'Tis simply... stay away from Chepstow, and stay away from Chateroy. Stay here, with your wife. 'Tis the best place for you."

Garren felt as if he were walking the edge of a cliff, unwilling to look down, but being inexplicably drawn towards the danger. "I cannot stay here," he said, wanting off the subject, unbalanced by the entire conversation. "My only concern, beyond my father, is that Derica is protected in my absence."

Fergus nodded. "I will protect her with my life. You know that."

"I know that," Garren said. "But it shan't be for long. I shall return as soon as I can."

"Christ, I hope not," Fergus muttered.

"What's that you say?"

"Nothing," Fergus said quickly. "And if you do not return, Garren? What then?"

Garren forgot about the past few moments of conversation, Fergus' oddly murmured words. He looked at Fergus as his oldest, closest friend. "Then I will trust you to take care of her, for all time. Will you do this for me?"

"Without question."

Garren left without another word.

CHAPTER THIRTEEN

He thundered in at dusk of the second day. Even from a distance away, Garren could see that the ambiance of Chepstow had changed. A heavy blanket of smoke hung over the castle and he knew that could only mean one thing; either Chepstow was under siege or there was an army in residence.

Fortunately for him, it was the lesser of the possibilities. Many of the men at arms recognized him as he pounded into the bailey, as they were loyal to the Marshal and had fought under Garren's command many a time. Somewhat perplexed as to the purpose of the amassing army, he tried to appear as if their presence was nothing new to him as he stowed his horse and made his way, somewhat wearily, into the keep. He was increasingly apprehensive of what he would find.

It was busier than usual inside. Commanders and noblemen that he recognized greeted him. Garren had to admit it was good to see the familiar faces. The Marshal was found in a sea of officers, clustered two deep around his table in the solar. There were plans on the table, and a map. When the old blue eyes lifted at the movement in the doorway, Garren saw the wave of surprise, then a flash of anger, then massive relief.

"Garren," William pushed his way between armored men in his haste to get to him. "Thank God, you have come."

Garren accepted the outstretched hand, unusual for the old man. He wasn't the warm kind. It was a gesture that put him on his guard.

"My lord," he was suddenly torn between the guilt of what he'd done and the gladness of seeing him again. "I came as soon as I was able."

The Marshal's pale eyes glittered at him, reprovingly, suspiciously. "Of course," he took Garren by the elbow. "Come with me. I would speak with you privately a moment."

That was not an unusual occurrence, and the men in the solar let them go without a thought. William pulled Garren into the adjoining room, a small chamber used by the servants, and closed the door. When he faced Garren again, the warmth was gone from his face and Garren felt the chill.

"Now," William grumbled. "I give you two minutes to satisfactorily explain to me what has happened over the past few weeks."

"My lord?"

"If you play me for a fool, so help me, I shall run you through myself. You know exactly what I mean, le Mon."

"I married Derica de Rosa."

"You eloped with her!"

"I did."

"To what purpose?"

"Because you ordered me to."

The Marshal was losing his patience. "Aye, I did. But under specific conditions and damn you for ignoring them. You, my friend, have violated my commands and have created a shambles out of your mission."

Garren wouldn't back down. "You ordered me to marry Derica de Rosa, my lord. I have done that. The circumstances on how it was done are not of issue."

The old man lost his patience then. "It is the issue. Are you living at Framlingham with your wife and her family?"

"No."

"Do you have any contact with Bertram de Rosa and his horde?"

"No."

"Then how can you possibly tell me that you are still within the guidelines of your mission? Your mission was to spy on them, Garren, nothing more or less. What information can you give me? Has all of my careful planning for you been in vain?"

"There are two thousand Teutonic mercenaries amassing north of Nottingham as we speak. The next few days with see two thousand more French. It is my guess that they plan to stranglehold England about the middle of the country and cut off the north from the south."

The Marshal stared at him. "Why do you think there is an army amassed in the bailey, Garren? I already know this."

Garren didn't flinch, though he felt as if he'd been struck. He felt like a fool. "Chateroy is under siege by the de Rosas because of what I have done."

That news gave the Marshal pause. "How do you know this?"

"I have my trusted sources. I must go and help my father."

William stared at Garren a moment longer before letting out a long, heavy sigh. Scratching his white head, he leaned back against a small table, pondering his course of action from this point. His anger had abated for the most part, though he was still rightfully upset. Mostly, he was disappointed.

"You realize that I have been quite angry with you."

Garren's guard came down somewhat. He could feel the disillusionment in the Marshal's voice and it hurt him. He had worked so hard to achieve the trust he had with William, though it was not completely lost, it had been damaged.

"Who told you?'

"It does not matter. I suppose what matters is that you have come back to face me as a man should. I expected nothing less."

"And I would never show such disrespect by not facing you."

"Then you admit your mistake."

"It was not a mistake."

William cast him a long look. "You failed."

"I did not."

"I am not going to argue technicalities, Garren."

"And I am not going to admit that marrying a woman I am deeply in love with was a mistake. I have done what I have done, for reasons you do not agree with. Rather than arguing about it, I am here to tell you what I have done and ask that I be given leave of Richard's service to be with my wife."

William's jaw dropped. "You're serious?"

"Never more so."

The fury returned to William's veins. He rose from his seated position, stiffly. "I have no intention of allowing my greatest emissary leave, in any circumstance. You were born, bred and trained to serve me, le Mon, and that is exactly what you shall do. Your marriage and personal feelings are secondary to the needs of our king at this moment. I need you now, more than ever. Is that clear?"

Garren stood his ground. "You have many capable commanders, my lord. I am inconsequential."

"You are my hammer."

For the first time since Garren had been a knight, he felt a surge of anger at a direct command. Never mind that it was coming from William Marshal; anyone who would keep him from his wife would be dealt with.

"Find another hammer, my lord. I am going back to my wife."

He spun on his heel, uncharacteristically defiant. He hadn't made it three steps when the Marshal spoke.

"Do you know Fergus de Edwin?"

Garren paused, massive confusion filling him. "Should I?"

William Marshal had achieved his position in life for a very good reason. He could be a cold and calculating when he needed to be. This was one of those moments. He knew even before the words spilled from his lips that the mood between him and Garren would change forever.

"I am the last person you need be evasive with."

"I am not being evasive."

"Then you will tell me that you know of him, for I know that you do."

"I do."

"Then I will tell you something else, Garren."

Garren couldn't help it; his eyes narrowed. "By all means, my lord. Tell me something else."

It was a tone that William had never heard from Garren before, threatening and deadly. But it did not deter him. "You will ride from Chepstow at the head of my army," he said quietly. "You will ride north to Nottingham and meet the mercenary army in battle. You will lead the armies of Richard to victory. Richard's reign is everything; you and I are nothing. Merely expendable figures in this great chess match of Life. And along with you and me as pawns, there are many other players. Your wife, for one. Fergus for another."

Garren hated the horror creeping into his veins. It was all he could do to keep his hands from wrapping around the Marshal's throat.

"What in the hell does that mean?"

"It means that Fergus de Edwin works for me. He has always worked for me. He befriended you on my orders and has been assigned to watch you since he was quite young. He has been my eyes on you, though I never truly believed you needed watching until recent events. It means that, even now, Fergus has orders. I assume he is at Cilgarren, is he not?"

Garren knew that all of the color had drained from his face. "How do you know this?"

"How do you suppose? Fergus suggested the place, and I agreed." The Marshal's gaze grew hard. "As you disobeyed me, I was one step ahead of you. Always one step ahead, Garren."

Something snapped inside Garren and he pushed forward, coming to within an inch of William's face. The expression on his face was sheer murder.

"If she is touched, I will kill you myself."

The Marshal wasn't the least bit intimidated. "She will be fine providing you do as you are told. And what you are told is to ride north at the head of my army. Any premature return to Cilgarren, any glimpse of you within the next six months in return for your wife, and Fergus has orders to kill her. She'll be dead before you can stop him. This is something you have forced me to do, Garren. As you love your wife, I love England more. I would do anything to protect and serve her, including blackmailing you."

Garren was struggling not to show his emotion, so much so that his lips were white. Suddenly, everything he had ever believed about his life was a masquerade. People he had trusted and loved did not trust him. He had been betrayed.

His mind began to swirl and he labored to stop the building madness. Had he stood there any longer gazing into William's eyes, he would have strangled him. With the greatest effort, he pulled himself away and paced the floor, slowly, struggling with every fiber of his being to clear his

thoughts. He had to regain control if he was going to get himself and
Derica out of this alive.

The conversation he had with Fergus in the gatehouse filled his brain. It
was the most peculiar conversation they had ever had. Unspoken words
and innuendos had brought Garren to the conclusion that Fergus may have
actually worked for the Prince. But that was not the case. He wondered
why the deception, the evasiveness. Fergus was trying to throw him off
track, yet he had been trying to protect him also. Garren began to realize
that Fergus was trying to steer him away from Chepstow. Fergus knew
what was waiting for him. He had been trying to convince him to stay at
Cilgarren and stay far away from Chepstow.

Fergus had known. Garren felt like a fool for not understanding what
his friend had been trying to tell him.

"Fergus promised me that he would protect her," he heard himself
mutter. "I cannot believe that he would betray his word."

William could feel himself weakening. He loved Garren like a son and it
was a difficult situation. He was a man, too, and could understand the
pangs that came with love. But he understood England more, and knew
what was necessary to preserve her future. Garren was, and always had
been, an integral part of that plan.

"He will protect her as long as you fulfill your duty," William said
quietly. "She could be in no better hands."

Garren didn't respond. He was shutting William out, killing all of the
feelings of admiration and affection he had ever experienced for the old
man. William sensed this.

"Garren," he got as close to him as he dared, afraid that in his turmoil
the knight might actually strike out. "I will promise you this; lead our
armies to victory and I will release you from Richard's service. I will
provide you with an army of your own, lands and title, so that you and
your wife may live your years in comfort and security. Do as I ask now and
your future is secure. Betray me and you shall lose everything."

Garren looked at him, his eyes full of venom and resignation. He knew
he had no choice and there was nothing left to say but the obvious.

"By your command, my lord."

It had been a struggle to speak the words. Garren's pride was wounded,
his heart damaged, but he knew what he must do. The Marshal was sad
and pleased at the same time that Garren's call of duty meant his liberation
and, quite possibly, his death.

"I am sorry it has to be this way, Garren."

"The hell you are, my lord."

William returned to his solar without another word, greeted by a host
of expectant faces as he resumed covering the plans of battle. Garren came

in behind him with no hint of what had transpired in that tiny room. For all the others knew, there had been a detailed war conference between the Marshal and his greatest knight. Garren and William would not let anyone think otherwise.

The stage was set

***

Fall was upon the land. The lush hills of Wales were turning shades of golds, some reds and browns, and the heavy fog that was normally so prevalent had been in reprieve a few weeks. It was a lovely time of year.

Derica sat at the top of the hill overlooking the River Teifi. The swollen waters rushed below her, echoing off the rock. She had a basket beside her, filled with wild turnips and blackberries she had harvested from the uncultivated vines that ran along the side of the castle. It wasn't food that was settling particularly well in her stomach these days, but nothing seemed to be. The child in her growing belly was particular about what he ate, making his mother miserable at times.

The child also made her cry or rage in an instant. Sometimes she could do both at the same time. Fergus had borne the brunt of her hysteria most of the time, in the dismal evenings when she would miss Garren horribly and she would demand Fergus go search for him. Fergus would try to soothe her, as did Emyl and Offa and David, but she would rage at all of them and cry pitifully. Then there would be periods of sunshine when she was the sweetest angel in the land. But the angel was giving way to the crazed woman more often than not, especially the more time passed and the more Garren did not return. Things were growing darker.

This morning seemed particularly bleak. Derica had done little but sit on the hill for most of it. She felt as if she had a great hole inside of her, impossible to fill except for the sight of Garren walking through the gatehouse. But nearly three months had passed since she last saw him on that rainy morning and the more time passed, the more desperation she felt. It was difficult to be continually optimistic, and to have faith in his promise. On this sweet morning, her confidence was in danger of disappearing completely. She had sat on the hill and cried.

She heard footsteps behind her, jolting her from her bleak thoughts. Quickly wiping her cheeks, she wasn't surprised to see David's dark eyes gazing shyly down at her.

"I thought I would take the basket from you," he said. "It looks like a fine harvest."

Derica smiled weakly, handing him the goods. "My thanks."

David stood there a moment, awkwardly. "Will you be coming back now?"

She shook her head. "Not now. I will in a while."

"I shall wait for you."

"Please don't. I shall be along shortly."

David didn't want to leave her alone, for he knew how it was with her these days. But he respected her wishes and left. He was a quiet man, very gentle, and his feelings for Derica were no secret even though he thought he concealed them quite nicely. He and Offa had gone out of their way to repair what was repairable for her, cleaning and roofing two rooms on the second floor of the north tower with a view overlooking the river. Fergus and Emyl lived below her on the first floor, while David and Offa maintained the loft in the great hall.

David was a good craftsman, using wood from the trees surrounding the castle and other items to fashion a bed for her. From wood, he had also fashioned bowls, eating utensils, a crude chest and chair, and a handloom. Then he had sold his dead brother's sword and purchased six sheep, carefully shearing them of their old wool so that Derica had something to make yarn and fabric with. Even though it was nearing winter and the sheep were cold without their wooly coats, the hair was growing back quickly.

Their life at Cilgarren was not as desolate as it could have been. They had food and were moderately comfortable, and the de Rosas had not come around in all the time they had been there. The only thing missing was Garren, and because Derica felt it like a knife, they all did.

David was crossing the bailey towards the kitchen when Emyl came hurrying in through the inner gatehouse. He was laden with items he had purchased in town with some of the money remaining from the sale of Guy's sword. He struggled towards David, who set the basket down and took the sack of grain from the old man's shoulders. Emyl wiped his forehead.

"Where is Fergus?" he demanded.

"In the hall, I think. Is something wrong?"

Emyl could only shake his head as he moved in the direction of the hall. "News. My son must hear of this."

David put the grain and vegetables in the kitchen. He went to find Offa and the two of them hurried to the hall. Emyl was sitting on a bench, wiping his forehead again and huffing about his age. Fergus, who had been mending a stool, sat on the table beside his father.

"You're sure about this, Da?"

"Sure enough."

Offa spoke. "What is it? What's happened?"

159

"News," Emyl said. "I heard in town. There were Welsh knights, talking to the smith."

"What news?"

The old man fixed the small group with a heady gaze. "A big battle, Richard against John. All the armies of the empire have been called to fight against each other."

The implication was not lost on Fergus; his eyes closed for a moment as if to ward off the very idea of it. "So it has begun."

"Aye, it has. And there is more. William Marshal rallied a huge army from the south and met John's mercenaries at Tick Hill Castle. It was an enormous battle with many lives lost. John's loyalists have captured thirteen castles about England's midsection and Richard's armies are struggling to regain ground lost. All of England is in turmoil."

Now, it all made sense. Fergus knew exactly where Garren was; if he wasn't dead already, he was in the middle of the great bloody war that had gripped the country. Feelings of dread and guilt swept him.

"How long has this been going on?" he asked.

"Since July."

Fergus ran a weary hand across his face, his thoughts racing. As a knight, he knew his only course of action would be to find the Marshal's army, find Garren, and join the fighting. But William Marshal had ordered him to watch over Derica. There was also the small matter of promising Garren that he would take care of his wife. Still, Derica had three men willing and able to see to her every need, and if the civil war was indeed raging, then the likelihood of Garren forsaking his duties to come back to Derica was slim.

Fergus had carried out his mission for the Marshal, in his opinion. Besides, he never could have truly killed her. The Marshal would have been wiser to assign that task to someone who hadn't known Garren like a brother. Now, the civil war they had feared for years was finally bearing fruition and Fergus knew where his place should be, as it had been many times; beside Garren in battle.

"Do we know where the fiercest fighting is at present? Did the Welsh knights say?"

"Northamptonshire, they say," Emyl replied. "Seems that John's loyalists are embedded at Rockingham Castle. Damn big place. Richard's army is trying to unseat them and regain the castle."

Fergus nodded in thought. The news was probably a few weeks old. The only thing to do would be to ride to Chepstow to find out what he could, and then follow the trail from there. He began to move as Emyl and the others watched him with closely.

"Where do you go?" Emyl demanded.

Fergus found his leather jerkin. "I go to war."

"Why?" the old man was distressed. "This is not your war, son."

Fergus looked at his father. "There are many things you do not know, things which I have not explained to you. Since I do not have the time, suffice it to say that any war of Richard's is a war of mine. It is also a war of Garren's and I can promise you that he has been in the midst of the fighting since it began."

The others passed glances between them. "What do you mean? He was to go to his father's aid against the de Rosas." Emyl said.

Fergus sighed, wondering how much he should tell them. "It is possible that he has. But my suspicion is that he is involved in the civil war now enveloping the county. I must go and help him."

His explanation only left them more confused. There was some bickering and chatter as Fergus gathered his possessions, only to turn to the doorway to see Derica standing there. From the expression on her face, Fergus knew she had heard far more than she should of. He silently cursed himself for not noticing her until this moment.

His manner softened dramatically. "How much did you hear, love?"

She stared at him. "Where are you going? What has happened to my husband?"

Fergus was truthful, yet he also wanted to reassure her very much that what he was doing was in her and Garren's best interest. "England is erupting into civil war," he said plainly. "If you know about your husband, and I suspect you do, then you know he is involved. I must go and help him. I do this so that he may return to you. Do you understand?"

Derica gazed at him, torn between horror and hope. Tears suddenly filled her eyes. "Oh... Fergus," she whispered. "He is fighting for William Marshal, isn't he?"

Fergus put his hands on her shoulders. "I believe so."

"This civil war I heard you speak of," she said. "Richard and John are fighting for rule of the country?"

"Aye," he nodded. "I cannot explain how it is that I know, but I can promise you that William Marshal has ordered Garren in to battle."

"You serve the Marshal, too."

His expression softened, winking at her when he was sure the others could not see. "You must trust me, Derica. I have to go find Garren and help him."

Tears spilled down her cheeks. "War," she murmured again, her knees suddenly weakening. Fergus took a good hold of her and helped her sit. "It is possible that he is already dead. That is why he has not returned to me."

"And it is equally possible that he is still fighting," Fergus would not give in to her gloom. "Wars have many battles. They move around like an army of ants, scuttling about, fighting, then pulling back to regroup and fighting again. I have seen your husband in battle, my lady. He is the one man that I have truly believed to be invulnerable."

"What do you mean?" she sniffled.

Fergus thought a moment; what he would tell her would not be embellishment on his part. It would be the truth. "There is something about your husband that draws men to him. He has a quiet strength about him, a power that is beyond mere mortal strength. When he gives a command, men trust him and they follow him. He has never been wrong that I have known. When he wields a sword, it is as if St. George himself is living through him. He is as clever as he is deadly. That is why the Marshal has ordered him to fight; the old man knows that with le Mon in command, victory is very nearly assured."

"He is a great warrior, then?"

"There has never been another like him."

Derica felt better, but she also felt worse. Her heart ached for Garren in a way that she could not describe. If she closed her eyes, she could still hear his voice, feel his touch, and smell the warm musk of his skin. The simple possibility of losing that delicious joy made her tears fall faster, no matter how Fergus tried to comfort her.

"Fergus," she sobbed gently. "Please... please find him. Help him fight his battles so that he may return to me."

"I swear on my life, my lady. I will do this."

Surprisingly, she wasn't hysterical. The tears on her face were from pure emotion, the hole in her heart bleeding for her husband's plight. Fergus held her hand as she rose, holding on to her soft flesh until she walked out of his reach. The men watched her leave the hall, wondering if one of them should follow her but opting not to. She needed time to regain her dignity and deal with the events in her life over which she had no control.

Derica sobbed quietly as she wandered to her favorite spot on the hill overlooking the river. Her sobbing deepened as she remembered Garren following her around on the slope, holding on to her skirt so she would not slide down the cliff and into the river.

Four months ago, she had been living a spoiled life at Framlingham, catered to by her father, uncles and brothers, living day by day without a care in the world. It seemed like an eternity ago. She remembered the day that Garren le Mon had come into her life. It was the day she had been reborn, though she hadn't known it at the time. All she had known was that the enormous man with the square jaw and sandy-copper hair intrigued her as no one else had. She couldn't remember the exact moment she had fallen in love with him, yet she couldn't remember when she hadn't love him. It seemed like always.

Her tears faded as she wandered down the slope, hearing the river rushing below. Thoughts of Owain and Bryndalyn came to her, recollecting the story Emyl had told her. Bryndalyn had thrown herself into the river upon hearing of her husband's demise, her grief far too strong for her to bear. Derica could now fully understand the woman's despair.

She tried to take heart in Fergus' words, rubbing her hand over the small bulge in her belly, praying that her unborn child would have the chance to know his father. Fergus said that Garren was a great fighter and that she should have faith in him. She must believe that. The more she wandered down and across the slope, the more her tears faded. She did have faith. She believed Garren would return to her. Somehow, somewhere, they would be together again. She knew it as surely as she knew he loved her.

It was her last pleasant thought as her footing gave way and she plummeted down the side of the cliff, into the churning waters of the River Teifi below.

CHAPTER FOURTEEN

The battle had been in full swing since first light. Even now, with hues of dusk streaming across the sky, men were fighting as if they were fresh, their screams of pain filling the air along with the sounds of metal against metal. The grounds surrounding Lincoln Castle were pooled with battle gore and the smell of death rang heavy in the air.

Garren was one of those who had been fighting since dawn, as had Hoyt de Rosa. Hoyt had been at his side from nearly the onset, joining Garren's command at William's orders. Garren hadn't been surprised to see him; in fact, he had been glad. It was an odd connection to his wife that comforted him, though he secretly wondered if William had sent him to make sure Garren lived up to his agreement. To be fighting alongside a de Rosa rather than against one seemed natural to him and they worked well together.

A rather large band of John's supporters had fled to Lincoln Castle and he had been ordered to take one thousand men to lay siege to the castle. Lincoln Castle wasn't even one of those held by John; it was the property of a loyalist, now held hostage by the Prince's supporters. It had an immense motte and thick walls, and Garren's men had been given a rough time trying to breach the defenses.

Having brought two trebuchets with them, they had taken to flinging flaming pots of expensive tar over the walls, hoping to burn the inhabitants out. Nothing beyond that had a hope of succeeding until they could penetrate the walls.

It was a strategy that had eventually worked. The portcullis had lifted to allow a screaming band of burning people out, and the hand-to-hand combat had been fierce for several hours. Garren lost count of the men he'd killed, though one of them had given him a nasty nick on his thigh. He didn't even remember how it happened, only that it had. The barber surgeon traveling with the army had cauterized it before it could bleed overly and he was back to the battle with hardly a step missed.

When the sun sat low and squat on the horizon, the battle began to lag. Garren and Hoyt wandered through the pockets of fighting while more socially ranking warriors invaded the interior of the castle to claim it for Richard once again. Garren's job was to make sure the major fighting was quelled and to discourage any further rebellion. He did so with exhaustive efficiency and demanded surrender from those still resisting. With Hoyt's assistance, he placed them under arrest and segregated the officers from the men into prisoner groups.

It was a long process that drug well on into the evening, and Garren had been grateful for Hoyt's presence. The man had been a fierce warrior, one of the best he'd ever seen. His respect for the man grew and a bond intensified.

The skirmish had truthfully taken less time than he had originally thought, mostly because the rebel force had been poorly supplied and poorly organized. True to form, Garren had come at them like a hammer and had quashed them soundly. He was the first one into battle, and the last one to leave. It had always been his mode of operation, something that continually endeared him to his men. He never expected them to do anything he wasn't willing to do himself.

It was after midnight when he sent Hoyt off to sleep. The old man was so exhausted he could barely stand. Garren lingered on the battlefield with the last few prisoners before returning to his own tent. The castle was quiet, the prisoners finally secured, and the squire that traveled with him had lit the fire in his tent and had food and drink waiting for him. Garren sat heavily on a sturdy stool, allowing himself a sweet moment to feel his exhaustion. The squire came back into the tent with a great piece of meat, some part of the cow that had been cooked to blackness. Garren wasn't particularly hungry, but he took it anyway. The squire, a young man to be knighted the next year, hovered before him.

"Will there be anything else, my lord?" he asked.

Garren set the beef down; he couldn't stomach it at the moment. He took his cup of wine instead. "Perhaps some water to wash my hands with," he took a long drink. "Where are my commanders?"

"Lord Payn and Lord Barnard have not yet returned from battle, my lord," the lad replied. "I have heard rumor that they have fallen."

Payn de Cantelupe and Barnard de Warrenne were young nobles from two of the more powerful families on the Welsh Marches. They had brought four hundred men-at-arms with them, men that would now fall to Garren's command if what the squire said was true. It would make his presence more critical than ever and his chances of returning home soon dwindle. Garren took another gulp of wine, pondering the information.

"Do we have any further news from Newark Castle?"

"Not since last eve, my lord. As far as we know, there is heavy fighting in and around the castle. They are expecting us as soon as this unpleasantness at Lincoln is finished."

Garren knew that. He was always expected somewhere, ready for battle at a moment's notice. It was one encounter after another, a never-ending parade of castles, villains, allies and action. Somewhere it had ceased to be a war between Richard and John and become an endless conflict between countrymen. When Garren had led the first charge at Tick Hill Castle, he was foolishly hoping that whatever battles there were would be short-lived, and that he could return to Derica within a few short weeks.

But the weeks had stretched into months. Two months, three weeks, three days, fifteen hours, and an odd number of minutes. He remembered to the last detail. He knew Derica would be frantic, thinking of committing herself to Yaxley Nene Abbey if she hadn't done so already. He felt a great deal of comfort in that, truthfully, for no matter how long the war waged, he knew where to find her, and he knew that she would be safe. He was desperately sorry that she would have to go through so much emotional turmoil in the meanwhile, thinking he was dead when he was very much alive and thinking of her every minute of every day. He longed for her as he had never longed for anything in his life.

But thoughts like that were useless. They simply made him hurt more. Pulling himself from the brink of emotional decline, as he had done so many times over the past several weeks, he drained his cup and reached for a piece of bread.

"We should be finished here tomorrow," he told the squire. "I do not anticipate Lincoln Castle taking any more of our time. We ship the prisoners south and move the army north by midday. Spread the word to whatever commanders I have left. Arrange a meeting in my tent in one hour."

The squire nodded and fled. Garren returned to his meal, emitting a heavy sigh as he forced himself to eat. After two bites, his thoughts turned to his pallet and a short nap before his officers arrived for conference. As he took one last drink from his cup, someone entered his tent.

Expecting the squire, it took Garren longer than usual to recognize Fergus. When recognition dawned, he stared at the man as if he had grown two heads. Fergus, seeing the shock, the suspicion, the anxiety, wasted no time.

"Garren," he muttered, true satisfaction in his voice. "They told me you were here. Thank Almighty God you are alive."

Garren wasn't sure how to react. He didn't know where to begin. But one thing was foremost in his mind; if Fergus was here, then....

"Where is my wife?"

The weary smile faded from Fergus' face. "My father heard about the wars between Richard and John. I knew you would be in the midst of them. I promised your wife that I would find you and make sure that you were safe."

Garren couldn't help but notice that his question hadn't been answered. "Where is she?"

There was no room for pleasantries or idle talk. Garren's expression was taut with anticipation. Fergus had hoped to ease his friend into the predominant reason for his visit, but he could see it would not happen. What he had to say would be the hardest words he ever had to bring forth.

"She is gone," he said quietly.

Garren stood up, his stool toppling over. "Gone? What do you mean?" He suddenly reached out, grabbing Fergus around the neck. "Did the de Rosas capture her?"

Fergus couldn't breathe, and there was no way he could contend against Garren's strength. "If you kill me, you will never know the rest," he gasped, and the grip loosened. "Nay, Garren, her family did not capture her. Please, won't you sit? 'Twould be better for us both if you did."

Garren's grip tightened again. "Damn you, Fergus, if you do not tell me what has happened to my wife, I will kill you where you stand and worry of the consequences later."

He meant every word, Fergus knew that. But he was not making this any easier. "Garren, please," he begged, trying to loosen the hold on his neck. "You must be calm, my friend."

"*Fergus!*"

Fergus could see there was no alternative than to tell him, quickly. "She knew you had gone to battle with the Marshal. She heard my father and me speaking of the civil wars. I tried to reassure her that it did not necessarily mean your death, but she was greatly distressed. She is easily distressed these days."

"What does that mean?"

Fergus' manner softened. "She carries your son, Garren. The child has turned her into a whirlwind of emotion."

Garren felt as if all of the wind had been knocked from him. A gambit of emotions raced over his features, delight and terror and everything in between.

"She is with child?" he gasped.

"Aye."

"Truly?"

"I would not lie about this, my friend."

"And she is well?"

Fergus was careful with his reply. "The child made her full of health, if that is what you mean. Otherwise, she drove us all mad with her raging and crying and smiles. We never knew what to expect from her." He watched Garren's eyes positively light with the news, a brief respite of joy from the horror that was about to follow. "When she found out about your whereabouts, she was upset, of course, but we did not believe overly so. We had seen her in a worse state. But... Garren, as closely as we can deduce, she must have thrown herself into the river in her grief. I swear that we never believed she would be capable of such a thing. The last we saw of her, she was standing on the hill overlooking the river, the hill where the wild lentils grow. You know the one. One moment she was there, the next she was gone."

Garren stared at him. It was an expression Fergus had never seen before. All of the color drained from Garren's face and Fergus found himself helping the man to sit so that he would not collapse. For the all-powerful Garren le Mon to collapse like a weakling was unthinkable. But Fergus could see the man cracking, right before his eyes.

"Perhaps she may have even slipped," Fergus tried to soften the blow now that the hammer had fallen. "She was close to the edge, as she always is, and we found tracks in the soft earth that had dragging movement to them. She was probably gone hours by the time we realized she was missing and we searched for days, Garren. I swear to you, we didn't sleep for several days or nights for search of her. We left no stone unturned."

Garren closed his eyes, falling forward to rest his head in his hands. "God, tell me this is a nightmare."

"I wish I could."

"You didn't find her?"

"Nay, my friend, we did not."

"No blood or... body?"

"We found nothing, Garren. She is simply," he shrugged helplessly, "gone."

Garren's head remained in his hands for several long moments. When he finally lifted his face, there were tears in his eyes.

"Just like Bryndalyn," he muttered. "Oh... God, tell me she didn't do what that woman did...."

A light of recognition came to Fergus' eye. "You know of Bryndalyn and Owain?" He knew the story, too, and horror suddenly swept him. "Just like the tale. Bryndalyn threw herself into the river when...."

A look from Garren made the words die in his throat. "Your father told us about it when we first went to Cilgarren," Garren mumbled. "She was so saddened by it, but I never imagined she would follow in the shadow of the legend. It never occurred to me that my not returning immediately would... Christ, that story was in her mind, ever lingering, planting the seed of despair that made her go mad when I did not come back as I would sworn to. How long has she been missing?"

"It has been nearly three weeks," Fergus said. "I looked for her as long as I dared before riding to Chepstow. They told me of the battles north and I came searching for you."

Garren's teeth abruptly clenched. "I know of your mission. The Marshal told me. Fergus, I swear to Almighty God, if you have done something to her and are trying to throw me off your scent, I shall...."

Fergus shook his head emphatically. "Do you truly believe I could harm a hair on her beautiful head? Garren, you are closer to me than a brother. "Tis true, years ago, the Marshal asked that I watch you, and as a fearful lad, I did as I was told. But as we grew older and our friendship blossomed, I put the Marshal's priorities behind yours. I would never betray you, not even for our country. I do not blame you if you never trust me again, but I assure you, my loyalty is and always has been with you. Haven't I proven that time and time again?" He could see that he wasn't making much of an impact. "If I truly wanted to harm her, I could have done it on that chaotic odyssey from Framlingham to the abbey. I could have easily turned her back over to her family, but I didn't. Does that not account for anything?"

Garren couldn't decide whether to kill him at that point or not. He decided against it, mostly because what Fergus said made sense. "Then why didn't you ever tell me who you were?"

"Why didn't you ever tell me?"

There was a tense silence as Garren pondered the obvious. He probably shouldn't have trusted Fergus, but years of experience and instinct took hold and the bond that had been established ages ago could not be broken. However, all of that was secondary to what had happened to Derica. Garren stood up, struggling to gain control; there was only one thought on his mind and he would kill Fergus if he tried to stop him. If Fergus were sincerely committed to their friendship, now would be the supreme test of that bond.

"I must go and search for her," Garren said.

"What of the Marshal? Surely he will not...."

Garren cast him a glare so deadly that Fergus swallowed the remainder of his words.

"This is where William Marshal and I come to an end," Garren growled. "I was foolish and weak to have let it come this far, but I did. I am going to find my wife and not all of the armies in England can stop me."

"But...."

"You are either with me or against me, Fergus. If you are against me, I will kill you where you stand."

"I am with you, of course. What can I do?"

Garren had a clear picture of what must happen. "We will go to the battlefield," he said in a low voice. "We will find a body; anybody that is near my size. If it is recognizable, then we will make it so that it cannot be identified. Onto this corpse will go my armor, my clothing, my weapon.... "

Fergus' eyes gleamed. "We will make it as though you were killed in battle."

"This man will be me. To the Marshal, I shall be dead."

"And then you can search for Derica without fear of reprisal."

"As much as I do not relish defacing a man who has given his life in battle, there are times when sacrifice is necessary. He will have died for two just causes this night."

Garren and Fergus blended into the night, like wraiths, completing their gruesome work with silence and efficiency. By morning, they were far from the battlefield as word of Garren le Mon's death spread like wildfire. When Hoyt de Rosa awoke to the news, he wept.

***

She didn't know how long she had been awake. She realized she was staring at the ceiling, a dense mixture of rushes and straw, woven tightly to create a barrier against the elements. When she tried to move, her entire body ached as if she had been pummeled. It was her groan of pain that stirred the others.

"Are ye awake?"

It was a soft female voice. Derica blinked her eyes, rolling her head with much effort to find herself gazing into a pair of pale blue eyes. She blinked again, disoriented, wondering why her head hurt so much.

"Who... where am I?" she rasped.

The woman smiled, reaching for a wooden pitcher. She poured something into a cup. "Here," she helped Derica lift her head. "Drink."

It was water, cool and clear. Derica took a sip, then gulped until she almost choked. When the coughing died down, she saw that the woman's face had been joined by two smaller ones. Derica gazed into children's eyes.

"Hello," she said softly.

The children, a boy and girl perhaps three and four years, respectively, giggled and did not reply. They were dark-eyed, dark haired little ones. They looked at their mother, who continued to smile.

"How do ye feel?" the woman asked.

Derica thought a moment. "I am not sure," she finally said. "What happened? Where am I?"

"Ye are in my house," the woman replied. "We found you."

"Found me?"

The woman nodded. "Aye. On the river bank. Ye were nearly dead when we came upon ye. How did ye get there?"

Derica tried to recall. "I do not remember." She put her hand to her head, wincing when she brushed the large lump on her forehead. "How long was I unconscious?"

"A few days," the woman replied. "Do ye remember where ye came from?"

"I... not really. A castle, I think."

"Ye're a lady, then."

"I... I do not know."

"I am sure ye are, by the look of ye. But ye canna remember what castle ye came from?"

"Nay."

The woman didn't ask any more questions. Derica's mind was shrouded in a foggy mist; it was alarming to realize that, until this very moment, she couldn't recall much of anything. Her memories were an enormous blur for the moment.

"Where is this place?" she looked around the small, neat hut. "What village is this?"

"It is called Rhos-hill," the woman said. "Do ye recognize the place?"

"Nay," Derica shook her head. "What is your name?"

"Mair," she said. "My children, Sian and Aneirin."

Derica smiled weakly at the children, who were still hiding behind their mother. It was apparent that Mair was waiting for Derica to introduce herself. A wisp of a name sprang to mind, familiar yet not. It hung there, like an unvoiced thought. Derica spoke it, not even sure if it was true.

"Bryndalyn," she whispered. "I... I think that is my name. But I am not... sure. I cannot seem to recall much of anything at the moment."

Mair put a sympathetic hand on her forehead. "Do not be troubled," she said. "Sleep, now. There will be time later for recollection."

Derica didn't particularly want to sleep, but she remained on her pallet. When she shifted to get more comfortable, sharp pains echoed through her lower torso. She gasped softly, putting her hand against her lower abdomen to rub away the pain. Mair saw what she was doing.

"I am sorry," she murmured. "The child did not survive."

Though Derica could remember little else, she had remembered the child. She touched her belly, feeling it soft where once she had known it to be rounded and firm. Tears instantly sprang to her eyes.

"No," she whispered. "Please... no."

Mair stroked her forehead again. "'Twas a blessing, my lady."

Derica sniffled. "Why would you say that?"

"I meant no harm. When we found ye, I would think that someone had beat you and thrown you in the river. Mayhap your husband. Any man that would beat his pregnant wife... 'tis a blessing, I say, not to bring a child into a world such as that."

Derica's tears were fading in lieu of her shock. "Why would you think someone has beaten me?"

"Because you are bruised all over your body. Someone thrashed you soundly, I would say. Do you not recall any of this?"

171

She didn't. But within the mists of her mind, she couldn't honestly recall if anyone had taken a hand to her, ever. Bits and pieces of a large castle and men who loved her came to mind, but she couldn't recall the names. Just faces. She closed her eyes and silent tears fell again.

"There, there," Mair said softly. "Sleep now, sweetheart. All will be well again."

When she turned away to prepare some manner of sleeping drink for Derica, the little boy with the black hair and dark eyes moved in to be a closer look. He had a sweet little face, his striking eyes gazing curiously at Derica. A tiny hand lifted and he resumed stroking Derica's head where his mother had left off. Derica sobbed deeply at the gentleness of his gesture, the longing for her own son that she would never know.

***

He was too old to be attending battle, but he was doing so nonetheless. The Marshal had never missed a battle; he was an old soldier, and they knew little else. If there was war waging, most especially his war, his presence was required.

Newark Castle was a small structure in a strategic location. William had arrived a few days ago to await word on the fate of Lincoln Castle and plot his next move. Two days ago had seen him receive word of victory in one breath and the loss of Garren le Mon in the next.

He had wept privately at the news, though he refused to feel guilt. Garren was a warrior and the vocation went hand in hand with death. Garren had known what his fate could be the first day he drew a sword. He had lived longer than most. Still, his passing had been a horrible blow, both personally and professionally.

Hoyt de Rosa had joined William at Newark. The man had abandoned his family and had joined Richard's cause in full. He had arrived a few months ago, pledging his service with a sudden strong loyalty that the Marshal was suspicious of, but that suspicion was lifted when he saw Hoyt in battle. The man was ferocious. The elder de Rosa had fought with Garren, and had been there when Garren had fallen. It had been Hoyt who had brought Garren's body to the Marshal. One look at the face and skull disfigured by a morning star, and William had ordered the body interred in the chapel at Newark with full honors.

William felt tremendous guilt for the state of their relationship when Garren had passed. It had been strained, though in William's estimation that could not have been helped. Still, he would have liked to have known that Garren harbored no permanent ill will. William had hoped that the marcher lordship of Buckton would have eased any hardship. The lordship came with two castles and a large chunk of land, something Garren deserved. Now that he was no longer in the land of the living to accept it, William could think of nothing else but granting it posthumously to his wife. Perhaps by making amends to Garren's widow, it would right things between them in the next life.

That was his guilt talking. He hated feeling the strange stirrings of indecision and regret. Hoyt had been at his side constantly since his return and the two of them had sparred with their philosophies on life and death. Even tonight, they shared a blood-red wine and discussed a variety of critical subjects, and the important subject, Lady le Mon's future.

"I never asked Garren where she was," Hoyt muttered, staring at the liquid in his cup. "In all of the months I fought at his side, I never asked. I did not want to know, as I thought it was best considering the circumstances. But you must know."

"Of course I do," William would not mention the entire ugly incident with Fergus and blackmailing Garren into service. "She is well taken care of at the moment, I assure you."

Hoyt glanced at him. "Then I will ask you. Where is she?"

"Wales."

"It is a big country."

"Cilgarren Castle. Near Pembroke."

"I must stand by my opinion, William. She should return to Framlingham."

"And I must stand by mine. She will be granted the titles and lands that were intended for Garren. That is suitable to his legacy. Should she return to Framlingham, the de Rosas will erase all memories of him from your niece's mind. That is an unacceptable end for such a man."

Hoyt couldn't completely disagree. "So you intend to grant her the lordship of Knighton?"

William's answer was to summon a messenger to the borrowed solar. The young, skinny lad was barely a man, but William had used him before. He was cunning and rode like the wind. Standing at the waist-high writing table, he authored two missives by himself in the flickering candlelight. He carefully sanded the ink, blew it away, rolled and sealed both missives. The messenger watched anxiously as William handed over one parchment.

"You will find your way to Pembroke Castle," he instructed. "Do you know it?"

The lad nodded. "Aye, my lord."

"Then go there with all haste. Find Keller de Poyer, the knight in charge of the garrison. He is an older man, with brown hair last I knew, and arms the size of battering rams. Give him this first missive." William handed the boy a second rolled parchment. "And give him this one as well. Tell him it is for Lady le Mon. Is this, in any way, unclear?"

"Nay, my lord."

"It is of the utmost importance that you deliver these safely to him."

"I will, my lord."

"Be gone, then."

The lad fled. William wandered to the lancet window, watching the bailey below as the young man leapt onto his long-legged horse and thundered through the gates. When the rider was out of view, William gazed into the misty night, struggling to release his guilt now that the deed was complete. He did not look at Hoyt, still seated by the empty bottle of claret.

"This does not ease the loss of Garren, to be sure, but it will ease the situation with time," William said.

"How do you mean?"

"I have provided well for the widow in two ways; titles and lands will be hers, making her a very wealthy woman. The second provision is to give her an attractive dowry to make my orders to de Poyer more palatable."

"Why should they be palatable to de Poyer?"

William believed he was doing the best thing for all concerned, but he had to remind himself that Hoyt was the Widow le Mon's uncle and, understandably, very fond of her. He needed to be diplomatic.

"I have known Keller for years, as had Garren," the Marshal replied. "In fact, they fought together on many campaigns and are of the same warrior fabric; powerful, cunning, and resourceful, though Keller does not have nearly the intelligence that Garren had. He is a large man with more strength than brains, but his nature is good and he is obedient to a fault. He will do as he was told, no matter what the order."

An inkling of suspicion came to Hoyt's mind as to the nature of the request. "And that would be?"

William looked at him. "The protection of a strong husband is necessary to a widowed woman, especially Garren's widow."

Hoyt knew instantly what was coming. "And you have asked de Poyer to marry her."

"Garren would want her well taken care of."

Hoyt stared at him, dumbfounded. "Christ, William," he hissed. "Garren is hardly cold in his grave and you have already married off his wife."

"I do not see the quandary in that."

Hoyt put down his empty glass, remembering the day that Garren and Derica met. He remembered the subsequent days that saw a magical attraction between them to the day when Garren ended up in the vault.

What his niece and the knight had went beyond simple attraction. There was genuine emotion involved, so strong that it eclipsed the sun.

"There is no possible way I can explain this to you, but I shall make an attempt," Hoyt said. "Garren and Derica's feelings for one another go beyond something that you and I can understand. It transcends time and sentiment, like the first, best love that ever touched the darkness of this earth. My niece was fortunate enough to experience something that few mortals do. You can't just push that aside with titles and another husband."

"I am not attempting to," William stressed. "But you cannot deny that Garren would want his wife well taken care of."

"Of course not."

"And she will be, I promise."

"She should go home to her family."

"She will not. My gift to Garren is to see that she sustains his legacy and doesn't end up back in that den of vipers."

Hoyt didn't argue further with him. He knew it was fruitless. But after William finally retired for the night, he summoned a messenger of his own and sent the man east to Framlingham.

CHAPTER FIFTEEN

Days passed into a week, and then two. Derica had grown strong enough to help with the chores, discovering she wasn't very good at cooking but that she was quite good at mending. The massive lump on her head had slowly subsided and with it, her memory had returned in bits and pieces. She could remember the large family of men and a few of their names – Hoyt was her uncle, Dixon and Daniel were her brothers, but she still had no idea where they all lived or who the rest of the nameless men were.

At night, she dreamt of a massive man with copper-gold hair who filled her with wondrous weakness. She awoke in the morning, expecting to see him sleeping beside her, and repeatedly disappointed when he wasn't there. Perhaps he was the husband who had beaten her and thrown her into the river, though her instinct told her the man was not the kind. Surely if he was her husband, he would come looking for her. But no man came all of these days.

Early one morning, Mair roused her from a deep, warm sleep. Derica yawned, rolling onto her back and searching for her clothes. The clothes that Mair had found her in had been unsalvageable, so the woman had given her what was probably her best clothing to wear. Considering the near-rags Mair wore, Derica could surmise nothing else.

Derica slept in her shift, a soft wool garment that hung to her ankles. Over her head, she pulled the dark blue woolen surcoat with long sleeves, and then she pulled on a plain fawn-colored sleeveless garment that was made for durability and warmth. These were her clothes, day in and day out, and Mair washed them once since giving them to her. They smelled like rushes, and a little smoke.

"Get up, get up," Mair apparently thought Derica was moving too slowly. "We must get up and go to the lake."

Derica ran a wooden comb through her hair, wincing when it caught a snag. "The lake? Why?"

Mair smiled, handing Sian a cup of warmed goat's milk. "For a winter's harvest. You will see."

Derica thought she meant fish. Pulling her hair into a braid at the nape of her neck, she put on her shoes and borrowed cloak, which was really more of a woolen blanket, and followed Mair and the children out into the early morning. Everything was damp and icy as they made their way through the trees and into the outskirts of the small village.

176

The sun rose steadily and smoke from cooking fires hung heavy in the misty air. Mair led them around the village and to a well-traveled road that headed to the east. Sian and Aneirin walked on either side of Derica, holding baskets for their harvest. They had decided over the past week that they liked Derica very much and had taken to following her everywhere. Sian was a sweet, protective little boy, while Aneirin was more aggressive in a big sisterly manner and liked to push her younger brother around a bit. They squabbled here and there, but had mostly made wonderful companions for Derica. She was quite fond of them.

"Bryndalyn?"

For the past few days, Derica had been having dreams and memories that suggested that wasn't her name, but she answered nonetheless. "Aye?"

Sian grinned up at her. He was always grinning at her. "Tell me of the knights."

They had been having a discussion for several days about knights. Sian was enamored with warriors. She smiled gently at him. "Men with big horses and bigger swords."

She held her arms up to indicate an enormous weapon, and Sian's grin broadened. "Tell me of a fight!"

Derica thought hard. She thought she could recall a tournament, events flowing through her mind of colors and lists and shouting people. Dixon had taken the melee prize at this particular one. Very slowly, she could recall the name York. This particular tournament had been in York, and she recollected how much she had loved gazing at the magnificent cathedral.

"Do you remember what I told you about tournaments?"

"Aye!"

"Then do you remember what I told you about the knight's weaponry?"

Sian nodded eagerly. "They use a lance for the jost."

"Joust," she corrected.

"Joust," Sian repeated. "They use their swords for the me.. me..."

"Melee."

"A fight!"

She laughed softly. "Aye, a fight, little man. They stick each other with swords until one man is left standing. It is a horrible, bloody spectacle, something I suspect you would love immensely."

Sian began swinging the basket around as if fighting for his life. "Behold, bad men," he said, swinging the basket so close to Derica's head that she had to duck. "Beware of my wrath!"

Derica took hold of Aneirin's hand, pulling her gently out of the way so she would not be struck by the flying basket. "All hail, Sir Sian of the Dark Woods."

Sian liked that name. Derica had come up with it one night when the young boy was expressing his desire to be the greatest knight in all the land. He paused in his basket swinging and bowed stiffly.

"I shall marry you when I am a knight."

Derica cocked an eyebrow. "I think that I shall be a bit old for you, but your offer is most flattering."

The boy suddenly looked very serious. He slipped his cold little hand into Derica's. "But who will take care of you?"

Derica had flashes of the man with the sandy-copper hair, straining with body and soul to remember who he was. In her heart, she already knew. "My husband will, when he finds me."

Sian looked confused. "Mam says he is bad for what he did to you. I will kill him if he tries to hurt you."

Derica stroked his dark head. "I am very fortunate to have a protector such as you. But he is my husband, and if he comes for me, I must go with him. I belong to him."

Sian didn't agree with her but he didn't know what to say. Aneirin looked frightened. Up ahead, Mair was leading them off the road and into some trees. Derica and the children followed. On the other side of a thin line of trees lay a large pond, swamped with too much water. Mair paused at the edge, and when Derica and the children reached her, she put her hand in the water up to the elbow, fished around, and came up with a handful of wet, red berries.

"Come on, help me," she encouraged them.

Soon, they were all harvesting the wet fruit from the swampy water. At Mair's urging, Derica popped one in her mouth and was delighted with the strong bitter-sweet flavor. They swept the edge of the pond until their baskets were full and their hands were freezing and wet. Derica dried off Sian's hands, while Mair dried off Aneirin's.

The children's teeth were chattering with cold, but they were thrilled with their booty, dancing around with the catch of red berries. As Derica bent over to pick up the little scarf that Sian had dropped, the little boy gleefully swung his basket around and hit her on the back. Derica pitched forward, unable to stop herself from ramming head-first into the decomposing tree directly behind her. Stars flashed before her eyes before everything went suddenly dark.

She hadn't been out very long, perhaps a few moments. Derica blinked her eyes, gazing up at Sian and Mair's worried faces. She put a hand up to her bruised forehead, struggling to sit.

"Are ye well?" Mair was beside herself with horror at what her son had done.

Derica nodded unsteadily. "I... I think so."

Sian, over the shock of having accidentally hit her, began to wail and Derica comforted him. "There, there," she hugged him. "I am fine. Do not be troubled."

"I am sorry, Bryndalyn," he sniffed.

Derica's expression slowly changed, as if a spark of flame slowly bloomed within her mind. She rubbed her forehead again, a weary smile on her lips.

"That's not my name," she said softly.

Sian's tears faded and he looked at her, confused. Mair, too, looked surprised. "It is not?"

Derica closed her eyes briefly, suddenly remembering everything in a waterfall of memories and feelings. They had been struggling to come through for several days and the knock on the head was apparently all she had needed. Her smile broadened as if the most wonderful thing in the world had just happened.

"My name is the Lady Derica de Rosa le Mon," she said, restraining her excitement lest she frighten the children with it. "My husband is Sir Garren le Mon, sworn to King Richard and vassal of William Marshal."

Mair squeezed her arm. "So ye do remember now."

Derica nodded. "I do." She hugged Sian tightly. "My thanks to you, Sian, for causing me to hit my head. 'Twas the best gift you could have given me."

The little boy was glad he was not in trouble, happy his friend was so joyful. But something occurred to him out of all the fuss and joy going on. "Your husband is a knight?"

Derica nodded, remembering the man with the sandy-copper hair and thrilled to remember every last detail about him. "He is a great knight," she said quietly. "And he did not beat me and throw me in the river. I was too close to the edge and slipped in. The bruises were from my fall."

"Ye recollect the fall that brought ye to us?" Mair asked. "Do ye also remember where ye're from?"

"We were at Cilgarren Castle," Derica said. "How far are we from there?"

Mair thought. "A goodly distance, I think. 'Tis to the north of us."

"But you know of it?"

"I have lived here all my life. I know the land."

Derica rubbed her head again and stood up, gripping the offending tree for support. But she didn't care that her head was swimming; all that mattered is that she could remember who she was again. It was deliriously liberating. She was seized with the desire to return to Cilgarren right away.

"I must go home," she said. "Will you help me?"

Mair nodded. "Of course we will."

"Can we make it in a day, if we start now? 'Tis still early."

Mair shrugged. "'Is it also possible yer husband is already looking for ye? Perhaps if we stay here, he will come to us."

Tears came to Derica's eyes, remembering her last conversation with Fergus. The good memories as well as the bad rejoined her. She wondered what had happened during her absence. "He is fighting the wars between Richard and John. I suspect he'll not come looking for me any time soon."

Mair understood. She didn't like the thought of wandering the dangerous countryside with her children, but she could not refuse her. "Very well," she said softly. "We will take you home."

Derica sensed the moment between them, the sacrifice Mair was willing to make for a woman she hardly knew. "I cannot tell you what you have meant to me, you and your children. You have taken me in and cared for me, and I will not forget your kindness. My family has much wealth and I swear I shall reward you for your trouble."

Mair's pale complexion flushed. "We have all we need. I did not help ye for the fortune to be gained by it."

"I know you didn't. But you shall be rewarded all the same. You have risked much."

There was nothing more to say. Rubbing her head again, Derica let go of the tree and took Sian's hand. Her heart was lighter than it had been since she came to this place. Together, the four of them made their way back through the trees, towards the road. The day was warming as the sun struggled through the clouds. Sian saw a rabbit with big white ears and ran off in pursuit. He wanted to play with it, but Aneirin wanted the fur for a coat. Derica and Mair reached the road, watching the children chase the rabbit through the bushes. A low rumble in the distance caught their attention.

"Rain is coming," Mair glanced up at the semi-cloudy sky.

Derica looked up, too. But the rumble didn't stop; it continued and seemed to grow louder. Her gaze moved to the road leading west.

"I do not think it is rain," she said. "Listen. It sounds more like horses. Many horses."

Mair's relaxed expression tensed. "An army?"

Derica was quiet a moment, thinking. "Where does this road lead?"

"To Pembroke."

There was a large castle in Pembroke. "Get the children," Derica said with quiet urgency.

They sprinted into the bramble. Derica came across Aneirin and grasped the little girl by the wrist, but the child didn't understand. She thought it was a game and pulled away from Derica, laughing. Derica chased her through a cluster of trees, panicked when she saw that the girl was heading back up towards the road. She called her name, trying to stop her, but the child dashed onward. By the time she hit the road, Derica was right behind her and finally grabbed her around the waist.

"Got you!" she breathed.

She noticed the dust first. Whirling around with the child still in her arms, her eyes fell on a large group of armed men several feet away. They were clad in expensive armor and rode massive chargers, animals built for the brutality of war. Having been around knights her entire life, she knew this particular group of men could be nothing other than seasoned warriors.

The group carried several Welsh crossbowmen with them, men renowned for their deadly accuracy. It was a war party. She prayed that Mair and Sian would stay to the bushes as she herself faced the horde, having no other choice. To run would be to surely invite them to follow, and that could result in the capture of all of them.

The group had come to a halt. Derica pushed Aneirin behind her, protectively, facing the men with courage. One knight flipped up his visor, studying her carefully.

"I have traveled this road many a time and have never seen a fairy, though I have heard tale of them," he said. When Derica didn't reply, he continued in a less friendly tone. "Your name, woman."

Derica knew her family name held much weight, on both sides of the realm. If these knights supported the Prince, then it would save her. If not, it may very well work against her. But it was her name, for better or worse.

"Who asks?" she questioned with polite authority.

"You will answer me, wench."

"I will. As soon as you answer me. And you will not call me wench."

The knight was working up another snappish retort, but the large knight next to him put out a hand, stopping the reaction. The knight who spoke reworded his reply.

"The Lord of Pembroke asks."

Derica knew she had to tell him. To be evasive would only pull her deeper into what could possibly be an unpleasant situation. She'd already been far bolder than she should have been.

"The Lady Derica de Rosa le Mon."

The knight snorted. "And I am the King of France. I will ask you one more time your name. Lie to me, and punishment shall be swift."

"I did not lie. I am the daughter of Bertram de Rosa of Framlingham Castle and wife to Garren le Mon, heir to the barony of Anglecynn and Ceri and descendent of Saxon kings. My father and uncles have crusaded with King Henry, and my godfather is Roger Bigod, second Earl of Norfolk. Shall I go on?"

The helmed heads looked at each other. The large knight who had held up a quelling hand lifted his visor, gaining a better look. His large brown eyes regarded her. He finally spurred his charger forward, an enormously hairy red horse with an abundance of cream-colored fur around its hooves. Derica didn't flinch as he came to within a few feet of her.

"You are Garren le Mon's widow?"

Derica felt as if she had been struck. "I am his wife," she replied steadily.

"What are you doing so far from Cilgarren, lady?"

Derica wasn't sure where to start with all of it, and her mind was still spinning with his words. Garren le Mon's widow. And how did this knight, whom she did not know, have the knowledge that she was at Cilgarren? "I... I was lost and preparing to make my way back home." It sounded like a lame excuse, even to her.

"Lost?"

"I wandered... too far and became lost." When he appeared as if he didn't believe a word, she grunted in frustration. "Suffice it to say that I was lost and am, even now, on my way home. I do not see how that is any concern of yours."

The knight regarded her carefully; he didn't doubt for a minute she was who she said she was. She was well spoken and exceedingly beautiful, even in the peasant clothing she was wearing. It was like looking at a diamond glistening in the dirt. But he was incredibly confused to find her wandering a road several miles south of Cilgarren Castle. She was surely as witless as she was lovely.

"William Marshal has ordered me to retrieve you, Lady le Mon."

"Why?"

"I am to take you back to Pembroke. He has sent a missive for you."

"A missive? What missive?"

"'Tis a private document, for your eyes only. I suspect it is news of some manner."

Derica's heart suddenly fell into her stomach; she knew what the missive was. The knight didn't have to say another word. It had to be a missive telling her of her husband's death, which is why the warrior referred to her as Garren's widow. Much had apparently happened in her absence. The world was suddenly very unsteady and her heart began pounding loudly in her ears. She was vaguely aware of falling to her knees, slightly less aware of the knight dismounting his charger and coming to her aid so that she would not fall on her face. Somewhere, she could hear Aneirin crying.

"No," she breathed. "God, please... no. He is not dead. He cannot be."

By this time, several of the knights had ridden forward. One of them took hold of the riderless charger, while two others dismounted, mostly to gain a better look at the beautiful lady rather than to actually lend assistance. The knight that held her pulled off his helm with his free hand and passed it off to the man standing next to him.

"Help me get her on my steed," he commanded softly.

"No!" Derica struggled weakly against him. "I will not go! I must go back to Cilgarren!"

The knight didn't reply as he swung her up into his arms. Aneirin was crying loudly now. Mair and Sian came running out of the bushes, protesting loudly at what was surely a kidnapping. Startled, one of the Welsh crossbowmen released his weapon, and an arrow sailed with deadly precision into Mair's chest. She was dead before she hit the ground.

The children screamed with horror. Derica, struggling for coherency, managed to angle her head around to see what had happened.

"You killed her!" she shrieked. "My God... Mair!"

The knight who held her cursed under his breath, hissing to the knight nearest him. "God's Bones, who released that arrow?"

"I do not know, my lord."

"Find out. And confiscate his weapon!"

"Aye, my lord."

The children were still screaming, crying over their mother's corpse. The knight that held Derica spoke steady orders to another knight.

"Collect the children. Bring them."

"Aye, my lord."

Derica had ceased to struggle. Her body went limp and she cried pitifully, tears for Garren, a few for Mair. She wished she could die, too, retreating into a world of incoherency and darkness. At the moment, she cared naught for her fate. All that mattered was that Garren was gone and her life was over.

The trip back to Pembroke passed in a blur. The knight with the big brown eyes carried her the entire way. A couple of times, she had tried to remove herself from his charger, but he had held her tightly and said little. She had asked about the children and he assured her they were well.

When they finally arrived at Pembroke, Derica was whisked into the keep by a pair of severe looking women. They hustled her into a chamber and shut the door. They chatted endlessly, asking her a myriad of questions, but she shut them out just as she had shut out the knights. She didn't want to talk, or think, or behave even remotely human. When the women stripped her down to her woolen shift, she didn't protest. When the women saw how dirty her shift was, and the skin beneath it, they called for a bath and gently, but firmly, coaxed the shift off of her.

The bath was hot. The women scrubbed her with an enormous sponge and soap that smelled of violets. They even washed her hair with a vinegar concoction and rinsed it out with flat ale. The scents and activity of the bath moved Derica from her numb depression to tears, and she cried with deep grief as the women removed her from the tub, rubbed her skin with oil so it would not crack, and brushed her wet hair. A heavy robe draped her body as maids scurried in and out of the chamber, bringing all manner of surcoats, bodices and shifts for the women's approval. There was apparently nothing of acceptable finery for a lady of her station at Pembroke, but the servants were trying desperately to find something.

Two hours later found Derica with dry hair and a clean body clad in a surcoat of deep blue brocade with a long-sleeved undershift of soft white linen. She had stopped crying for the moment, but her eyes were red and swollen. Truthfully, she didn't have the energy to cry. Everything seemed drained. The numbness had returned and she sat in her borrowed chamber, neither feeling nor seeing. The women had tried to feed her, but she would accept nothing they offered.

The flames of the fire became her friend. She stared into the golden licks, the soft light offering some warmth and physical comfort. She became one with the fire, a few stolen moments where there was no pain, no sorrow, only the warmth and light she craved at the moment. Yet, every so often an errant tear would stream down her cheek and she would dully wipe it away.

Her entire world revolved around memories of Garren, of his deep voice, his gentle laughter, now forever silenced. The fire couldn't soothe away the pain entirely. His death was a crime, she decided. God had committed a crime against her and she would never forgive him for it. Besides, he must hate her. Why else would he bring her such happiness and then abruptly take it away.

There was a knock at the chamber door, rousing her from her thoughts. She had been dreading this moment, for she knew what was to come. The knight who had brought her to Pembroke entered, a long ecru-colored scroll in his hand. He had cleaned up somewhat since their return, no longer wearing his armor. A tunic and leather breeches replaced the chain mail suit. He walked over to where she sat, lingering by her chair as if suddenly uncomfortable in her presence. Derica ignored him, uninterested in whatever he had to say.

"I see that you are feeling better, my lady," he commented.

Derica didn't look up. "I want to go back to Cilgarren."

He knew he needed to be careful with her, unsure of himself. "There is no reason for you to return, my lady."

"There is every reason for me to return. I have friends there that are missing me."

"What friends, my lady?"

"Friends who are in charge of my welfare while my husband is... gone."

"I am assuming charge of your welfare now."

She did look up at him, then, a hateful look on her face. She hadn't the strength to argue with him, her mind a whirlwind of anguish and confusion. Her gaze trailed to the missive in his hand. "You have brought me something. Read it and be done."

The knight looked down at the parchment as if he had forgotten he held it. Truthfully, he had been so captivated by the lady's clean and shining beauty when he entered the chamber, he nearly had. He felt stupid.

The knight promptly rolled open the vellum, his gaze fixing on the carefully written words. Before he could start, Derica interrupted.

"Your name, sir knight."

It occurred to him that he'd not told her. He had never been one for social pleasantries. "Sir Keller de Poyer, my lady. I am the garrison commander of Pembroke Castle."

"Proceed, Sir Keller."

Keller could barely read, though he'd not let on to the lady. He personally had a scribe who both wrote and read his missives. Somehow, he didn't feel right leaving this to the scribe. He read slowly.

"'Be it known this twenty eighth day of September, Year of our Lord 1192, I, William Marshal, Chancellor to King Richard I, Supreme Majesty of the British Realm, do hereby grant to the Lady Derica de Rosa le Mon the marcher lordship of Knighton, and all privileges, lands and wealth related hereto, in honour of the sacrifice her husband, Sir Garren le Mon, has made for the King's cause.'"

Derica sat there as the words sank it. There was no mistaking that the missive was notifying her of Garren's death, but it was as if the notification was secondary to the granting of title and lands. She continued to sit, unmoving, and Keller wondered if she had even heard him.

"He goes on to list your lands," he said. "Hopton Castle belongs to you and the lordship that stretches to the marches on the east, Adforton to the south, and Craven Arms to the north, and includes four towns, two fiefdoms, and about five thousand vassals. Additionally, you have possession of Clun Castle and her lands, although the castle was burned by the Welsh a year ago and is now an abandoned shell. The Marshal is also providing you with your own army of four hundred men, as well as ten thousand gold marks as a dowry."

Still, Derica sat with no outward reaction. Any person in their right mind would have been delirious with joy. Keller was hesitant to say what had to come next.

"He is also providing you with a husband."

Derica looked at him with disbelief, shock, and then anger. It was enough to get her out of the chair.

"I have a husband," she hissed. "I do not want another."

Keller took offense, although he should not have. From the moment he saw her, he had actually been pleased at the thought of acquiring such a beautiful bride, lands and title notwithstanding. He would have taken her with just the clothes on her back. Being somewhat inexperienced when it came to any manner of personal emotion, he matched her anger with some of his own.

"You will have to take it up with the Marshal," he growled.

She was particularly lovely with her fury-colored cheeks. "I intend to, have no doubt." She reached out and grabbed the vellum from him, looking at the scribble as if she could read it. "Who does he demand I marry? Who is this fool?"

Keller's anger cooled to droll resignation. "A knight in rather good standing with some wealth of his own."

"Who?"

"Keller de Poyer."

Derica's eyes widened. "You?"

"Aye," he could read her expression. "And before you go any further, I certainly had nothing to do with this. I was only informed that I was to have a bride two days ago. Do not imagine that it brought me any great happiness to assume this burden."

Rather than explode, Derica seemed to calm. She grasped for her chair, sitting heavily as she absorbed the information. Keller regretted his last few words the moment they left his mouth; he hadn't meant them. The lady looked so pitifully lost at the moment. He wasn't very good with women and right now was a prime example. He attempted to ease her in his own clumsy way.

"I fought with your husband in a few campaigns, my lady," he said quietly. "He was a good man and an excellent knight. I have nothing but the greatest admiration for him and his death saddens me deeply. To be asked to take care of his widow is something of a tremendous honor for me."

Derica closed her eyes, struggling not to cry. When she finally opened them, it was to look at Keller. She took a moment to study his features for the first time; he had short, thick brown hair with some gray mixed into it. His face had been marred by pimples at one time, leaving some scars on the tanned skin. He wasn't particularly ugly, nor was he particularly handsome. He was somewhere in between. He had a big, muscular body and enormous hands, but Derica sensed a gentleness about him. He was fairly soft-spoken and seemed nervous around her. The comparison of him against Garren was inevitable; there truly was no comparison. Garren was a god, and this man was a mortal.

"I will apologize if I offended you, then," she murmured. "You must know that my husband and I loved each other. I do not want another husband."

"That is understandable," he said. "You have only just been told of his death. Please do not hold it against me that I was the one to tell you. It was only by chance."

"I know that."

"When I saw you out on the road, earlier today, I am sorry if I was harsh in addressing you as his widow. I did not know that you were unaware."

"You were not harsh. You do not need to apologize."

He stood there, growing uncomfortable, unsure what to say. He didn't want to leave her alone, but suspected he should. Still, he wanted to reassure her that he would attempt to make as fine a husband as Garren le Mon. Perhaps it would help her grief and uncertainty right now.

"My lady, may I speak?"

"Aye."

He scratched his head before continuing. "Perhaps this is not the right time to say this, but I am not sure if there will ever be a right time, so I must speak." His hands, unconsciously, were cracking knuckles. "I am not Sir Garren, nor could I ever be, but I swear to you that I will never raise a hand to you, nor speak harshly to you, and I will provide you with comfort and gifts and protection as well as, or better than, any man alive. You will never want for anything. Perhaps... perhaps with time, you will grow accustomed to the idea of me as your husband, a poor substitute for Sir Garren."

It was a kind thing to say, gently spoken. Derica could only nod, as she felt the tears coming again. Keller realized he had been expecting a reaction from her, something favorable. But she gave him nothing. Not knowing what else to say, he turned to leave.

"Thank you," Derica whispered. "For your kindness and hospitality, I thank you."

Keller paused, dipping his head graciously in response to her words. He also felt emboldened by them.

"If I were to bring you some food, would you eat it?"

Derica didn't want to give him the kind of encouragement she suspected he was looking for. She refused to even think about it.

"I would like to have the children brought to me," she said. "And perhaps some food for all of us."

A hint of a smile crossed Keller's lips. "It shall be done, my lady."

***

Sian and Aneirin slept with Derica that night in the great bed, and for the next several nights afterward. She would not let them out of her sight. Keller would come every morning as their meal was brought and would attempt to engage her in small talk, which he wasn't very good at. Although Derica could sense his conversational ineptness, she hadn't a greater desire to lead their conversations. So Keller would leave within a few minutes, saying he had duties to attend to, which he did, but it was obvious he was disappointed that his future bride had no interest in him. Derica was never rude, but she wasn't particularly receptive, either. Keller would return two or three more times throughout the day just to see if she required anything, but she never did. At least, not from him.

Whether or not she required anything, Keller saw to it that she had an entirely fitting noblewoman's wardrobe by week's end. The two severe women who aided Derica were the chatelaines of the castle and had set an armada of women sewing garments for Derica and the children. Keller had personally escorted the severe women to the town of Penfro to barter with the merchants for fabric. While the women tended to the dressing needs, he had wandered to the silverworker's hovel and had come away with several lovely pieces of jewelry.

Keller had never bought jewelry in his life and had gone over the top with his first purchase. Either the silversmith had been very persuasive, or Keller had been very weak to resist the sales pitch. At any rate, there were three brooches with different colored semi-precious stones, one necklace with Citrine stone and one with Garnet stone, each necklace with a matching ring, and finally a filigree belt inlaid with pale purple stones that he had sewn into a gown of heavy lavender brocade.

On the guise that they were wedding gifts to his bride, Keller had delivered everything to Derica after sup one evening. He'd simply thrown all of the gowns on the bed and then handed her the jewelry in a great awkward bunch. While Derica stood there with her hands overflowing with silver and stones, Keller gave the children little trinkets he had also picked up on his shopping tour. Sian had a wooden horse and cart and a tiny sword, while Aneirin had a doll. Before they could properly thank him, Keller predictably fled the room.

Stunned with the gifts and his fast disappearance, Derica put the jewelry on the table against the wall and went through the pieces one at a time. Aneirin came to stand beside her, inspecting each item carefully. The little girl had never seen such things. She put one of the necklaces around the doll's neck and Derica smiled her approval. The jewelry was finely made, Derica knew; she had possessed a great deal of it, left behind at Framlingham. This small horde must have cost Keller a sizable amount of money.

She turned to the gowns, lying in a heap upon the bed. She could see at least five different colors of garments. There was a lavender, a pale blue, a deep green, a rich yellow, and a soft red. While Sian crawled on the ground alternately playing with his cart and his wonderful sword, Derica and Aneirin inspected the clothes. They were well made. Since she had come to Pembroke in nothing but peasant rags, Keller had been more than thoughtful to her needs. More than that, he had gone out his way to be kind to her and the children.

Derica fingered the gowns, feeling guilty for the way she was behaving towards him, but she didn't want to give the man any encouragement. Her heart forever belonged to Garren. But that should not prevent her from being nice to Keller, who was doing all he could to make her life comfortable.

It was late when Derica finally put the children to sleep. Sian liked to fall asleep in her arms, so disengaging herself from him when he was finally asleep was something of a tricky effort. She managed to do so without rousing him. The fire in the chamber burned low, giving off a good deal of heat as she silently changed into one of the new gowns Keller had given her.

The soft red surcoat made from finely polished cotton fit her very well over a delicate linen long-sleeved sheath. To it, Derica attached one of the brooches Keller had given her, a silver piece worked into the shape of a flower with a large garnet set deep into it. She then brushed her hair and plaited a long braid, which fell luxuriously down her back.

Looking at herself in the polished bronze mirror, she didn't see the same woman she had known once, the young girl who had run away from Framlingham into the arms of the man she loved. Gazing back at her was someone with the sad maturity to have loved and lost at a young age. If she looked long enough, she could see her broken heart bleeding out all over herself. It was a sobering moment in a week that had been full of them. Depressed, she quit the room.

It occurred to her half way down the hall that she hadn't left her room since her arrival and was somewhat lost in the vast labyrinth of Pembroke. It was a massive place that smelt of dampness. She found the stairs and ended up on the living level, which held the great hall. There was some light and voices coming from the great room, drawing her into it.

Keller was standing by a hearth that was taller than he was. A fire blazed brightly in it. There was a cup in his hand as he spoke softly to a shorter man next to him, his strong features silhouetted by the light. When Keller looked over and saw her standing in the doorway, he nearly dropped his cup.

"My lady," there was concern in his voice as he walked towards her. "Is something the matter?"

"Nay," Derica shook her head. "The children are asleep and I wish to speak with you."

He couldn't set the cup down fast enough or walk quickly enough to her side. "Of course," he gestured to the small room across from the great hall. "We may speak in the solar."

The solar was dark, no fire in the hearth. Keller quickly set to lighting a blaze, but Derica stopped him. "There is no need for that," she said. "I will only take a moment."

"Very well," he stood up, too fast, and dropped the kindling on his boot. Rather than look the fool and reach down to pick it up, he simply kicked it away and pretended not to care. "What did you wish to speak to me about?"

"About your gifts."

"The gowns? Are they not to your liking?"

"They're fine."

"Then the jewelry. You'd rather pick out your own? The silversmith said that garnet and citrine were of the latest fashion. I bought what he suggested."

He was turning into that nervous boy again. Derica put her hands up to stop his chatter.

"The jewelry is lovely, Sir Keller. Absolutely lovely."

He looked confused and relieved at the same time. "I see." He started popping his knuckles again. "Then what did you wish...?"

"If you'd let me get a word in, I simply wanted to thank you for your generosity. You left the chamber so quickly that we did not get the chance."

A twinkle came to his brown eyes. "Oh," he said. "I left because I did not want to intrude. I feel as if I intrude far too much on your time as it is."

It was rather humorous watching the seasoned knight pop his knuckles and shift around nervously. "May I ask you a question, Sir Keller?" she finally said.

"Of course."

"Do I frighten you?"

The twinkle in his eyes grew. "Aye."

"I thought so. But why?"

The man shrugged his big shoulders and stopped cracking his knuckles. "Because... because you're so beautiful, I suppose."

"But why does that scare you?"

He pursed his lips. "I didn't say I was scared. Merely terrified. There is a difference."

He was trying to make a smooth explanation, but it wasn't conveying what he hoped. He was looking befuddled and Derica couldn't help but feel sorry for him.

"Sir Keller," she reached out and put a hand on his arm. "I do not wish to terrify you. I am not the sort to terrify anyone, truly. I am quite approachable under normal circumstances, but this week has not seen normal circumstances. If I have been distant, or even rude, then I am sorry. But my mind is elsewhere. Much has happened."

He was gazing at her with a look on his face like the man who had just been given the greatest gift of his life. "There's no need to apologize, my lady," he said softly. "'Tis only that it seems to me that you and I find ourselves in an unexpected situation and I am simply trying to make it easier for the both of us."

She removed her hand from his arm. The cold of the solar was getting to her as she turned away from him, shivering, and sat in the nearest chair.

"I know you are," she said after a moment. "And I suppose my attitude should be the same. But I am still very much married to my husband, in heart and mind and body, and I cannot give that up."

Keller didn't say anything. After a moment, he left the room, leaving Derica sitting in the cold darkness. She thought she had offended him. Just as she was preparing to leave herself, Keller returned with a heavy woolen blanket and swung it over her shoulders.

"'Tis cold in here and since you will not let me start a fire, perhaps you will let me bring you a blanket."

Derica was touched by his gesture. "You really are too kind, Sir Keller."

He sat on a stool opposite her, his rugged face barely visible in the darkness. "I would be honored if you would simply call me Keller."

That was not too much to ask, and Derica nodded her head in agreement. The silence grew heavy and Keller began popping his knuckles again.

"Is your chamber comfortable?" he began with the idle chatter again because he didn't know what else to talk about. "Should we move the children to their own chamber now?"

Derica shook her head. "I still prefer them with me, thank you." She fell silent again, watching the knight fidget. "Keller?"

His head snapped up as if she had ordered him to attention. "My lady?"

"There is something you can do for me, if you would be so inclined."

"Name it and it shall be done."

"You can find where my husband's body is buried and bring it back to me."

He paused, indecision on his features. But he was a man sworn to obedience and his word was his bond. "If that is your wish, my lady."

Indescribable relief swept over Derica. She hadn't realized what that gesture would mean to her. The thought of Garren's precious remains being within her grasp, something she could reconcile herself to, was almost too much to take. She simply wanted to see him one last time, to say a proper good bye to the man who meant everything to her. Before she could thank Keller, the tears came and she was unable to speak.

He was stricken with her soft sobs. "Have no fear," he attempted to comfort her. "I shall find him. I shall go tonight."

Derica could only reach out and touch his arm again, silent thanks for a deeply meaningful promise. Keller dared to put his big hand over hers in comfort and, feeling that her hand was like ice, took it into his big, warm palm. She was freezing and he gently coaxed her other hand away from her. When he had both of them in his grasp, he rubbed briskly to warm her.

"Do not weep," he murmured. "I will not return until I find him."

She sniffled, her big green eyes overflowing at him. "But how will you do this?"

"I will go to Chepstow. The Marshal will know where he is."

"I do not know how to repay your kindness to me."

He was in deep territory and unsure how to navigate. "Our marriage will be repayment enough. And perhaps a strong son or two."

Derica's smile faded and Keller knew he had said something terribly wrong. "I didn't mean...." he stammered.

She pulled her hands away from him. "I know you did not. Your statement was not unreasonable."

"But I did not mean to...."

"You did not." She stood up, abruptly, and the blanket fell away from her. "I will bid you a good eve, then. And I thank you again for your kindness."

She was to the door before he could stop her. "My lady," he said, almost pleading. "Please do not leave. I did not mean to offend you. I would never knowingly do that."

Derica paused, feeling foolish, feeling overwhelmed. The thought of bearing another man's children had not yet occurred to her. To let this man, no matter how kind he had been to her, touch her in such an intimate fashion made her sick to her stomach. The only man she would ever want to touch her in that manner was dead. She forced herself to look at him, smiling weakly.

"There may be days when I behave abruptly, for reasons I can hardly explain at the moment," she said quietly. "You did not offend me. It is just difficult for me to think of another marriage right now, much less children."

Keller was relieved he had not insulted her. He gave her a lopsided smile. "And you have to ask me why you make me nervous? I live in constant fear to say something that will upset you, and I do not want to do that."

"I realize that, and I am sorry. I shall try to do better."

He looked at her a moment. "I should not want you to do better."

"Why not?"

He tried to put his thoughts into words. "Because if you were grieving for me, I should want the same devotion. I shall not take any measure of loyalty away from Garren le Mon."

Derica thought on that. "Sir Keller, I suspect that you are a truly remarkable man somewhere underneath all of that knightly solemnity."

He smiled, embarrassed. "I cannot say, my lady."

"I can." She flashed him a genuine smile. "Good night to you."

CHAPTER SIXTEEN

"If she fell into the river, there is no knowing how far down stream she is drifted," Emyl said quietly. "You must face facts, Garren. Your wife is dead."

Garren's jaw flexed dangerously. In the great hall of Cilgarren, he stood his ground, unwilling to give in to the resignation the others had. It had been nearly four weeks since Derica's disappearance and, for as much as they had searched, they were convinced she had drowned in the river and her body would not be found. It had been a painful realization for Offa and Emyl, a devastating one for David. Their world had been a dark and dreary place as of late.

"I understand your logic," Garren said steadily. "But if nobody has been located, then there is still hope. I have seen too many incidents of alleged death in my life to be so easily convinced that death has come. Show me her body and I shall believe it."

Emyl cast his son a long look before turning away. He was too old to give in to false hopes. Fergus, however, had been listening to unrealistic expectations for the better part of a week.

"We'll go look for her, you and me," he told Garren. "Perhaps, somehow, she made it out of the water and was kidnapped by peasants. Perhaps she is being held hostage somewhere. Who knows?"

"Nonsense!" Offa snorted. "More than likely, if she made out of the water, she is in the hands of bandits who will..."

A deadly look from Garren stopped him. Fergus smoothed the situation. "There is a possibility she escaped your search," he said. "Garren is like a hound. He'll track her until he finds her."

"What if he doesn't find her?"

It was David's soft question. They all looked at him, the tall, slender man with the haunting dark eyes, knowing how smitten he had been with Derica. He had, so far, looked the most for her out of all of them. Even with her husband returned, the enormous knight with the recent battle scars, he was still feeling her loss and was inadequately hiding his feelings.

"Unless God himself has reached down and pulled her into the heavens, I will find her," Garren growled at him.

No one had the courage to say another negative word. Garren was exhausted from battle, exhausted from riding for days on end, and in no mood to be disputed. He wouldn't even wait to eat and rest, as Fergus had strongly suggested. Finally reaching Cilgarren had empowered him,

194

renewed his resolve to find Derica alive. He was back where he had left her, and he could feel her presence as strongly as if she was standing next to him. Nothing was going to stop him from finding his wife. In a flash of armor and steel, he quit the hall.

Fergus followed him outside, as did the others. Near the kitchens, he slowed to observe the sloping hillside that abruptly disappeared into the river below. The weather had long since worn away any clues that might have told him what had happened to his wife on that fateful day. Still, he inspected the slope, walked among the wild garden, glancing down to the murky riverbed.

"She was here, we think."

Garren turned to Fergus, who was standing very close to the edge of the cliff. The man was looking sadly into the gray waters. He made his way over to the place where Fergus stood and paced around, inspecting the rim.

"Had it been raining that day?"

"It had been raining for weeks."

"So the ground was slippery."

"Verily. Which is why I am more inclined to believe that she did not throw herself into the river as much as she slipped in."

Garren took a long, slow breath, his mind working. "Damn her for standing so close. Too many times did I warn her."

"We all did. She was fearless about it, unfortunately."

Garren was quiet a moment. "The fall itself should not have killed her," he said. "My concern is that perhaps she hit her head somehow and was knocked unconscious."

"And drowned," Fergus was barely audible.

Garren couldn't refute the obvious. He turned away from the cliff, heading back towards the bailey. "It is my hope that we will find out," he said with more determination than he felt. "I intend to comb down river inch by inch until I find something that leads me to believe she is either alive or dead."

"That could take time," Fergus followed him. "If we only had more help."

Garren paused. "Your father and Offa and David have already been through this," he said. "We will use them again to search, as futile as they believe it may be. And..."

"And what?"

Garren suddenly looked thoughtful. "The nearest garrison is Pembroke. You could ride there and ask for assistance."

"Pembroke is held for the Marshal. Won't some of those who serve there know you on sight?"

"Probably."

"If they see you alive…."

Garren put up his hands, moving forward again in search of his horse. "I know, I know. All would be for waste if someone from the garrison saw me and reported back to the Marshal. But they don't know you, and I could direct their efforts through you."

"True enough," Fergus agreed. His steed was nearby and he wearily sought the animal's reins. "Very well, then. I shall ride to Pembroke for help. Perhaps a dozen men or so to cover more ground than you and I can alone. But you need to stay out of sight."

"I will."

"I shall return as quickly as I can."

Garren watched him ride out, mounting his own charger and fighting his exhaustion as he did so. He felt better knowing that aid was coming, hoping he was that much closer to finding his wife. He could only pray it would be soon enough.

***

Derica had never had so many gifts. As if the floodgates of a mythical Aladdin's Cave had suddenly burst open, she had more jewelry and belts and dresses and shoes than she knew what to do with. Keller apparently thought that the best way to ease her grief was to ply her with gifts, and he did so with exhaustive efficiency. Not a day passed that he didn't present her with something soft, shiny, or otherwise. It was becoming an endless parade.

Sian and Aneirin had more possessions than they had ever known to exist, too. Toys, food, clothing was all theirs for the squandering if they wished it. Keller had taken a particular liking to Aneirin, and she to him. Since Derica was distant, he lavished attention on the little girl instead. He wished he could lavish it on Derica, but he knew he had to be patient with her. She wasn't remotely ready for his interest, so he bided his time with the brown-haired little girl. Sian seemed more intent to be Derica's shadow, no matter how much Keller tried to interact with him.

On a morning during her second week at Pembroke, Derica awoke to a bright day and the children playing silently near her bed. They had been up for hours. Yawning, she climbed from the bed, kissed them both, and went about preparing herself for the day. She had always been one to rise and dress immediately, not to lag about lazily.

One of the severe women, whom she had yet to be able to tell apart from one another, brought her warmed rosewater to wash the sleep from her face with. She brushed her teeth with a soft reed brush and rinsed it with a breath sweetener. Pulling off her woolen night shift, she replaced it with a shift of soft lamb's wool. Over that, she donned a long sleeved linen shift of deep blue and a sleeveless surcoat of contrasting pale blue broadcloth. It was some of the less ornate clothing she owned, but highly fashionable and very comfortable.

Her dresser was overflowing with belts and jewels that Keller had given her. The severe servant encouraged her to wear something rich and gaudy to compensate for the plain dress she wore, but Derica pushed her suggestions aside and chose a simple gold cross on a golden chain that hung between her breasts. When the servant attempted to braid her hair in an elaborate style, Derica insisted on one simple braid that draped over one shoulder. Every time the woman tried to dress her up, she would dress down.

The children were ready to go outside and run about. They had been caged in the bedchamber far too long since awakening and were bouncing about like animals. With one child in each hand, Derica ascended to the hall below and was met by the majordomo of the castle, a kindly man named Sims. He ushered her to one of two heavy dining tables that lined the hall of Pembroke and quickly ordered the morning meal delivered. Within a very short time, there was more food than they could possibly eat covering the table.

Derica sipped the boiled water with a hint of rose and apples in it; she didn't like ale for breakfast, which was a common drink. It made her sleepy. She nibbled on a wedge of white tart cheese while the children gobbled gruel with honey. Her mind, for the first time in several days, didn't seem gripped by anguish this morning.

All of the agonizing grief she felt had dulled to a throbbing ache at the moment, but the tears were still close by. They were always near the surface, ready to be released at the slightest provocation. She dare not look at the silver band around her finger; it was a sure-fire trigger, yet she refused to remove it. She was sure she would never be able to.

"I see that you are eating this morning," Keller had come up behind her, silently. "A good sign, my lady."

Derica glanced up into his weathered face, realizing whatever appetite she may have had inexplicably fled. "I suppose it would not be good for me to starve myself to death."

Keller smiled timidly. "May I sit?"

"Of course."

He sat down on the bench beside her, a proper distance separating them. It had been two days since he had promised to go in search of Garren's body and Derica couldn't help but notice he'd not yet left. Every time she saw him, she wondered when he was going to go about fulfilling his vow. Even now, as he sat next to her, she realized her curiosity was turning to bitterness. Perhaps he had no intention of going, after all, and had only agreed to stop her tears.

"I was hoping to see you this morning before I left," he said.

Derica wondered if he had read her mind. "You are leaving?"

He nodded. "I have a long journey to Chepstow before me. I apologize that I did not leave right away, but there were some issues at hand that needed my attention."

She began to feel guilty that she had thought badly of him. "What issues?"

"Nothing to worry over. Local grumblings, 'tis all."

It occurred to her what local grumblings might mean. "The Welsh are planning to attack?"

He laughed softly. "Not so much as that. Besides, they could never breach Pembroke. Our position is so strategic that it would take intervention by God himself on their behalf. But they are unhappy as of late. That is normal. Their moods surge with the moon, it seems, and I find myself in the position of soothing local chieftains."

Aneirin wriggled her way onto Keller's lap, bread in hand. He squeezed the girl affectionately. Derica watched the two of them, thinking that they would all make a fine family one day and feeling torn that she wanted no part of it. She wanted the children, of course; with Mair's death, they had understandably fallen under her care. But Keller seemed more than willing to impart himself as their father and it was that thought she had such difficulty with.

Aneirin suddenly jumped up, with Sian on her tail. They ran over by the great hearth where the dogs were gathered. One mutt had a litter of puppies and the children scooped up happy armfuls of licking tongues and wagging tails. Derica watched them, wishing she could be so happy and carefree. The only time in her life she had ever felt that way was when she had been with Garren. Dear God, she missed him.

The ever-threatening tears filled her eyes and she looked away so that Keller would not see. But he caught the gesture.

"My lady, do not fret," he said quietly. "I shall return as soon as I possibly can. I promised you that I would find Sir Garren, and I shall. Have no doubt."

She wiped her eyes, struggling for control. "I have faith in you, Sir Keller."

"I am glad," he said. "Would you do me the honor, then?"

She looked at him, not sure what he meant. "For what?"

"Escort me to the door of the keep. I would like my last vision of this place as I leave to be your lovely face."

Derica surmised it was the very least she could do. Rising from the bench, she accepted Keller's arm when he offered it. As they proceeded across the hall, a distant horn sounded signaling that a rider had entered the through the main gates. Neither Derica nor Keller spared the noise any heed. By the time they reached the door, Derica glanced up into the blue sky and thought it was an exceptionally lovely day. She decided to escort him down into the bailey because she felt like walking in the sunshine. By the time she and Keller were halfway down the retractable wooden staircase, she glanced up into a familiar face in the midst of the bailey. Derica stopped dead in her tracks.

"Fergus!"

Fergus thought he was seeing a ghost. But no ghost ever looked so lovely. Before he could stop himself, he leapt up the stairs and threw his arms around her. He almost fell, roughly pulling her from Keller's grip. Derica shrieked in delight, which Keller took to be a scream.

The sword came out in the blink of an eye. "To your death, fool," he snarled.

Derica caught the flash of metal. "No!" she cried. "Sir Keller, I beg you! I know him!"

Keller was far too close to slicing through Fergus' neck. He almost nicked him in his haste to stop the blade. Fergus, however, was unaware of anything other than Derica in his arms. He held her out at arm's length, his joyful gaze drinking in every feature.

"Sweet Jesus, it is you," he murmured. "Are you truly alive or am I seeing a delicious spirit, sent to assault my weary senses?"

Derica was weeping with happiness. "I am alive, truly I am."

He looked her up and down, still unbelieving. "You look real enough, I shall grant you," he said joyfully. "You look... wonderful, my lady, just wonderful. But you look so slim. The last I saw you, you had...."

He froze, realizing he was babbling, suddenly aware that the last time he saw her she had the rounded belly of a pregnant woman. He paled as Derica caught his meaning.

"It was not meant to be, not this time," she murmured. Her grip on Fergus tightened. "But they told me of Garren. Dear God, they told me."

Fergus shook off the shock of the lost baby, trying to focus on what she was saying. "They told you of...?"

She nodded before he could finish his sentence. "Did you see for yourself? Did you see him? Is that what you have come to tell me?"

"Tell you...?" Fergus noticed the big knight in his peripheral vision; the man didn't look happy. He struggled not to say too much. "What have you been told?"

"That he is dead." Derica burst into soft sobs. "Oh, Fergus... I simply don't want to live any longer...."

She fell against him for comfort. Fergus could see the big knight turn away as she did so. He had no idea how jealous Keller was, or how hurt, watching Fergus comfort her the way he had wanted to.

She was crying as if her heart was broken into a million fragile pieces. Fergus held her gently. "Take heed, my lady," he murmured in her ear. "All will be well, have no fear."

Derica sobbed. "This damnable war," she suddenly grew angry and pulled herself from his comforting embrace. "This is all William Marshal's fault. He murdered Garren as if he had taken the sword to him personally. And to grant me titles and land in compensation for Garren's loss is... is an insult. It is worse. It is an affront to all that Garren stood for. I would rather have my husband than a bunch of dirt and a pile of cold, heartless rocks."

Fergus was hearing a good deal of overwhelming information, struggling to maintain his composure and piece the puzzle together. So the Marshal knew of Garren's death, as they'd planned. But what the old man did was unexpected if what Derica said was true. There was more going on here than Fergus, or Garren for that matter, could have anticipated.

"But the lowest blow of all is the betrothal," Derica was wiping her nose and eyes. "My feelings are in no way reflective of Sir Keller's worthiness, but I am apparently to become a pawn in William Marshal's game for some inconceivable reason. Why on earth should he...?"

Fergus cut her off then. He had to. Taking her firmly by the arm, he turned her in the direction of the keep. "Perhaps we should speak of this inside, so that all the world cannot hear us." He glanced at the big knight. "My apologies for my dramatic entrance, sir knight. I am Sir Fergus de Edwin, a friend of the lady's husband. Up until a moment ago, I believed the lady dead. You will understand my astonished reaction to her."

It didn't make any sense to Keller, but at the moment, he didn't much care. He was more concerned with Derica's emotional outburst with the blond knight and struggling with the envy it provoked. He tried to be civil.

"I am Keller de Poyer, garrison commander of Pembroke Castle," he said. "You seem to have caught us at an awkward moment, as I was just on my way to fulfill a promise to my lady."

Derica spoke before Fergus could ask. "He is going to find Garren's body, Fergus. He promised me that he would."

Fergus just looked at her, trying to conceal his reaction to two very startling points; the big knight had the same name as the man Derica had mentioned in the same breath as her betrothal. Furthermore, he wasn't at all sure what promise the knight was planning to fulfill, but Derica's statement had answered that. There were wheels in motion here that he was adamant to stop.

"That will not be necessary," Fergus said quietly.

Derica searched his eyes, her tears renewing. "You know where he is, don't you?"

"I do."

"Oh... Fergus," she began to sob again. "Where is he? I must go to him."

Fergus was pleased that he didn't have to lie to her. "I brought him back to Cilgarren."

"Sweet Jesus!" Derica gasped. "I must go there at once, do you hear? At once!"

"You shall," Fergus soothed her. "I shall return you today."

Keller let out a piercing whistle. Fergus looked over to see that he was hailing some men-at-arms in the bailey. Keller quickly issued some orders to them, his intentions obvious.

"There is no need for your escort, sir knight," Fergus said steadily. "I shall escort the lady to Cilgarren myself."

Keller cast him a long look. "Though I thank you for your offer, you will not be offended if I insist on personally escorting my betrothed."

Fergus stood his ground. "I am not offended in the least. But I assure you that I am quite trustworthy and capable of protecting my lady. There is no need to pull you from your duties here at Pembroke."

"I have no other duties as important as my lady's wishes."

Fergus didn't know what to do. Quickly, he ran all avenues in his mind and kept coming back to the same one. He had to tell them both the truth before this grew out of hand. The Marshal be damned; he could see a very bad situation rising. For Garren's sake, he had to spill the truth.

"May we speak inside, privately?"

It was a question directed at both Keller and Derica. Keller's reply was to cast him another long look before turning to lead them inside the keep. Fergus had hold of Derica as they entered the enormous structure. To the right, they entered the solar and Keller closed the doors. It was cold, like a tomb, but Keller didn't light a fire, not even for Derica. He didn't want Fergus to get too comfortable.

Fergus had been given little time to think of what he was about to say, but he knew for certain that he had to be clear. Keller de Poyer was in the more powerful position to refuse him everything. He wisely surmised that he had to plead to Derica; it was the only hope they would have of being allowed to leave Pembroke.

He therefore focused on her. Putting both hands on her arms, he physically braced her for what he was about to say.

"There is something you must know," he said softly, glancing at Keller as he spoke. "Something you both should know."

"What, Fergus?" Derica asked earnestly. "Is it something about Garren?"

Fergus nodded, somewhat ironically. "Yes, love." He could feel Keller tense as he used the affectionate term, but he paid it no heed. He focused deeply into Derica's eyes. "I want you to listen to me and understand every word I say."

"Of course, Fergus."

"What were you told of Garren's death?"

She wasn't sure how to answer. "Simply that he gave his life in the service of the king."

"Nothing else?"

"No," she shook her head, sudden fear in her eyes. "Why? Did something awful happen to him?"

Before Fergus could answer, Keller spoke. "Don't frighten her, de Edwin," he growled. "There are things she does not need to hear."

"I realize that," Fergus said patiently. "I would not dream of frightening or horrifying her. But I must tell you both the truth."

"Truth of what?" Derica insisted.

Fergus chose his words carefully. He pulled Derica to sit in the nearest chair, kneeling before her, his hands holding hers.

"The Marshal was mistaken, love," he said quietly, steadily. "Garren is at Cilgarren Castle. He is very much alive and in excellent health. He has come home to you."

Slowly, Derica's eyes widened. Then they widened more. It seemed to be the only reaction she was capable of. Suddenly, she bolted out of the chair, screaming at the top of her lungs. It startled Keller. Fergus had hold of her hands; otherwise, she would have surely bolted away.

"He is alive?" she cried.

"The ibis has returned. The alligators could not keep him from you, no matter what you have been told."

"The ibis... my God, the ibis!" The old reference sang in her ears once again. "Fergus, take me to him now!"

She was like a wild horse as he tried to keep hold of her. "I will, love, I will. We'll go this instant."

"Alive?" Keller repeated, both confused and stunned. "I don't understand. How could the Marshal have been mistaken?"

Fergus thought to lie at this point, if only to gain Garren and Derica sometime before word reached the Marshal and the man sent his troops after them.

"Garren sustained a flesh wound during the battle of Lincoln," he said. "Whilst having the wound tended, someone stole his armor. We never did find it. It is quite possible that the thief was killed in battle and mistaken for Garren."

Clearly, Keller was shocked. Fergus couldn't tell if he believed him or not. But the more pressing issue was Derica as she continued to shriek. She was pulling him out of the room, insisting that they would leave this very second for Cilgarren. Her face was a mixture of madness and euphoria. But Keller was firmly in the way.

"I don't understand any of this," he persisted, more strongly. "How did you know to find the lady here? Did the Marshal tell Sir Garren she would be with me?"

"Nay," Fergus was being yanked from the solar. "The lady went missing weeks ago. Even now, her husband and others are searching for her. 'Twas Sir Garren who asked me to ride to Pembroke and ask for assistance in our search for her. But, as I discovered, you had already found her."

"Missing?" Keller looked at Derica. "I found her wandering on a road not far from here. She would not tell me what she was doing there."

Through the chaos of Derica's mind, she understood the crux of the conversation. For the moment, it diverted her thoughts of a living Garren. "I fell into the river and nearly killed myself in the process. A peasant woman and her children found me and nursed me back to health. That is why Sir Keller found me wandering on the road." She looked stricken. "The children! Keller, get the children, please!"

Keller started to move, as was natural when doing her bidding, but he just as quickly stopped himself.

"Wait," his voice had returned to a growl. "No one is going anywhere at the moment. Not to Cilgarren, or to heaven or hell until I have satisfactory answers. How do I know this isn't some ploy to abduct my lady? I don't know you, de Edwin. You could be a murderer and thief for all I know."

"But I know him," Derica countered. "I know him well, and he has risked his life for me on many occasions. I have faith in him completely and you will do me the courtesy of trusting my judgment."

Keller was torn, that much was obvious. "You are my betrothed, my lady, and my responsibility until God himself deems otherwise."

"My husband is alive, Sir Keller," she whispered urgently. "God has spoken, can you not understand? He had returned him to me. I am no longer your concern."

Keller's confusion in the entire situation was quickly being overtaken by fury and disappointment. He could hardly believe the devastation he felt. "Not until I see Sir Garren myself," he said quietly, "will I relinquish you."

"Then come and see him," Derica growled. "And bring the children."

Derica matched his stony demeanor; Fergus knew she was determined enough to kill should Keller try to stand in her way. Perhaps the knight sensed that, for he did not stand in her path. He simply stared at her, matching her gaze, feeling emotions he had no right to feel. After what seemed like a small eternity, Derica tore her eyes from Keller and quit the solar, taking Fergus with her. Keller dutifully went in search of children he instinctively knew he was about to lose.

Sian and Aneirin each held a hand when Keller finally returned to the bailey. The children were dressed against the chill, their eyes wide at the commotion of the courtyard. The two severe women had accompanied them, bringing a heavy wrap for Derica. She was already mounted on a small gray palfrey and they fussed over her, making sure she stayed bundled against the cold. Derica took Sian on the horse with her and Keller took Aneirin.

Keller tried not to think about what was happening as he adjusted his reins around the little girl and glanced up at the sky. It looked like it would rain. He wouldn't look at Derica, and she had no interest in looking at him. She never had. She had been kind, as much as she could, but he knew she had never truly been his, betrothal or no. He felt cheated by Garren's appearance, if it was true. He couldn't help wonder if he was riding in to some sort of trap set up by de Edwin and made sure to arm them dozen soldiers accompanying them. A couple of knights were also suited up for the ride. He didn't want to take any chances.

Fergus, for his part, was immensely curious about the two brown-eyed children that Derica seemed to have inherited. They were adorable children, to be sure, but he couldn't help thinking what Garren would say to all of this. He caught her attention.

"Am I to understand that these are the peasant children you mentioned earlier?"

Derica nodded. "Aye. Their mother pulled me from the river and took care of me until I regained my strength. She was accidentally killed. The least I can do is care for her children, and gladly so."

Fergus looked at the little boy, who was now staring at him. "I see," he smiled at the boy. Sian responded by sticking a finger in his nose. "Charming."

Derica loved the children but didn't want to talk about them at the moment. "How is he really, Fergus? Garren, I mean."

"He is very well," Fergus' thoughts were diverted from the children, thinking of Garren and the trouble they would all be in soon. "He is thought of nothing but you, so much so that he has risked all to come home to you."

"What does that mean?"

Fergus didn't want to alarm her. "Nothing," he assured her, sorry he had to lie to her. "Suffice it to say that his joy in seeing that you are alive will eclipse the sun."

Derica smiled at him. "I can still hardly believe. Tell me again, Fergus. Swear it to me."

"I swear to you on my oath as a knight that Garren is alive and well."

Her smiled broadened, her eyes closing briefly as if to dream him yet again. "And you have come to bring me to him again, just as you did those months ago."

"'Twould seem to be my calling in life, to unite the two of you."

Derica didn't want to wait any longer to see her husband and Keller was dragging his heels. She spurred the palfrey toward the gate.

"If we hurry, we can be to Cilgarren in a few hours, don't you think?" she asked.

Fergus moved after her. "Two hours at the most."

Keller had been talking to one of his knights, waiting for the two Welsh crossbowmen he had requested to join the party. When he saw Derica and Fergus already moving towards the gate, he spurred his charger in their direction.

"Hold," he commanded.

Fergus didn't listen; he waited for Derica to respond. She did so by simply turning her head, not stopping her horse.

"Why?" she asked innocently.

Keller was beside her on his red-and-cream beast. "Another moment and the escort party shall be complete. If you will simply wait, we shall...."

"I do not want to wait," Derica told him. "I have waited long enough. I am riding to Cilgarren Castle at this very moment. You may ride with me or not. It makes no difference to me, but if you choose not to, then give me Aneirin so that I may take her."

Keller's expression darkened. He made a surprising move by reaching out and grasping her horse's reins, effectively stopping the animal.

"You're not going anywhere until our escort is complete," he rumbled. "I am assembling my men to protect you and you will do me the courtesy of complying."

Derica's voice was like ice. "You do not want me to go to Cilgarren; that much is clear. Any more attempts to delay me and you shall suffer Garren's wrath in this. Be assured that I will tell him of your reluctance to return me to him."

It threatened to grow ugly. They had come too far to have it turn bad at this moment and possibly cause Keller to forbid either of them to leave Pembroke.

"My lady," Fergus said quietly. "Sir Keller is merely trying to protect you. Your statement was harsh."

Derica had a moment of doubt that what Fergus said was true. Her remorse grew. "I apologize, Keller," she murmured. "I am not quite myself at the moment. My desire to see my husband seems to be taking over all of my senses until I cannot think clearly."

Keller forgave her, of course. "As I told you before, were you married to me, I should expect the same devotion. I can only admire your determination." He glanced over his shoulder at the assembled escort party. "It seems we are complete, after all. By your command, my lady, we shall depart."

He let go of the reins and Derica's little horse danced forward. Sian thought it was great fun and giggled as the horse shook him about. Derica's heart was soaring, her joy in seeing Garren too delirious for words. Two hours seemed like an eternity to wait, but wait she would have to. As they neared the great gates of Pembroke, a familiar figure caught Derica's attention. A small, cloaked wisp of a figure was walking towards her, the face pale and the blue eyes red-rimmed. Derica nearly fell off her horse when she realized she was looking at her maid.

"Aglette," she hissed. "Dear God… Aglette!"

She slid from the palfrey, careful not to take Sian with her. The women fell into each other's arms, the red-haired maid sobbing pitifully. Derica was seized with fear, with surprise, and shook the woman gently.

"What is it?" she demanded. "Why are you here? How did you know…?"

"Your father," Aglette sputtered. "He and his army lie beyond the gates. They sent me in to tell you…."

Her weeping cut her short and Derica was filled with terror. She shook Aglette hard enough to snap her neck. "What are you to tell me?"

The maid struggled to control herself. "That the garrison commander is to turn you over to the army of the Earl of Norfolk, 'else they will raze Pembroke and kill all who stand in their way."

Derica knew her face went pale. She looked at Fergus. "No," she breathed. "Not here, not now. How did they find me?"

Fergus' face was grim. He dismounted his charger and focused on the hysterical maid. "How many men did de Rosa bring?"

Aglette shook her head. "I do not know exactly, my lord. We stopped to pick up more men at Hereford Castle. I heard one of the men say that the total army was about one thousand fools and men."

It was a massive army. Fergus looked at Keller; he would give the man credit, for he held no discernible expression even though his castle was grievously threatened. It took Keller a moment to realize everyone was looking at him, expecting some manner of response. His first response was to look at Derica.

"Your father is the Earl of Norfolk?" he asked, quite calmly.

She shook her head. "He serves Norfolk. He is garrison commander of Framlingham Castle."

"Framlingham?" Keller almost looked amused. "The Marshal neglected to mention that."

Derica knew that she should explain; the man was at risk for reasons he knew nothing of. "My father is loyal to Prince John and Garren is loyal to Richard. We ran off and were married against my father's wishes."

"I see," Keller said." That being the case, your father has come to retrieve you. However, the better question would be, how did he know you were here?"

"I do not know."

"Nor do I," Keller didn't seem overly concerned. "Spies abound, my lady. Even now, I am sure that Pembroke is littered with them."

Derica couldn't tell what he was thinking. "What do you plan to do?"

Keller sighed heavily, dismounting his charger. There was much on his mind; that was evident.

"What do you want me to do?"

"I will speak with my father. But I want you to help Fergus escape to Cilgarren to warn Garren."

"And hold off the horde to buy him enough time?"

To hear Keller say it made it sound as if she was asking the world of him. And he was getting absolutely nothing in return. Fear crept into her veins.

"I know it is an enormous request, Keller, but I would be eternally grateful to you if you would...." she trailed off, feeling stupid and desperate at the same time. "There is no way I can repay you and nothing I can promise you in return other than my undying gratitude. But if you would do this for me, I swear that I would repay the favor if ever I were able. So would Garren."

He smiled at her, ironically. "What I would have from you, you could not repay. I know Sir Garren certainly wouldn't." He didn't look the least bit distressed as he lifted his helm, propping it up on his forehead as if that made it easier for him to think. "Let me assure you that your father cannot destroy Pembroke, no matter how he believes otherwise. I invite him to try. But getting you out of here is another matter altogether."

Derica felt a tremendous amount of relief and fear, one after the other. "Then you will help me?"

Keller looked at her, feeling himself weaken as he stared into the green eyes. "I believe we should think about this for a moment and come up with a plan," he said. "But the first order of business is to close the gates and arm my men. I have a feeling this is going to be a long day."

Derica felt more relieve than she could express. She put her hand on Keller's arm. "Thank you, Keller," she whispered. "From the bottom of my heart, I thank you."

Keller couldn't decide whether he felt noble or like a fool.

CHAPTER SEVENTEEN

Keller didn't waste any time in ordering the timber hoards erected on the battlements. Timber hoards were wooden platforms that extended beyond the tower battlements from the corner of the walls, providing a fighting platform that was well above the heads of the enemy. The entire east wall was protected by a cliff, rendering it a non-threat, and Keller ordered the massive catapult on the northeast tower wall to be loaded and cocked. Normally, the catapult was directed at the sea should the attack come from that direction, but Keller had it directed at the northwest towards the trees that would undoubtedly shield the de Rosa army.

The story Aglette gave Derica was a sad one; Bertram had received a message that Derica was at Pembroke almost three weeks prior, but she couldn't say who had sent the missive. Bertram, contrary to his nature, had spent a day and a night drinking in indulgent self-pity until he finally made the decision to march on Pembroke. More than anything, he wanted his daughter home. He didn't care about Garren le Mon, revenge or reckoning; all he wanted was his only girl-child home where she belonged. He had missed her terribly, and her absence cut at him like a knife. Knowing how well she might not respond to him, he commandeered her servant and childhood friend to march with the army and relay his terms of her surrender.

Derica had cried at the tale. She loved her father very much. The situation at their parting had been difficult for her, but she had been overwhelmed with her desire to be with Garren. She still was. Nothing Aglette told her could take that away. She was angry with her father for so many reasons that she couldn't seem to pick just one.

It was late in the day when Derica sent Aglette back to her father with the message that she wished to negotiate. She retreated to her chamber with the children and removed the simple clothing she wore in favor of something more elaborate. She thought that, perhaps, if her father saw her good fortune and good health that he would not be so inclined to remove her from a situation that obviously agreed with her. She wanted to present a strong, collected front.

She was nervous. Everything seemed to hinge on this day and what would be said. She dressed in a sheath of the softest white linen and topped it with a heavy brocade surcoat in rich green. The full skirt swept the floor and gold thread in designs ran throughout. The bodice was laced tight, giving her a glorious figure. Around her neck she wore a necklace of pale cut emeralds that Keller had given her, and her long hair was pinned at the nape of her neck and secured with a golden web. She made an absolutely stunning sight. She only hoped her beauty would dazzle them if her courage would not. The tension was rising and the stakes were enormously high.

Fergus knocked on the door and she let him in. He had been with Keller in the courtyard, discussing his retreat from Pembroke. One look at Derica and he found he had never seen anything quite so beautiful. It was enough to cause him to impulsively take her hand and kiss it.

"You know," he said, "if Garren saw me do that, he would run me through. In fact, I am not so sure how He is going to take any of this."

"What do you mean?"

"You, here, living in the same keep with a man who is not your husband."

He said it rather dramatically, wagging a finger at her. She knew he wasn't serious, attempting in his own annoying way to lessen a tense situation.

"Fergus, may I remind you that I slept next to you on the ground for several days and you were not my husband. What makes this any different?"

"Garren doesn't know about that one."

"He will if I tell him."

"You wouldn't dare."

"If you tell him anything other than the truth about this situation, you can be assured that I will tell him the story of our flight from Framlingham in a far more impressive fashion. It will not reflect well on you."

Good-natured threats were about. Fergus snickered at her. "On a serious note, I had a bit of a chat with Keller down in the bailey. The man opened up surprisingly well after he got over his envy of me. It seems that he is quite smitten by you and those children."

"He'll get over us. He'll have to."

"That's a rather cold attitude, don't you think?"

She looked puzzled. "What would you have me say? I was betrothed to the man by force. I have no feelings for him other than gratitude."

"Make sure he knows it. He is risking much to help you."

The point was taken. Derica changed the subject. "How are you getting out of here?"

"Keller is going to lower me over the east wall while you speak with your father. I can escape on the sea side while the army is occupied."

Derica's expression turned wistful. "I wish I could go with you, but it is better if I don't. The last thing we need is to have the army track you and I back to Cilgarren, and there is no reason to believe that they won't. My father won't be made a fool of again."

"You should stay here, anyway. I shouldn't like to think of some mishap befalling you as we flee back to Cilgarren. Leave it to Garren to figure out a way to get you out of here without risking your life fleeing from your father again."

"Agreed. Besides, I cannot leave the children."

"A noble thought, especially since I understand how badly you wish to be with your husband."

Her expression turned wistful at the thought. "How long will it take you to reach Cilgarren?"

"Unless I find a horse, it should be at least seven or eight hours. I can run fast, but it is still several miles away."

Derica had to be realistic. "Then let us hope you find a horse so you don't run yourself to death before you get there."

Fergus could only nod in agreement; he wasn't keen on running the full thirty miles to Cilgarren.

"Hold off your father as best you can. Garren will think of something."

They stood there a moment, a silence filled with uncertainty. There was so much to say in this fragile situation but neither of them knew where to start. Sian left his cart and horse over the corner, coming to stand beside Derica. He gazed up at Fergus, the big man with the bright blue eyes. It was the first time the child had dared to as much as look at him.

"You are a knight?" he asked Fergus.

Fergus smiled gently. "I am, little man."

From behind his back, Sian brought out the small wooden sword that Keller had given him. He held it up for Fergus to see. "I have this."

Fergus pretended to examine it. "So I see. A fine weapon," he said, and Sian lowered it. "What name do you answer to, little man?"

"Sian," he child whispered.

"Sir Sian of the Dark Woods," Derica reminded him, smiling.

Sian grinned at her, embarrassed, pushing his face into her skirt to hide. Aneirin wandered over, not wanting to be left out. She, too, had not had the courage to look at the strange man, but her brother emboldened her. Fergus studied both of the children.

"Garren will undoubtedly feel the loss of the child you carried," he said quietly, "but I can almost assure you that these two moppets will help ease his pain. Perhaps they have been left to you for a reason."

Derica looked at him, surprised. "Garren knew about his child?"

"I told him."

She felt sad, trying not to dwell on what could not have been helped. "I can hardly wait to hold him again, Fergus," she murmured. "When you see him, give him something for me."

She reached up and kissed him on the lips, something so soft and sensual that Fergus lost his balance. But he knew it wasn't a kiss directed at him; it was full of warmth and love and longing for Garren. He could feel all of that and more. It made his heart pound as he gazed back at her.

"I understand your meaning perfectly," he muttered. "But you can wait and give that to him personally. And I swear that you shall."

They left the severe women with the children. With a silence filled with apprehension and determination, Fergus escorted Derica down to the bailey. There were soldiers everywhere, prepared for battle, their grim faces set. Derica tried not to look any of them in the eye, fearful that they would accuse her of condemning them to their fate. All of this was because of her. Keller saw her from the battlements and descended the stairs in the northwest tower down to the ward.

"Your father and two men are waiting just outside the gates," he told her, then looked at Fergus. "One of my men will lower you over the west wall. He'll keep watch there for your return with Sir Garren. 'Twill be the easiest way in and out of the castle."

"Excellent," Fergus nodded. With the plans solidified, there was nothing more to say and he looked at Derica. "Good luck to you, my lady."

"And to you, Fergus."

One of Keller's knights went off with him, moving to the eastern wall with plans to carryout. Keller, with a deep sigh he hoped she didn't see, held out his hand. It would probably be the last time he would be able to do so. When she put her warm palm in his, he stole a split second to enjoy a feeling that would very quickly leave him.

"Ready?" he asked.

"Ready," she replied.

He took her to the outer concentric wall facing east. The de Rosa army lay beyond, like locusts on the land. It would have been foolish to open the gates and lower the drawbridge, even during the course of a negotiation. It left Pembroke too vulnerable. He continued to hold her hand until they reached the top of the battlements of the great gatehouse. Nervous, feeling slightly ill, Derica looked to the ground below.

In the dusk, she could see her father, her Uncle Lon and her Uncle Alger. They were atop their chargers, clad in colors of Norfolk. It was enough to bring tears to her eyes. She hadn't realized until that moment how much she had missed them. Keller stood there, watching her, waiting for her to summon both courage and composure.

"I am here, Father," Derica called from above.

Three helmed heads snapped up. Bertram removed his helm, his face as naked with emotion as Derica had ever seen. It took all of her self-control to keep from turning sentimental.

"Derica," her father drank in the sight of her. "So you truly are here. Though we had hoped, I did not truly believe."

"Aglette told me of your demands."

"I only wish you home and safe, daughter."

"I am home and I am safe. You must understand that I have no wish to return to Framlingham with you. I have my own life now."

Bertram was quiet a moment, reflecting on what he was going to say next. The conversation was moving faster than he'd hoped; it had been his wish to move slower, to play on her sentiment, before moving forward with demands. But the Derica that faced him was unwilling to entertain even the slightest pleasantries. He had to admit that he was not surprised.

"I know that le Mon is dead," he said. "I also know that William Marshal plans to marry you off to some knight, someone I know nothing of. At least I knew something of le Mon."

"You knew something of him, yet you showed him as little respect as you would the lowliest serf." Derica could feel herself harden. "How dare you show so little regard for the man I loved."

"It is my duty to protect you. I believe I was attempting to do that."

"As you can see, I do not need protecting. I am safe, healthy and reasonably content. Garren took the best of care of me, and my future husband is continuing the tradition. It is my wish that you return to Framlingham and leave me to my new life."

Bertram's stubborn streak, seen so strongly in his daughter, came forth. "I can promise you a wonderful life at Framlingham. Norfolk has graciously arranged a betrothal that will promise you comfort and security the rest of your life. I have met and approve of this man."

Derica thought it ironic that she had more than her share of betrothals now that Garren was presumed dead. "Who is he? A mercenary with plenty of money and no political connections?"

"The nephew of the Duke of Savoy, Alessandro Donatello Ettore di Savoy. He is very wealthy and well-connected in Rome."

Derica was silent a moment. When she finally spoke, it was with bitterness.

"You do not want me to marry a man of my choosing, but a man of your choosing so that you may save your foolish pride." She shook her head, sadly. "Go home, Father. Go home and forget you ever had a daughter."

"Derica, please," her father pleaded. "I only desire what is best for you, truly. By running away with le Mon, you severely limited your choices of a mate. Savoy is an excellent match and willing to overlook your female indiscretions."

"Go home," Derica exploded at him. "I have no desire to be swept under the rug because you are ashamed of me. If I had it to do over again a thousand times, I would do it the same way every single time. Nothing you can say will change how I feel about Garren."

"You're tired. You have been running too long, without the comforts of home and family. I can forgive your mistake, but I cannot forgive blind stupidity. Come home with me now, please, before any more damage is done."

It was like talking to a wall. "I realize this is foreign to your thinking and God forgive me to saying this to you, but this is a battle you have lost, Father. With all of your wealth and strength, you could not win against me or against Garren. You must understand that."

"Derica, listen to me. I..."

Derica didn't hear the end of the conversation; she had turned away from the wall, in tears and anger. Keller chipped off commands to his sergeant before following her. He took hold of her elbow, helping her down the stairs so that she would not trip in her heavy gown. When they reached the bottom, she was wiping her face, struggling to regain her composure.

"I fear I have put Pembroke in a bad situation," she apologized. "My father will lay siege, of that I am sure. If you want to lower me over the west side and let me take my chances, then I understand."

Keller watched her, every gesture, and every move like fluid poetry. She was graceful and ladylike even in turmoil.

"'Tis been a while since I have tasted battle with the English," he said. "Let your father attack if he wants to. Frankly, when the Welsh catch wind of a battle, it may very well anger them and your father could find himself fighting on two fronts. I will wager your father is in a good deal more danger than Pembroke is. We can hold out."

He sounded so sure. Derica was moved by his chivalry. "You are a good man, Keller. I want you to know that if Garren was not alive, then I should have been very proud to be your wife."

"Then never have I been more tempted to commit murder."

He meant it as a joke. Derica smiled at his attempt, worried over the fate of Pembroke and praying that Fergus would reach Garren to deliver the news. So much could happen to ruin all she hoped for. Keller sensed her distress and took her by the elbow.

"Come," he said softly. "I would have you retreat to the keep so that I may accept your father's invitation to dance."

"Invitation to dance?"

"Battle is like a dance, carefully planned, carefully executed. It all depends on who will lead and who will follow."

She thought on that. "An interesting comparison. I have been around knights my entire life and have never heard it put quite that way."

He took her to the steps of the keep. "There is one thing your father doesn't know about my dancing skills, however."

"What is that?"

His expression took on a shadow of dark determination. "I can trip a partner in that careful choreography. He'll hit the ground and lay there, dazed and vulnerable, before even realizes he has fallen."

Derica hesitated. "Keller," she said softly. "This is my father. I do not wish him... killed if it can be helped. I just want him to go away."

"I understand and shall do my best to accommodate your wishes."

She smiled in thanks. With nothing more to say to a man she was deeply grateful to, she impulsively leaned over to kiss him gently on the cheek. Keller grasped her face before she could pull away and covered her mouth with his own, overwhelming her with his power and desire for a flash of a moment. When he released her, it was as quickly as he had taken her. Derica stumbled back, her eyes wide at him. Keller looked equally surprised but managed to shrug weakly.

"I had to know what I would miss."

It was as much as an explanation as he could give her. Derica, having no reply, went up the stairs to the keep and disappeared inside. Keller stood there, watching until she vanished.

He probably would have been better off if he'd not kissed her, for his own sake.

***

It had started raining again the moment Fergus left Pembroke. It had been rather harrowing being lowered over the western wall into the sea cliff below, but they had intentionally waited until low tide so he wouldn't be swept away by the pounding surf. Still, he was wet and cold by the time he slipped along the cliffs and beaches to the north before daring to make his way back up onto the land.

It was dark as he made his way inland, racing through the shadowed landscape as fast as his freezing legs would carry him. With the cloud cover, there was no moon by which to see. More than once he tripped over something, muffling his curses as he stubbed a toe or whacked a knee.

Fergus had always had a knack for physical activity and running did not tire him easily, but the conditions were cold and wet and he could feel his muscles tightening after a few miles. Pushing on at the pace he was, he reckoned that it would take him between seven and eight hours to reach Cilgarren, thirty miles to the northeast. However, if he kept crashing into things in the dark, no telling how much longer it would take, if he made it at all. Settling himself down into a rhythm, he moved along at a steady pace.

He was glad when the rain eased. The supper hour came and went because his stomach was rumbling and it was never wrong. He kept running, unable to tell the difference now between the sweat rolling off his body and the blobs of rain still pelting him. On the outskirts of Jeffreystown, he slowed his pace, thinking now would be a good time to borrow a horse. It was by sheer luck that he passed near a tavern, the occupants barricaded in for the night. There was a stable behind the tavern and he silently made his way to it. It was pitch black inside when he opened the door, careful not to wake the lad sleeping just inside. The boy was snoring. Keeping his eyes on the lad, Fergus took the nearest horse he could find, good or bad or indifferent, and quietly led it from the stall.

It was a hairy brown steed, fairly well fed. Fergus took a rope hanging on the side of the fence and fashioned a bridle out of it. Slipping it over the horse's ears and nose, he leapt onto the animal's back and inaudibly walked it from the barn and through the grass. When he reached the trees near the road, he spurred the animal into a run.

He reached Cilgarren by midnight. Unable to cross the destroyed drawbridge on the horse, he tethered the animal and plunged into the muck-filled ditch, climbing up on the other side and into the gatehouse. He raced across the outer bailey and into the inner bailey. Suspecting Garren would be in the great hall, he barreled into the cavernous room and shouted for his friend. In a moment's breath, he sensed a body behind him and whirled in a start.

Garren's blue eyes glittered at him in the light of the dying hearth. He had a dagger in his hand, aimed at Fergus' midsection.

"Christ, Fergus," he hissed, lowering the knife. "I heard you coming. I thought we were being raided."

Fergus put both hands on Garren's massive arms, bracing him for the news to come. "Garren, I found her."

Garren dropped the knife in shock. "Is she...?"

"She is alive and well at Pembroke Castle."

The information was coming too strong, too fast. Garren nearly choked on the breath in his lungs, wanting to shout his joy but unable to form a coherent thought. After making a gagging sound in an attempt to speak, he settled for a snort of pure relief.

"Thanks be to God," he breathed fervently. "I can hardly believe it. I thought surely...."

Fergus cut him off. "There is no time for your happiness, my friend. There is far more to the tale."

He could see Garren stiffen. "What is it?"

Fergus didn't know where to begin. But he knew one thing; they had to go to Pembroke at that very moment.

"Get your horse," he shoved Garren towards the door. "I shall tell you everything on the way."

"You will tell me now."

"I can't tell you everything now. All I can tell you is that it is a matter of life and death to go and retrieve your wife at this very moment."

Garren froze. "Is she in danger?"

Fergus could see that Garren was going to be difficult until he had some answers. He quickly tried to surmise the situation.

"Her father is laying siege to Pembroke as we speak. He wants his daughter back."

"De Rosa?" Garren wondered how much worse this could get. "How did he find her?"

"I don't know," Fergus managed to get him out into the bailey. "But suffice it to say that he knows. And he is there. You must go and retrieve your wife."

Garren was on the move. Offa and David, having heard the noise, were up and apprised of the situation. David ran for the horse so Garren could don his armor. Offa went to get Emyl. There was excitement in the air, and anxiety. Garren knew it was bleeding out of every pore of his body; his mind was swimming, his limbs shaking as he strapped on his protection. It was difficult to focus.

"She is well, then?" he asked as he slapped at a fasten on his breastplate.

"Very well."

"How did she get to Pembroke?"

Fergus helped him with the heavy armor. "The story of her trip to Pembroke is amazing. Apparently, it was as we surmised. She did not throw herself off the cliff as much as she slipped and fell. As she tells the story, she drifted down the river and by sheer fortune washed ashore. A peasant woman and her children found her and took care of her."

Garren absorbed the information. "I cannot tell you how happy I am to hear this," his voice was husky with emotion. "Although I insisted she was still alive, I must admit that I did not believe it. God has been looking out for her."

"Indeed he has, for the both of you."

"But how did she end up at Pembroke?"

Fergus cocked an eyebrow. "Here is where the story grows complicated. As I understand it, William Marshal, wracked with guilt over your death, has granted Lady le Mon lands and titles in reward for your services."

Garren stopped, mid-strap. "So the Marshal knows of my death," he said it almost thoughtfully. "It is as we planned, then."

"There is more," Fergus went on. "Now that Lady le Mon is a wealthy, titled woman, it is logical that she would be in need of a husband for protection and equal status."

Garren's blood turned cold. "What husband?"

"The Marshal betrothed her to Keller de Poyer, garrison commander of Pembroke Castle. De Poyer, rightfully so, was en route to Cilgarren to retrieve his bride when he happened across her and her peasant saviors upon the road. If there was ever so strange a coincidence, Garren, that was it. Naturally, he took her back to Pembroke, where she is at this very moment."

Along with a myriad of other emotions he had experienced this day, now he was dealing with jealousy and possessiveness.

"How in God's name did he know she was at Cilgarren?" he returned to securing his armor, furiously and quickly. "And how did the de Rosa's know she would be at Pembroke? I do not understand that bizarre forces at work, either for or against us."

Fergus shook his head. "I do not know, either. There are some elements to this tale that make no sense at the moment. Perhaps they never will."

Garren forced the most difficult question he had ever had to ask. "They... they didn't marry, did they?"

"Nay. Derica has kept him at arm's length, much to his disappointment. De Poyer is quite taken with her, and he has been quite good to her. Before you go riding in there to slay the man for showing attention to your wife, you should consider thanking him instead. He has been remarkably gallant."

Garren didn't know what to feel. "How is that?"

"He is fighting off the de Rosas and he helped me escape to come and tell you everything. That should be quite enough."

The last piece of metal that Garren collected was his sword, massive and lethal. He looked at it, thinking that he would soon be raising it for the greatest cause he had ever known. Fergus saw the deadly gleam to his eye as he spoke.

"Not hell nor William Marshal nor the de Rosas will keep me from claiming what is rightfully mine," he growled. "Fergus, I swear to you, by the time this night is through, I shall have my wife. If I do not, it is because I was killed trying."

Fergus could see a recklessness about him that was frightening. "You have come too far to die," he said firmly. "Derica would never recover. She went for weeks thinking you were dead and it nearly destroyed her. For you to die within sight of her would be too much for her to bear. You must think of her, Garren."

"She is all I think of."

"Then temper yourself. We need your cold logic, not your fury."

Garren's jaw ticked. There was too much happening for him to be rational at the moment. Without another word, he and Fergus went back into the inner courtyard where surprise met them; Offa and Emyl, dressed in their ragged armor and weapons, stood silently in wait. Garren eyed them as he approached.

"Where do you go?" he indicated their dress.

"With you," Emyl said steadily. "You will need our help."

They were old knights and due their respect. Garren tried to be careful in his reply.

"Although I am most grateful for your offer, I fear this is a job for me alone. Four of us would be too many and not enough, all at the same time."

"But there is an army in wait for you, Garren," Offa said. "You must have aid."

Garren couldn't help but think how pathetic they looked, though noble were their intentions. The de Rosa knights would cut them to ribbons.

"Gentle knights, I am riding to reclaim my wife. I must do this alone. Pray that you understand and are not offended."

Offa shrugged. "We were obligated to offer. We are knights, after all."

"And your loyalty is appreciated. But for now, I need you here to shore up Cilgarren for a de Rosa attack. If I am successful in retrieving Derica, it is quite possible they will follow us here in their zeal to kill me and take back their daughter."

It was an honorable duty requested of them, and a necessary one. Emyl was perhaps more disappointed that Offa was; there was a time when he lived for a good fight. But he forced down his disappointment.

"We shall be ready, Garren. Godspeed to you."

Garren laid a hand on the old man's shoulder as he walked away, glad they understood, now better able to refocus on what he must do. By the time he reached his charger, he was quivering with the anticipation of seeing Derica again. It seemed like a dream he'd held so closely to his heart that she was nearly nebulous, like a ghost. He could remember the smell of her, the taste of her, but the feel of her soft flesh in his hands was slipping from his memory. It had been too long. The more he struggled to keep the memory, the further it moved away from him. His whole being cried out for her.

It had been less than an hour since Fergus' arrival at Cilgarren. In the dark of night, Garren and Fergus were back on the road, riding southwest to Pembroke.

CHAPTER EIGHTEEN

Bertram de Rosa unleashed hell.

Keller, a man who was not easily impressed with battle tactics, had to admit he was somewhat respectful of not only Bertram's cunning, but of his power. The maid that had come with de Rosa's terms had not exaggerated when she had said the army carried around one thousand fools and men. It had to be at least that, if not more. But Keller was ready for them.

The first phase of the battle had consisted of archers, aimed high at close range so that they sailed up and over the outerwall of Pembroke but had less luck breaching the inner wall because of its distance from the outerwall and the great gatehouse. Because the archers were so close, they were in range of Keller's Welsh archers, the finest bowmen in the world. After Bertram's first volley, Keller let loose with his own barrage that effectively sent Bertram's archers running for cover. But it had been a shrewd move on de Rosa's part, designed to give Keller an overabundance of confidence and invite the hope that he would follow it up with something foolish.

But Keller held his confidence in check as he watched the de Rosa archers scatter; it was tempting to want to chase them, but he suspected a man as experienced as de Rosa would not have made such a foolish mistake. He had been correct; a few moments later, he was glad that he had restrained himself. Parting the trees as they moved towards Pembroke were two massive siege towers being pulled by teams of oxen. Keller had been momentarily surprised; so had his men up on the wall. All eyes were fixed on the siege towers that were as tall as the outerwall, lumbering steadily towards them. Once the shock wore off, Keller snorted. Then he applauded.

But his jovial mood was short lived. He knew they were in for a serious siege. He set his archers on the outer wall battlements, taking aim at the oxen pulling the siege towers. Rather than try to kill the beasts, he ordered his men to take out their legs. It was careful hunting and by the time the siege towers came to within several feet of the moat, more than half of the teams on both towers were crippled and the remaining oxen were panicking.

The de Rosa men cut the injured animals loose and took up the pulling themselves, creating gangs of men that began to inch the towers forward again. Keller and his men watched as the giant towers inched closer; he seriously wondered how they were going to bring the siege engines close enough to the castle walls to breach them. The castle was protected on three sides, leaving the fourth side heavily fortified with ditches and the great gatehouse. If Bertram seriously had it in his mind to penetrate Pembroke, then he had his work cut out for him. Keller was very curious how the man was going to accomplish it.

But he wasn't so fascinated that he wasn't focused on the castle as a whole. He had a heavy concentration of men on the south side of the castle, but he had the west, north and east sides covered as well. He had been fighting against the wily Welsh too long to be fooled into thinking that a frontal assault was all Bertram would attempt. He kept the entire castle under vigilant watch.

As the siege towers drew closer, Keller had lost his curiosity on Bertram's tactics. In a sharp command to his Welsh archers, he had them concentrate on taking out the gang of men now pulling the siege towers. Soon enough, Bertram lost many men to the archers. But there were more to take their place. As many as Keller would order taken out, Bertram was there to replace them.

And so the deadly dance continued.

***

Holed up in her luxurious bower, Derica could hear the shouts and screams from the battle. The noise and stench seemed to waft upon the wind in deadly breezes, filling all of Pembroke with tension and fear. The children played on the floor near the hearth, not entirely oblivious to what was going on but not particularly understanding it, either. Derica was thankful they were too young and too naïve to understand the severity of the situation.

Sian seemed to be fascinated with the knights on the walls but Derica kept urging him away from the window and back to his toys. He wanted to know why he could not go outside and fight with Sir Keller, something that was rather tricky to explain without insulting his fighting abilities. Derica assured Sian that Sir Keller was quite capable of defending the castle without him and she further explained that Sir Keller had left him with the women to protect them should the castle be breached. That seemed to pacify the little boy, who went back to his cart and horse, wondering aloud if he was going to get to use his sword today.

As the hours dragged on and the day turned into night, Derica became increasingly uneasy. Changing out of the fine surcoat she had worn to greet her father, she put on a simple surcoat with a deep neckline, the color of violets. Pulling her hair into a single braid, she wound it up at the nape of her neck to keep it out of her way, emphasizing her lovely neck and shoulders.

But she wasn't thinking on how lovely she looked as she moved to the lancet window that overlooked the outer bailey; she was thinking of her father and brothers fighting to gain her, and of Keller fighting to protect her. There was increasing guilt over the man who would never receive her love or affection yet was more than willing to sacrifice himself. But she was mostly thinking of Garren. She wondered if Fergus had reached him yet.

The night wore on and so did the battle. Derica had given up trying to sleep as she sat vigilant watch over the slumbering children. The severe women had taken up station in a small servants' alcove that adjoined Derica's chamber, sitting in a frightened huddle, not moving from the stone bench built into the wall. As the battle dragged on and dawn began to approach, Derica found an excuse to leave the children in their care as she left the chamber, taking the stairs quickly to the main level of the keep.

Fortunately, the wooden stairs leading into the keep had not been retracted or burned to prevent the enemy from storming the keep. Gathering her skirts, Derica rushed outside, ignoring the soldiers calling to her. In her deep violet surcoat, her skin was pale and porcelain in the early morning hours as the sun and fog began to blend.

Breath coming in great puffs in the cold dawn, she made her way to the inner gatehouse but the soldiers on the battlements refused to open it for her. They had the inner ward bottled up tightly. Frustrated, she went to mount the stairs to the wall and ran straight into Keller.

He looked weary and stubbled, his dark eyes intense upon her. He grasped her by the elbow.

"What are you doing out here?" he asked. "Is there trouble in the keep?"

Derica shook her head. "Nay," she replied. "Everyone is sleeping. I came to see if my husband has arrived yet."

Keller's gaze moved over her, the way she had her hair pinned back and the gentle slope of her neck and shoulders. She looked exquisite, more exquisite than he had ever seen her. Her words, although reasonable, cut at him; the more time he spent with her, the easier it was to pretend that they would be together when all of this was over. He knew that was not the case but, for the sake of his morale, he did not want to think on it. Her words had rudely reminded him.

"He has not," he replied, trying not to sound bitter. "Return to the keep and rest. I will let you know when Garren arrives."

He was trying to gently push her back towards the keep but she resisted, finally breaking his hold on her elbow.

"I do not want to return to the keep," she said staunchly, cutting him off when he attempted to insist. "Keller, if you were in my position and waiting for the arrival of someone you were told was dead, someone you loved very much, would you be able to remain calm? I cannot rest and I cannot remain calm. I want to be on the walls and wait for Garren."

Keller's sense of hurt was increasing. "You cannot wait upon the walls," he said flatly. "Your father is shooting arrows over the walls and I do not want to take the chance that you will be hit. Go back inside."

He seemed gruff; Derica couldn't really blame him but she didn't want to return to the keep. She reached out and grabbed his hand as he tried to shove her back.

"Please," she begged softly. "Please let me stay out here. Just for a short while. I promise that I will not be any trouble."

His expression grew frustrated. Just as he opened his mouth, a shout came from the western wall. Derica wasn't sure what had been said but Keller suddenly bolted.

Derica ran after him and followed him up the narrow tower stairs, taking two at a time, before emerging onto the narrow wall walk. There were dozens of soldiers and two additional knights, armed to the teeth, all peering down into the river below.

It took several moments before two heads could be made out, swimming the cold river in the early dawn hours towards the castle. Keller hadn't realized that Derica was next to him, heart in her throat as she strained to identify the swimmers. But it didn't take a genius to deduce who would be making their way across the swift, silty river towards the castle; it was the same path Fergus had taken when he had left. It would only make sense that he was retracing his steps.

Before Keller could clearly identify the shapes in the muddy river, he began waving a big gloved hand towards the great gatehouse on the south side of the castle.

"Ready the archers," he boomed. "Start launching everything we have at them. Keep their attention away from this wall."

The two knights and about a dozen soldiers ran to do his bidding as the orders were shouted down the line and across the castle. In short time, the archers were launching great flaming long arrows over the walls and into Bertram's front lines. The two siege engines that had been threatening for most of the night remained on station about thirty feet from the walls, because none of Bertram's men were brave enough to attempt moving them towards the walls again. All who had tried had been cut down or otherwise injured by de Poyer's defense. Now, no one attempted to go near them as they all dove for cover.

With the main gatehouse alive with a renewed offense, Keller snapped orders to the men remaining around him.

"Lower a rope," his voice was quick and controlled. "Get ready to pull them up."

Derica was still hovering over the side of the wall, watching as a figure she recognized emerged from the river. She would have known that tall, powerful form anywhere. Joy at the confirmation surged and forgetting herself, she suddenly waved her arms and screamed.

"Garren!" she cried.

Startled, Keller ran at her and threw her in a bear hug, pulling her away from the wall. Derica struggled violently against him.

"Are you mad?" he hissed. "Do you want to attract your father's attention?"

Her initial fury at being grabbed morphed into terror. She immediately stopped struggling.

"My God," she breathed. "I... I am so sorry. I did not think."

Keller gazed into her beautiful eyes, his thoughts moving to those not of battle. He was suddenly thinking of the woman in his arms, her soft lips, and the marriage that would not take place. It would be so easy to allow le Mon to fall from the rope or succumb to de Rosa's attack. But he simply couldn't do it. As quickly as he grabbed her, he released her and returned to the wall where his men were lowering a fat, scratchy rope.

Derica hovered back out of the way, watching the men work the rope and praying she hadn't, in her zeal, attracted unwanted attention. It had been stupid in hindsight; she knew that. But she was so thrilled to see her husband that her excitement had gotten the better of her.

Quietly, she wandered to the edge of the wall walk again, peering over the side and seeing Garren and Fergus at much closer range. They were both sopping, scrambling up the embankment that led to the tower. Thrilled, Derica clapped a hand over her mouth so she wouldn't make any noise. She began jumping up and down, hand over her mouth, as far below, Garren reached for the rope. He was so close she could almost taste him and her desperation to touch him, feel him, was palpable.

But horror struck as a high-pitched wail suddenly filled the early morning air. Derica saw Garren duck, realizing that someone had launched an arrow at him. Everyone on the wall walk shifted their focus to the south side to see that several dozen de Rosa men were scaling the slopes of the western wall, making their way from the south side of the castle, and they were heading straight for Garren and Fergus.

Keller was suddenly next to Derica, his dark eyes riveted to the incoming men.

"Damn," he hissed, turning to the men on the wall who held the rope. "Get le Mon up here. He will not survive long down there. Move!"

"My God," Derica was watching her father's men approach, the tears in her eyes now spilling over. "I did not mean to alert them. I did not mean to do it!"

Keller heard her. He grabbed the tail end of the rope, anchoring it with his big body. "You did not," he replied calmly. "The arrow assault over the southern wall drove them men to seek shelter. I would surmise they scattered to the west side to hide, saw what we were doing, and decided to investigate. I... I should have considered that possibility. It is my fault."

Derica's hand was at her mouth in fear as her gaze lingered on Keller a moment before returning her focus to the incoming de Rosa men. Then she looked to Garren, who had by this time grabbed the rope. She could see that he was waving at Fergus to join him, but Fergus refused. Garren then held out the rope to Fergus, indicating for the man to go first. Derica could see what was happening and her terror mounted. The de Rosa men were coming closer and more arrows were flying.

Before Keller could stop her, Derica screamed again at the top of her lungs. She just couldn't stand there any longer and watch the indecision that had her own life hanging in the balance. He had to hurry.

"Garren! Take the rope!"

***

Garren heard the scream. It startled the hell out of him. His body jerked as if he had been struck and his shocked gaze moved to the wall. Though there was twenty feet of rock and dozens of men in his field of vision, all he could see was a vision in violet.

After that, he remembered very little except an overwhelming need to get to her. He grabbed the rope, yanking Fergus by the neck to follow him.

"Come on," he roared. "Grab the rope!"

But Fergus still begged off. "The weight will be too much," he insisted, shoving Garren at the rope and waving to the men high on the wall. "If I latch on, chances are neither of us will survive. You must go. Your wife is waiting."

Garren could see de Rosa's men rushing at them from the south. They weren't firing off as many arrows as they had initially but they were closer now, swords flashing in the early morning light.

He knew Fergus was correct; God help him, he knew it. He heard his wife scream again and a grunt of frustration escaped his lips, turning to her panicked face before looking to Fergus again.

"Fergus," he rasped, feeling the rope lift even as he held on to it. "I simply cannot leave you to your death."

Fergus' blue eyes glittered. "And so you are not," he assured him, motioning to the men high atop the wall to hurry up the rope. "I shall be here when you reach the top of the wall. There will be opportunity still."

Garren knew it wasn't the truth and his anguish tore at him. His gaze met with Fergus' bright blue, a million words of thanks and friendship passing between them. This was where they parted and they both knew it. The time for heroics was over.

"Get back in the water, then," he hissed. "Swim as fast as you can and get out of here."

The rope was pulling Garren up, out of arm's reach. Fergus gazed up at him, eyeing the de Rosa men that were far closer now.

"I believe that would be wise," Fergus agreed, darting back down the slope towards the river.

Garren was several feet above even the tallest man's arm reach. The soldiers on the wall were heaving him upward, upward still as the de Rosa men swarmed below him. As he watched, several took off after Fergus, who had reached the water. Just as Fergus dove into the cold, muddy river, two men dove in after him. As Fergus came up for air, one man surged atop him and plunged his head under the water.

Upon the wall walk, Derica screamed again as she watched the man attempt to drown Fergus. The second de Rosa soldier reached him and soon, Fergus was being pushed down by two men. Derica was positive she was watching the man drown when suddenly, an arrow sailed by her ear and plowed into one of the men wrestling with Fergus.

Startled, she looked to see Keller with a double-shot crossbow in his hand. His dark eyes were focused on the second man fighting with Fergus and, as Derica watched, he dropped the second man with another well-aimed arrow.

Fergus swam away with only a few men several feet behind him, too far away to do any damage. They eventually turned back as Fergus kept swimming for the safety of the opposite shore. He eventually climbed out and ran off, free as a bird.

Mouth hanging open, Derica turned to Keller to thank him for assisting Fergus but the man was already gone. To her right, the soldiers hauling her husband up the wall had gotten him to within a few feet of the summit and her focus returned to Garren.

She forgot about Keller and his dead-eye aim, instead rushing to the group of men now pulling Garren up over the side of the wall walk. She tried to push her way through the group but there were too many men, so she hung back, heart in her throat, struggling for a glimpse of his copper-blond hair. All she could see was a sea of soldiers. But suddenly, the armor parted and Garren appeared, unwrapping the rope from his arm. The moment their eyes met, the rope fell to the ground.

Derica hadn't seen him move; one moment she was standing looking at him and in the next, she was aloft in his arms. When she realized this, the tears came and she wrapped her arms around his neck tightly enough to strangle him.

"You are not dead," she gasped over and over. "You are not dead!"

Garren held her so tightly that he swore he heard bones cracking. He was only aware of her soft body in his arms, her hot breath in his ear. He couldn't seem to hold her tightly enough, closely enough, feeling her hair tickle his face. It was like heaven. Before he realized it, he was kissing her cheeks, her nose, her eyes now wet with tears. All the while, Derica gasped, something between a laugh and a sob.

"Nay," he breathed in between heated kisses. "I am not dead. And neither are you."

Derica laughed joyously, meeting his feverish kisses with delight. Her hands were on his stubbled face as he literally kissed every pore on her face. He didn't seem to want to do anything other than kiss her. But as the initial shock of delirium began to fade, Derica wanted answers.

"What happened?" she asked in between furious kisses. "Why did the Marshal send me a missive telling me of your death? Fergus said that he was mistaken. How could he make a mistake like that?"

Garren sighed, his kisses slowing considerably. It occurred to him that they were on the wall walk, not the best place to be in the midst of a battle. He stopped kissing her long enough to look around, noticing the nearby turret and taking Derica along with him as he made haste for it.

His arms were around her as they entered the cool shelter of the tower. His hands moved to her face, touching her reverently as if to confirm that she was indeed real. He still couldn't believe it. But the question hung in the air between them, the massive implications becoming reality. He didn't even know where to start.

"What else did Fergus tell you?" he asked softly.

Derica shook her head, her eyes wide with anxiety. "Not much more," she told him. "He simply said that the Marshal was mistaken about your death. But how can this be?"

Garren thought on that question, taking her hands between his own and kissing them reverently.

"I told you that nothing could keep me from you," he murmured. "Not the Marshal nor your father nor even death. I meant it. Fergus came to me when I was on the battlefield at Lincoln to tell me that you had disappeared from Cilgarren. At that moment, there was nothing more important on earth than finding you and I was determined to do so. Dead or alive, I would find you. But I knew the Marshal would not let me go so easily so I faked my own death so that I would be free to return to Wales to search for you. I had no idea that the Marshal would find you before I would, sending you missives of my death."

Derica stared at him, shocked by the story. "So the Marshal still believes you are dead?"

He nodded slowly. "If he finds out that I faked my death, then my death might not be such a mistake after all. He will not be pleased."

Derica clutched at him. "What are you going to do?"

He kissed her fingers again, still gripped between his two enormous palms. "Truthfully, I had not thought on it. My only focus has been to reclaim you. Now that I have you, I suppose I must make plans for our future."

"What future?"

His blue eyes glimmered. "A glorious one now that you and I are together again. What does it matter with kings and princes? The only thing that matters is you. Trust that I will do what is necessary to build a fine legacy for our son." His gaze drifted over her slender body. "I must say, you do not appear to be with child."

Derica's soft expression faded somewhat, realizing that Fergus, or someone, must have told him that she had been pregnant. She sighed softly, putting a tender hand to his cheek. "I am not," she murmured. "Not any longer."

His brow flickered with confusion. "But Fergus said...."

She cut him off gently. "It was not meant to be. The fall into the river saw to that." She saw his expression wash with sorrow and she turned the tables on him, kissing his big hands instead. "Do you know how I ended up at Pembroke?"

He nodded, distressed, and she pressed him. "Did Fergus tell you?"

"He did."

"Then you know that I slipped from the hill at Cilgarren and into the river. I was found by a woman and her two children. They nursed me back to health." She smiled timidly at him. "There will be more children, my love. Do not grieve for the one lost. It simply was not meant to be, not this time."

He nodded reluctantly, pulling her back into his embrace once again. For several moments, he fell silent, rocking her gently against him and relishing the feel of her in his arms once more. He felt extremely blessed for her life yet sorrowful for the one she lost. Still, they were together and that was the only thing of import now. He murmured prayers of thanks as he stood there and held her.

Outside of the tower, the sounds of battle were growing. Men were shouting and arrows were slinging over the walls. Garren's gaze moved to the portion of the wall walk he could see, watching the battle grow more intense.

Derica noted where his focus lay and she, too, gazed out of the tower, watching the activity upon it. Then she looked up at her husband, his handsome profile as he watched the action. She could tell that he was anxious, pensive, torn. Now that they had found each other, bigger issues loomed.

"What will we do now?" she asked softly. "My father is here to retrieve me. Keller is doing all he can to protect us."

Garren looked at her. "De Poyer is a good man," he said. "I have known him for years. He would have made a good husband for you."

She could see the mirth in his eyes and she shook her head, a faint smile on her lips. "Perhaps. But I would rather have you."

His smile broke through and he kissed her tenderly. "How fortunate for me," he murmured against her lips. "In answer to your question, however, I do not know what we are going to do right now. But I can do one of two things; I can return to the Marshal and beg his forgiveness, or we can leave England entirely and start a new life somewhere else."

She gazed at him seriously. "You said the Marshal would kill you if he found out you faked your death."

"It is entirely possible. But an honorable man would hone up to his actions. They were, after all, in pursuit of a noble cause and I have always considered myself a man of honor."

She fell silent, pondering the greater implications. "I would be honest when I say that I do not want to risk it," she whispered. "I would rather have you alive, Garren. Is your honor worth more than your life with me?"

He took a long, pensive breath. "Nay," he murmured. "I do believe that I have demonstrated that. I have destroyed everything I have ever worked for but it matters not. I am nothing without you."

"Then we will flee England?"

He looked at her, seeing the light of hope in her eyes. He knew, as he lived and breathed, that he could not return to the Marshal to tell him why he had faked his death. He was fairly certain the Marshal would never trust him again and he could no longer continue as an agent for the king. All of that was destroyed the moment they dressed that old, rotted corpse in his battle armor at Lincoln. Garren realized, as he gazed into Derica's eyes, that a whole new life was before him, something richer and more wonderful than he could ever imagine. He was very eager to know it.

"Aye," he whispered. "We will leave and never look back."

Derica threw her arms around his neck, holding him close against her and praying they were making the correct choice. All she knew was that he was alive and they were together, forever, whatever may come. He had given up everything he had ever worked for because of her. She would spend the rest of her life making sure he did not regret it.

As night fell on another brutal and bloody day, the de Rosa army camped at a safe distance around the walls of Pembroke with the exception of the area of the swampy marsh that surrounded the water gate on the northeast side of the castle. There was no way to cover that area without getting too close to the castle and too close to the archer's range. Bertram saw no reason to cover the old, mossy iron grate that sat half-buried in the water, instead choosing to focus his attention on the south and west sides. The decision would cost him.

By the cover of darkness as the sliver moon barely illuminated the velvet expanse of sky, Garren, Derica, Aneirin and Sian escaped in the chest-deep water that filled the swamp. Garren carried both children in his arms and his wife was tethered to him with a rope that Keller had tied about the two of them. Fortunately, Aneirin and Sian were good swimmers and when Garren told them to hold their breath, they did. Into the river they went, through the dark and murky water to safety on the other side.

Keller watched the four heads cross the ghostly gray river in the dead of night, more sorrow in his heart than he could comprehend. But seeing the joy in Derica's face, and seeing the love in Garren's, told him that he was doing the right thing. Heartbreaking or not, it was the correct thing to do.

Bertram de Rosa laid siege to Pembroke for four more days before finally giving up and going home.

He knew he would never see his daughter again.

CHAPTER NINETEEN

Beaucaire Castle
Languedoc, Southern France
1220 A.D.

The day was bright, warm and beautiful. Just a few miles from the Mediterranean Sea, Beaucaire was normally bright, warm and beautiful, something that Derica loved about her adopted home. Norfolk had been such a cold, wet place that the balmy warmth of the Languegoc region of France was something she had taken to immediately. She adored the climate.

Gazing up into the blue, blue sky, she was startled when two out of her four sons came barreling out of the stable yard astride new Belgian chargers that their father had recently purchased for them. Derica moved out of the way as her eldest son, Weston, came too close to her, wrestling with a big blond beast that was unwilling to be tamed. When the horse began to buck, she leapt up onto the flight of stone steps that led into Beaucaire's resident hall.

"West," she scolded. "If that horse throws you, I'll not lift a finger to help. Do you hear me? Break your neck and I'll not weep for you, not one tear."

Weston le Mon smiled at his mother; an extremely handsome man with his father's good looks and his mother's bright green eyes, he continued to happily wrestle with the animal.

"Not to worry, sweetheart," he told his mother. "I will not keep this animal, although I would dearly like to. I plan to give him to Rose's betrothed as a wedding gift."

"Ha!"

The shout came from the gaping entry into the gray-stoned resident hall of Beaucaire. Stunningly beautiful at seventeen years of age and awaiting the arrival of her betrothed, Roselyn le Mon scowled menacingly at her brother.

"You will do no such thing, Weston le Mon," she gathered her skirts and took the stairs angrily. "I'll not be made a widow before I even become a bride."

As Weston laughed softly at his sister, his younger brother by fourteen months came up beside him on an equally fired-up war horse. Davin le Mon, the only sibling with dark hair in a family of light-haired people, grinned at his sister.

"You worry overly, love," he told her. "Your new husband will be thrilled with this gift. 'Tis exactly what a new bridegroom wants – a wild horse to tame."

The brothers laughed lewdly but Roselyn was on to their game. "He shall be thrilled until the beast bucks him off and kills him," she shook a finger at the brothers. "No tricks, you two; do you hear me? No chasing this one off. I think I should like to marry him."

The brothers passed wry expressions at each other, preparing to respond until they were distracted by a yell from the stable yards. Their youngest brother suddenly came shooting out of the yard astride a massive white horse, struggling to control the beast. As the family watched with a mixture of horror and bemusement, Austin le Mon let the horse take him on a couple of wild circles around the bailey of Beaucaire until finally managing to pull the horse to a halt.

The biggest of the four le Mon brothers, Austin was the mirror image of their father in his youth. He finally brought the horse to a stop, wiping his brow to the laughter of his brothers.

"I thought I was a dead man," he breathed, slapping the big white neck affectionately. "He shall make a wonderful wedding gift for Roselyn's beau, don't you think?"

"No!" Roselyn threw her hands up. "No wild horses!"

"But...," Austin began.

"I say not!" Roselyn turned to Derica, grasping her mother by the arm. "Please, Mother; tell them to leave my betrothed alone. No wild horses, no swords that are weighted with lead, and no wine that has been mixed with pepper so that he will cry for days. Please make them stop!"

Derica looked at her boys, the exact image of her own brothers in spirit and demeanor. Daniel, Donat and Dixon would have been proud. She had grown up with this kind of madness, never dreaming she would also breed it. Weston, Davin and Austin were loving, strong and powerful, but with a wild streak in them that would test God's patience.

"Your sister has requested you not chase her intended away," she lifted an eyebrow at the handsome faces. "You will kindly obey her wishes or my punishment shall be swift. Do we, in any way, misunderstand one another?"

Davin was the first to shake his head. "Nay, Mother," he assured her. "We understand perfectly."

Weston and Austin nodded sincerely but there wasn't a bit of truth to it. Derica lifted the other eyebrow at her boys to reinforce her request just as Austin's white stallion reared up and dumped him onto the dirt of the bailey. The horse ran off as Weston and Davin laughed uproariously.

"Austin, I find you in this position far too often," Garren suddenly emerged from the resident hall, pulling on his massive leather gloves as he descended the stairs. He had missed the bucking stallion. "One would think with your size and strength, you would be able to best your brothers when they toss you around."

Austin picked himself up, brushing off his bum. "It wasn't my brothers," he lifted his hand in the direction of the open portcullis. "It was the horse."

"The new one I just purchased for you?"

"Aye, Da."

Garren came to a halt next to his wife and daughter, still fumbling with his gloves. He lifted a threatening eyebrow at his youngest son.

"Then what are you doing still standing here?" he asked. "Go get that animal. It cost a small fortune."

As Weston and Davin snorted, Austin turned for the stable yard, making a face at his brothers. Davin made one in return, Austin rushed him, and soon the two of them were rolling around in the dirt throwing punches. Derica rolled her eyes and looked at her husband, suddenly noticing a little body standing behind him. She motioned to the tiny figure.

"I did not see you, sweetheart," Derica said. "Come to me."

Twelve year old Lily le Mon went to her mother, allowing herself to be cuddled. As the youngest child in the family, she was sweet and spoiled. If her mother wasn't cuddling her, her father was. In fact, Garren was rarely without his little shadow. Lily was as beautiful as a new spring morning with her blond hair and big blue eyes. While Roselyn had a lush, seductive beauty, Lily looked like a sweet little poppet. At twelve years of age, she should have left to foster long ago but her parents couldn't bear to part with her, so she remained at Beaucaire.

As Derica hugged her youngest, a tall, black-haired young man suddenly emerged from the resident. He, too, was pulling on his leather gloves, much like Garren had been. In fact, their actions were almost identical. Sian le Mon had grown up idolizing the big, blond knight, so much so that he was very nearly the spitting image of him in action and mindset. As the eldest of the le Mon brothers, he acted more like Garren than any of his brothers did. Even if he wasn't Garren's son by blood, he was certainly his son by spirit and nature.

"We should get going before the day grows any deeper," he said to his father as he came down the stairs. "The shops in town will be closing early for Vespers."

"Where are you going?" Derica wanted to know.

Sian leaned over, kissed her cheek, and continued down the steps to the bailey. "Into town," he replied. "The tavern keeper at the Pig and the Fife said that he received a massive shipment of St. Cloven ale all the way from England. Father and I are going to buy as much as we can for Roselyn's wedding feast."

"If the groom ever gets here," Davin was picking himself out of the dirt as Austin struggled to his knees. "Maybe he is not even coming. Maybe he has decided to marry someone else."

Roselyn's big green eyes welled up. "Dada," she sniffed. "Tell them to stop being so hateful."

Garren stopped messing with his gloves and eyed his middle son. "Enough, Davy," he ordered quietly. "Upset your sister again and I shall take it out on your hide."

He didn't mean it but the threat was enough to silence Davin as he rose to his feet. Austin stood up next to him, weaving unsteadily in the wake of a righteous punch to the head from his brother.

"She was hateful to us first," Austin pointed out. "She told us that her new husband would fight us if we did not ply her with gifts every day for the next year."

Derica fought off a grin, as did Garren. He pointed a thick finger at his sons. "That is because you have much to make up for," he said sternly. "You three have harassed your sister since the day she was born. 'Tis a wonder I didn't throw you all to the wolves with all of the havoc you have wrought."

Roselyn stood next to her father, nodding vehemently. "Putting honey in my bed," she sneered. "And saffron in rosewater so it turned my teeth yellow. And...!"

Garren put his hand on her copper-blond head to silence her. "And probably more that I do not even know about so, if I were you, I would listen to her. Be kind to your sister on the event of her wedding. And if you go anywhere near her marriage bed, you shall rue the day you were born. Is that understood?"

Roselyn stuck her tongue out at her brothers for good measure; with her father's support, she was brave enough to antagonize them. As she continued to make faces at them, Derica grasped her husband by the arm when he turned to walk away.

"Would you please bring me a selection of fabric while you are in town?" she asked. "I want to make some more garments for Aneirin's child."

Garren struggled not to roll his eyes at her. "Sweetheart, you have already made that child a massive wardrobe and he is not even born yet," he said, then relented when he saw the look on her face. He threw up his hands and turned away from her. "Oh, very well; I know he is our first grandchild. Surely the Christ Child was not so anticipated or revered as Aneirin's first child."

Derica watched him go, knowing he felt the same way about Aneirin's first baby as she did. They were both so excited they could barely stand it. Aneirin had been married to a fine knight for seven years, childless until this past year when she discovered that she was pregnant. Derica thought that Garren was perhaps more excited about it than Aneirin was although he pretended otherwise. It was a wonderful addition to their already wonderful world.

The sound of distant horses suddenly interrupted her thoughts. In fact, Garren came to a halt, turning towards the wide-open portcullis as the sounds of hooves grew louder. The portcullis of the castle was almost never closed, and that was usually only at night. Beaucaire had been at peace for four years since the Count of Toulouse had captured it, putting Garren in charge of the garrison.

Garren had served the Count since fleeing England some twenty three years earlier, having come to the Count with his father's reference. Although Chateroy hadn't been destroyed those years ago by the de Rosas, it had been heavily damaged and Garren's father was thankful it hadn't been razed altogether. He also understood, clearly, why Garren needed to leave England. So the Count accepted Garren into his service based on former service from Sir Allan le Mon of Anglecynn and Ceri. The Count never asked why Garren had left England and Garren had never offered. For over twenty years, it had been the perfect arrangement.

Therefore, Garren wasn't particularly concerned with the sounds of approaching hooves but he did order his soldiers on the wall to lower the first of the double-portcullises about half-way. That was so men on horses couldn't suddenly storm in and rush the bailey without getting their heads cut off. He approached the open gate as the sounds grew louder. Behind him, the four le Mon brothers were already moving to arm themselves; as trained knights, like their father, they were always prepared.

As Garren wait for the horsemen to make an appearance, Lily suddenly ran to her father before Derica could stop her, grasping her father's hand tightly and smiling up into his concerned face. Although Garren knew he should send her back with her mother and sister into the keep, he relented when he beheld her lovely face, going so far as to wink at her and squeeze her hand. Happy, Lily pressed herself against her father, half-hidden behind his massive bulk, as three riders suddenly appeared at the half-lowered portcullis.

The riders immediately came to a halt; to go any further would mean getting knocked off their horses by the half-lowered iron grate. The horses danced about nervously as the riders eventually dismounted. One man handed his reins to the man next to him and ducked underneath the lowered portcullis.

"Stop," Garren boomed. "Come no further before you announce yourself."

The armored man came to a halt. After a long, tense pause, he finally off his helm. Garren's eyes nearly popped from his skull in astonishment as he recognized the face.

"Fergus!" he hissed.

Fergus de Edwin flashed his toothy grin; he was older, perhaps thinner, but there was no mistaking the bright blue eyes or graying blond hair.

"I see that I have come to the right place," he said. "You are as ugly as ever, Garren."

"And you are still as stupid."

It was their traditional greeting, much missed and much revered. Garren was already making his way towards Fergus, who met him somewhere near the raise second portcullis. In lieu of an extended verbal greeting, Garren simply threw his arms around the man. Fergus returned the gesture and they hugged each other to reaffirm old bonds. The affection, the friendship, was still there and as strong as it had ever been. Words, at the moment, were fairly useless.

"I do not even know where to start," Garren said as he pulled back, gazing into Fergus' face with complete, utter amazement. "How on earth did you find me?"

Fergus clapped Garren on the side of the face. "Your father told me," he said, catching a glimpse of a pretty young girl half-hidden behind Garren. His focus turned to her, startled. "And who is this pretty faerie princess? Is she magic, perhaps?"

He was looking at Lily as he spoke. Lily flushed bright red and shook her head, pressing her face into her father's side. Fergus watched her a moment longer before returning his focus to Garren.

"Surely she must belong to you," he said softly.

Garren grinned, lifting his arm so he could get a glimpse of Lily with her face buried in his torso.

"She does," he said. "This is the Lady Lily le Mon. And the rest of the group behind me also belongs to me. I believe you know my wife."

Fergus hadn't noticed Derica standing on the steps with a lovely young woman beside her. As their eyes met, Derica smiled broadly and descended the stone stairs into the bailey, coming upon Fergus and doing just as her husband had; she hugged him fiercely. Fergus seemed a bit overwhelmed at everything, studying the faces of the young men and women looking back at him. He gestured to the group.

"All yours?" he asked Garren and Derica, incredulous.

Garren nodded, glancing over his shoulder at his children. "All ours; Weston, Davin, Austin, Sian and Roselyn. You remember Sian, of course."

Fergus thought back through the years to that dark-haired little boy from Pembroke. "I do."

"His sister is married and about to have her first child."

Fergus shook his head in amazement. "Quite a brood, I must say," he was still in disbelief. "And they are all grown. Has it been so long between us, Garren?"

Garren nodded slowly, so very glad to see the man. "It has been too long," he murmured, his expression growing intense. "Tell me why you have come."

Fergus took a deep breath; he was still amazed with Garren and Derica and all of their children. He could not believe how much time had passed. But he focused on Garren's question, on the reason for his visit. It was important.

"I come bearing news, Garren," he lowered his voice. "Much has happened recently."

"Recently?" Garren's brow furrowed. "What has happened?"

Fergus clapped a hand on Garren's enormous shoulder. "The Marshal passed away not long ago," he replied. "His son is now the new Earl of Pembroke."

Garren felt a flash of sadness for the man he had once served. He nodded in acceptance, acknowledgement. "I will pray for him," he said softly. "But never did I doubt my decision to leave his service and, consequently England, was the correct one. I could not have lived in peace had I stayed."

Fergus sighed faintly, scratching his forehead, eyeing the little girl now peeking out from behind her father.

"He knew where you were, you know," he muttered.

"Who?"

"The Marshal. He knew where you had gone almost the moment you left. Had he truly been out for vengeance, he could have done it long ago. I would not be too bitter towards him if I were you."

Garren's brow furrowed. "How did he know?"

Fergus lifted his eyebrows. "Do not forget that de Poyer and I knew you were alive, as did my father. The Marshal came to Pembroke shortly after you fled England and, after a night and day of drinking, my father told the Marshal everything. So he knew from nearly the beginning."

Garren's eyebrows lifted. "And he never sought to find me? Not ever?"

Fergus shook his head slowly. "All he ever said to me about you was that he hoped you were finally happy, wherever you were. No more than that."

Garren looked at Derica, who gazed back at him with wide-eyes. All of these years he thought he had been hiding from William Marshal when the truth was that the Marshal knew where he was the entire time. Upon reflection, it didn't surprise him. The Marshal made it a habit of knowing everything. He turned back to Fergus.

"So why have you come?" he asked. "Surely not to tell me of the Marshal's passing. It is of no consequence to me, truly. My life is here at Beaucaire and I have no intention of leaving."

Fergus wriggled his eyebrows. "Perhaps not," he said. "But I have not come for that reason alone. I have also come to tell you that your father passed away last month. You are now the new baron of Anglecynn and Ceri. Chateroy Castle is now yours."

Garren stared at him a long moment, feeling Derica's hand on his arm comfortingly. "My father passed away?"

"Aye. I am sorry, Garren. I know you loved him."

Garren nodded faintly, saddened by the fact that his father would never get to see his strong grandsons or beautiful granddaughters. But he had known that the moment he fled English soil. Still, it was a sad moment.

Fergus could see the sorrow in his expression but he continued. "There is more," he said softly. "I have brought with me documents from the Marshal. He told me to give them to you should I ever see you, so I suppose now is the time. Do you recall that he granted your wife lands and title upon your death at the Battle of Lincoln?"

Garren nodded vaguely, not particularly remembering the details. "What of it?"

Fergus' bright blue eyes began to gleam. "He never took them back, you know. Once he gave them to Derica, they became hers forever. She is a very wealthy heiress of the Buckton Marcher lordship that stretches from Hopton Castle on the east, Adforton to the south, Craven Arms to the north, and includes four towns, two fiefdoms, and about five thousand vassals. She also has possession of Clun Castle, four hundred soldiers and ten thousand gold marks. William Marshal the Younger is holding all of this for your return, should you ever decide to return."

Garren and Derica stared at him with big eyes before turning to each other, a thousand unspoken words between them. Garren finally shook his head and turned to Fergus, confused and bordering on irritation.

"So you come to France to tell me of my father's death, the Marshal's death, and of vast wealth awaiting my wife and I should we return to England?" he reiterated. "Fergus, you could have done yourself a favor, remained in England, and simply sent me a missive. All of this does not change the way I feel about my life; I have been deliriously happy for the past twenty three years and have no intention of returning to England."

Before Fergus could reply, Derica put her hand on her husband's arm.

"But your family home is now yours, Garren," she said quietly. "Do you not want your sons to return to Chateroy to continue the le Mon legacy? Surely you do not want it to die out with you."

Garren looked at her; Derica had only grown more beautiful with the years, her lovely face hardly lined and her green eyes just as bright. She was literally his heart and soul. He didn't know what he would do without her.

"Are you not happy here?" he asked softly. "Must we uproot our family because of old ties and old memories?"

She smiled at him, wrapping her arms around him and Lily, was still pressed against her father.

"Of course I am," she said. "But Chateroy is your legacy and has been in your family for two hundred years. You do not want to see it end with you. As for the rest, well... perhaps it will make a fine gift to our children, don't you think? We can divide up the Buckton lordship among them and they will have lands upon which to build their own legacies."

Garren didn't look entirely sure but he respected his wife's opinion. Still, there was much to talk about. In just a few short minutes, his life had changed dramatically and he wasn't sure how to feel about any of it.

Lost in thought, he failed to notice that the two other men who had accompanied Fergus had dismounted their horses. Lily had somehow unhinged herself from her father and had wandered over to them, gazing up at them with her bottomless blue eyes. The two men looked down at the little girl, inspecting her as she was inspecting them.

Lily was not usually so bold with strangers, which made her behavior odd. But she didn't seem particularly wary of these strangers for some reason. She stared up at them curiously.

"Who are you?" she finally asked.

The men in armor were big, one bigger than the other. The larger of the pair stiffly knelt down in front of Lily, almost eye-level with her. Then he removed his helm

Hoyt de Rosa's tired old face gazed at Lily as if she was the most beautiful creature on the face of the earth. The old eyes were soft with emotion.

"My name is Hoyt," he said in his soft, deep voice. "Who are you?"

Hearing Hoyt's voice brought a gasp from Derica, followed by instant tears when she saw him. But Lily ignored her mother, instead, focused on the very old man in front of her.

"I am Lily Elspeth de Rosa le Mon," she said her name very quickly and fluidly. "Why are you here?"

"I am your mother's uncle," Hoyt replied. "You are very pretty, Lily. You look a good deal like your mother when she was young."

Lily eyed him a moment, finally pointing to the other young lady who was standing slightly behind her mother.

"That is my sister, Roselyn," she said. "She is awaiting her betrothed today but my brothers have said he is probably not coming because he is probably marrying someone else."

"What?" Hoyt roared softly, rising to his feet as he gazed at the very beautiful Roselyn. "How is this possible? Your sister is too beautiful to be jilted. Who is this bridegroom that would shame my grand-niece?"

Although he was big and scary, Lily didn't sense bad from the man. In fact, she rather liked him. She slipped her hand into his massive gauntlet and continued to study him curiously. When he looked down at her, she smiled. Next to Hoyt, the last helmed man lifted his visor, revealing his face to the world.

"No man will shame my granddaughter so," Bertram de Rosa said softly. "Lily, you will tell me his name so that I may champion your sister."

Derica went from soft tears to great sobs as she rushed to her father, throwing herself into his arms. Bertram, very old and very tired, hugged his daughter tightly.

"Da," she wept. "How... how...?"

She couldn't finish and Bertram didn't let her; he held her back at arm's length, holding her sweet face in his hands and drinking in the sight of her. Although his eyesight was failing him and he was nearly crippled, he still felt the need to come and see to his daughter after all of these years. The past twenty three years had not caused him to forget her. He had missed her every day.

"Every night I prayed for your happiness and safety," he murmured, watching tears spill down her cheeks. "Every day, I would wonder where you were and if you were happy. I see that God has answered my prayers; you are as happy as you are beautiful, and I am thankful."

Derica kissed her father's cheeks, struggling to still her tears. "But how did you know where to find me?" she looked between Hoyt and Fergus and her husband. "I do not understand how."

Bertram smiled wearily, putting his arm around her shoulder and leaning heavily on her. Derica could see as well as feel how exhausted her father was and it concerned her, overshadowing her joy. Everything aside, he was an old man who had traveled a very long way.

"Hoyt told me," Bertram said quietly. "He discovered your whereabouts through your husband's friend, Fergus."

Derica knew the greater implications of Hoyt's, and Fergus', loyalties but she said nothing, Perhaps her father didn't know their connection; perhaps he did. Either way, it didn't seem to matter any longer. Loyalties or politics could not trump family and friendship bonds.

"And so you came with Fergus and Hoyt to see me?" she asked softly.

Bertram nodded. "When I caught Hoyt sneaking out in the middle of the night nearly a month ago, I demanded to know where he was going. After much discussion, he finally confessed. I knew I had to come. I know there was much dissention the last we saw each other, Derica... I was hoping that with time you have forgiven a selfish old man."

Derica shook her head emphatically. "Of course I have," she assured him. "I am so happy you have come. You have, in fact, come at a most opportune time. As Lily told you, Roselyn is expecting her betrothed any moment. She will be more than pleased to have her grandfather attend her wedding."

By this time, the boys had begun to gather around the emotional group near the portcullis and Derica took the time to introduce her and Garren's sons. It was apparent that the boys were of de Rosa stock and Bertram was deeply touched to be greeted by grandsons he never knew he had. Roselyn even gave him a kiss on the cheek, causing the old man to get misty-eyed. Derica watched it all with tears in her eyes, never imagining it was something she would ever witness. Family, and life, had come full circle.

But she could see the sheer exhaustion in her father as he spoke with his grandchildren and she was determined to get him inside to rest. She took his elbow gently, firmly.

"Come along, now," she urged her father towards the gray-stoned resident hall. "There is all the time in the world to become acquainted later. Right now, I want you to rest and recover. It has been a long trip for all of you."

Bertram resisted. "I am more interested in meeting my granddaughter's betrothed," he said, sounding very much like the Bertram de Rosa of old. "Who is this man? What of his family and loyalties?"

Derica looked at Garren, shaking her head ironically. "Do you remember the last time my father met a bridegroom?"

Garren lifted an eyebrow. "I do indeed."

"The situation could get ugly."

Garren merely shook his head and snorted, having a difficult time believing the irony of history repeating itself. Roselyn was at his side, grasping his big hand tightly.

"Tell me, Dada," she begged. "When was it? What happened?"

Garren looked at his daughter, fearful to tell her. "Well," he began slowly. "It was...."

"His name is Paul le Velle," Davin suddenly piped up as they all walked towards the resident hall. "His father is the local sheriff and he comes from a family of all women."

Bertram looked at his grandson, his eyebrows lifted. "All women?"

Davin nodded eagerly. "His mother is a shrew and his sisters are hags," he made a face, completely riling his sister. "They live like a pack of animals on the other side of town."

Roselyn let out a shriek and began chasing Davin around the bailey, swatting at him with her hands. Lily was tugging on Hoyt, pulling him up the stairs towards the entry, as everyone else followed. Bertram watched Roselyn make contact with Davin's head, grinning when the young man began to howl. When Austin and Weston took up the face-making complete with witch sound effects, all three boys ended up running from their furious sister.

Only Sian was left out of the fun; he was more serious, like his father, and watched the antics as the taunting boys and furious sister made their way into the keep. Derica noticed that her father was grinning from ear to ear.

"Why do you look like that?" she asked.

Bertram shook his head faintly. "'Tis as if I am watching you and your brothers thirty years ago," he replied. "Brothers and sisters never change."

Derica laughed softly. "Well, those boys had better change or Roselyn will have their hides."

Bertram lifted his eyebrows. "They have de Rosa blood in them, daughter. They will never change."

Derica laughed softly. Lily, still attached to Hoyt, reached out to take Bertram's hand, escorting both elderly gentlemen into the resident hall, leaving Derica and Garren bringing up the rear. Garren smiled down at his wife, wrapping his arms around her affectionately.

"It looks as if Roselyn's betrothed must endure what I had to go through," he murmured, kissing her on the forehead. "Four brothers, a grandfather and a grand uncle to scrutinize him like an ibis among alligators. God help us all."

Derica laughed softly at the old reference, gazing into his strong face, more handsome than she had ever remembered him.

"Thank God that the alligators did not eat the ibis those years ago," she murmured. "I would have never have known such joy."

Garren's features softened. "Nor would I," he leaned down, kissing her lips tenderly. "We have much to be thankful for."

When Paul le Velle arrived less than an hour later, he found himself surrounded by a new generation of alligators. But this time, the ibis wasn't set upon. He was scrutinized but not devoured, and Roselyn managed to have a wedding night without nails in the mattress or eggs in the pillow. Her father saw to that.

Garren le Mon never again saw the green fields of England or Chateroy Castle. But, then again, he didn't much care. His legacy did not include anything left to him by his ancestors. A missive sent to his aged sister, Gabrielle, had bequeathed Chateroy Castle to her, which she in turn deeded to Yaxley Nene. That was how Chateroy Castle became a Benedictine monastery for the next three hundred and forty two years, until fire burned it to the ground.

Garren had created his own legacy, safe in the bosom of Beaucaire Castle. He was eventually buried in the same crypt as his wife and, as the centuries passed, surrounded by his descendants. And in Wales, Cilgarren Castle remained standing into the new millennium. It is still called by its rightful name, no longer bearing tales of Owain and Brendalyn, but of the mysterious Lord Garren and his wife who vanished into the river only to be saved by good faeries. All of these things were left to the ages by Garren and Derica.

It was the best legacy either could have ever imagined.

ABOUT THE AUTHOR

Kathryn Le Veque has been a prolific writer of Medieval Romance Novels for twenty years.

The Whispering Night was a story that followed an odd path. Written several years ago to completion, the last several pages were lost due to a defective hard drive. The author then had to not only remember what she had written, but sit down and actually do it. Anyone who writes knows that rewriting a book can be extremely difficult. Thoughts and feelings sometimes aren't the same and one must recapture the 'mood' of the book. Additionally, Fergus was killed in the last version and the author wasn't so sure she wanted to kill him off again. As you can see, everyone lives happily ever after. The last time anything was written in the manuscript of *The Whispering Night*, it was 2003. The last chapter(s) were written in 2010. The author thinks it turned out much better the second time around.

As a note of interest, there really is a Cilgarren Castle in Wales that fit conveniently into the novel. Look it up on the Castles of Wales website.

Visit Kathryn's website at www.kathrynleveque.com for more information including ordering more novels. Kathryn lives in La Verne, California.

CPSIA information can be obtained
at www.ICGtesting.com
Printed in the USA
BVHW041729030521
606361BV00006B/101